KŌKUA

Kōkua

is the Polynesian word used to describe the spirit of kindness accompanied by a desire to help one another, without expecting anything in return. More specifically, it translates to extending loving and sacrificial help to others for their benefit, and not for personal gain.

KŌKUA

Stephanie Hoffman

SALT & SAND
PUBLISHING
LA JOLLA, CA, USA

KŌKUA.
Copyright 2020 by Stephanie Hoffman.
All Rights Reserved.

Published by Salt & Sand Publishing,
La Jolla, CA, USA

www.stephaniehoffmanbooks.com

Graphic Design and Layout by Karl Hunt
Artwork and illustrations by Stacy Vosberg & Brett Hoffman
Edited by Neva Sullaway

Printed in the United States of America

Library of Congress Cataloguing-in-Publication Data has been applied for.

p. cm

ISBN 978-1-7347681-0-7 (pbk.)

Women—Fiji—Fiction
Woman—Doctor—Fiction
Leprosy—Islanders—Fiction
Pacific Islands—Fiction
Australia—Medical—Fiction
U.S—Medical—Fiction
I. Title

Inspired by those I've worked with, who are born with or acquire health disparities, straddling the axis between strength and depletion, isolation and exposure, disability and despair; there remains a need to reach out, hold hands and open our hearts to you.

Part 1

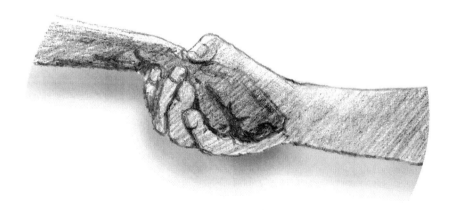

1

*R*EAGAN tried not to focus too closely on the syringe as the vial needed her undivided attention. She drew the needle out of the inverted glass vessel with one fluid motion, then tapped the air bubbles so the liquid venom would settle. This time the bubble distribution would not affect the end result. Reagan took several deep breaths and contemplated what the end result would mean, not only for her but for the whole tribe. She hesitated, staring at the chief who had entrusted his life to her. His ashen skin and bloated body were visible reminders of his terminal struggle.

"Don't wait too long," the chief's wife urged.

Maintaining her heart rate and rhythmic breathing, Reagan refocused in order to carry out the next move. She pierced the tough, mottled skin, not with a sharp stinging prick but with the slow, gentle touch of an artist. After guiding the syringe into the distended vein until the last drop had evacuated, she placed the stethoscope over Chief Toro's heart, waiting patiently while he succumbed to the lethal chemistry of the medication. Reagan kept her glance on her own hands and away from Maura's, fearful of being shaken by her emotion.

"How long will it take?" Maura asked.

"Not much longer." Reagan hoped the end would come quickly. She had seen too much suffering and understood the chief's dire need to be released from his terminal illness. Maura whispered words that Reagan didn't understand. Her prayer spoke to the Spirits and was different from Reagan's: "Let go, my friend, no more suffering, no more pain, your brave fight is over."

Reagan inhaled deeply again. She let the air, and the emotion, out in one slow and silent release. To her right, Maura's knob-like fingers entwined with her husband's lifeless hands. A sense of calm and peacefulness lingered around them.

Exhaustion tightened Reagan's shoulders. The chief's illness had taken a toll on everyone. It had been such a long journey, caring for all the islanders over the years. She whispered to Maura, "I'll go to the children."

Reagan heard the girls from where she knelt—the sucking sound of repressed crying, the oxygen flowing in, then trapped inside immeasurable sadness. She struggled to stand up against the inertia of loss, torn between wanting to comfort Maura and knowing the children would not be allowed inside the bure. Traditional Fijian ways would supersede their need to see their father, to say goodbye, to kiss him on the cheek one more time. They were under the age limit set by the elders who carried on the time-honored customs.

Maura would direct the cleansing when his Spirit left. Reagan looked back at the chief's wife one more time, concerned about her vacant stare, transfixed on her husband's breathless body. Her eyes were red-rimmed, but there was something missing. Reagan couldn't put a word on it. Was Maura not accepting the inevitable?

Pushing open the bamboo separation and stepping outside, Reagan found the chief's daughters holding hands. Their cheeks were wet with salted tears. Intense brown eyes fixed on Reagan, waiting for the answer, needing to be told the end had arrived. And there she stood, usually so bold and strong, so full of energy. Reagan's laughter had always thrilled them to tears, but this moment was a silent abyss she had trouble crossing.

"The chief has gone to the Spirit Side. Your mother prays with him as he passes over. She will tell you when it is your turn to see him."

The girls accepted Reagan's straightforward instructions. She delivered the message clearly and calmly, just as the islanders would speak to their children. She mustn't break, or cower in the face of death. It was the necessary release from unbearable pain. But the children . . . they had so much beauty and love in their hearts. Reagan surrendered to their emotion. Walking forward, she scooped them up as she always did and kissed each wet cheek while pushing back the straggly hair from their penetrating eyes. She said what came to her, "I love you so much." She pressed the children into her body. "The chief is leaving to a place where he will be safe. He will be happy, no more sickness. He would not want you to be sad. Your mother and father love you so much. They will never leave you alone."

Joni, the youngest, squirmed between her sisters, trying to be closest to Reagan. "Auntie Reagan, where is Papa now? What does the place look like?"

Reagan could not help but make a shallow grin. Joni was special. Her eyes were always big and round with questions; her smile was full of white teeth gleaming with a childish joy that seemed to run through every fiber of her being. Masina and Lelei were older and had an air of seriousness about them. Perhaps they had seen and experienced too much tragedy.

This was a sad, difficult time, and the girls looked to Reagan to explain it and take away the sadness. She pointed to the sky. An albatross soared high above making its way seaward.

"The chief is going home." Reagan raised her hand, mimicking the flight of the bird. "See, he is free."

The girls marveled at the beautiful, winged creature, dipping its long, graceful wings as it soared away from them.

2

*J*EREMY BLACK had become a household name in the States, and two of his recent films had been released internationally. He'd worked his way up the "B" list and had finally cracked into the "A" list. He no longer had to scour the streets for parts or hang out at useless Hollywood parties. Jeremy Black was there, in the midst of it all, and people seemed to like him . . . all of them.

He was naturally charismatic and knew how to package his arrogance into a captivating little-boy smile. His looks were as expected, perfectly hewn to master any role scripted for him. Jeremy had a reputation for being easy to work with—he did what he was told. And as long as he had a script in his hand or someone to impress, his confident alter ego appeared.

"Mr. Black, can I bring you another cocktail?" The flight attendant blushed as she leaned toward him, taking away his second empty vodka and tonic.

Jeremy stopped his nervous heel tapping and raised his eyebrows. He intentionally let his index finger hold onto the glass as she reached for it, allowing his skin to make contact with hers.

"Same, sir?" Her voice cracked.

"Oh, please, we're all on this flight together. I'm Jeremy . . . Jeremy Black."

"Yes, sir, I know who you are."

Jeremy turned up the edge of his lip seductively. "What do you recommend?" His hazel green eyes captured hers.

She looked over her shoulder. "Maybe champagne, sir?"

"Do you have any Dom?"

"Yes, of course. What year?"

"How 'bout 1999?" He glanced at her, letting his lips part and drawing her into his path.

"Oh, I'm sorry, sir, our oldest is 2000. I recommend 2004. Will that do?"

"Certainly, and bring a few glasses—"

Jeremy awaited his manager's reaction and list of rules . . . *keep a lid on it, no screwing around, keep your head in the game.* He was used to Jones' interceptions. But the remote island shoot would be a prime place to invite a private jet flight attendant to hang around for a drink or two—a perfect distraction.

His manager interrupted the flirtation. "The script seems arduous. Have you run through it yet?"

Jones—Jonesy to those who worked with him—had been Jeremy's manager for ten years. Jones interrupted anyone and anything that appeared to draw Jeremy's attention away from an impending project, or anything that might complicate his life, usually women. He'd hired a fleet of handlers for Jeremy, some spurious types who were observers meant to keep bad press away. Others did the opposite, they hyped the paparazzi and scripted social media moments. Jeremy remained oblivious to it all. He liked acting, made money, got loads of attention, and had a big house in Malibu to escape to at the end of the day.

Jeremy looked around for the flight attendant. "Jesus, Jonesy, why do you always have to do that?"

"Do what, my friend?"

"Interrupt . . . I was just talkin' to the lady. I'm not doing anything. I'm bored and tired and we're going to the end of the earth for this movie. Just leave me be." Jeremy's heel picked up its pace again, this time louder.

"Well, have you . . . run through the script yet?" Jones stared disapprovingly at Jeremy's noise-making leg.

"Yeah," Jeremy planted his heel on the ground. "Seems pretty straight-forward. I'm sure someone will prompt my lines, right?"

Jones leaned toward Jeremy like a father, a brother, and a con artist. "Look, we took this project because of Raava. He's got the bucks and he's not afraid to pay for talent—you, my friend."

Jeremy waved his hand with one finger pointed skyward, signaling the Dom needed to arrive quickly. "What do you mean by arduous anyway?" Jeremy focused for a moment on the troublesome word.

Jones offered a less than accurate definition, while flipping through the script's pages. "Arduous . . . you know, a pain in the ass. We gotta get permission to film on this island. Something about a leper colony. What the hell is Raava up to? This role isn't really our thing, it could mess with your image . . . our image."

The flight attendant brought the glasses of champagne and Jones grabbed the closest flute. She shot him a disapproving sneer.

"Thanks, doll, that's just perfect," Jones added, dripping in condescension.

"Oh, for chrissakes." Jeremy looked away.

"Stop sulking and get a grip. You know Dominique and Bianca agreed to this ménage just as long as you're on board. It's not all bad— those two beauties on the same shoot. You know what I'm saying." Jones downed the champagne in one gulp.

Jeremy shrugged off the whole conversation, the twisted logic seemed to work. "Yeah, cool, I haven't worked with either of them in ages. An island resort, how bad can it be?" He emptied his glass. The vodka tonics and champagne had smoothed the edges of the long flight. Turning to the window, Jeremy dropped his head against the glass and sighed. He captured the distant view—a smattering of tropical islands through the distortion of the plane's window. *How bad can it be. . . .*

3

REAGAN pulled the cord on the outboard engine and was relieved when it started on the first stroke. She dropped the lines, pushed off, and steered the small boat toward open sea. A heaviness crushed her chest. She tried not to look back at the children and Maura on the rickety dock, but she felt the pull of emotion in their expressions.

Masina, the middle daughter, swayed back and forth, hypnotically humming the ancient Bird Song. She scraped her big toe along the edge of the splintered surface as if needing a physical reminder of her pain. Lelei, the eldest daughter, held Joni firmly with both arms, physically restraining her from jumping into the ocean to follow Reagan.

Joni cried out, over and over again, "Auntie, Auntie, we need you . . . please."

The islanders' grieving process and traditional ways were second nature to Reagan. She would return soon, but only after the private cleansing and release. She waved to Joni, a familiar gesture between them. Reagan whirled her arm in the air as if signaling a helicopter pilot to start the propellers, meaning she'd be back soon.

Joni broke free of her sister's strong grip and ran to the water's edge.

Reagan powered down, waiting for Joni to return the signal.

They shared the same message: *I will see you soon. I love you and I will not leave you stranded.*

Pushing the throttle forward, Reagan guided the boat to make way against the contrary currents. Her heart, like Maura's and her children's, pounded with grief.

She went to her sacred place. Once outside the reef, Reagan lowered the plow anchor and secured the boat to the sandy bottom, away from the breaking waves and coral entanglements. She waxed her surfboard with methodical, mindless circles. The waves looked a bit different, sliding in from the northwest corner. *Cyclone season's coming.*

Reagan picked up her board. Just as she was about to lay it into the crystalline sea, she was overcome by an emotion she didn't understand. She had followed her beliefs and Chief Toro's request to end his life. His wife, Maura, was close by, urging her on. Her children knew the end was imminent and Reagan had adhered to the Hippocratic Oath: *Do No Harm.*

She held the six-foot surfboard in her shaking hands. *What are you doing? Put it in the water. Just drop it, for godsakes, put it in.*

Frozen in time, there were too many voices yelling: "You can't leave medicine, prescribe what you want . . . do what you want . . . you can't. . . ." Her colleague back in L.A. had scoffed, incredulous that she would leave it all behind to practice medicine on a tiny island.

A few playful bottlenose dolphins broke through the surface. Her shaking subsided and she tossed the surfboard in the ocean. Reagan opened her chest and put both arms in the air to welcome them. "There you are, my friends." A powerful sense of joy swept through her as she stood on the rail, unsteady for an instant, arms balanced in midair. She flew through the air, spreading her arms like the albatross' wings. Suspended in a dream-like state, she glided in slow motion, before landing in the healing, warm water.

The dolphins came to her, bumping against her skin. She stretched out her hands to them, stroking their slippery gray bodies. She let go of the first layer of stress. Reagan coaxed them to play. "Yes, I need you both today. This was a difficult one. He was family."

Reagan's smile broadened at the loud thunder of waves breaking over the reef. Hopping onto her board, she paddled toward the offshore break with the dolphins gliding next to her.

She pushed through each wave scratching for the outside line-up, but something was wrong. Her arms felt weak; her heart was beating too fast. She ducked under the next wave and it crashed over her head, pressing her down toward the spiky reef. Choking out salty foam, she got back on her board.

The dolphins continued guiding her toward the next set, but another wave closed right in front of her. Out of nowhere an intense sadness walled up, just as the last wave had. *Shake it off . . . shake it off . . . think about it later. No sense in going over it. It's done.*

Behind her, the dolphins' silhouettes streamed through the teal tapestry of the oncoming wave. She spun her board around and refocused, caught in the sheer magic of the wave—perfect size and shape. Matching the wave's intensity with her own revitalized strength, she paddled with two deep strokes with the proficiency of a lifelong surfer.

Timing perfect, a steep drop down the glassy face, she flexed her knees into a deep bend to absorb the rolling thunder now chasing her, then a clean carve to the left. Reagan tucked smaller to allow the sheer curtain of saltwater to surround her. Its power enveloped her and thrust her into a deep and narrow glass tube that could fracture at any moment. Her heart pounded, adrenalin flooding her system; this was her moment, her lifeblood, her longing, as it had always been.

She needed the ocean and its creatures to help her grieve and refuel her body and soul. In return, she promised to look after the precious creatures that surrounded her. She caught a few more waves, each as exhilarating and renewing as the one before. The sea washed away the sadness and anger once again.

As she was about to take one last wave, a swish powerboat roared into the narrow channel, swerving out of control toward the reef and surf break. *What the hell? Who has that kinda—* It wasn't like the usual runabouts the locals used. It was ostentatious, oversized, and racing its engines. She threw her arms in the air. *What are they doing? This is insane . . . such idiots.*

As the boat neared the line-up, it veered out of the breaking swell section at the very last second. It was nearly swallowed by the set wave.

What are they doing? Holy shit!

The boat whipped around her, throwing a huge plume of water off the bow, directly toward Reagan. The crash of the boat's wake with the oncoming set knocked her off her board and sent it flying in the air. Then the diesel-spewing monster ran over the reef, tearing off the top shelf, shredding it to bits. The sound of the reef being severed and the crush of metal along the ancient columns of stony coral tore through Reagan. It was like witnessing a murder.

4

*W*HEN Jones told Jeremy he wanted to rent a boat for the transit from the mainland to the island resort, Jeremy didn't think twice about it. But as he braced himself against the pounding of the forty-foot cigar boat swerving out of control through the wind swells, a queasy fear upwelled in his stomach.

"Hey, Jonesy, cool it on the testosterone," Jeremy yelled over the noise of the roaring engines. He gripped the side of the runaway powerboat wondering what would happen if he fell overboard. He couldn't swim that well, at least not offshore. *Sure, land is right over there, but where is the resort . . . what about sharks? Where the hell are we?*

"No way. This is how you handle these babies, with full throttle!" Jones cocked his head, yelling over the harsh discordant racket.

"Then at least slow down so I don't lose my lunch, or worse—Hey, watch out!" Jeremy shouted as a green body flew through the air not far off their starboard bow.

Jones cranked the wheel and spun the boat into a tight turn. At the same moment, a wretched noise and jarring motion shook the boat. It sounded like two race cars crashing into each other, with metal bits scraping and ripping apart into useless bits of carnage.

"What was that?" Jeremy tried to catch a glimpse of the body that had been hurled through the air, but the radiant streaks of light bouncing off the water made it difficult.

Someone yelled at them, but the noise of the over-revving engines obliterated the words. Jones pulled away as fast as he'd come in and proceeded on his course, spewing a huge wake as he cranked the wheel into another sharp turn.

"Goddammit, Jonesy, turn around, go back. We gotta check him out."

"Grow up, Jeremy. The guy's fine. We didn't get near him. Look, that's probably his crappy boat over there . . . a local. They know how to swim . . . not our problem."

"Not cool, definitely not cool!" Jeremy tried to maintain his composure while hiding his anger and clenched fists. He looked back to see if the surfer was okay, but as they sped away the churned up water obliterated his view—no lime green color anywhere.

REAGAN gasped for air as she tried to scream. She kept her head above the whirlwind of water and pulled herself back onto her board. Paddling to her boat, she shook off impending shock while assessing her condition like a doctor . . . *no blood, no broken bones . . . breathing . . . pulse settling. Asshole . . . I'm gonna cook your sorry ass. I can't wait to get ahold of you . . . you moron.*

She opened up the small engine on her fifteen-foot whaler, pressing its speed to the max, but it was no contest for the massive twin engines on the swanky boat. It was out of sight in seconds.

Reagan slowed the boat to an idle, letting the boat drift in the current. Her stomach muscles spasmed and a sharp pain shot to her side making it difficult to get a full breath.

The thoughts she was avoiding flooded back in—the enormity

of the chief's life. Maura and the children. She couldn't stop the onslaught, or the rush of tears and the gulping for air.

He was in terrible pain . . . no hope . . . that's why I'm here . . . comfort . . . protect . . . do no harm. Reagan took a long deep settling breath, while wiping the moisture from her face—half tears, half saltwater—a good mixture for calming her. She exhaled, repeating the mantra: "His chains are broken, his spirit now free." She motored back to the harbor in a trance-like state.

5

*J*EREMY was relieved when they arrived at the resort. The upsetting experience at the reef had left him feeling like the ugly American. Jones still managed to come in too fast and bump up against the dock causing further damage to the rub rail.

"Hey, J, let's go check out the digs." Noticing the torn-off rub rail dangling in the water, Jones kicked it with his foot, showing little concern.

"What about the damage to the boat?" Jeremy shook his head and pointed to the long scrapes and indents along the side and bottom of the boat, clearly visible because all the glossy finish was now a patchwork of scratches and dents. "Look at that mess."

Jones waved his hand. "Come on, let's get to the bar. Someone else will deal with it."

Jeremy was irked by Jones's disregard and carelessness. He was tempted to mention they weren't in Marina del Rey where someone else usually dealt with his reckless behavior. He wanted to say, "Hey, man, this is Fiji, for godsakes, and we nearly ran over a surfer out there." But instead, Jeremy's throat got dry with anxiety and his clenched fists trembled. He stood there feeling useless and guilty that he didn't have the nerve to say what he felt.

"HEY, asshole," a female voice came from the landing. "What the hell . . . who the hell do you think you are?" Reagan stormed at them like a tinder fire ready to catch hold, her chest heaving in anger, underneath a lime-green rash guard.

"Jonesy, hang on and get ready to be schooled." Jeremy welcomed the interruption and relished the thought of the solid rebuke he'd been unable to deliver to Jones. He recognized her by the day-glow green—the surfer they'd cut off. He certainly hadn't noticed while swerving through the waves, the surfer was female.

Reagan marched straight to Jones, wrenching her neck to look up, stopping only a few inches from his face, and continued on her rampage. "Who the hell gives you the right to drive over a protected reef, rip it to shreds, and haul ass like nothing ever happened? Not to mention, nearly running over me." She fumed on without hesitation, "You are either really drunk or really stupid. So which is it?"

"Get out of my way, li'l lady," Jones snapped, puffing up his chest against her assault. "Off you go, if that's all you got."

Jeremy stood motionless, immersed in the spectacle.

"Really? Is that how you want to play it?" Reagan fumed. "Just try to move me out of your way and I'll make sure you never get this close to another female, cuz I'll be rearranging your face. You get where I'm coming from?"

"Where do you come from, surfer girl . . . you got quite a mouth for such a small gal on this tiny piece of crap island."

"Listen up, I'm only gonna say this once. Only once! Hire a local boat captain and don't you dare get behind that wheel again." Reagan glared at Jones.

"Okay, I get it." It dawned on Jeremy that maybe the surfer had been flown in as an extra for the film, and Jones had acted out the whole escapade—this was an impromptu screen test. But she was too natural and confident, nothing like the actresses he'd ever come across. He could never play opposite her; it would be unnerving. Surely this was a classic Jonesy prank, all a setup, but Jones looked worried.

Reagan turned away grumbling, "What idiots."

After a bit of hesitation, Jeremy stepped in to smooth things over, to play the hero. "We're here to make a film. It'll be great for your island. You know, we'll need extras and this place will get a chunk of cash. Looks like it could do with some fixing up." The minute the words left his smooth lips, Jeremy sensed her stiffness and resurgence of anger. He had only managed to reignite the fire.

"Not while I'm around," Reagan sparked. "The last film crew left this place in shambles—poisoned the island with their trash, nasty habits, and insensitivity. You are not welcome here. End of story."

A tall man with overgrown facial hair, broad shoulders and a captain's hat approached, "Reagan, my dear, it's okay. They are guests here."

"What! They are guests?" She flared, her fire now fully lit. "This is ridiculous. He ran over the manta-ray reef, destroying a recent outcropping and nearly ran over me! Roger, you can't be serious. He could have killed us."

Roger was her close friend, confidant, and the owner of the resort who had welcomed her years ago. He had made Reagan part of the family knowing she was a great asset to the islanders who were afflicted with leprosy. The nearest emergency medical care was miles away and only accessible by boat or air.

"Gentlemen, perhaps it's best we leave this for now and take it up at another time. I'm sure everyone is tired from traveling," Roger added diplomatically.

"That's a good idea," Jeremy chimed in, trying to cut the tension between Jones and Reagan. He had never witnessed such strength in a woman, entangled with emotion. *This is not a game to her; she's not playing a part.*

Caught off guard, he was uncertain as to what to say next. "We didn't mean to—"

"Didn't mean to what? I don't care who you are or what you do, just hire a boat driver and stay out of my way!" She looked back at Jones, then stormed away, while Jeremy stood speechless.

Jones turned to Roger. "Is she part of your staff here?"

"Not exactly, but Reagan, like all of our staff and the islanders, will be treated respectfully. You did read the contract, right? It was right there in big print. We certainly appreciate your business, but I won't put anyone or the resort at risk." Roger downplayed his disapproval. The truth was, Roger did need an influx of U.S. dollars; the tourist season, like the cyclone season, was very unpredictable. Other resorts closer to Nadi airport had invested in trending sports and luxury tours. Roger had depended on returning guests who sought seclusion for whatever reasons.

"So is the huffy chick staff or not?" Jones was annoyed and ready to give up on the evasive answers.

"Well, actually—" Roger nodded toward Reagan, who was sitting at the bar, "she is your contact for the tribe on the island, so all your filming rights have to go through her. You do nothing without Reagan Caldwell's approval."

"You've got to be joking!" Jones leaned toward Jeremy, "Well then, Romeo, we need you for a cameo appearance at the bar. Try to win over the vixen who has our future in her hands."

Jeremy moved toward Reagan. She was sorting and organizing something in a big bag. He admired her composure after being rattled by Jones. Watching her intense focus, he couldn't fathom how his normal tactics were going to work.

"Go on!" Jones nudged him. "Go do your Jeremy thing."

6

_A_S Jeremy approached Reagan, he noticed her body language first. Her muscular legs crossed at the ankles, tapping her sandal to some rhythm he couldn't hear. She scribbled with quick movements on a notepad. Her sun-streaked hair fell over her tan, bare shoulders in unkempt, lazy twists of blond. She looked up from the paper, nodding her head, as if she was talking to someone. But no one was there.

Jeremy moved in, "Hey there, mind if I sit down for a sec?" His throat closed up and went dry, his words—stuck. Embarrassed, he tried to continue, but no scripted lines surfaced.

"Sorry, I don't have a _sec_, and you can't fix your buddy's mess. He needs to do that, so sending the messenger boy won't work." Reagan avoided looking at him.

"What are you scribbling there? Are you a writer?"

She shook her head, not engaging in the conversation.

"Well, how 'bout I buy you a drink and call it even."

"You know this resort's all inclusive, right? Drinks are free."

"Oh, yeah, well then. . . ."

"Hey, I'm busy and you guys nearly killed me today, and you did tear up a part of an endangered reef out there. So I'm pretty sure I'm not having a drink with you."

"Well, I ju-just thought, maybe—"

"Let me guess. You're an actor in the so-called film, and you are supposed to win me over so you can have the rights to film on the island. Correct?"

"Sorta, well, but—" Jeremy looked into her blue-gray eyes and softened his voice to a near whisper, "Look, I'm sorry, my manager can be a real jerk. He was definitely out of control and I apologize."

He waited for a response.

Reagan mumbled something about a med . . . dilates blood vessels quicker.

"What?" Jeremy moved closer. "What about a med?" Jeremy waited again for some kind of response, but she remained focused on the vials and papers in front of her. She wrote down numbers and other symbols then shuffled the bottles of liquid around in a frenetic fashion.

"So maybe if the blood flow were regulated . . . double that number. . . ." Her voice was softer than before.

"Excuse me?" Jeremy tried to understand.

"Nothing. I was talking to myself." She waved a hand in his direction.

"But I ju-ju . . . just thought . . . I mean I . . . I was going to say—" Jeremy tripped over his words like a toddler learning to walk. Sweat trickled down the side of his face and dripped onto his silk shirt. He had soaked it through, as the tropical heat pressed into the open-air bar. "Well then, what is your name?" Jeremy blurted out.

Reagan glanced back at him. "Reagan. And yours?"

Jeremy looked stunned. "Are you kidding me?" The words escaped his mouth before he could censor them. *How could she not know. . . .*

"No, I'm not kidding you; my name is Reagan."

He surrendered and walked away in defeat, shoulders slumped forward with his chin pinned to his chest. Jeremy slouched back to his manager like a cowering pup. Jones sat at a hardwood table, a safe distance from Reagan. He was already on his second round of drinks.

"J, you look beat up. What happened? Did you smooth out our road?" Jones regaled Jeremy as he sat down.

"Not exactly." Jeremy slumped into the wicker chair.

"Well, we start shooting in two days so keep turning on your charm. And by the way, one of your leading ladies should be here shortly and she is expecting to have dinner with you privately in your room."

Jeremy was only half listening. He couldn't stop thinking about his stilted conversation with Reagan and how inept he'd felt. He sat down facing the bar so he could catch another glimpse of her.

BIANCA REVERE was the first leading lady to arrive. Jeremy walked to the edge of the deck to greet her. The first thing he noticed was her ruby-red lipstick. She wore a revealing blouse, exposing a scarlet-red bra, and a tight skirt shrunk to her hips. Behind the scenes, much help was required to maintain her youthful façade, but that didn't matter to Jeremy. He was aware of her affection for him, albeit contrived and superficial. She had been in one film that landed her a nomination for Best Supporting Actress playing a sleazy alcoholic who preyed on men. Although the role suited her, she was acknowledged largely due to Jeremy's success in the film.

He stood with his hands in his pockets, peering down the ramp, entertained by Bianca's travails getting off the boat and onto the landing. Two inches of her right high heel disappeared into the crossties of the wooden dock. Jeremy surprised himself by smirking rather than feeling any immediate worry for her safety. Her assistant would surely take the brunt of the fall, but Bianca showed a bit of dexterity by skipping out of her Jimmy Choo and landing flat-footed.

"Jeremy, my God, what is this place? This is hideous. Where on earth are we?" The other shoe mimicked its counterpart and Bianca yelled at her assistant, "What is wrong with you? This is ridiculous, get my shoes and hurry up."

Instead of running over to assist her, Jeremy waited at the top of the ramp leading into the octagonal, open-air dining area. He liked the layout of the place; he could walk off the boat and be at the bar in a few steps.

"Don't worry, you'll be fine." But Jeremy wondered how she would survive, so far from Rodeo Drive.

As if on cue, the trade winds caught Bianca's long, flowing scarf and swept it off her neck, rattling her even more. She scolded her assistant, "Damn you, girl, can't you do anything right?"

Jeremy chuckled as the scarf flew out to sea. He sent out a welcoming wave with a measured grin.

"Oh, my darling Jeremy, please come help me get as far away as possible from that wretched boat. It was dreadful coming all the way over here. I've had too many cocktails and I need to lie down," Bianca whined incessantly, before she was even up the ramp.

Jeremy fell comfortably into his role. "My dear, I've missed you terribly. I thought we were going to try to stay in better touch." He approached her, kissing each of her cheeks as if from a scene out of his last movie. "You know I adore you and I only said yes to this film because you were in it."

Bianca succumbed to the flattery and blushed. "But what is this place? Jones said we'd be staying at a resort. Tell me this is the set that's just been built for the film."

Jeremy realized Jones's bit of subterfuge. "Well, this is part of the set. We will be filming around this area and the dining area. The bures aren't bad, you'll see."

"Is that a cocktail?"

"No, it's a traditional Fijian shelter, a home, so to speak. Beautiful, actually. They have everything you'll need, and they are all handmade with palm fronds and local wood."

"I really don't care." Bianca pouted. "I'm exhausted. I need a nap. How do I get somewhere? Is there a golf cart of some sort?"

"Everything is in walking distance. Your bure is just down this path . . . Go along the beach and one of the guys will help you. I have to check on a few things. See you tonight for dinner."

Bianca's assistant handed her the broken heel. "I'm sorry, it broke right off when I pulled it out."

She glared at the assistant. "That's your only job, honey, and you can't even keep my shoe in one piece." Bianca twisted her lipstick open and reapplied it in front of Jeremy. She puckered her lips and adjusted the color, accentuating the movement of her mouth for his pleasure. "I can't wait to see what they serve up for dinner. I'll see you then, darling."

Jeremy was surprised at his lack of attraction to Bianca this time. Her attention span was minimal. And he had remembered her as being more beautiful. Now, under the bright tropical sun, he wondered if she'd had a few too many plastic surgeries, leaving her facial features frozen and unable to keep up with her remarks. He made a brief comparison to Reagan, and it was almost as if they were different species. Reagan seemed real. This woman in front of him was robotic, like she'd been popped out of a plastic doll mold.

Bianca huffed off with the assistant grappling with her bags, tripping along behind, while Bianca carried only her cigarette.

Jeremy felt a strange void. Usually he looked forward to these sideline affairs when shooting a film, but this time was different. He glanced out at the ocean searching for something or someone. The sun was setting in hues of pink and red, mixed with a pastel glow. He wondered why he had never noticed sunsets back at home. He was now drawn to the changing shades projected on the water. As the final glow disappeared, Jeremy headed to his room where he prepared for his performance with Bianca.

Let the charade begin.

7

REAGAN fell onto her bed exhausted from the visit to the island and the death of Chief Toro. She shut her eyes trying not to relive the big boat coming at her and its shredding the reef. Drifting off, she dreamt she was trapped in an underwater cave. Her tank was almost out of air. There had to be a way out of what seemed like a shadowy maze. At first it appeared as though there was an outlet, but no, it was another cold and dark corridor of seawater.

Bang. Bang. Bang.

She swam faster trying to escape the darkness.

Bang. Bang.

Reagan bolted upright to a sitting position.

"Miss Reagan, Miss Reagan, please get up. Come quick!" She identified Angus' voice right away; he was one of the resort's boatmen.

She answered the door not realizing she was half-dressed. "What is it?"

"It's the chief. He needs you," Angus said anxiously, out of breath.

"What are you talking about? He died yesterday."

"No, the chief is alive and he is crazy." Angus avoided looking at her as he urged her toward the doorway.

Reagan couldn't believe what she was hearing. Was this possibly part of her dream? She felt even more disoriented.

"Come, come, Miss Reagan. We go now." He tugged her arm. "I do know a crazy man when I see him. We have to go now!"

Grabbing a sarong and wrapping it around her body Fijian style, Reagan then hurled the emergency backpack over her shoulder. They sprinted out of her bure leaping over koi ponds and headed down the path toward the boat landing.

There was a shed near the dock for emergency supplies. Shoving boxes aside in the dim light, Reagan unlocked a large wooden box. Inside were a variety of bottles with pharmaceutical labels on them. She filled medical syringes one after another with a swift and methodical technique. Not an ounce of liquid escaped.

"Come on, Miss Reagan, we go now, get in," Angus yelled out while holding the boat fast to the dock with his foot.

"Coming, coming, one more sec." Reagan grabbed a few bottles of Lidocaine and threw them in her bag, zipped up her backpack and ran to the boat. "Wait!" She ran back to the shed and box, and latched each with a secure lock.

SMOKE billowed from afar as they approached the small island. "What happened?" Reagan asked, squinting in disbelief. A charcoal-like odor seeped over the trees. As the boat neared the dock, she choked on the thick fumes.

"Angus, I don't understand . . . what could have happened? What's going on?"

He slowed the boat just enough to avoid a collision with the rickety dock.

Reagan leapt out of the whaler, barely throwing the bowline over the dock cleat, yelling back at Angus, "I've got to get there."

She ran up the shaky dock onto the dirt path; her legs trembled as she made a sharp turn toward the raging flames, now in full view.

Finally, she could see the rampage. "Oh, my God, what went wrong?"

After securing the boat, Angus caught up to her.

"Was it the propranolol mixture? The high concentration could have penetrated the blood-brain barrier and had an adverse effect causing night terrors. Maybe the chief's bradycardia was overstimulated, jump-starting his heart. The nonselective beta-blocker has been known to have adverse effects. It is so lethal, how could he—I don't get it."

And then as if her own heart had stopped, she gasped in disbelief. The chief's six-foot-five frame—seeping in anointed oil and caked in mud—was illuminated by the fire. His arms held a small wooden table, which he raised over his head before launching into the growing blaze.

"Moro . . . moro . . . Kalougata . . . he's comin', he's comin'." The words were cryptic yet still Fijian. Chief Toro's pupils were constricted, and the glow of the flames made the whites of his eyes seem expansive.

"He's coming for you. Repent . . . Kalougata serpent." The words weren't familiar to Reagan, but she made out *serpent*.

"Oh no, not the reverse effect. He's gone mad. The meds must have stimulated his amygdala."

Angus was by her side. "What's the migdala?"

"It's the part of the brain responsible for aggression and emotional reaction, which must have sent him into a rage."

Maura was now by her side, hysterical and distraught. "He jus' up and open his eyes, gasping for breath." She choked on the smoke around her. "The oil . . . really hot . . . happen' so fast . . . no one believes he get up . . . it was jus' so fast."

Reagan put her sarong over her nose and mouth. "Get back, Maura, back from—"

Maura pushed her way toward the chief. "His eyes so big, he's screamin', the devil come to get me. No! He tells the devil, I'm not goin'."

"Maura . . . let me handle . . . you're too close to the fire . . . get back."

"He said he come back to save himself from the devil. Then he come out of the bure and start throwin' things . . . anything . . . in fire." Maura ranted on and on, as spirals of smoke and wind fueled the area.

Reagan whipped the backpack from her shoulders. Coughing forcefully, she grabbed a small red bag marked *emergency only*. She prepared a syringe of phenobarbital to calm him down. She ran at him like a savage, digging her toes into the ground, then plunging the needle into his thigh. She leaned in with all of her body weight to ensure the med was delivered. She held her breath, unsure if his strength would overcome her. Chief Toro collapsed slowly to the ground with his eyes open and fixed on Reagan. She checked his pulse and heart rate.

"Move him into his bed and restrain his hands," Reagan directed the men who were standing motionless in shock. "The rest of you . . . handle this fire."

"He is asleep now." She turned to Maura whose skin had gone pasty, as if she were about to faint. "I'll stay here until he is conscious and assess the situation. Go be with your children. I will let you know when he awakens."

Reagan went to the chief's side trying to figure out what had happened. He seemed lifeless, although the chest still expanded as it should. His skin was thick with tension. She untied his hands and placed them on his chest.

"I'm so sorry, my friend. I had no idea. . . ."

A hand reached for hers. Chief Toro opened his eyes and looked deep into Reagan's. "I wasn't ready," he whispered. "You are the

29

one," he coughed. "You . . . change their path. . . ." His voice was disintegrating. "Maura . . . my love." Each word came painfully. "She taught me . . . no ugliness, just love . . . she is your family now." His eyelids fluttered as if too heavy to keep open. "My children are yours."

The sedative defeated his struggle to stay awake, to speak. His spirit was leaving. "Please, Reagan, it is done."

She drew the fatal dose of barbiturate needed to supplement the sedative. "Maura is already my family, as you are. Now rest."

The chamber was empty, the process complete.

Reagan shut his eyelids and listened until his breathing ceased. She held his hand for a long time—not wanting the profound and intimate moment to cease. Her breaths were slow, helping her own lungs to perfuse at a steady rate. Putting both earpieces in place, she rested the stethoscope over the chief's chest—and waited, she must be certain this time. Then she straightened her posture, composing her strength to lift herself to a standing position to go look for Maura.

8

*J*EREMY awoke the next morning to a blinding headache and the stench of red wine and cigarettes looming about. Slumped over a wooden Adirondack chair, he propped his elbows on his knees holding his head in his hands. The pulse from his temples penetrated the palms of his hands. Jeremy tried to wash the previous eight hours from his memory, and although Bianca hadn't slept with him, he felt emptied of any emotion. There was no connection or attraction with the woman. He suddenly remembered another scene in the middle of the night when he was awoken by a sudden series of hurried footsteps—*that woman, Reagan . . . where did she go? In the dark, in a boat?*

He walked out onto the lanai. It was still early and the predawn rays cast long shadows across the water. Looking out to sea, Jeremy noticed the small boat cruising back into the harbor. The same boat that had sped away last night now idled at a snail's pace. As the boat approached the dock, he strained to make out the silhouette of Reagan but quickly decided it wasn't her. Jeremy moved to the edge of the lanai to get a better look, stretching his body across the rail, then walked across to the other side. He rubbed his forehead and was about to walk back inside when the hood of the sweatshirt fell back uncovering Reagan's face. He stopped and stared as she hobbled off the boat.

Walking in small shuffling steps, Reagan paused halfway up the dock and grabbed hold of the rail. Her knees buckled and Jeremy stiffened. He could get there in a few minutes, but suddenly Roger appeared, consoling her, holding her. The shuddering movements of Reagan's body were visible from Jeremy's viewpoint. He gripped the railing, watching the scene from afar.

Jeremy had never witnessed anything so poignant, so honest, and so attractive. He felt a strong urge to go hold her and protect her from whatever hardship she had endured. This woman who was still a stranger to him seemed so familiar and so alive. He was envious of Roger comforting her while she convulsed in his embrace. Jeremy straightened his posture, extending his neck as she said something to Roger, using her entire body expressively. His curiosity was further piqued as other staff members joined in a circle hugging and holding her. There was no point in moving—his legs were heavy and the return of his headache threatened. He relied on the lanai rail to hold him upright.

The circle dissipated and Reagan headed on the dirt path leading to her bure. Jeremy saw Jones approaching her and tried to warn him. But it was too late.

"Hey, Miss Caldwell," Jones started smugly. "We really need you to cooperate with us and not get in our way. There is a lot of money at stake here, and—"

She interrupted him with a penetrating stare of unspoken derision that quieted him. She walked right past without saying a word—emotions masked.

Jeremy braced himself as she took the fork in the path towards her bure, which was beyond his. Relieved to see her downward gaze, he stayed focused on her—something of great significance had happened. He was curious and deeply drawn to her. Moving to the center of his lanai away from the discrete planter, he stood in full view. Within feet of his bure, she stopped and faced him.

"Where did you go?" Jeremy surprised himself.

Reagan stood motionless. "Who, me?"

"No, the other guy who sailed away into the dark night." He kept it light.

Reagan scuffed her sandal on the back of her leg. She swallowed. "Nowhere."

"Really!" Jeremy chuckled. "Well, you went nowhere awfully fast, and for a long time." A heartfelt silence changed his tone. "I'm sorry for my friend. Jones can be very demanding, and he is under immense pressure to get this film wrapped up fast."

Jeremy was more at ease with her this time. He sensed her need of something or someone, which was different from their last encounter at the bar. Her body continued to hide from something—her avoidance of his glance and incessant head movement told him something was affecting her. He was concerned for her, a feeling unfamiliar to him.

"What is it?" Jeremy asked in a soft voice. He moved forward, stepping over an imaginary line into her space.

Reagan shifted her weight back and forth, like on her surfboard, to regain balance. She looked toward him, still avoiding his eyes, his questions. The intrusion was penetrating. Taking several steps backward, she finally looked directly at Jeremy. "You can have the rights to film on the island as long as you don't film anyone against their will and above all you stay true to who they are. No mockery, no insults, no negative portrayal."

Bianca walked up to Jeremy's bure and interrupted the conversation. "Morning, Darling. Did I leave my wrap here last night?" She planted a kiss on Jeremy's cheek.

Reagan proceeded down the path toward her own room, without a word.

Jeremy felt a rush of red heat snake through his system. He was embarrassed to be seen with Bianca this way and tried to free himself from her arms. "Wait . . . Reagan, right? Is that your name?" Jeremy tried desperately to hang on to the conversation, even though she was already several bures away.

Bianca blurted out, "Jeremy, I am right here, you know."

Reagan turned back to answer, "Yes, and I still didn't get yours."

Bianca was flabbergasted. "What rock do you live on?"

"Jeremy, my name is Jeremy," he blurted out like a child who all of a sudden knows the right answer.

Reagan turned toward the shell pathway. "Well then, good luck and have fun."

"It's *under*—what rock do you live *under*," Jeremy scolded Bianca.

9

*J*EAN MICHAEL RAVAA was a late arrival on the island. Looking bedraggled in a striped cotton shirt, which hung half-tucked into his wrinkled khaki pants, he looked more like a worn-down father-of-five on holiday than a well-respected director of edgy humanitarian documentaries. He walked around the bar, hoping to find a familiar face.

"Ravaa!" Jones yelled over in a boisterous voice. "You made it. Come on over and have a cold one with us." Jones pointed to their favorite drinking spot, close enough to the bar for constant service, with a perfect viewing angle toward the gangway and all the comings and goings.

"How was your flight?" Jeremy asked.

"Long. I don't think I'll ever get used to these junkets."

After they had settled into their chairs and a round of drinks, Jones was the first to broach the subject.

"So tell me, Jean, why this place, of all places . . . what's this film really about? I'm just not clear—" Jones took a swig of his cold Fiji Bitter.

Jean Michael lunged at the question, quick to deflect it, "Molokai . . . Molokai would have been better, I know. Would have been closer to home and definitely the feeling I was looking for, but we couldn't get the rights to film there."

"Why not?" Jeremy asked naively.

"Too many films there already . . . you know, the leper colony and all. But here, we can have the same tropical setting and—"

Jeremy interrupted, ". . . but the script, I don't get what the story is about."

"Well, Bianca's here, right? And Dominique should be here in a few hours . . . missed her connecting flight again."

"You mean they didn't hold the plane for her? What's wrong with those guys?" Jeremy rocked back in his chair amused, downing another Fiji Bitter.

"No need to worry about all this, J . . . we got the details all covered. You just show up for the shoots, okay?" Jones reversed the ground rules, like he always did, when needed.

Jean Michael watched for Jeremy's reaction, hoping he would accept the superficial explanations. "It's a love triangle, Jeremy, with your two favorite actresses. Should be a natural for you."

"But, why here? I can do that anywhere. What's the thing about lepers and the island and needing special permission from this surfer we . . . met?"

The director shifted from side to side in his chair. There was more to the story than he was willing to explain to Jeremy.

"Why do you care?" Beer foam spewed from the corner of Jones's mouth. "As long as we make you look good, the money rolls."

"Forget it, I don't care." Jeremy feigned a smile.

"Great, so we'll figure out the filming rights and you take good care of our leading ladies." Jean Michael held his beer in the air.

The three toasted to success for their "arduous" film.

After an hour, Jean Michael staggered off to his bure, swaying from too much heat and drink. He'd traveled through a full day's time change, with a bag full of serious doubts. Could he really make a meaningful film out of a twisted plot? Telling the longstanding tale of human suffering—the forced exile from society and horrific stigmatization had been on his list for a while. But, he was short on funding and harangued by his production manager before leaving LAX. He remembered the conversation.

"What about using Rooney's production company? He's had some big wins and has deep pockets. He might go for it. After all, you got Jeremy Black."

Jean Michael crossed his arms and shook his head when his manager interrupted.

"I know what you're gonna say, he cuts corners, no integrity. But he brings in the dough again and again. I know he's ruthless, but—"

Jean Michael had to resist the urge to say, "But he's an asshole." His churning stomach told him so. "I don't know, Tom . . . not sure I'm up for it. Rooney's been known to really screw people."

"Well, it's your call, but he has the bucks we need."

Jean Michael was apprehensive about using Rooney, knowing he would have to give up some control, but the payoff would be getting the film made and distributed. "I guess I can work with him." He uncrossed his arms. "I just don't want to end up with a half-baked story that goes nowhere."

"I know what you're sayin', but I'll start workin' on Rooney and let you know how it goes."

Grateful to be away from L.A., Jean Michael opened the hand-carved door to his bure and laughed from exhaustion because of the simplicity of the space before him. The spartan room, with a low-slung queen-size bed shrouded in a mosquito net, a clamshell washbasin off to the side next to a double-drawer table for his belongings, tossed off all the complexities of his project, making it appear simple, clean, and straightforward.

10

$\sim\!\!\sim\!\!\sim$

*R*EAGAN resisted the need to get out of bed. An unusual lethargy held her motionless. She looked around the room trying to find something to brighten the feeling of loss. Her sketchpad lay abandoned on the thatched stool near her small table. She raised her eyebrows, *Huh, that could work.* But first she needed to tend to the daily inspection.

Standing fully naked, the search for altered pigmentation began under the fluorescent light. Reagan was cautious not to be too hasty in the process since carelessness could be costly. Although most cases of Hansen's disease weren't as contagious as once believed, some were. More alarming, she had heard via a satellite news station that there was a recent outbreak of Hansen's in the States and some cases had shown up in L.A.

Reagan finished by turning forty-five degrees in each direction to inspect the backside of her body, lifting the golden hair off of her neck. She took a regimen of herbs from the backyard garden, boosting her immune system, and cleansing any micro-bacteria. Reagan had been fairly healthy back in the States, but a variety of tropical diseases surrounded her, so vigilance was imperative. She also took special care in handling all bodily fluids of anyone sick or injured. This wasn't because of any fear of contracting Hansen's, but rather avoidance of staph infection, which was highly contagious. The islanders already had such suppressed immune systems.

She continually reminded the resort staff. "As you know, staph infections can be serious here, but fortunately none of it is turning into MRSA. I don't intend to compromise anyone by dolling out excessive antibiotics like sugar. I think you understand what I mean. I saw enough of that back in the States."

Roger, Sachi, and Angus were among those instructed about the locked medicine box. Their heads were bowed in deference to Reagan's umpteenth lecture on the topic. She varied her lessons slightly, but the message was clear: Meds are powerful and not to be abused.

Having gone through her morning to-do list, Reagan reached for the sketchpad, eager to escape her thoughts and focus on the beauty that surrounded her . . . *work on the old stuff or something new?* Art was a simple outlet from the intensity of her profession. Though she never felt particularly talented, the movement of the pencil on the page released the emotion and creativity. It felt uncomfortable when others admired her work. If someone peered over her shoulder, she was quick to close the pad and hide what she considered private.

Reagan flipped over a new page. Her hand moved dexterously across the thick paper, in swift motions, lines appearing on the page, creating an unknown shape, a new idea. She tilted her head, turning the sketchpad in all directions, gauging what the sketch would become.

Ah, of course, the devil ray. As if on its own, the pencil formed the shape of the hornlike projection of the ray's mouth. Reagan smiled thinking of the creature's fluid flight breaking through the ocean's surface. A few more upward lines with the lead—*I'll finish this later.* The devil ray had reminded her there was much work to be done at the reef. She rummaged through her tackle gear searching for supplies to help repair the reef. *This salvaged surgical tubing is biodegradable . . . it should do the trick.*

Grabbing her dive gear and surfboard, Reagan headed for the boat. Walking past the restaurant, she did a double take. There was Jeremy sitting at the corner table—the one with the best breeze—this time with a different woman. He was holding her hands and leaning in toward her.

He sure gets around. What a poser. No wonder he stutters. He doesn't know which way is up.

Reagan's gaze caught Jeremy's as she walked by. Hands full of surfboard, dive fins, and gear; she kept moving toward the bar, overhearing their conversation even though her earbuds were in place. She had resisted turning on the music. Instead, Reagan caught the words of the newest female arrival.

"Hey, I'm over here, are you listening to me?" The woman waved her hand in front of Jeremy's face.

The words were aimed at Jeremy. Reagan tried to shake off his stare and walk faster, but the conversation from the open-air bar followed her around the corner.

"Yes, yes, I'm so glad you made it safely . . . rough ride . . . it's not an easy crossing."

"Jeremy, the trip was dreadful. I hate boats. I only came to this pathetic place for you. I knew you'd take care of me. How did Bianca get here first?"

"I think there was a mixup with the flights or something—"

Reagan stepped around behind the edge of the bar to get to the main water faucet. She pretended not to listen—it was a small place after all. *Looks like a young one this time.*

The woman twirled strands of her copper ringlets between her fingers while pawing at Jeremy's thigh under the table with the other hand. She wore a flimsy silk blouse and skin-tight pants, exposing the woman's bony pelvis.

Reagan restrained her desire to gawk while filling up the water jug. Bending over, her view of the couple became inverted and added a certain humorous tilt to the scene.

A shadow crossed over her.

"Are you gonna see Maura today?"

Startled by the voice, Reagan tipped over her jug and water cascaded over the polished wood counter, saturating a stack of napkins before dripping onto the concrete floor. "Oh, sorry Roger, didn't see you there." She snatched the bar towel from his hands and soaked up the trail of wet. "Headed there now, as a matter of fact." Reagan was relieved. "Walk me down?"

"Please, let me help." Roger grabbed the half-filled jug and topped it off.

"Roger, what the heck is going on here? All these shallow people in their edgy clothes."

"Now, now, Reagan, you know I've gotta make a living. Cyclone season is right around the corner. This place will be empty for months. Come on, don't let them bother you."

"I know. I get it. Can you promise me they won't run me over again?"

"Yes, in fact, I can. I had the big bad boat towed this morning to the main island for repairs . . . not coming back. How are you doing? You don't seem yourself."

Reagan spun her hair in a makeshift knot. "I'm good. Just need to get in the water. I'll be okay."

"Got some fresh huauchinango for dinner. We'll cook it how you like it. Sound good?" He handed her the water jug.

Reagan boarded the whaler, placing her equipment and supplies so that the boat would be balanced and move through the water with ease. "Snapper sounds great, Rog."

He released the bow and stern lines and cast her off.

Reagan mouthed 'thank you' and headed toward open sea.

AFTER assessing the damage at the reef, Reagan prepared the tools she needed for the surgery beneath the surface. She carefully anchored the boat and prepared a buoy to mark the spot where she intended to dive. It was a tedious job creating a cross-stitch pattern using hemp twine, fishing line weights and bits of broken coral. She sewed them together to create a natural textile habitat—an abode that no fish could refuse. The prosthetic reef angled upward to reach for the sun, as it would have done before its amputation. She scattered chopped bait around the reef to draw fish in to feed, knowing she'd have to return daily to convince them to settle in and nourish the reef back to health.

The dolphins dove and swam around her while she worked on the coral heads. Reagan stroked their skin. *So sleek. I love you guys. You are so simple, so innocent.* She held out the baitfish for them to grab. *There you go, Juliet, like you needed my help with this snack. And you too, Romeo.*

Holding another fish up for Juliet to take, Reagan waited for the expected next move. The dolphin took the fish with the edge of its mouth and swam to the other dolphin, placing it in his mouth. Then Juliet came back to Reagan and nudged her for another. "Oh, such a smart girl, you want more for your boy, huh?"

Reagan wore extra-long dive fins, pretending to have the same underwater agility. She played and worked . . . and played some more, for hours. The reef was a labyrinth of exquisite beauty in delicate balance. She embraced it all.

After heaving her gear into the boat, Reagan pulled herself up and over the gunnel effortlessly. As the boat shifted, the surfboard slid forward and Reagan caught it with her palm. *Sure, why not?* She looked at a glassy set approaching at the tip of the reef. The tide would fill in soon and there was just enough time to catch a few waves before heading to Maura's. Reagan waxed her board in circular patterns while another reeling wave raced over the reef, lifting its crest and folding over itself—perfection. Layers of pink pastel reflected off the mirror-like glass, landing on a cloud of foam as the wave broke.

Reagan paddled out with ease even though the swell was building. It was only shoulder high but the rising tide was sure to push some power. Diving deeper through the approaching sets made it easy to conserve energy for what was to come. The tranquility beneath the surface slowed the sensation of time. It calmed her. Eyes wide open, Reagan waited patiently while the roar passed over her body. Then she was catapulted above the surface to rejoin the commotion of white water. Gasping for air, she exhaled forcefully and pushed through four more waves, duck diving seamlessly each time looking for the quiet beneath it all.

The sun's marmalade tints splayed toward the clouds, as it approached the horizon—the day was dissolving. Reagan still had to get to the island to see her patients before the slight onshore breeze picked up. She gathered her buoy, lines, and reef-building tools, packed up for the day and powered to the island.

Maura greeted her first. Reagan could see the lightness in her body. The enormity of the stress of Chief Toro's death was behind her. They hugged for moments too long for most people's comfort. Reagan felt her friend's tremor and knew her own legs were supporting them both.

"He loved you so much, Reagan," Maura said. "You give 'im so much before he leave us. You bring his soul back, fight the devil . . . so he leave in peace."

Reagan hugged her again, supporting her deformed spine and short leg. It wouldn't be much longer for Maura as well.

"You know it was suppose to be my time, not his." Maura welled up as she buried herself into Reagan's chest. "He be callin' me home soon."

"Your love for your husband is like no other." Reagan believed every word. "You were there for his every need as he was for yours. I envy what you've both shared."

Reagan remembered how Chief Toro had fallen in love with Maura's overall beauty. It was as if he hadn't noticed her speckled skin, lesions, and knobby fingers. When Reagan told the chief he should probably not have children due to Maura's leprosy, he didn't know what she was referring to. He hadn't noticed Maura's disease; he simply fell in love with her spirit. Reagan admired this most about him.

"Auntie Reagan, Auntie Reagan," Maura's eldest daughter yelled.

"Hi, Reagan, hi. Over here," came another petite voice. Lelei, Masina and Joni, the three children of Maura and Chief Toro, ran to Reagan squealing with laughter. They climbed on her, jostling for the best position to be scooped up in her strong hugs.

Maura turned to Reagan. "You stay for dinner . . . the children, they need you tonight."

Darkness was fast descending and Reagan had no urgent need to return to the resort. One of the running lights on the boat was broken, making line-of-sight navigation on a moonless night a bit dicey.

"Sure, I'd love to," Reagan answered, knowing they needed to be together.

11

$$\sim\!\!\sim\!\!\sim$$

*J*EREMY walked toward the bar and stopped. He hesitated, turned to go, halted in mid stance and waited. Roger was busy talking to the barmen, who signaled that somebody stood behind him.

"Ah, Mr. Black. May I help you?"

"Well, actually, I need—" Jeremy momentarily reconsidered his question. "I was just curious, what does the surfer, uh, Reagan, do here? I mean what is her position?"

Roger dismissed the barmen and looked directly at Jeremy. "Sounds like you already know she surfs. And she helps out around here."

Jeremy shifted his stance, getting closer to Roger with each word spoken. "I see, but what I mean is, what's her job exactly?"

"No job really, just a helper. They call her Kōkua." Roger remained evasive.

"Where does she go on the boat?" Jeremy persisted.

"She surfs or dives—you know, recreational activities."

"At night?" Jeremy asked, this time in a more direct tone, looking for an honest answer.

"Sometimes if it gets too late to make it back, she camps on a neighboring island."

This wasn't the first time someone had asked questions about Reagan. The staff at the resort understood they shouldn't discuss with guests what she did on the island, and they knew never to discuss her work, even among themselves, in case someone overheard and took it out of context. Her work there was sacred and well-protected.

"How long has she lived here?" Jeremy pressed further.

"Sounds like you have a lot of questions about Reagan. Why don't you ask her yourself?"

"Well, is she single?"

"Ah, okay, let's cut to the chase, my friend." Roger's words carried a hint of irritation.

"What I mean is . . . could you arrange a dinner for us?" Jeremy asked, in a softer, almost meek voice.

Roger laughed out loud. "I'm sorry, sir, you'll have to catch your own fish."

"Ah . . . well . . . I don't usually arrange my own . . . Oh never mind." Jeremy backtracked, trying to mask his intentions.

"Well, you'll need to talk to her about your film . . . if you want it to go well. Maybe you should just be straight up and ask her yourself."

Jeremy smiled in agreement with Roger, even though the film was the last thing on his mind. He felt like a schoolboy entangled in his first crush, asking his buddy to find out if she liked him. "Maybe I will." He spun awkwardly, his words twisting in the air, landing in the vacuous space between him and Roger.

Roger stood up and followed a few steps behind him. "Hey, Reagan is special. She's not one of your Hollywood trollops, if you know what I mean. You are out of your league." Roger's gray and wiry brows furrowed. "And by that I mean you're not to go near her with trashy intentions. We protect her, and if you were to attempt anything that might harm her in any way you *will* see consequences."

Jeremy let out a reassuring sigh. "That's not my intention, just curious about her, that's all. Forget I even asked about her."

12

~~~~~~

*A*S Reagan pulled up to the dock the following morning, Jeremy was there to greet her. "Long night?" he asked.

Reagan was not only caught off guard, she was rattled by his sudden appearance. She had hoped to idle in early, undetected, and get to her bure without notice, but there he stood, his sea-green eyes looking at hers. His light brown hair, usually coiffed to perfection, was tussled by the sea breeze.

"Yes, long night," she answered bluntly. Reagan stared at him for a moment, the bowline still in her hand. It wasn't so much that she felt attracted to him, but she tried to imagine capturing the errant wisps of color in his eyes on her sketch pad. She loved the intricacies of their patterns and the challenge of re-creating them on paper. Reagan couldn't pull away from his eyes—their oceanic design—feathered with green and orange highlights, like the evening sun reflected on the emerald sea. They absorbed her against her will.

Reagan tied off the bowline and gathered a net of fruit and two freshly caught wahoo that the tribe had given her. The herringbone net was heavy but she lifted it with ease. Her sinuous muscles became more defined as she transferred the weight from the boat to the dock.

"Can I help with that?" Jeremy stepped forward.

"Uh, that's a pretty fancy shirt you're wearing. Doesn't pair well with fish."

Jeremy scanned his pressed Tommy Bahama shirt, already scattered with evidence of salty sweat, but he had seven more like it, tags still on, in his bure. "I'm good." He extended his open arms.

Reagan handed over the spear gun, knife, and a bag of fruit. She blushed thinking of her slight attraction to him.

Jeremy held up the banana stalk with one hand, not quite sure how to equate the spear gun with the catch. "Wow, I hope you gave these bananas a fighting chance with that big gun."

Reagan stared at him. She didn't smile or laugh. "Can you carry this too?" She handed him a mesh dive bag with her weight belt, regulator, and extra slings.

Jeremy swayed under the weight of it all. His silk shirt clung to his skin. "What do you do with all this stuff?"

Reagan carried the two wahoo by their tails as Jeremy followed her up the gangway. He tripped on the edge of an upended wooden plank sending the banana stalk flying in the air.

"You okay back there?" Reagan finally cracked a smile.

Jeremy dropped all the gear at the top of the ramp and headed back down the dock to pick up the escapees.

Reagan didn't let up. "Hey, that's my breakfast, don't bruise them, please."

He gathered them up and met her at a large saltwater tub at the top of the gangway.

"Can you clean?" Reagan asked.

"Clean what?"

Reagan held up the thirty-pound fish.

"No, not a chance . . . not where I come from."

Entertained by the notion of teaching the polished actor how to gut a fish, Reagan pulled out her knife, wiped it back and forth on the sharpener, and positioned the wahoo on a large koa cutting board.

Jeremy stood, galvanized by the action. "You are amazing."

"Great, well, let's get this guy cleaned. It's breakfast and it's only fresh for so long."

She was in close proximity with Jeremy's arm. Her eyes swept down to his hands, first noticing his clean manicured nails. Then the freshly pressed dress shirt, already wet with the day's steam, but still didn't even have an island wrinkle. *Silk!*

"Don't you just rinse it under some water and throw it in a pan?"

"Okay, get in here. Take your knife . . . careful it's sharp." She placed her hand over his, showing the position of his grip at the top of the blade's handle.

"My knife?" Jeremy winced.

Reagan pierced the fleshy part of the fish, just under the gills. "You got this?" Thickened fluid oozed from the fish's belly.

Jeremy lifted the knife in midair and his hand shook. "No, not exactly. I've never been good with knives. I have cooks at home . . . why would I bother—"

"Here, watch me." She took the knife from Jeremy's quivering hand and directed the blade along the centerline of the fish. Once sliced open, she pulled out the entrails and tossed them over the top of the platform into the ocean. She placed her thumb along the tissue barrier at the spine and scraped out the blood and remaining guts with her nail. Holding the empty fish under the faucet, she rinsed the remaining loose pieces down the deep-bellied cleaning tub.

"See, that's not so hard."

"Well, you probably do this every day."

"Close . . . almost every day." Reagan rinsed the knife and positioned the second fish. "You try this one."

"I'm not so sure about this—" Jeremy's hand shook so violently the knife fell to the ground. "I'm sorry . . . it's not the fish . . . or anything. . . ."

Reagan looked at him curiously. It was odd, she thought, he seemed such a cool and slick character, but here he was—he couldn't hold a simple fillet knife.

"Come on. I'll show you." Reagan picked up the knife and placed it in his hand. She put her hand over his, firmly—to quiet the tremor, and guided the knife below the fish's throat. She drew it down the centerline and then took her hand away to let him finish the surgery.

Blood seeped onto Jeremy's hand. He froze. "I—"

"You got it, keep going. It's okay."

Jeremy looked at the inner makings of the fish then back to her. Exhaling, he slowly scraped out the guts with the knife, unwilling to touch the slimy bits.

Reagan looked at Jeremy; the saltwater smears on his silk shirt were now laced with drops of red. His hands were drenched and the lower edge of his shirt stained in blood.

Jeremy's voice was barely audible, "I can do this."

"Just like in the movies, eh," Reagan tried to keep it light, but she sensed something disturbing in his behavior, a fear of some sort. It seemed silly to be scared of cleaning a fish. Was it the fish? The blood?

Jeremy wiped off his hands and placed the knife on the platform. He took a few steps back. Clearing his voice, he looked at Reagan relieved. "So you surf and clean fish. What else do you do on this island? It's kind of . . . well, off the grid."

"I ended up here on a surf trip and . . . I don't know . . . it's a hard place to leave. And there's lots I can do here."

"Like what?"

Reagan's tone changed, redirecting his prying. "Reef restoration and conservation. Like fixing the reef you guys broke."

"Hey, I'm really sorry, I couldn't be more—"

"Yeah, I know. Anyway, I keep track of different species. The manta rays are endangered, so I look after their count. I work with the fishermen and we share ideas about sustainable fishing. They don't call it that, but their practices are naturally responsible. They don't take 100,000 tons of tuna a day like the big commercial trawlers that plow through here."

"So what do you do for fun?" Jeremy shifted over to the open faucet and rinsed the fish in the streaming water.

"What do you mean *for fun*?" That word wasn't in Reagan's lexicon. She was a doctor, she lived a meaningful life . . . she helped people. Mitigating unbearable suffering for the neglected population of patients on the island didn't leave much room for any extras. *Fun* for her was jumping in the ocean, surfing, playing with her dolphin friends, and doing her artwork. She suspected Jeremy's *fun* meant something different.

"You know, go out with friends, get a few drinks or whatever."

"No, that's not really me—"

A loud voice descended from above. "What the hell are you doing?" Jones stood with his shoulders hunched up toward his ears. "I can smell that fish skank from up here. Look at yourself, you're a bloody mess." He emphasized the word "bloody" with an English accent.

"It's breakfast, Jonesy."

"Ah, hell, get your ass up here. First shoot is in ten minutes and here you are, cleaning a gored fish. That's disgusting."

Jeremy's fist clenched. "I'm coming, for chrissake." He turned to Reagan. "I'm sorry, I've gotta get to work."

"No worries, I get it." Reagan took the fish from him, noticing the return of the slight tremor in his hand.

Jeremy made it to the entrance of the restaurant and turned back to her, "Where do you go at night?"

The sudden intensity in his eyes and the strength in his voice set Reagan off balance. She took a deep inhale, hoping to find the right words.

The voice from above saved Reagan from responding.

"Jeremy, now," Jones barked.

Reagan shifted back and forth. Her lips were sealed tight, her eyes shifted away from his, avoiding the question. It was all too complicated to explain. When she looked up, he was gone.

13

IN tune to the social and medical inequities back in the States, Reagan had only worked for nonprofit institutions. She felt strongly that the commodification of medicine was rapidly growing, so she dedicated her energies to helping those who needed it most. Coming to this remote island in Fiji and helping the most underserved population reflected what she held most sacred. Now, witnessing the pretentious actors at her resort, her protective instincts kicked in.

"So what is this film about anyway?" Reagan's hands sat squarely on her hips.

Roger took a sip of his coffee and one more bite of the eggs benedict. He leaned back in his chair and sighed. "It's a story about someone who gets leprosy from a leper who was his lover and then carries it back to his wife, eventually killing her from the disease. The director thought it was a good topic to teach the public. He says there's been a recurrence in the States, so he's got an interest in it."

"That's it? A story that demonstrates one of the biggest misconceptions in medicine? And, come on Roger . . . don't use that word. Have they done their homework? Do they have any idea of the social injustice it will perpetuate?" Reagan lowered her voice. "I'm sorry, Roger. You know I didn't mean that toward you."

Roger raised his hands. "No offense taken."

She collapsed in the chair beside him. "It's just that I've been doing this for so long, and the early intervention treatment is working. Look at Joni. The empirical evidence is obvious!"

"I know." Roger shook his head. He was prepared for the lecture.

"My loose statistics have about thirty percent of the islanders affected, but most of them came to the island already showing signs."

Roger continued to shake his head. "I know, dear."

Reagan stood up with quick and renewed angst. "The chief was clean, not a scratch, with Maura fully lit up. Joni just recently showed her first marks and that's where the dapsone is doing its thing." She paced in front of Roger.

"Well, yah know—" Roger started.

"Well, nothing. What I know is that there seems to be a correlation with the immune system—those that are suppressed are most susceptible."

He tried again. "I get it, but—"

"I don't think anyone gets it." Her hands flew in the air. "I suspect there might be a defect in cell-mediated immunity making certain people more susceptible to leprosy." Her pacing became frantic. "That's why we're trying to boost their immune systems. That's why I always ask guests to leave their vitamins and supplements behind, so we can give them a leg up, since the nutrition is so marginalized here."

Roger let her vent, let her teach, as she always did. He simply nodded and somehow understood her frustration, even though he didn't always understand her analysis.

"Miss Reagan," a soft voice interrupted, "Maura says Joni is sick. They need you now." The resort staff had grown accustomed to alerting Reagan. They were the intake personnel, similar to a hospital admittance staff. They learned over the years which messages were more urgent than others and adjusted their tones accordingly. "She's so hot, they say she burning up . . . no eat, no drink . . . come quick." Sachi recited the vitals and summary of symptoms.

"Load my boat." Reagan had calmed down, but felt shaken after her long speech defending her beliefs. Would Joni prove her wrong?

She checked the med bag for levels of dapsone and rifampicin, the sulfone drugs used to treat Hansen's disease—the supplies were depleted. Going back to the States to beg for more donations was inevitable. As needs grew dire, she would also need more morphine and fentanyl. She grabbed prednisone to control the inflammation and some tamarind seed to accomplish the same thing holistically, cautious not to fully rely on Western medicine. She had witnessed the power of medicinal plants and the harmonious connection between nature and nurture. Killing the bacteria was one thing, but controlling the life-altering symptoms from the chronic inflammation was now the priority.

"Sachi, please add more green beans if you have them." Reagan continued her med count. "Those kids need to keep their iron levels up."

"Got 'em, and these come yesterday from Aus." Sachi held up a bunch of rich hibiscus spinach. "Did you say these have red bean flavor?"

Reagan chuckled. "Yes, Sachi, they have riboflavin."

"Do you want your surfboard loaded also, Miss Reagan?"

She raised an eyebrow toward Roger. "Of course, Sachi. What if—"

For Reagan this meant she might as well be prepared—her surfboard, the one tool she needed to replenish her soul and wash away her anguish and suffering. She pushed the boat away from the dock and headed toward the island.

JEREMY had finished his run through the script with both actresses. He found it peculiar that he wasn't as infatuated with Dominique as he once was. She was full of the youth that he was starting to relinquish; her look was less plastic than Bianca's, and her sensuality was more inviting, yet Jeremy found himself distracted and inattentive. He was relieved to be heading back to his bure alone.

The familiar sound of the outboard motor caught Jeremy's attention . . . there was Reagan again, packing up the small boat with crates of food and equipment, preparing to cast off. He changed his direction so he could watch her movements. The boat idled away from the dock with Reagan at the helm.

As her distance from shore increased, Jeremy ran to the dock and offered the boatman one hundred dollars to take him out on a boat.

Sachi's mouth fell open in a wide grin. "No need for the money, sir, I take you to fish, dive . . . whatever you wish."

Jeremy knew he couldn't answer honestly, as stalking Reagan was probably frowned upon. "Yes, fishing."

"Okay, I get poles an' bait, come back here in a bit. You get clothes betta for fishing." Sachi exposed his slightly irregular row of white teeth in a huge grin.

"No, we must go now!" Jeremy was already in the boat as Sachi hurried to gather a pole, bait, net, and knife; anything he could quickly grab.

"We go now." He nodded, not fully understanding Jeremy's urgency.

Jeremy could see the island in the distance and the small boat outlined against the harsh tropical sun making its way there.

Sachi slowed the boat. "Fish good here, see the reef?"

"No. Is there another fishing hole closer to that big island?" He pointed in Reagan's direction.

"Sorry to correct, sir, all sand, no reason for fish to live there." Sachi pointed around the reef. "I know these waters, sir, grew up here . . . no reason go to island."

"Actually, I'm not feelin' that good. I need to get off this boat for a few minutes, quickly, or I might heave." Jeremy bent over, acting the part.

"Oh, okay, sir, why didn't you say so? Yes the waves coming bigger. I get you to land."

Jeremy was relieved that Sachi obliged him so easily, turning the bow toward the island.

"I'll just be a moment. It's happened before, just need to stop rockin' for a bit. How about rigging the poles while I'm on land?"

"Yes, I'll bait 'em up." Sachi inched the boat up to the dock.

Jeremy hopped out and headed into the bushes that acted like a security gate for the island. The lingering sound of Sachi's whistling faded in the background. He didn't look back.

14

$$\sim\sim\sim$$

SIX-YEAR-OLD Joni had a high fever and labored breathing in addition to the swelling around her reddened wound. Reagan sifted through her medical bag for a compression sleeve to help with Joni's edema. She came up with a cut-off wetsuit sleeve, often used for this very purpose. She placed it around Joni's arm and adjusted the volume on the IV bag. It was still too sluggish.

"A little higher, Maura, if you can." Reagan stood up to show Maura how high she needed the lifesaving bag of fluids.

Reagan bit the side of her lower lip looking at Maura's hands, which had become severely crippled over the years—the crusty nodules that were once fingers were now thick and stiff, unable to bend to hold onto anything. Maura was only forty-five and already showing advanced stages of tissue degeneration.

Ruthlessly, her debilitating disease had stolen the use of her hands, which were needed for everyday chores and for caring for her children. It was hard embracing them without feeling some sense of loss. It was impossible to untangle the daily knots in their seaborne hair, or to chop up much needed fruit for their meals. Now, Maura insisted on holding the broad-based bag overhead, delivering life-saving nutrients to her daughter. But her hands were shaking, causing her to lower the bag, making delivery of the fluids sluggish and interrupted.

"Let me take it." Reagan took the IV bag from Maura. "Just need to make it easier for you. . . . Here, how about pressing your elbows against the bag on the wall." Reagan took the slippery bag from her stubbed fingers and propped it for her. "It just needs to be a few inches higher to let those fluids move, if it's not too painful for you."

"I can't feel it anyway, too numb and dead, not steady." Drips of sweat rolled down her arm. "Jus' can't hold it up. I'm sorry, I keep trying. . . ."

Reagan understood—Maura was a mother and needed to do her job. She would make it work, as she always did—the need to care for others was so vital. This would be Reagan's first early intervention case, and if successful she could spread the word of success to other physicians who could share the knowledge and treatment worldwide.

But success meant lowering Joni's fever, which had originated from a recent cut, now rotting and festering. Reagan had to prevent the bacterial infection in her wound from spreading throughout her body. The fluids were vital for this to work.

"Just a little higher, Maura, if you can." Reagan spoke softly although the girl's life depended on it.

Maura's hands continued to shake; beads of sweat dripped off her forehead, rolling into her eyes. "I love her more than my world," Maura whispered. Her voice was now trembling, as she spoke with intense physical pain.

Reagan had to intervene before she had two patients to treat.

"Maybe if I massage the blood vessels near the port of the IV insertion, the fluids will start moving." Reagan stretched and released the tissue, like delicate dough, to create a pump for the fluid to move through.

"Huh, it's working, the flow is increasing. Okay, I got this, it might work. . . ." Without looking up, Reagan continued, "That's the way,

Maura. Keep it up. We've got it working now . . . just a little bit longer. . . ."

Reagan glanced toward Maura to offer reassurance. She almost dropped the task at hand. It wasn't Maura holding the bag upright to allow the flow of life, it was Jeremy.

"What in God's name—" Reagan was speechless. Her mouth dropped open as he spoke.

"So this is what you do." Jeremy held the bag of fluid, high in the air.

"What are you doing here?"

She looked back at Joni to assure the fluid was still flowing. She adjusted the flow to decrease it since there was a backflow starting. Joni's pulse raced, and the small heart rate monitor she was hooked up to set off the auditory warning alarm. Reagan was back at Joni's side in an instant. The child could arrest if she wasn't careful. The fast pulse persisted. Reagan grabbed her med bag and prepared an anti-arrhythmic injection to slow down her heart rate. She moved swiftly, drawing the fluid from a vial, tapping it twice, and injecting it into the small port inserted in Joni's wrist. The beeps went away.

Reagan adjusted the IV.

"So this is what you do!" Jeremy repeated. "I didn't realize . . . I had no idea . . . I was just curious. You're a doctor! I thought you were a—"

"How did you get here?" Reagan kept her eyes on Joni.

"By boat," he responded.

At that moment, Sachi ran in. "I'm so sorry, Miss Reagan. He tricked me into dropping him off. We were supposed to—"

Beep, beep, beep. . . .

Stethoscope in hand, Reagan refocused, assessing the heartbeats. "Bag up," she barked at Jeremy.

"Sachi, extend her head, now." Reagan started CPR, confident in her abilities and stable in her wits. Again the distress of the cardiac alarm terminated its warning sound. "Sachi, release. I have a pulse," she announced.

Jeremy remained quiet.

"Hang on, my dearest. It is not your time," Maura whispered, grasping her daughter's hand—with her palms, as if her own life depended on it.

Reagan sat back and waited, *please stabilize . . . please stabilize.* She took in a deep breath, realizing how tense her own muscles had become. "It's not her time. . . ." she repeated again. "Not her time." She glanced at Jeremy with uncertainty, feeling angry and grateful at the same time.

Her thoughts were overwhelmed with emotions. . . . *Why did he follow me here? What does he want? Oh yeah, the film, of course,* but she was mostly suspicious of the slick actor. Once she saw Joni was stable, she stood up and paced in the small room.

"You shouldn't have come here," Reagan scolded Jeremy as they exited the bure. "You must be invited. It is their private island and not for gawkers." She avoided his eyes as she walked in front of him, heading toward the dock. "Do you understand me?"

Sachi was close behind, masking Jeremy's response. "It won't happen again, Miss Reagan."

They walked down the path in silence, with Reagan leading the way. Jeremy followed each footstep with caution. There was a deathly silence.

"Reagan, I'm sorry, I shouldn't have barged in. I didn't realize. . . ."

"There are quite a few things you don't realize," she fired back.

They got in the boat. Reagan went straight to the stern and pulled the throttle. It always took a few tries before the engine fired up. Sachi looked on, embarrassed; it was his job.

Jeremy slumped into the seat at the front of the boat not knowing a bow wake would soak him once underway. She didn't bother telling him.

Reagan hopped out and kicked away the gunnel. "Thanks for your help, Sachi. Please tell Roger we are okay and I'll be back when Joni is settled."

Sachi took over the controls as Jeremy looked up, adrift.

15

~~~~~~~~~

EAGAN sat through the night with Joni, checking her vitals, stroking her forehead, keeping her comfortable. The heaviness of loss stayed with her as she watched Joni sleep fitfully. Short clips of memories raced through her mind—leaving the U.S., or was it escaping . . . her infamous surf trip ending—her boat in distress and her rescue by the islanders who suffered from leprosy and now she battled to save them.

She wavered between fatigue, sleep, and a subtle memory of her last relationship with an attorney, ten years prior. The worst of her waking memories assaulted her—the man she so loved had all the qualities she'd hoped for in a relationship: strength, compassion, integrity, intelligence, and he was polished, good-looking—the whole dreamy package. How could she have deceived herself? The answer was always the same—her work. Reagan had always been absorbed in work, love of medicine, her dedication to her patients.

Those memories were fading—more than ten years had passed since her residency in geriatrics, and her total immersion in working with aging patients. She had lived with the well-respected attorney boyfriend for two years. Never thinking that his interest in her work was disingenuous, she trusted him. He listened to every detail of

Reagan's day as if it was precious. She wondered about his endless questions about her patients, but she never thought . . . never considered the point of them.

One Saturday morning Reagan was off-duty, breezing through the morning paper, sipping slow-brewed coffee, when she scanned a headline: Corruption, Medicare Fraud, Elder Abuse. For no apparent reason, her heart rate increased, she read more closely, and there it was—his name, the lawyer providing legal defense for the corporate conglomerate who owned the chain of senior care facilities. Reagan's hands shook as she read the list of abuses reported by patients and their family members.

No . . . No . . . this can't be true. Reagan screamed as she ripped the paper to shreds. It was the end—not just to a relationship, it was the end to believing that things would change, that those who were afflicted with a disease, or just old age, could be safe.

The ancient fight-or-flight instinct took hold. Reagan decided at that moment she needed to leave; she needed to see the world anew, surf and feel a modicum of joy. She needed to cleanse herself of the pain, if that was even possible.

The wound and memory ran deep. Reagan felt it creep up every time she saw Jeremy. He was busy making his film with the dilettantes, and it was no concern of hers, except to keep the islanders out of harm's way. It was unnerving the way he appeared at odd times and in different places, as if he was always watching her.

I must be an idiot. Who is this actor guy? Sure, he's attractive . . . first a lawyer, now an actor, what is wrong with me? On and on her thoughts tumbled like a coffee grinder, around and around.

But why does he keep appearing? Why do I care? I don't care and that's it. Reagan was used to talking to herself, used to working out all sorts of problems in her head, agreeing and disagreeing, arranging and rearranging thoughts, measuring correct amounts of medicine and remeasuring; it was a system that kept her nicely focused.

Joni is stable. Best to go for a surf . . . rinse the emotions.

The morning light chased away her thoughts. Reagan left Joni briefly, to find Maura and let her know she was leaving. She watched Maura rise from her thick woven matt; it was such an effort. She had to balance on her crippled hands and try to gain enough strength to push upward. Reagan knew better—not to help her up. It would only upset Maura, who said over and over again to Reagan, "I need to do it myself."

Reagan stepped over to her and gave her a morning hug, whispering, "Joni's fever is gone. She needs to rest and take in as much water as possible. Coconut milk is fine too. Tell her Auntie said no running about for a few days."

Maura smiled. "I'll keep her close. You off to the dolphins now?"

Reagan laughed. "Yes, time to visit my other friends."

After dropping anchor on the sandy bottom, Reagan jumped into the warm sea hoping for some answers, seeking some solitude so she could listen to her own inner voice. But instead, her beloved dolphin friends appeared, racing through the waves, laughing at her as they dove underneath her, spiraling upward and making her laugh in return. They represented her faith, her belief system—the ocean, the animals, humans, the environment—all bound together in a universal energy, entwined, inextricable.

16

～～～

*J*EREMY walked up the gangway, his eyes cast down at the wooden slats, hoping to avoid the angry glare and impending assault of words from Jones and Bianca, who waited on the deck above.

"Damn it, Jeremy, you're late for our morning run-through."

Jones' fury was cut off by Bianca's fuming. "What happened to dinner last night? Did you forget? I'll leave this film so fast if you pull that stunt again. You are really pushing the prettyboy envelope."

Jones picked up where he'd left off. "Where the hell have you been? You split on us yesterday, and now you show up two hours late?" His voice escalated, since Jeremy was avoiding eye contact. "This isn't a Disney film where Jeremy gets to go play on his island whenever he wants. Time's a-wastin' brother, and it's my time you're wasting."

Jeremy tried to drown their muffled chatter. "Sorry, guys, I apologize, won't happen again. I had a problem with—"

"Hey, are you listening to me? You're blowin' it, dude." Jones yelled at him like a belligerent parent. "You have no idea how much I've slaved for you . . . and to pull a stunt like this."

"And what about me?" Bianca chimed in, the pitch in her voice up a few octaves. "You only think of yourself. The world doesn't revolve—"

"Come on, just get movin'. You're both driving me crazy." Jeremy shoved both hands in his pockets.

Like a referee, Jones stepped between Jeremy and Bianca. "Let's just get through the damn shot."

Jeremy suddenly felt tired, not from any physical exertion, but from what felt like an endless roadshow—the circus that surrounded him. There was something deep and indefinable he was reaching for but couldn't quite get to. He'd seen the islanders with leprosy but wasn't horrified or disgusted by them; he had looked to them for guidance. He watched as Reagan practiced medicine in the most compromising of circumstances, no white lab coats or sterile instruments—just a child in dire need of her skills.

He hadn't experienced much physical discomfort in his adult life, and this brief glimpse into Reagan's life was painstakingly honest. He thought of Bianca and Jones; they both seemed part of a silly charade, but he was still part of it too.

Conflicting emotions battled each other. *What is real and what is fiction? What is this film about anyway?* The neurons in his brain seemed overloaded—the voices too piercing, the decibels exceeding his comfort level. He tried to retrieve the feeling of the quiet boat ride back to the resort, but the feeling was gone. Instead, short vignettes from his childhood flooded in—neglected by his alcoholic father, a neurotically jealous mother, pushing his father toward endless affairs. Oh, how the neighbors loved to gossip about them. Jeremy created his own world where the yelling, hitting, crying, and throwing things were part of a theatrical play. He would become the hero and save his mother, but he never did. The bloodstains on his hands forever etched in his memory. He had tried to take the knife from his father's hands, but he couldn't stop the powerful arm lunging toward her. He wasn't strong enough or fast enough. It was over in seconds. Jeremy had felt powerless from that moment on. No longer a child, the only way he could gain control was by holding a script and escaping reality.

Snapping back, Jeremy read the script like a hollow man. He recited words that felt foreign and artificial. He had always been able to fall into character with ease, somehow knowing the story being read was fuller than his own life, but he felt adrift, without purpose. Jeremy tripped on one of his lines, losing track of the script in front of him.

"What is wrong with you, dear? Did that moon keep you up all night? Do you need some coffee?" Bianca tried to sound sympathetic, but the words came out as mockery.

Jeremy repeated the line, trying to focus on the connection of words. "You are for me complete—Wait, let me try that again. What does this say? I don't get it." There was no meaning, no feeling. It was a love scene and he needed to portray intimacy, which he had always been able to fake.

"You are the only one for me. My life is not complete without you in it, Reag—uh, Roxanne." The name of the character that Bianca was playing hadn't adjusted in his head yet.

Jones gave him a sideways look. "Where the hell are you, Jeremy? Pull it together. Jean Michael is coming our way."

Jeremy glanced up to catch the approaching director.

"Are we ready to roll?" Jean Michael asked.

Bianca looked at Jeremy for an answer. Her head shook back and forth. "I need a few minutes," she said demurely to the director.

Jones pulled Jeremy aside and whispered in his ear, "Look, you either get it together fast or he'll bury us. Bianca's not the only one who needs this to go well. Jean knows plenty of other guys out there eager to take this script away from you. So what's it gonna be?"

Wiping Jones' spit off his cheek and ear, Jeremy took a deep breath. "Yeah, all good here. Let's roll." He faced Bianca with his chest touching hers. "My life is not complete without you in it, Roxanne." He held Bianca in his arms and pulled off a star performance. He kissed her plastic red lips and closed his eyes holding a different vision in his head. Just as he released his mouth from hers, he glanced over his shoulder and noticed Reagan passing by, her eyes shifting from his as soon as he caught her stare. She picked up her pace and left.

"Cut!" the director announced. "Let's do it again, without taking your eyes off her."

17

$\mathcal{E}$XHAUSTION overtook her. Reagan's head touched the pillow and her spine melted into the dense mattress. She was mesmerized by the revolving fan overhead, unable to look away. Her eyes followed its circular and hypnotic path until she couldn't hold her eyelids open anymore. She'd been up all night with Joni, chasing her fever, flushing the infection, and holding it together for Maura. Then out to the reef for a surf to rinse out her toxic thoughts. Although her eyes were shut and sleep was close, something kept her tossing and turning in the narrow bed. It was a new and uncomfortable feeling—fueled by fear and loneliness. She hadn't felt attracted to anyone since she'd arrived on the island and wasn't even sure how she felt about Jeremy. Perhaps she was simply intrigued by his sudden appearance in her day. She squelched the thought and drifted into a deep sleep.

A waterspout was approaching Reagan in the surf. Its swirling pattern pulled at her body, drawing her out of the water. The clouds acted like a cushion intending to protect her, but the pull of the spout kept her out of reach. The vortex was fast approaching and she panicked. She held tight to her surfboard, not willing to let it go. It was her lifeline. But her grip was giving way—her fingers thick and stiff, were not able to hold on to the rails any longer. She was about to let go when she was awakened by a loud commotion outside her bure.

Bianca and Dominique were arguing about something. Reagan could barely hear their words.

"Yeah, well, he can't focus on nothin' cuz of you."

"Don't you dare make this about me, he brought it all on himself."

Reagan turned over, hiding under her pillow, reassuring herself she was just dreaming. The voices turned into yelling and she couldn't help but hear Jeremy's name tossed about.

"You kept him up all night!" Bianca yelled. "Just because you're . . . well . . . younger, doesn't mean you get him all to yourself."

Reagan got up and pulled back the bamboo shade over the window. She rubbed her eyes and refocused in time to catch Bianca raise her hands in the air and yell something at Dominique.

Watching in disbelief, Reagan witnessed the two bicker back and forth. "Don't touch me. No wonder he's done with you. You pushy, pathetic bitch."

Reagan was appalled by the banter. Closing the window shade, she went back to bed . . . *those days are over . . . never again.* She swatted away the memory of her lawyer boyfriend turned fraud and womanizer. Coming home late smelling of whiskey and someone else's perfume . . . disgusting, yes and pathetic. Here it was being played out again right in front of her. Reagan put on her headphones and adjusted the volume to enhance the violin chords, blocking out the noise pollution outside her window. The thought of Jeremy's piercing eyes entered her thoughts momentarily as she dozed back to sleep.

JEREMY flipped the pages of the script for his next scene. Taking an oversized bite of his fresh ahi sandwich, he tried to envision the scene he was reading. He was distracted by the incident with Reagan the day before. The little girl lying there drenched in sweat and fever, he could practically see her heart beating dangerously fast. Then the CPR, a young life was in Reagan's hands . . . *she's a doctor . . . huh . . . a surfing doctor.* . . . His thoughts collapsed as Dominique approached.

"Hey, I need to talk with you. She's really senile, you know, forgets everything, talks too much . . . I'm fed up!"

Jeremy, still thinking of Reagan, took another sip of the Fiji Bitter and stared vacantly out to sea. "Say what? What's the problem? Calm down, Domi. Who's senile?"

Jeremy knew Dominique had been hesitant to commit to this film with Bianca playing a bigger role. Even though Dominique was to be the main love interest, Bianca got superior billing and a heftier paycheck.

"Pathetic Bianca, that's who's senile."

"Sit and join me, Domi. How 'bout a glass of wine?" Jeremy pushed his plate away and summoned for a bottle of wine. "Relax, it's great to have you here. You know you'll always be my favorite leading lady." He needed to keep her happy, keep her on script. Dominique had a natural beauty, with long auburn tresses and high cheekbones accentuating her oval eyes. There was plenty for Bianca to be jealous about. Aside from her looks, Dominique could poke fun at everything and even tell a joke if she had to. She had a base sense of humor that film crews usually found entertaining.

Calming down, Dominique twirled her hair. "What do you think of my hair color?"

Jeremy filled up their wine glasses—hers more than his.

"I read an article in Ms. mag that said I shouldn't go too dark or else it will make me look older." She pulled on a long twine of hair. "Do you think it's too dark? How 'bout mysterious? Does it make me look mysterious?"

Jeremy leaned back in his chair as if trying to decide. "Nope."

"What's 'nope' mean? Seriously, baby, what do you think? Do you like my hair color?" She went back to twirling, and leaned in, letting her silk blouse fall off her shoulder.

Jeremy chuckled. "It's fine . . . dark, or whatever . . . it's just fine." He was distracted by her hand rubbing his thigh under the table.

"How about we go to my room and finish this bottle, or better yet, get some champagne?" Dominique slurred her words as she drained her half glass of Zinfandel.

"Nice idea, but we still have some work today and gotta feel half decent tomorrow." He shifted his chair away from her and her roving hand.

"What's with the new Jeremy, so serious, no fun. What's up with that?"

"I'm just—" Jeremy regrouped and tried to explain the inexplicable. "I'm tired, that's all, a bit off my game."

He told the truth and lied at the same time. He was tired . . . tired of fake love, fake happiness, fake tears, colored hair, rosy-red lips, breasts hardened by implants, kissing botox frozen faces and, most of all, he was tired of faking who he was. His arousal had crashed and burned, right there, right then—a hundred-dollar bottle of wine, a voluptuous woman, on a remote tropical island—*nothing*.

18

$\sim\!\!\sim\!\!\sim$

EAGAN woke to the sounds of fruit bats in the trees pulling at grape seedlings on their branches. Their crisp chirp was distinctive and refreshing. As she walked out to the lanai, one of them dove and clenched a grape in its mouth, swallowing it whole.

"Nice catch," Reagan said, sipping her morning brew. The robust flavor of the coffee piqued her senses, accentuated by the swallows' screech high above the trees as they looked for prey. She picked up her sketchpad and began the graceful dance of sketching. She guided the pencil to initiate a shape—the upward angles felt easy and soothing. The shape of a flower took place without any conscious effort. A few minutes later, she closed the pad, not quite finishing her single hibiscus petal.

Reagan was about to make her third visit to a young man on the island to confirm his will to die. She held fast to her required five visits, each time noticing how introspective each person became. At first they were filled with uncertainty, which progressed to absolute intention, and then settled into gratitude and forgiveness. When this final stage was apparent and their conditions affected their daily quality of living so that life was essentially unbearable, Reagan succumbed to their will. Then elders and family were notified and plans on the day of finality ensued.

Reagan had found peace in the decisions of individuals choosing when they wanted to die. She acknowledged the empowerment in letting people have some control over a disease that robbed them of their freedom and joy in life. She had also watched older patients live with the painful progression of leprosy and fight for survival, only to be replaced by a torturous, slow death that no human deserved. Their ability to breathe was the first challenge, followed by respiratory failure and finally cardiac distress. All of this, while their loved ones watched and writhed in their painful observation of what their family member was enduring.

"It's not fair," Chief Toro had said when he first met Reagan. "Their suffering is beyond a normal person's death. They not only have a difficult life, but even death is unbearable." The chief was wise beyond his years, and he promised those who suffered to make their days more enjoyable or at least, purposeful. Reagan was witness to the endless inspiration that Chief Toro offered, encouraging the islanders to build their own bures, dig the gardens, mind the chickens, improve their fishing skills, and sew the nets if they could. Reagan was welcomed by them, not as an outsider, but as Kōkua—helper, healer.

Now as she packed her bags for the third visit with Geoffrey, who was only thirty-two years old, she was prepared for his final gesture of gratitude. She finished her daily inspection in the mirror, paying close attention to any changes in her pigmentation. She never experienced fear with these inspections; it was just a tedious necessity like flossing teeth. She grabbed her backpack, then a bunch of fresh bananas from the tree, and headed to the dock.

As she loaded the last of her supply bags, Reagan looked up. There he was again.

Jeremy was walking down the dock toward her boat. "Can I join you?"

"Not today." She untied the lines.

Just like the first time they met, Jeremy fumbled over his words. He tried to appear unaffected. "I can hold an IV bag up all day long," he said, searching for his worth.

"Sorry, this one I do alone." She avoided his eyes, not wanting to give an explanation.

"Why don't you like me?"

"That's not it. I simply don't need your help today," she answered in a firm tone used years ago for volunteer hospital interns. Yet she felt for him, his insecurities. She softened. "Toss me that line." She nodded in the direction of the stern cleat. "Now, tie a half-hitch across the top into the crate." His blank stare and open mouth said everything.

"You see, if this end were to get snagged, then it would release the stress," she said, demonstrating how to tie a half-hitch slipknot. Her elbow brushed against his and she felt a slight tingle. "Okay, good, you're getting it, fasten the end of the coil with this bevel."

Reagan's voice had a strange quiver as she absorbed the warmth of his skin.

"When you pull both ends of the rope in opposite directions, you secure the rope in place." She tried steadying her voice while explaining the purpose of the knot.

Reagan had almost forgotten the signs of increased heartbeat, the uncomfortable warmth developing into a sweat, both internally and in her shaky hands. She redirected her body language back to the task. Her heart felt deconditioned to arousal. Reagan's level of compassion to end a life had exercised her heart in a different way.

"Secure the rope in place. Pull it in opposite directions."

"What does that even mean?" Jeremy ran his fingers through his hair.

"Here, try it again." She placed her hand on top of his, guiding it gently, moving, twisting, and reaching for the other end of the rope. "See where this goes?"

The magician-like movement of their arms together was a slow-motion dance. When the knot was complete, Jeremy's hands were the only ones on the rope. His eyes were fixed on hers.

"Did you see that?"

Reagan held her breath.

"What next?" Jeremy stood tall, facing her—still holding onto the rope.

"Jeremy, where are you, honey?" Dominique's voice echoed through the resort entry.

Reagan let out an audible exhale. "Sounds like you're needed somewhere else." Relieved for the interruption, she moved to the back of the boat. She knew he couldn't join her today and she needed to get going. Her sigh of relief helped her heart rate regulate to its normal pace and rhythm.

"There you are," Dominique huffed, peering over the top of the dock. "It's time to go over lines."

Reagan cringed at the sound of Dominique's whiny voice, but on it went. The second woman showed up, and standing next to each other, they looked like clones but at different stages in life. One porcelain doll was a bit more cracked than the other.

"Oh, Jeremy, honey, time to go."

"Many women in your life I see," Reagan commented.

Jeremy dropped the rope and his head in one movement. "Are you kidding?" He turned toward the two women above.

"Seems complicated." Reagan started the whaler's engine and released the dock lines. Her boat turned seaward and she pressed the throttle forward.

"No, it's not what it seems," Jeremy blurted out. "Have dinner with me tonight."

Reagan knew he had said something but couldn't hear over the blasts of engine noise. More serious matters lay ahead.

19

~~~

"WHAT happened?" Reagan asked Geoffrey's wife, Eve. Rushing to their side, Reagan attempted to stop the hemorrhagic bleed. The amount of blood covering both of them made it difficult for Reagan to fully assess. Eve had both hands over her husband's stomach holding the massive wound together. Reagan took his pulse.

"He's still alive."

"He tried to kill himself." Eve sobbed.

Reagan wondered what stage Geoffrey was in—way past fear and denial. She quickly concluded—anger.

Geoffrey was a severe case, showing early signs of leprosy as a young child, only to be robbed of any humane life until he met Eve. They had married and had two children. He loved them with all his being, but Geoffrey had severe deformities, including loss of vision in one eye, disfigured extremities, and extreme peripheral nerve damage. He hadn't felt his right arm since he was fifteen years old, and his most recent progression was a failing lung that had led to pneumonia.

"Only one steady lung, small pneumothorax in the other," Reagan recited as if she was in a hospital talking to a colleague.

"What does that mean?" Eve's voice was barely audible. She had used her last ounce of energy holding the wound together for thirty minutes before Reagan raced in.

"It's like a tire that has a leak in it." She didn't elaborate on the part about his lung collapsing; the high-pitched whistle sound made it apparent even without a stethoscope.

"He's wheezin' the whole night. No air . . . so much pain. Then he cough an' cough, 'til his face turned red as that blood."

Reagan imagined the unproductive cough that resulted from the damaged lung tissue. It couldn't keep up with the imbalance of air pressure in his chest. The panic must have been massive. She checked his vitals, assessed the wound, and reached for the med bag.

Eve went on. "He grabbed those shears and jus' kept stabbin' and stabbin'." She was shaking as she looked over at the bloody weapon on the floor. "He said it mus' stop. I try to take 'em, but he too angry, the pain too much. . . ." Her sobs replaced the words.

The blades on the shears were soaked in dark purple and black blood—the oxygen had left the bloodstream long before it left his body. "Dear God," she whispered, "how does it get this bad?" She pictured the scene of Geoffrey gasping for air with a partially collapsed drowning lung, in dire pain from the carbon dioxide overload, with no end in sight. As far as she knew, no one had ever tried to end their own life on the island.

Reagan administered an IV of albuterol. "This will help, my friend, this will help." Grabbing a large bundle of gauze from her med kit, she packed the wound and held pressure for several minutes until the white gauze turned dark red. With no more gauze in her kit, she placed a large surgical bandage over the massive wound and then wrapped her sarong over the top, fastening it tourniquet-tight.

"Is he gone?" Eve pleaded.

"No, just relieving the compression in his lungs so he can relax. He should be out for a few hours. Just watch him and make sure he doesn't pull the bandage off." She didn't dare administer the fatal dose of propofol without his permission, although the consent was desperate and implied. She had to get it right. She couldn't bear to go through another mishap. *Do no harm, do no harm.* This was her oath, her commitment to medicine.

How can I help? I can't do it without his consent. I must wait . . . Do no harm. He must wait.

She paced outside of Geoffrey's bure when Maura approached her.

"Maura, tell me about how bad it gets," Reagan began. "I know I've been here awhile, but this is the first attempted suicide I've seen."

Glancing back and forth in the direction of Geoffrey's bure, Maura took a breath and bowed her head. Her hands were crossed at the wrists. "It's not the pain or ugliness we fear, it's the hatin'. The others look at us . . . jus' the wrong way, like we did somethin' to them. Not lookin' in our eyes, we just not like them, so they jus' hate us." Maura welled up with tears. "It's like someone grabbin' at your heart all day long, not knowing how bad you'll become and how alone you'll be—that is my greatest fear."

Sitting on the edge of a bamboo chair, Reagan listened and absorbed the powerful words. There was a pause in Maura's answer to the difficult question. Reagan's eyes followed Maura's swaying movements—a mixture of back and forth, side to side shifts in her body, resulting in a semicircular sway. She finally came to a stop and her eyes blinked excessively.

"I'm jus' a prisoner, trapped in this body with no escape, with no hope or nothin'. And yes, I would end it myself if I could, if it weren't for my girls."

Reagan looked out at the ocean trying to process Maura's honest words. The trade winds had shifted and swirled in contradictory directions. Her hair whipped across her face and regardless of how much she swept it away, the restless strands returned, clouding her view. She closed her eyes and wept internally for Geoffrey, the chief, and all the others. She felt helpless and skeptical about how to repair the wounds of the human spirit. Although Reagan realized words would not do justice to the prejudices of the world, she attempted. "Maura, it's just not fair . . . it's—"

The lump in her throat squelched her from saying how repulsed she was by the shunning of the disfigured, or for that matter, the rejection of any human being for simply being different. She held Maura close to her chest, weeping together—silent at first, but then deeper. The horrors of the chronic oppression haunted her. Reagan gripped her chest like a cardiac patient sensing a heart attack. The stabbing pain was intense and her heart rate was going into fibrillations. It was as if she was reliving Geoffrey's own experience. She gasped for oxygen, unable to fill her own lungs. The edge of panic set in.

"I need to help Geoffrey." She gave Maura one last empathetic hug. "I know what to do now . . . the right thing to do." She grabbed her med bag, searching for a specific vial; the one that would help "do no harm." Emptying the bag of all its contents on the floor, she realized it wasn't there. The propofol was back at the resort. She had a standard practice of not bringing it with her until the end-of-life plan was concrete and agreed upon by the patient and immediate family. Reagan held this as a safeguard against hasty decision-making, which she hoped she was not doing now. No, this was not a hasty decision. She needed to help Geoffrey end his suffering at once.

"Maura, is there any emergency propofol in the chief's medical chest?"

Maura shook her head.

"I need to get to the resort. I'll be back as soon as I can. Will you go sit with Geoffrey and Eve and assure them I'm coming?" It was a request more than a question. Reagan raced away in her boat, desperate to shorten the time span ahead of her and return to end Geoffrey's suffering.

The strong tail wind accelerated her boat speed back to the resort—it would be a challenge returning to the island, to get back to Geoffrey in time. He would wake soon and the panic would return. She pressed the throttle all the way down—hard, and leaned into the wheel. Once lined up with the small harbor pylons, Reagan didn't decelerate as she normally would. The boat's wake slammed into the dock as she made a sharp turn, narrowly missing it.

Cutting the engine, Reagan caught Roger on the approach. "Roger, hang onto the boat, I need meds quick . . . it's Geoffrey."

"What do you need?" Roger caught the bowline that Reagan had tossed his way. He fended the boat with his foot and settled the rocking chaos with both arms on the side rail.

She leapt out and scrambled up the gangway to unlock the shed where the emergency supplies were housed. *Where is it? Where is the*— She was frantic in her search.

Muffled voices emanated from the deck and bar area—Jean Michael was directing someone to move closer, more light, less chatter. . . .

Reagan heard a commotion then felt his heat behind her.

"Hey, what's the rush? You okay?" Jeremy hovered over her.

"Oh . . . Jeremy, I gotta go, no time to chat."

"What about dinner, are we still on for tonight?" He stayed close to her.

"Not likely." She avoided his glare, but felt the heat of his body. Slamming the lid of the medical kit, she checked the lock and darted back to the boat.

Jeremy followed but stopped to pick up an empty syringe she had dropped.

"This is different." Reagan reprimanded Roger. "This is why I'm here. It can't happen again. Those meds are not for others' recreation."

Jeremy stood at the edge of the boat holding up the empty syringe. She grabbed it from his hand without looking at him.

"Are you sure you're okay?" His hand was left hanging in the air.

Reagan moved fast, her legs lurched back and forth, from bag to bag, and bow to stern. She ignored Jeremy, who hovered over her asking something. She threw a dark drawstring bag at the center console, and it made a stark clanging noise. She pushed the boat away with such a force that the stern hit the edge of the wooden platform.

"WHAT was that all about?" Jeremy looked to Roger who was already walking up the gangway.

Roger waved his hand in the air. "Oh nothing, just a little hiccup. No worries."

"But what's going on?" Jeremy followed Roger then stopped as he heard the voice overhead.

"Jeremy, let's get back to the script," Jones yelled over the top of the dock.

Roger turned around and faced Jeremy. "Really, it's all fine, just get back to your film."

Jeremy and Roger both turned their heads as Jones' voice assailed them.

"You've done it again, Jeremy. Get your ass back up here."

Roger rolled his eyes. "Go on, she'll be fine. She always is." He walked away leaving Jeremy alone in the middle of the gangway.

"Jeremy, now!"

Jeremy put his hands in his pockets and slinked back up the gangway toward the impatient cast and crew. Stopping midstride, he mumbled, "I can't . . . I have to go back. That's it, I have to find her."

Jean Michael leaned over the dock railing. "Come on, Jeremy, we're almost done with this scene."

"I can't . . . I mean I've got something I have to do. Sorry, Jean." He choked out the words, tangled in fear. "What am I doing . . . I don't know . . . I've got to get to her." Jeremy turned on his heels and ran back down the dock.

A blur of voices chased him but the impulse overrode them. Jeremy threw off the dock lines of one of the small runabouts and started the engine. It revved on the first try and he headed the boat toward open water, just as he had seen Reagan do many times.

He'd had his hands on the wheel of a boat a few times in movies, but he'd never really handled one. Someone usually stood next to him and instructed him for the shot and was ready to take over. He knew how to turn a boat like a car with the steering wheel, but that was about it. Now as he made a sharp right turn out of the protected harbor, the boat tipped and jerked in answer to the abrupt changes of conditions. The waves were short and choppy; the headwind tested him and tossed him in all directions.

Oh crap, I can do this, he whispered into the wind, unsure if he could. He fought the wheel, first too hard to the left, then he swung it too hard to the right, overcorrecting on each turn. He'd watched Reagan leave the cove with such control. He imagined how to be calm—like her. His hands relaxed and the boat settled into a straight course toward the island. He didn't look back.

20

$\sim\!\!\!\sim\!\!\!\sim$

*R*EAGAN arrived back at Geoffrey's side; he had deteriorated to critical condition. His pulse was faint and his breaths frantic; his cold body had surrendered hours ago. He was no longer coherent or talking. His suffering was affecting everyone.

"Maura, will you help me?" Reagan knew Maura understood.

"Of course, I do what I can, I do what you need. I know you'll help him." Maura's gaze looked upward. She pressed her wrists together in prayer.

Reagan usually kept her personal emotions in check and maintained her composure to stay focused on her patient. She also considered the timing of the lethal delivery based on how the family members were doing. But these circumstances were different. Geoffrey's suffering was complicated by his wound and the determination to end his own life. There were no rational conversations or final phase of acceptance. There was no gratefulness on behalf of the patient. This time Reagan would have to end the suffering on her own terms.

Stick to your oath, she reminded herself, *do no harm. His suffering is over. Do your job.*

Reagan prepared the vial and syringe, noting the small amount of propofol available.

How could he . . . how could Roger breach the narcotics storage . . . for a sleepless guest? This has never happened, how could he? She estimated how much additional sedative she would have to use from another form, crushing and liquefying it to add to the vial. It was unprecedented. Her colleagues would strongly disapprove, not only of the chemistry corruption, but for choosing when to inject the lethal dose without patient consent. Her moral compass was strong and would guide her. She thought only of Geoffrey and his need to let go.

Maura's hands shook as usual. It was times like these that Reagan wished she had a steady partner not only to assist her, but also to provide the much-needed colleague support in decision-making.

UNSURE how to gauge the boat speed approaching the island dock, Jeremy plowed straight into it, hoping to stop his forward momentum. The boat ricocheted off a few times before he realized he had to cut the engine. He threw the bowline over the upright stanchion and circled it a few times then threw the rest on the platform, neglecting the stern altogether. He ran up the plank and was soon surrounded by a small group of islanders.

"Miss Reagan say no before. You trick us," one of the islanders warned Jeremy. He had severe facial deformities in addition to clubbed hands and feet. Jeremy looked away for a moment, but then overcame his reaction, remembering why he was there. The other two men had severely impaired hands and towered in size. The word "thugs" came to mind, and Jeremy convinced himself it was similar to great Hollywood artistry. He had certainly seen scarier disfigured faces than these, though never without the help of a talented makeup artist.

Jeremy blurted out his intentions. "I'm here for Reagan. I was supposed to be on her boat but needed to wait for some medications for her." He was proud of his quick thinking and ability to manipulate others when needed. "Honestly, no trick, she needs me."

"I'll show you," the man offered warily.

Jeremy was relieved, convinced his fabricated excuse lowered the islanders' guard. He needed to get to Reagan, and that justified his white lies.

21

$\sim\!\!\sim\!\!\sim$

REAGAN focused on the chemistry in front of her. "Seventy-five percent dilution of propofol with another sedative should decrease my dilation time by half. Or is it one-quarter?" She spoke out loud, as if discussing the options with a colleague. Her independence served her well on this island, but she often questioned her objectivity when it came to new practices. "This has to work," she whispered. "No mistakes. Don't overthink this . . . do no harm." Reagan looked to Maura for support, but her head was already bowed in respect.

Geoffrey's wife knelt at his head chanting a prayer with an even melody. "Yashee . . . mammmiiiii . . . naaammmaaass . . . hmmm hmmm Yashee hmmm hmmm praise him in your name . . . hmm . . . hmm."

Reagan didn't know the meaning of their prayers, but she felt at ease when they were hummed or recited. Her emotions settled as they sang. The melodic contour shaped her sense of belonging, while the tone nurtured and encouraged her. She felt comfort knowing they were ready for the end-of-life transition.

Reagan finished the mixture and prepared the flesh. It was tense and full of distress. She could already feel the skin shriveling from all the blood loss. She massaged it gently, trying to expose a viable vein. Geoffrey suddenly became lucid and aware. He looked into Reagan's eyes and nodded with gratitude. She responded with a similar look. "No more suffering, Geoffrey," was all she could say as she plunged the syringe forward with a steady pressure to empty the chamber of poison. All three of the women bowed their heads in silence and held each other's hands.

Standing at the opening of the bure, Jeremy was silent. The air was still—the sea glass chimes at the edge of the window barely swayed. The room seemed crowded with four people in such a small place, so focused on a body. There was dampness on Jeremy's cheeks—a combination of sweat, fear, and shock. He grabbed at his chest in response to a strap-like pressure across his body and gasped for air.

Reagan whirled around to see him and the shocked look on his face. She was surprised at her initial feelings of ease. She tried to conjure up anger to let him know his presence wasn't okay, but she couldn't. It was okay that he was there.

Maura took Jeremy's hand in her gnarled one and gripped it gently.

Jeremy looked at each of the women and then to Geoffrey. "Is he dead?" The direct question seemed like that of a child's, unaware of what death was or looked like, yet he did. A brief flash of his mother's blood-soaked chest ran through him. He swallowed hard.

Maura lifted her eyes. "Yes, his suffering is over."

Reagan stood up slowly, hearing Maura's words. She hesitated, "He doesn't . . . understand." Reagan walked out of the bure confused. Her emotions had now shifted to Jeremy's unveiling of her secret. She wasn't ashamed but rather protective of her motives—the deep desire to help patients on a level at which most physicians weren't willing to assist. Jeremy followed and took hold of her arm.

"I don't want to be judged." Standing erect, Reagan raised her hands in the air. "His suffering was unbearable . . . I mean, he just couldn't—"

Reagan tried to explain her actions and Geoffrey's painful act of bludgeoning to take his own life. Desperate to put into words the years of deafening silence that this colony had endured, she was compelled to stand up for them and all their endless suffering. But instead, she stumbled over words that were mangled in a wreckage of thoughts, mixed up in exaggerated gestures.

Jeremy put his index finger on her lips, silencing her, calming her. "I understand. Really."

Her thoughts wanted to rage. *You can't possibly understand*, but the gentle pressure of his finger on her lips immobilized her. Reagan was transfixed almost against her will. Once again, she was drawn to the curious patterns in his eyes, an unusual mix of green and brown that created a soft glow around his iris. But there was no time for an exchange. Geoffrey's blood was still on her hands and all over her sarong.

Maura peered out of the bure, and in a low voice, asked Reagan to help her clean Geoffrey. She looked up at Jeremy with an intense gaze. "I'm sorry. Thank you, this is a difficult moment."

Turning away from him, Reagan touched her lower lip, wondering why there remained a slight sensation of heat.

JEREMY stood alone, perplexed by his own actions, and not sure what to do next. He felt embarrassed that he'd made the gesture, intent on kissing her. He was momentarily caught between a selfish need and a profound urge he could not silence. He was sincere in his words; he did understand the man's suffering needed to end. Jeremy's sense of confusion came from within himself; his inner numbness was slowly wearing down. A sense of quiet embraced him.

The islanders convened to move Geoffrey's body and prepare for the burial. Things were handled quickly after a death. Even in this case, which wasn't planned in advance, they were all there to lay the body to rest and start the healing process.

"There will be a small ceremony now with all the islanders," Reagan explained to Jeremy. "His name is Geoffrey." She smiled at all the people gathering to help. "He was loved by everyone."

Jeremy remained silent. His hands were clasped with his gaze downward.

"Are you okay?" Reagan touched his hands. She saw the pain, the sorrow, the invisible bruise of tragedy.

Jeremy looked directly at Reagan, his shoulders hunched forward. His mouth opened, then shut again. He looked beyond Reagan and down at her hands holding his. "Can I help?" Jeremy had never offered to help anyone, since his path was always handled. The words caught him by surprise, but they came out so naturally.

"Can you help carry his body to the shrine up the hill?" Reagan pointed to a steep incline with random boulders scattered in the path.

"Anything, anything at all. I need to help."

The half-mile journey up the path was arduous, but the five men assisting distracted Jeremy from his fatigue. Their bodies were all disfigured and disabled to some extent, yet they stepped forward without complaint. One man had a considerably shorter leg than the other and moved more easily than Jeremy as they ascended along the difficult terrain.

At the crest of the hill, a makeshift shrine was being built. Intricate carvings on totems, painted bird skulls, and a variety of feathers decorated the shrine. Some of Geoffrey's Sunday clothes were placed at the bottom and young children were picking off plumeria petals and spreading them along the path. The air was filled with an intoxicating scent of a sugary butter. Across the way, people were digging a grave with small shovels and picks, rudimentary tools ill-suited for the task. But the job progressed in an efficient manner. Those looking on hummed with the workers. It had a familiar timbre, but Jeremy couldn't quite identify it.

Reagan also hummed, and he couldn't believe how well she blended into the crowd. She almost looked like them, though not disfigured in any way. In fact, she was more beautiful than any woman he had ever seen. Jeremy stood motionless, yet engulfed in waves of unexpected emotion.

The elder leader held his arms upward. "We gather to offer our son Geoffrey to his beloved creator, and now he looks down on us, his family. We pray for his safe journey home, from dust to dust. . . ."

Jeremy found himself making the sign of the cross as if he had done it before, yet he hadn't. He wasn't sure how he knew the gestures, but they simply fell into place. He bowed his head.

"Your son Geoffrey gave up his life for us. He taught us well and placed others before him," the elder said. "May his soul rest and his spirit take flight."

Thinking about these words, Jeremy froze. He rarely gave consideration to others' feelings or needs. What had he become? A selfish, spoiled actor. No one had told him . . . no one had said anything. He shook his head thinking of the years centered only on himself and his career. He simply lived from film to film, taking on different characters, not ever giving a thought to the message that character or film was delivering. It was always about the fame and fortune, never about virtue or respect.

Tension ran throughout Jeremy's body—his shoulders and hands tightened and his brows inched toward each other. There was deep remorse and reflection, both foreign notions for him. He dropped his gaze to the dirt path and rocked side to side as if searching for something lost.

"You okay, son?" An older woman hobbled next to Jeremy and nudged him with her elbow. "The sadness come to you . . . let it go." She motioned to the men digging the grave.

Wiping the sweat off his face, Jeremy nodded. He cleared his voice. "Uh, yeah, I'm good."

Jeremy's eyes met Reagan's from across the crowd as he spoke with the old woman. He swallowed back an emotion and tried to keep it together. The weight of it all affected him. For the first time he could remember, he felt calm in a crowd. He suddenly envisioned his mother from years before her death. She was carrying a birthday cake to him and singing, *Oh the singing, her voice, her smile.* He now remembered the good, not just the blood on her chest.

A small child standing next to Jeremy reached for his hand and then held it with both of her tiny ones. She was precious in her handling of his imposing yet fragile spirit. The girl glanced at his tearful eyes and, making a gesture, she said, "Can you make me big, I need to see Uncle Geoffrey . . . and say goodbye now."

Jeremy lifted her onto his hip, and the small girl put her arm around him. This simple gesture caused tears to well up and a confluence of emotion Jeremy could barely conceal. His grieving wasn't over the loss of another human being, but over the loss of himself. He seemed to be in physical pain as he focused on the years of not being a better person, the years thinking he should have saved his own mother from the rage of his alcoholic father. He had only lived the lives of his characters and never the role of Jeremy Black.

Fatherhood had never entered his mind, and now he tried to recollect if he had ever starred in any films with a child, realizing he had not. He cherished the little girl's embrace and her need of his support. He felt a loss at having missed the experience of a simple hug from a child. He had always shied away from kids; their dirty and sticky hands were a turn-off. They just never served a purpose in his life. He had even avoided dating women who already had children, as they seemed like an unwelcome hassle. The shame of these thoughts assailed him.

"I'm Aerin," the girl said proudly, showing off her missing front teeth. "I'm five. How old are you?"

"I'm forty years older than you." Jeremy changed his voice to match her tone. "Do you know how old that makes me?"

"Too many coconuts." She giggled.

Reagan approached. She let out a small chuckle. "I see you have a new friend."

Jeremy looked at the girl in a fatherly fashion that surprised them both. "What have you discovered here?" Jeremy asked Reagan.

"Something extraordinary, and beyond words or explanations. It's a fountain of hope." She smiled at Aerin.

Aerin wiggled free of Jeremy and ran to meet her cousins.

Jeremy stood next to Reagan as they were audience to the vibrant island songs and dances. He brushed up against her arm several times, swaying to the hymns. His own humming voice grew with the crowds' new volume. The celebratory hymns went on for another thirty minutes until, one by one, people made their way back down the hill.

As they walked away from the rousing inner circle, Jeremy asked Reagan, "What happens next?"

She stopped and stared at him. "Uh, what do you—?"

Jeremy took her hand into his and responded to her quizzical look. "With all of this."

There was a warmth to her skin, and Jeremy tenderly pulled the back of her hand to his cheek.

Reagan took a deep breath. "Time to head back home."

Jeremy stopped walking. "Home?"

"Back to the resort . . . home."

Jeremy tried to hold onto her wrist as it slipped out of his hand, but it fell to her side. They walked through the village and Reagan pointed to the various families' bures, explaining their daily routine and lifestyle. "Everyone lives communally. They contribute what they are good at and share their abundance with each other. There is very little strife here; they depend on each other for survival. It's only when the outside world infringes that things seem to get upset."

Jeremy listened intently to every word, catching her subtle message, while admiring everything he was witnessing. There was a natural flow of movement—no rush, no harshness, rather a simple and symbiotic gathering. He had never seen anything like it.

Reagan smiled as they passed an older couple holding each other's disfigured hands. "The only hierarchy is respect for the elders. There is also a shared acknowledgment that nature and the environment dictate everyone's health."

They walked through the lush landscape of foliage, which collectively created a blend of green, yellow, orange, and pink. "The indigenous plants of the South Pacific are rich in antioxidants as well as toxins. Knowing each one is imperative for survival here." She smiled at the significance of her explanation. "The psychotropic properties were used for centuries before modern pharmacology. Much of the flora is endangered, including these creeping lianas right here."

"Be careful." She grabbed his arm to protect the fallen flora in their path. "That flower is so delicate, yet lethal." Reagan's hand stayed on his for several seconds.

Jeremy was perplexed. "How could something so beautiful be so dangerous?" Their eyes met and held an intense glance. His pulse quickened.

"Its compound is used in poison arrows but also has important medicinal benefits." Reagan broke the connection, glancing down at the ornamental bloom. "It's Aphrodite meets Temptress."

They headed to the resort in their own boats. Reagan waved, indicating to slow down. "It's the manta ray passage, and they swim shallow, so be cautious of their crossing," she yelled to him.

He looked around the crystal-clear turquoise lagoon and noticed fish of all colors feeding on a shallow reef. "What are those?" He pointed to the beautiful fanlike fish with spiky twines of projections coming off their bodies.

"Lionfish," Reagan answered. "Extremely venomous, but beautiful. They flaunt their tentacles and blow jets of water at their prey to disorient them, making them an easy catch."

He smiled, "Aphrodite meets Temptress," excited to reiterate his recent lesson. He pointed to the spiky and colorful tentacles swaying through the current. "Those colors and stripes, they're a little hypnotic."

Their boats were now in contact. Jeremy held them together so he could hear her. He found himself in the student role, eager to listen and learn. He was enamored by her expression—her eyes so eager to teach.

She went on, "Lionfish also respect the hierarchy of seniority and elders. The more colorful the fish, the higher they sit in the food chain."

"Social order and common sense, interesting." He kept his gaze on her.

She pointed to a school of fish hovering over a reef shark. "We have so much to learn from the ocean and its inhabitants. They tell us when the environment is off, when the world is in danger, if we would only listen."

He was struck by Reagan's physical beauty as she reached her hand in the water. Her shirt fell loosely off her shoulder as she patted the water, calling her sea friends. He was drawn to her sun-kissed tan and silky skin. She blended in so naturally.

Reagan smiled at the two dolphins circling her boat. She took off her sarong, exposing her bikini, and jumped in the water, frolicking around for several minutes.

Jeremy couldn't believe his eyes. Reagan was interacting with two bottlenose dolphins as if they were two Labradors. She threw the boat bumper and said, "Go get it," and they brought it back playfully.

"Come in. They're pretty friendly!" Reagan dove deep, dancing around her aquatic friends, laughing with ease when she resurfaced. Her laugh was infectious, creating an alluring affect on him.

Jeremy was apprehensive about moving from the safety of his boat. He took off his shirt, exposing his skin to the sun. The tropical warmth was different from the arid climate where he lived. The moisture in the air joined the salty sediment from the water and left a crusty residue on his skin that he welcomed. "How do I get in?"

Reagan raised her eyebrows as she treaded water off the starboard bow.

He looked aghast at the open space of ocean—land too far to escape to—so the boat was the closest thing to secure footing.

"What about the boat?" Jeremy continued with decoys while trying to quell his fear. "Is it anchored okay?"

"Just jump in."

Jeremy emptied his pockets and took off his Rolex. He glanced around again looking for an excuse to stay put. He considered taking off his shorts but hesitated just long enough to notice she was now staring at him. He steadied himself on the gunnel of the boat and gripped the rail with a heightened degree of fear. This was new territory for him—the deep blue ocean, wild dolphins, no resort and then . . . *her*.

His jump into the water was like a boy's first leap into the summer pool to escape the sultry sun. He had never felt this kind of exhilaration before. But again, he had never been around Reagan before these last few weeks. Was she the effect he was experiencing? He came up for air and gasped in laughter as she joined him; they giggled like naive adventurers.

The dolphins circled them, investigating Jeremy's presence. Jeremy felt their supple, sleek skin and muscular torsos. The flow of the water became turbulent and powerful as the dolphins kicked their powerful tails. Their energy was provoking and enticing.

Swift in their movements, the dolphins kept a slight barrier between Reagan and Jeremy. He was amazed by the Homeric display of their power.

Reagan grinned. "Meet my best friends, Romeo and Juliet. They are inseparable and quite passionate in each other's presence. He protects her, never leaving her side. I've never seen one without the other."

"Let's hope their ending isn't the same as the real Romeo and Juliet's," Jeremy choked, treading water the best he could.

His eyes fixed on her as they both bobbed in the ocean. The dolphins swam out to the reef, leaving them on their own. It was an awkward and quiet moment.

Reagan broke the silence. "We should get back before sunset." She swam toward the boat. "Roger worries if I get back too late."

Jeremy couldn't help but stare at Reagan as she pulled herself back into the boat with ease, flexing her lean, sinuous body. He found every part of her beautiful, even the faint row of freckles on her back. He grappled with his feelings for her. The entire day felt surreal, beyond his grasp. He desperately wanted to hold her, but she was already hauling up the anchor and motioning him to do the same.

They motored back to the resort in separate boats, lost in separate thoughts.

22

~~~~~~~~~~

*R*EAGAN contemplated the day; Jeremy's sudden appearance with Geoffrey's last breath, little Aerin in his arms, his childlike approach to just about everything—his enthusiasm for driving the runabout and reluctance to hop into the Fijian sea. And . . . his finger on her lips. A hesitant smile overtook Reagan's face as she steered toward the entrance to the resort—it had been an extraordinary day.

She made her usual soft landing, inches from the dock. Tying off the lines, she gauged where Jeremy might land. He was coming in fast and at too steep an angle. She motioned to him to slow down and turn slightly to port, which he almost managed before slamming into the dock.

"Sorry, I did the best I could." The wide grin across his face warmed her.

Taking the boat lines, Reagan secured the small boat to the dock. She returned his smile. "No worries, that's why the dock fenders are there. You're getting it."

While Jeremy hopped out of the boat, Reagan stepped in and turned off the engine.

"Oh, shoot, forgot that."

"Like I said, you're getting it. There's a bit of detail with boats."

As Jeremy extended his hand to assist her onto the dock, a voice overhead shouted, "Perfect, hold that shot. Roll cameras on Jeremy."

Jean Michael and two cameramen leaned over the ledge of the railing of the upper deck.

"Keep rolling."

"Jeremy, darling, where have you been?" One of the actresses interrupted the shot.

"Cut!" Jean Michael sulked. "Take two. Jeremy, get the girl to step out of the boat again . . . it was perfect . . . and quiet on the set."

Reagan glared at Jeremy, cutting through the levity. "Not on your life."

"I don't have all day," the director commanded.

"She's in a hurry, Jean. I don't think she's up for it." Jeremy attempted to stay with Reagan's pace as she walked away.

"Dominique, take her place, and cameras ready to roll."

"What about me?" Bianca whined. "I'm his lover. I should be the one on the boat!"

"Okay, Bianca, you go get on the boat." Jean Michael regretted the whole idea.

Dominique chimed in. "Oh, aren't you the prima donna. Spoiled little worn-out, dried-up Bianca always gets her way." The scene escalated with both women fighting for attention, trying to claw their way into the scene with Jeremy.

Reagan walked around the two actresses whose voices had elevated to new levels of catfight. She circled past Jeremy and whispered, "Looks like you have your hands full."

Jeremy shrugged. "They always fight over me."

Reagan shot back a disapproving stare, seeing a different Jeremy than the person she had been with all day. Something had shifted. His eyes looked shallow and empty rather than the richness she had observed while swimming with him. The softer glance she had seen all day was gone, replaced by a peculiar slant of his eyes and a stiffening of the edges of his mouth. In an instant he was someone different.

"Come on, somebody take her place!" Jean Michael yelled.

Reagan faced the director. *It's just that easy, huh?* She surveyed the crew—the empty looks on their faces—frozen. Maybe it was boredom, fatigue, too much humidity, or was it dread? Reagan continued to examine the entire scene—the cameramen looked spent, there was a void in the faces of the lighting crew, and even the makeup artists sat in a sullen manner. Again she glanced at Jeremy for support—nothing.

Picking up her backpack and medical bag, water jug and towels, she walked away from the chaos. Reagan headed to her bure with confused emotions: *Maybe that magical afternoon was standard procedure for him. What have I gotten myself into . . . when will I learn?*

23

*A*TRANSLUCENT wall of water threatened Reagan. It grew more powerful as it rolled toward her from the horizon. She grabbed the rail of her surfboard and tucked into a protective ball. The rogue wave was about to close out. The power was overwhelming. She lost control of her board and succumbed to the ball of white water. Grabbing one last breath before the wave enveloped her body, she was pulled down to the ocean floor. Reagan tried to swim toward the surface but couldn't propel herself upward. Held down by some unseen force, she panicked and her lungs screamed in agony. She needed air. The pressure increased as she hung onto her last bit of oxygen before surrendering. Strange images streamed by—a butterfly with shocking orange and yellow wings, floating dandelion heads, and then a faceless figure wavering in front of her. The surreal images were comforting— she no longer felt threatened. A certain peacefulness surrounded her. Reagan's family entered her mind—Mom, Dad, Maura, Chief Toro, Jeremy—a surge of energy spiraled around her like a whirlpool. *Reagan, fight, Reagan—we need you.* She stroked toward the surface, pulling at the thick kelp strands as if she were climbing a ladder. The light shone through the surface, she was getting closer, kicking harder, then she burst through the aqueous space. Breathe.

Reagan awoke startled and gasping for air. She looked around the room and tried to settle her panic, realizing it was just another disturbing dream. They were becoming more regular and vivid. When Reagan was a child, she'd been diagnosed with night terrors, but as she grew older the dreams had intensified with illusions of life-and-death situations. Awake, with her heart still pounding, she contemplated the dream. *What does it mean?* She thought of Andy. It had been five years since his death—her childhood friend and surf partner. They had often explored SoCal's best surf spots, breaking their parents' boundaries and pushing their limits—two young surfers seeking the oceans' energy. She wondered if the dreams were related to Andy's death. *I miss him so much. If only I could have been there. . . .*

"Reagan," she heard again, this time realizing the voice wasn't from her dream. "Reagan, Maura needs you. Joni is sick again." The familiar voice of Roger, with his light tap on the thin wooden door, brought her to a seated position.

Reoriented from the dream, she packed her bag for the day's journey. She'd been spending more time on the island than at the resort and wondered why she didn't leave some personal items at Maura's house to make it easier to come and go. She shook off the leftover tension from her dream and moved forward, but the sensation of loss lingered.

Leaving her bure and passing by the deck, she noticed Jeremy and Dominique in close contact. He was leaning forward, elbows on knees, sitting on the wooden Adirondack chair and facing the skinny actress.

What the hell? I knew he was no different. She looked away, avoiding his glance and the subsequent jealousy that might rear its ugly head. *I don't care. . . .* The tightness in her chest and rapid heartbeat said the opposite. Reagan resisted the urge to look back, to see if he'd noticed her. *No, definitely no . . . I can't fall for him . . . they are all the same. . . .* She jumped in the whaler and sped off toward the island trying to scrub away the thoughts that assailed her.

BY the time Reagan reached Joni, her fever was already down and manageable. Checking her other vitals, she filled the coconut shell with water and finely ground turmeric.

"Masina, will you stay with your sister and keep giving her sips of this golden milk? She can also have ice chips, but no up and about. It's story time."

"Yes, Auntie. I for sure keep her down." Masina picked up a few books and sat next to her sister in bed, putting Joni's loose strands of hair behind her ear.

Reagan's smile widened witnessing the natural kōkua in Masina.

"We'll be back soon. Your mama and I are going to meet with an elder high on the hill. Might be a few hours or so."

Masina's eyebrows shot upward. "But why? Why would you and Mama go to him? He might eat you."

Maura laughed. "No, my dear Masina, big stories rise from the mountain."

Reagan looked at Maura who shrugged and made a strange face.

"We'll see." Maura laughed again, but it was an uncomfortable, off-pitch sound. The two women walked toward the single-track trail.

"When did you last see him?"

"Oh, many sunsets. Maybe last time was with Chief. We brought the old man supplies. You know, things he don't grow 'imself."

"Does he ever come down to the village?"

"Not if he don't have to. Too much island sickness on 'im. Too tired to come down. But before Chief pass on, he really wanted you to meet Phaeole. Thought you could help."

"What was Masina concerned about?"

"Well, some believe he still practice cannibalism, cuz that's what they used to do long, long time ago."

Reagan stopped walking and turned to face Maura, giving her a slanted look.

"Chief say never approach him during the changing moons. He will turn you into long pig," Maura deepened the tone of her voice.

Reagan didn't verbalize how far-fetched it sounded, because the lurid tales had permeated the island. Others had expressed similar concerns. "Our hide is too thick, the taro root and fresh ahi are better. We'll make sure he doesn't eat us both," Reagan joked as they climbed up the steep ascent toward Phaeole's home.

Reagan looked back periodically to see how Maura was handling the climb on the uneven path, littered with stones and tangled vines. Her clubbed feet and uneven legs didn't seem to impede her progress. Reagan admired what could only be an inner strength that kept Maura's awkward body ascending the windy hillside. They lifted their legs high over fallen branches and slopped through the mud.

"The mountain doesn't want us . . . go up . . . today," Maura said out of breath.

"We'll get there. I can see the top, but it sure looks like no one's been up this way for a while." Reagan pulled some green creepers off her legs. "How does Phaeole get by without going down to the village?"

"I don't know . . . he has water . . . grows his food." Maura puffed.

"But what about people? Doesn't he miss people?"

"He not like us . . . no . . . no . . . you see."

As they neared the crest of the hill, Reagan sensed someone watching them. She could feel a presence but could not see anyone.

They slowed their pace and looked in all directions.

"Phaeole, it's Maura and Doctor Reagan."

A rickety set of stairs leading up to the modest thatched shelter was in full view.

"Maura . . . here . . . we come to talk."

A faint rustle of bushes preceded a gruff voice. "Who?"

"It's Reagan and Maura from the valley. The chief told us to come." Reagan looked in all directions wondering when the old man would appear. She heard the shuffling of feet, a wheezing sound and the slap of woven palm fronds at the makeshift doorway.

"I'm coming. You wait."

Maura and Reagan looked at each other before turning toward Phaeole.

There was a grisly edge to his features, and his surly attitude was obvious. "You'd better not be here to steal anything."

"May we come in?" Reagan caught herself raising her voice and adjusted, "We'd love to visit."

His only response was, "Humf."

Reagan took three steps up the stairway and extended her hand to Phaeole. "I'm honored to meet—"

Phaeole had turned away and walked back through the clanging palm fronds, waving them to follow.

Moving forward, Reagan kept up with the shuffling steps while Maura trailed cautiously behind.

"Who'd you say? Who's Reagan from the valley? I haven't seen the chief in many sunsets."

Maura looked down at the mention of her husband.

Reagan did her best to carry the conversation. "I'm Reagan, the doctor who helps in the village. The chief asked Maura to bring me here . . . to talk to you. I'm sorry to say Chief Toro has passed to the other side. He is finally at peace."

"How long ago?"

"In the last full moon." Maura's voice trembled.

"Then we sit, have kava."

Maura and Reagan exchanged glances and moved to the simple wooden table next to the window.

Phaeole's eyes stared straight ahead. "There's kava already boiled in there," He pointed across the room. "Bring it here with three bowls."

Reagan watched his every move and realized he couldn't see, even though he motioned in the correct direction of the small kitchen. She gladly followed his instructions to make three bowls of tea and have a look around.

They sat for a long time, drinking kava tea and discussing village matters—births and deaths and food sources.

Reagan was eager to find out how and why Phaeole had managed to survive in such desperate isolation. "It's beautiful up here. Do you have a garden?" She glanced at the wild ferns creeping in and around the windowsills.

He remained gruff and on guard. "I killed the chickens . . . they eat too much."

"Then how do you survive?"

"I have enough from the ground and the trees."

Reagan pressed for more answers, but the old man sat still wearing an angry expression.

"What about water? Is there a well around here?"

"The stream. Don't you hear it?"

She strained to hear anything beyond the birds' kakaaw and constant rustling of bushes. "No, I don't hear any water. Is it close by?"

"Close enough." Phaeole slurped from the wooden bowl.

"You can walk there on your own?"

The elder stiffened as if Reagan was taunting him. "I know the way. I see it in my mind."

Maura interrupted, "Phaeole, we come to you to help. Reagan can help . . . she's a doctor . . . knows how . . . to help."

"Help? You see colors on the mountain as the sun circles . . . the way it plays off my porch like rainbow? You hear the stream? And do you see my friends, do you know each bird, each lizard? And how 'bout my favorite: the poptail etsy toad with his hideous hide, diving into the blissful waterfall to his death, only to be kissed by the stoneyfish omptipide?"

Reagan and Maura were mystified by his sudden turn—his talk of strange, whimsical creatures.

Maura tilted her head. "What is a poptail . . . whatever you said?"

"Oh, you know the kind, the ones that no one ever sees or hears about, the ones who go unnoticed in life yet they are still there . . . every ounce of them . . . still there."

Reagan glanced at Maura with full understanding. She looked down at her hands, straightening each finger, wondering what it was like. Changing the subject to something simpler, she asked, "Are you an artist?"

There were unfinished paintings all around his home: plummeting waterfalls, overgrown trumpet vines, jacarandas and plumerias . . . the images mirrored his outside surroundings. On smaller pieces of material there were sketches of hands with finely formed fingers, hands holding hands, fingers touching fingers—replicas of what he imagined were perfection. Half-filled water glasses with paint residue and dried-up brushes that once were partners in his passion for art lay lifeless and scattered.

Wondering where Phaeole got his supplies, Reagan noticed bits of bark lying around the rough sketches and half-filled wooden bowls with dried colored residues. "You mix your colors from tree bark." Reagan's voice energized the room, filling it with a lightness, a tangible sense of surprise and admiration. "This is astounding. Your world is beautiful."

Her voice wrapped around Phaeole like a warm hug. His body relaxed, a faint glimmer of a smile formed around his hardened lips.

"You see the truth. That is good. I prepare to leave and go to the Spirit world."

Reagan's voice dropped, her exuberance compressed to a low whisper, "I know."

Phaeole turned his sightless eyes directly toward Reagan. "This body is done."

She nodded, acknowledging his condition—his gnarled hands no longer functioned, pustules and ulcers oozed, with toxic odors and his shortness of breath limited his ability to finish a full sentence. Reagan asked, "You are far from the village. You will need help at some point. How can I help you?"

"I want to sleep. You can help release my spirit . . . like the chief." Phaeole leaned in toward Reagan.

"But why?" She waited, holding her breath.

He glanced in her direction and answered in a low tone, "I'm blind and can no longer feel my hands. There is nothing more for me here." He turned his head to face the window finishing, "Soon I will not be able to find my way . . . to the stream . . . or to my seeds. I am useless."

Maura stood up and shuffled to Phaeole. Reagan witnessed the tender and considerate gesture of picking up his hands and holding them in hers. Maura closed her scarred and thick fingers over Phaeole's.

He bowed his head and accepted the gesture. Tears flowed down his cheeks like the stream that wound downhill from the waterfall. He wept for some time—not just for himself but for others like him, like all the other poptail etsy toads.

Maura shared his sentiment, understanding the pain of having leprosy and living in solitary confinement for life. He finally glanced at Maura's eyes, even though he could not see them, before drawing in a deep breath. "I am tired now. I just want to sleep."

Reagan saw the cast of colors drape across the floor—a mixture of yellow, orange, and green that appeared like a kaleidoscope. The sun was setting and they needed to get back to the village before dark. "We must go now. May we come back?"

Phaeole nodded and closed his eyes, settling into the deep crook of the chair.

24

$\approx\approx$

*D*ARK clouds loomed overhead as if merging with Reagan's thoughts about Phaeole. The outside world would assail her with criticism for helping to end desperate lives. As she maneuvered the boat toward the dock, she saw Jeremy walk down the gangway. Gathering the bowline and stepping onto the dock, she avoided his glance. She wasn't in the mood.

"Hey, there you are." Jeremy pulled on the stern line, simultaneously matching the tension with her bowline, snugging it to the dock. He attempted a quick figure eight around the cleat but settled with big circles. He threw the unfinished line on the dock. "I've been looking all over for you. You are a tough one to keep track of."

Reagan uncoiled the stern line and fastened it correctly. Becoming more solemn, her eyes penetrated his. "What would happen if you could no longer do what you loved?" She held his glance, feeling the dance of energy between them. Her conflicting thoughts about him earlier in the day had settled. Their last encounter had left her questioning everything about him, but now she liked how she felt around him.

"I'm not sure what you're talking about, but tell me more." The words appeared script-like and contrived coming from Jeremy. But he faced her, less than a foot between them, and he did not back away from her questions.

"Well, say you loved pineapple," she paused, "and suddenly there was no more pineapple for you to taste, no more for you to eat and enjoy its juice running down your throat. No more pineapple to enjoy for the rest of your life. How would you feel?"

Jeremy shrugged.

"Well, what if you couldn't act anymore?"

"You mean when I age out?"

"No, I mean what if something happened and you couldn't act anymore now?"

Jeremy sighed. "I don't know. I never really thought about it. I guess I'd go broke fast. What's goin' on, Reagan?"

"Nothing really . . . I was just thinking of what it would be like— not surfing or doing my artwork or swimming with the dolphins. It's just that all I see on the island is illness, isolation, and devastation and no answers, except to end the suffering."

Jeremy whisked a loose strand of blond hair from Reagan's face. "Why do you worry so much?"

Reagan shook her head to the side, releasing his hand. "This is my life. It is what I do."

The sky cast its darkest shade of achromatic gray, with the blue, green, and red codes exactly equal. The winds blew from the leeward side of the island, an unusual direction for this time of day. Reagan felt the hair rise on her skin and shuddered a bit, not as a response to the changing weather but as a reaction to her deepest thoughts concerning loss.

Jeremy took hold of her hands to steady her movement, to get her attention, and draw her out of her trance.

"What if the only thing you ever loved was taken from you?" Reagan continued.

He pulled her closer and steadied his grip on both of her hands. He took a deep breath, and Reagan did the same in response.

"What is it you're so afraid of?" Jeremy asked in a whisper.

His movement jolted her, thoughts of a canned script returned—all the re-enactments of love scenes she'd accidentally observed in the last week. She released his hands and turned to the ocean. "I am afraid of losing who I am." She pulled the windswept hair out of her mouth and avoided his glance. "If I get too close to someone, I lose my center, my focus, being able to help where I'm needed. To be selfish is not a virtue."

Jeremy listened intently. "So, you are saying, you can't do anything just for yourself?"

"Not at all. Look at what I've surrounded myself with. I surf, swim, dive, hike the mountain. Really anything I want. It's just that—"

A crack of lightning interrupted her words. Reagan looked up at the stark light as it swept over the water. In the distance there was an impending squall sweeping over the ocean, heading toward them. A tropical downpour arrived within seconds and they were chased up the gangway, where the cast and crew hunkered under the broad thatched ceiling of the restaurant. Another loud roll of thunder and lightning lit up the sky. Chaos erupted as the film crew rushed to protect their equipment. The resort staff battened down the canvas side covers. Reagan knew the drill and helped draw the protective siding.

The tropical storm thundered in, breaking their connection.

25

$\sim\sim\sim$

OVER the course of the next week, Reagan had arranged for the actors and film crew to transit to the island for limited access and filming. She had some brief encounters with Jeremy, but filming always interrupted any viable exchange.

"How about a drink tonight, back at the resort?" Jeremy asked her when the crew was preoccupied with lunch.

"I may be around later." Reagan was guarded.

Jones stepped in. "Night shoot tonight. Won't be back 'til midnight."

"Maybe tomorrow?" Jeremy kept his focus on her, ignoring Jones' intrusion.

"Five minutes guys, five minutes." The cameraman announced.

A woman with makeup brushes staged herself between Reagan and Jeremy, and touched up his face. Someone else unrolled, then re-rolled the sleeve of his shirt and brushed off some dirt. Reagan couldn't see Jeremy's eyes, but heard, "I'll see you tomorrow then—"

Reagan avoided the rest of the cast the best she could, but when she was leaving Maura's bure she overheard a comment from Bianca to the director. "These lepers are repulsive. What if I catch something here? I refuse to get near them." Bianca pointed at a crowd of islanders watching from the side, all in earshot of her cruel comments.

Reagan looked to Jeremy for rescue, but he was out of range.

Instead Jean Michael responded, "Just pretend it's good Hollywood makeup."

Bianca looked mystified. "So I should imagine them as zombies?"

Reagan froze. She expanded her lungs to get enough air to keep her wits about her. The word "leper" cut deeply enough, but "zombie" was over the edge. She took another deep breath, her rage seeped through her pores.

Jean Michael shook his head apologetically toward Reagan. "She doesn't know any better."

Reagan held back her need to school the woman on her insensitive and prejudiced words. She looked to Jeremy for support as he entered the scene.

"Get back, Jeremy," Bianca half-screamed as if on script. "They will infect you, my dearest. If you get too close, they could breathe on you." Her fabricated hysteria didn't alarm the rest of the cast or crew. It probably wasn't the first time the actress had said something off-color. But it was the first time Reagan had heard it and the fire in her belly raged.

Reagan looked to Jeremy—he would certainly speak up. He'd met the islanders, sang and grieved with them; he had to understand the damage this woman was doing. She waited patiently, ready with a barrage of words to launch at the crude actress—*imbecile, idiotic moron, half-wit, brainless, cretin* . . . the list grew with each irritating moment.

Keeping her lips shut tight and her feet firmly in place, Reagan stared at Jeremy. *Come on, come on . . . just say something.* But . . . no words came. Reagan closed her eyes and hunched forward—her hopes were severed, leaving her confused and disappointed. She turned away in disgust.

"Come, my dear Bianca, let me help you through this." Jeremy's words felt like a knife in the gut to Reagan and the islanders.

Reagan kept moving to avoid his eyes, fearing that anything he added would only infuriate her more. She walked down the dusty salt-laden path, reminding herself that prejudice, ignorance, and hatred were alive and real, even here on the small, protected island. *And he didn't even stick up for them, or me. I'm out!*

JEREMY'S chest tightened as he watched Reagan walk away. His hands flexed into a strained clench as if holding onto something that wasn't quite his. He would have to find her back at the resort later to explain the need to keep Bianca calm and get the scene done, or worse yet, she might continue to insult the islanders.

As the final day of filming wound down, Jeremy took a break from his scene with Dominique at the resort. The scene seemed contrived and superficial like all the others, and he thought of Reagan. His feelings for her had progressed to longing. For the first time, Jeremy needed something richer in a relationship, something more intimate and with greater purpose. He couldn't get Reagan out of his head. He couldn't do the simplest tasks without wondering where she was and what she was doing. The word *manic* came to mind as his thoughts raced around without direction.

He hadn't seen Reagan for the last few days and he knew she was upset about Bianca's comments. He still hadn't had the chance to explain his actions during the scene with the insensitive actress.

He searched for Reagan all afternoon. Jeremy was desperate to see her. He paced endlessly along the crossties of the dock.

One, two, three, four. . . . He counted the truss frames numerous times, not realizing the compulsion. *One, two, three, four . . . Where is she? Is she avoiding me? What is this tightness in my chest?* He clenched his hands. *One, two, three, four. . . .* The wooden beams supporting the dock creaked underfoot, echoing his anxious longing for her.

The cast and crew had cleaned up the set—no tripods or boom poles left for the next day's shooting, no shirts or hats left behind on the restaurant tables, everyone was packing. The place already looked deserted. They were heading back to the States the next day and Jeremy needed to see Reagan one more time. He wanted desperately to tell her that he was sorry and how much he admired her. He found Roger at the dock, inside a boat hatch working on an engine.

"Roger, any idea where Reagan is?" Jeremy tried to cover any urgency in his voice.

Lifting his head slowly from the oily machine, Roger raised his eyebrows and put the wrench down on the deck. He let out a slow sigh. "I think she's off fishing for the day. Probably back tonight." He wiped his hands on the grease-ridden towel and glanced toward the outer island.

Jeremy wandered the rest of the day, staying within visual reach of the dock and adjacent areas. He stayed up all night watching for her boat. He was reminded of his days as a child when he sat up all night waiting for his dad to come home not knowing if he would be drunk, and not knowing if his mother would be okay. That was the last time he was concerned for anyone else in his life. Now he cared for this woman, Reagan, who he'd only known for a few weeks. He needed her to know how he felt about her. Would it matter? He'd be thousands of miles away.

"Hey, Jeremy, what's going on?" Jean Michael walked down the dock around midnight. "I saw you pacing. Something up?"

"Oh, nothing." Jeremy was startled. He'd thought he was alone. "Hard time sleeping, so I'm just admiring this place before we leave."

"Bar's still open. Wanna get a drink?" Jean Michael tried coaxing him back up the gangway. "You look agitated."

Jeremy stood at the back of the chair and looked around the restaurant. It was empty except for the two of them. The lights were dim except for the subtle spotlight above him. "Do you think this profession changes us?" Jeremy bit the edge of his bottom lip.

Jean Michael let out a cynical "huh." He offered Jeremy a chair to sit. "Hopefully any profession changes you to become something better than you were before, otherwise why bother?"

"But what if it changes you for the worse? What if it corrupts you . . . leaves you empty?"

Jean Michael shifted in his chair. "Are we talking about anybody I know?"

"There's got to be more than just this." Their eyes met and Jeremy stood with clarity. "Why are you in this profession?"

"I try to deliver a worthwhile message, even if it gets tangled in a love story." He paused. "And if we strike a chord . . . well, then we've done our job."

"Is that enough?" Jeremy's question hung in the air, unanswered.

There was silence for several minutes. The light flickered above and a few dock crabs scurried across the floor.

Jean Michael stood up and put his hand on Jeremy's shoulder. "Come on, bud, let's get some shut-eye, long travel day tomorrow."

Jeremy remained seated, his gaze fixed on the feathered whitecaps in the distance.

ISLANDERS loaded baggage and oversized containers onto the private inter-island yacht. Jeremy realized that he would be leaving without seeing Reagan. The void was all-consuming. He'd never had regrets leaving any woman. If anything, he welcomed easy escapes to end his superficial relationships.

The captain announced in a commanding voice, "Time to board. We cast off in fifteen minutes."

Jeremy walked down the gangway. He took small steps, glancing at his cell phone as if it could help him. He slid the phone into his pocket and looked toward the horizon for one last time. Walking toward the boat, he heard the reluctant creaking of the wooden boards under his footfall. *I'll miss that sound . . . I'll miss everything about this place . . . I'll miss—*

The captain interrupted, "Step carefully, eh. Watch your step."

26

$\approx$

REAGAN'S worries about Joni and her fluctuating temperature went on for three days. Just when her fever was almost normal, it would spike again within hours. By the end of the second day, Reagan was exhausted and could only think of sleep. She laid down next to Joni listening to her settled breathing.

Reagan opened her eyes to find Maura and Joni smiling. Joni sipped fresh coconut milk from a wooden bowl.

"Auntie Reagan, I'm better! And you snore."

"I do not."

Maura giggled from the wicker chair near the window, nodding.

Reagan smiled, instinctively putting the back of her hand on Joni's forehead. "You are better. I think we did it." She placed the stethoscope over Joni's chest. "Lungs sound clear too."

"Now you need to eat poi, get strong again. Feed these chicken legs." Maura poked at Joni's thigh.

"Eat some for me too. I'll make a run to the resort and check on things. I'll send Angus over with more greens . . . then I'll be back to check on you." Reagan felt relieved and refreshed, and looked forward to a quick swim with her buddies on the way home. Strangely, Romeo and Juliet did not appear when she anchored in the small alcove near the surf break. *Odd, they're always here.*

Pulling herself up and over the boat's gunnel, she thought of Jeremy. She brushed the thought away . . . *I should at least say goodbye. . . .* Reagan wiped the salt out of her eyes and started the engine. She took one final look for her dolphins . . . *huh* . . . then headed toward the resort.

As she pulled into the dock, an eerie quiet surrounded the resort. No hustle of the film crew, no bustle of scenes being shot. In fact, no one was in the restaurant where they tended to congregate.

"Hey, Reagan," Roger called over from the top of the gangway. "Wondered when you'd get back. You had an admirer looking to say goodbye."

"What?" she yelled back, cutting the engine noise.

"I said, Jeremy was looking for you before he left."

"He's gone? They're gone?" She tried to disguise her disappointment. *What about closure, a firm and clear goodbye?* While she knew he wasn't staying forever and a relationship between them was unrealistic, in her organized fashion she'd wanted to confirm her feelings were temporary, useless, and more importantly, over him.

"Yes, they loaded and hauled out of here. Just in time, huh? Good to get rid of those whiny—"

Roger's voice had dwindled. Reagan only heard her harsh regrets throbbing at her head. *He hadn't even defended the islanders,* she rationalized.

"Everything alright on the island . . . the little girl?" Roger stood in front of her.

Reagan resumed her boat duties, avoiding his glare. "Yeah, all okay. Joni's better. I'm a bit tired, is all."

TWO months rolled by and although the memories of Jeremy hadn't ceased, they were becoming more distant. Reagan stopped looking toward the corner table of the restaurant every time she came up the dock ramp. She could walk by his bure and not wonder what could have been. But a pressing nudge beneath her skin still crept up periodically. One afternoon Reagan walked into the bar to find the small gathering around the large screen. Roger, Angus, Sachi, and the bartender were laughing.

"Hey, guys, what's all this? Football season's still another month—" Reagan stood behind them just long enough to see the title running above the trailer: *Hidden Beings*.

Surprised by Reagan's presence, Roger motioned to the barman to turn off the TV. He avoided her eyes. "One of the cameramen sent us the trailer. He figured he got all those free beers and all."

The room fell silent. Reagan stood still.

"It's really awful, Reagan. Not what we imagined, for sure." Roger sipped his beer. "More sleaze than substance, really—"

"I can only imagine." Something stirred in her gut. She walked away mumbling, "Why did I ever concern myself with any of it?"

27

$\sim\!\!\sim\!\!\sim$

*J*EREMY paced back and forth in his home office. It looked less like an office and more like an elegant reception area decorated with contemporary art and midcentury modern furniture. The wet bar extended well beyond the center of the room. There were no computers, no scattered papers, no books, pens or desk accessories—only a clean, organized, and unused space. His six-foot-long desk made of one hundred percent Indonesian-sourced teak, supported a digital phone and answering machine. He took five steps and turned back, staring at the phone. He repeated the path again and again, cursing before finally picking up the phone.

"Jean Michael here." The words were sharp.

"What the hell?" Jeremy laid into him without hesitation.

"I'm fine. Thanks for asking." Jean Michael matched his tone for the moment then softened. "How's it goin', Jeremy?"

"I think you know how it's going. I've sat through several rounds of clips. Even the trailer sucks, Jean. What the hell happened?"

Jeremy heard Jean Michael suck in a deep breath. "Yeah, well, it sucks for both of us. Creative differences. Things got a little out of hand—out of my hands anyway."

Jeremy let out a loud "Huh!" He cleared his voice. "Out of hand? Why didn't you stop it? Why the hell—"

"Get off your high horse, Jeremy, and give me a break. You know how this goes—usually not well."

"But what about them? The island scenes . . . Christ . . . you made it into a freak show, and we look like jerks—"

Jean Michael interrupted. "I know, I know, but look . . . we needed the bucks and Rooney had the deep pockets—he had the say and the editors went to town."

The two men talked all over each other, one not hearing—the other not listening.

"Look, Jeremy, I can't go around in circles with you. What's done is done. We screwed up and got screwed in the process, end of story. Your career will be fine. Now, I gotta get back to work . . . new scripts to read, new. . . ." The line went silent.

Staring down at the phone in the receiver, Jeremy hunched over the desk. *Can't believe it.* He resumed his pacing. *My career? Who cares? I'm done being a puppet, no more charades.*

"Sir, would you like lunch soon?" the interruption from the chef startled Jeremy.

"No, I'm done, no more." Jeremy verbalized his thoughts.

"No more what sir? Certainly you need to eat."

Jeremy waved the chef away, and looked back at the phone. *I'll call her again . . . I've got to explain. She can't see this. . . .* But he'd been calling for five months. He picked up the receiver and held it up for an instant before placing it back down. He sighed. Jeremy walked around to the front of the desk, surveying the drawers. He picked the top one on the right to open. Inside lay a stack of unused stationery and a pen. He sat down and pulled out a single piece of embossed stationery and clicked open the pen.

REAGAN stared at the handwritten envelope with the airmail stamp on the front. She was accustomed to emails and phone calls, if the resort was lucky enough to get a slip of wifi or cell signal. The thin lightweight letter—with no return address—was disturbing. Her family came to mind. She realized she hadn't spoken with her parents in a while. What if something hap— A sense of dread took hold of her as she ripped open the envelope.

Dear Reagan,

I know this must seem odd, at least to me it is. I've never written a letter before. I tried to get ahold of you, emails, phone call; you guys don't have a message machine. Anyway, I'm just going to say what I have to say. I hope you will read this. I know we only had a short time together and I didn't get to say goodbye. I wanted to. I waited and waited. Anyway, I really do care for you. I miss you every day. I've never known anyone like you.

Reagan's hand trembled. It was hard enough absorbing Jeremy's words, and unbelievable that he would write them down in the first place. She glanced out at the ocean, and taking a deep breath continued to read:

Your world is so different than mine, but I learned so much, you have no idea. I'm afraid of losing that . . . it's hard to explain. I miss you. I miss your world. I miss your eyes and smile and even the row of freckles on your back.

She stopped, unable to read any further. Clenching her chest, the words were like a thundering tidal wave. Reagan dropped the letter and ran toward her room. Hyperventilating, she ripped off her shirt, grabbed a hand mirror, and strained to look at the reflection. She moved from side to side for a broader view. *Oh, God, Please! Nothing,*

nothing. She strained to reach up high on her spine to palpate anything that might be there. "Nothing, nothing"—the words were frenetic. Her breaths escalated, the accumulation of carbon dioxide caused her to gasp for air.

Reagan ran to Roger's bure. "Roger, I need your help." She was frantic, forcing the mirror into his hands. "Hold this up and don't move." She rotated again, not quite seeing anything.

"What is going on, Reagan?" Roger's voice reflected her distress.

"Where are there freckles?" She yelled, although Roger was within inches of her.

"What do you mean? I don't see any freckles." Roger scanned her back and neck. "You're imagining—" His sentence halted; his eyes dilated.

Reagan strained to see the evidence in the mirror. Her eyes closed and her world slowed. She had hoped never to see them—three small patches of brown, clearly not freckles.

"Oh, yes . . . oh." Roger was speechless at first. He lowered the mirror. "I'll book you on the first flight to Sydney. Pack your bags and I'll handle the rest," Roger insisted.

"I can't do that. You know I can't."

"Yes, actually, you can, and you must." Roger remained calm but stern.

Reagan couldn't open her eyes; the vision was too much. Her fateful dreams flashed before her—instinctual images and messages she had denied. The disease that she fought daily had found its way in. Her dedication, research, practice, theories about the cure—now all in question. Doubt swirled about her like the waterspouts in her dreams. Even Jeremy had seen what she could not.

Reagan had conducted regular skin tests throughout her years on the island. Never a patch or even a blemish. She opened her eyes, hoping the nightmare would vanish—what was real and what was fiction?

Roger repeated his order. "You have no choice. You need to get help. You said so yourself. Early detection, remember?"

Reagan counted on her fingers how many months it had been since she had seen Jeremy. Five—no, six months ago he left. *He saw the markers then.* She was already past the incubation period and well into stage two, according to this timeline. Supplies were low—both dapsone and clofazimine, the two early intervention medications needed. She wouldn't get another shipment from the World Health Organization for at least two to three months. That would put her well beyond the early stage of treatment.

Looking up at Roger's glaring stare, she hesitated, "Rog, I don't see how I can go, it's not realistic, and Joni and the others . . . who will look after . . . well, it's just not good timing."

"Never is, that's what you always tell us. Disease, illness, breakups, bad storms . . . you always tell us hardship is never convenient, it doesn't wait for a good time to pick yah, it just picks yah when it does. Isn't that what you taught us?" Roger's eyes remained fully open.

There was a quiet moment where even the breeze halted.

"I see. Well, I'm gonna look into some arrangements cuz. . . ." Roger's voice cracked and he turned away.

Reagan didn't push the issue. His words sat heavy on her mind. She turned to see his expression, but Roger had left the bure.

Roger summoned Sachi to get Maura. "Tell her she can come. Tell her it's okay to come all the way to Reagan's room."

Sachi put his hand up. "But what about the guests? What about—"

"Now, Sachi. Hurry." Roger's voice screeched.

"SHE has three brown marks in a row on her back," Roger explained to Maura as she struggled to get out of the boat. "She needs an accurate diagnosis and skin biopsy immediately and won't leave here to go get it."

He extended his hand to help her, but Maura kept both hands tight in her pockets. "Please, let me help you." He stepped into the boat and took Maura by the elbow, steadying her as she lifted her clubbed foot onto the ledge of the boat. She made a sound, "ahhha-umphhh," and Roger lifted her onto the dock.

"There you go. I'm sorry to have to rush you, but Reagan won't listen to me. She needs you." He held her arm securely in his and led her up the gangway.

Maura smiled as she kept up with his pace. "I see you a good man, jus' like Reagan say."

Hobbling up the dock at the resort, the stares of guests fell upon Maura. She hadn't been off her island in a long time and didn't miss the demeaning looks others gave in her presence. The empty feeling was also still there as they whispered within a few feet, just loud enough to be heard.

Roger glared at them and barked, "What are you looking at? She's a guest here."

Maura blushed. "Thank you, Roger."

The door was open to Reagan's bure. Maura took one step in and stopped. The room was simple, not an item in the open space was frivolous or unnecessary. The colors were reminiscent of the ocean, the fragrance like the flowers of the island, and the fruit on her table had been freshly picked that morning.

A sketch pad lay open exposing a profile of a man. It was stunning, the bold and powerful expression on his face. Maura pointed to the unfinished piece. "You do this?" She embraced Reagan.

"How did you—"

"I hear we go on a lil' vacation." Maura held Reagan's shoulders. "How far is this Australia place?"

"What on earth are you saying, Maura? We can't leave. We both have our family, our work . . . we don't leave. What if Joni's fever comes back? And the expense, it's just not—"

"I've already handled it and I'm paying." Roger stepped forward. "It's all arranged, if Maura agrees. Sachi and Angus are ready to step in. God only knows they are capable. They've shadowed you for years, been in numerous emergencies. Got all the sat phones charged up to talk to you for daily advice."

Reagan looked at Maura hoping she'd offer a rebuttal.

"Lelei can handle Joni. She's becoming beautiful Kōkua, like her Auntie. She does more than me, even now. All be fine while we go."

Roger moved forward. "It will be a short trip, not even a week."

"I don't like it. This is crazy," Reagan pleaded like a child.

Maura fixed her dark brown eyes on Reagan's. "No better choice. We go."

WITHIN a week, Roger had arranged the logistics, getting them by boat to the main island, then a direct flight to Sydney, Australia. He tried to make arrangements with a specialist at Sydney General, but the numerous questions were beyond Roger's ability. He settled with making an appointment with the first available doctor and left it at that. There was one more thing to do, one errant, needling thought that kept circling around him.

Sitting at his desk, Roger stared at the satellite phone. He picked it up and dialed 001 . . . *this is crazy . . . I shouldn't interfere . . . 213. . . .* It was a very clear moment. He had to—

"This is Sheila, how may I help you?" The woman's voice seemed distant.

Roger took a deep breath, his voice quivering. "My name is Roger Thorne. May I speak with Jeremy Black?"

"I'm sorry, Mr. Black isn't available. Can I take a message?"

Roger hesitated. His eyes darted back and forth. "Tell him . . . uh, tell him Reagan called and needs his help."

"Is that all, sir?"

"Tell him Reagan is sick at Sydney General Hospital. It's quite urgent—" The line went dead. *Too much distance . . . Jeremy's not going to be able to piece this together . . . damn phone.* Roger slammed down the receiver.

Sheila jotted down: *Reagan at Sydney General Hospital.*

"That's a new one, alright . . . Sydney, why on earth Sydney? Must be code for something? These gals think they are so clever. . . ." Jeremy had never mentioned a "Reagan" and Sheila was paid to know all of the female names that he would respond to, so she drew a big red X through the note and tossed it onto the recycle pile.

28

JEREMY paced the hardwood floor of his office half listening to his manager read the script outline for a new movie. He had struggled with his purpose since his return from Fiji—a nervous anxiety took over large parts of his day. *1 . . . 2 . . . 3 . . . 4. . . .* The counting wasn't helping to calm or distract him. *1 . . . 2 . . . 3 . . . 4. . . .* He momentarily stopped the compulsive steps. "Sounds like another piece of crap. What's wrong with these writers, Jonesy? I just need a break. I've been thinking—"

Jones snapped back, "Oh, buddy, don't start thinkin' too much now. It's not your strong suit. Leave the plotting to me."

"I'm serious. I need a break. I'm thinking of maybe going back to Fiji. What do yah think?"

"No way am I going back to that plunging sinkhole of a place." Jones waved his hand in the air. "What the hell's goin' on in your head? Don't tell me . . . no please . . . it's not the surfer chick . . . please . . . J, get a grip. She's just another gal. Focus on this new project. Do you think you can handle this director?"

"She's not just another—" Jeremy resumed his pacing, with a mixture of emotions. *1 . . . 2 . . . 3 . . . 4. . . .* Where was the confidence and self-sufficiency he'd found back on the island? The sense of intuition and feeling alive—now dead. He felt like a well-dressed manikin posing in the shop window. Then back to pacing. *1 . . . 2 . . . 3 . . . 4. . . .*

"Do you need more time to consider this film?" Jones asked. "What about if we—"

Jeremy heard Jones' litany, but he wasn't listening to the meaning of his words. He was distracted by a small message pad on his assistant's desk. The message was upside down, but he read it clearly, even though it had a stark red X through one of the slips of paper. The words grabbed him—he read it over and over again: *Reagan at Sydney General Hospital.*

The words registered: "Reagan . . . at Sydney . . . General . . . Hospital. . . . *Dear God* . . . Sheila!"

"She took lunch." Jones looked at him quizzically. "What's up?"

Jeremy was frantic as he dialed Sheila's cell. No answer. He slammed the phone down on the desk and left the room without explanation. Last he heard was Jones yelling at him, "J . . . come on . . . don't be a fool."

DRIVING his convertible roadster down Pacific Coast Highway, Jeremy's thoughts raced as he accelerated. He needed to escape somewhere, anywhere, without Jones and his unrelenting pressure to sell him to the next producer. Exhaustion, agitation, and confusion were choking him.

Jeremy took one turn too fast, his heart pumping, a headache building behind his temples. He pulled the roadster off of Pacific Coast Highway and shut down the engine. He kicked off his loafers and walked toward the beach. The first sense of relief came when he drew a deep breath of sea breeze. He stepped forward carefully. The coarse sand embedded between his toes, slivers of broken seashells stabbed at his soles.

He was drawn to the ocean landscape, gazing beyond the shoreline. He pictured Reagan and could almost smell her salty skin. *What's happened to you? I miss you . . .* he whispered into the breezy air.

Jeremy's thoughts collided. He regretted not saying goodbye. Why hadn't he gone looking for her? His head throbbed with confused emotions. A dagger-like pain twisted in his gut. He thought of Geoffrey's desperate act. Surreal. Jeremy put both hands over his eyes attempting not to see, not to remember. The memory of Reagan, Maura, Joni, Geoffrey's burial, little Aerin twisting her fingers in his— all landed heavy on his emotions. And then the memory of Bianca's outburst and her reference to the islanders as zombies—why hadn't he stuck up for the islanders . . . stood up for Reagan?

"Hey, mister." The calm and softly spoken words took Jeremy by surprise. "You got any change?"

Jeremy turned in slow motion toward the man whose eyes were cast downward. Although the man's cheeks were recessed, with skin slipping off the sunken arch of bones, his facial features were strongly defined and angular. Jeremy followed his stare to the man's filthy bare feet—stained with street tar and asphalt residue. His clothes hung off him in a smelly mess of ripped and tattered cloth.

Jeremy stared at the man for a bit too long. "What's that?"

Something about the man was striking. Jeremy focused on the unfortunate man's empty stare. His eyes were opaque, like the upper levels of a tropic sea. The warmth in his smile was peculiarly refreshing, or unsettling. It didn't reflect the appearance of the man. Something about him seemed finely sculpted and not at all as ragged as his clothes. He stood straight with his muscular shoulders squared against his harsh reality.

Jeremy hesitated, grabbing at words, uncomfortable in his own skin. "What's your name?"

"Uh . . . it's Mike . . . Mike Peters. What's yours?"

Jeremy laughed out loud. "Mike Peters, nice to meet you. I'm Jeremy, Jeremy Black." He extended his hand to the man.

Looking downward at his blackened hand, the man declined Jeremy's greeting.

"I didn't mean to laugh, sorry for that, it's just—what I meant was . . . it's a relief to meet you."

The ragged man looked up. "Sorry, sir, I'll move along. I didn't mean to annoy you."

"No, no, not at all. I was just thinking of someone I lost and suddenly you appeared."

"Yes, sir, but that's okay. I'll move along."

Jeremy placed his hand on the man's shoulder. "Why are you calling me *sir*?"

"Not sure, sir. It's a habit."

"Were you in the military?"

"Yes, sir."

Jeremy had never talked to a homeless person before, but he was drawn to this man. He was also desperate to talk to someone who might understand *his* loss.

"How long you been out?"

The man kept his glance downward.

"Don't want to talk about it?"

"Not really, sir."

"Would you like to have something to eat?"

He raised his eyes. "Yes, sir . . . please."

Jeremy moved toward uncharted waters. "Come join me for dinner." He pointed to the only car in the parking lot.

"Sir, I'm really dirty. I can't get in that car. I couldn't possibly—"

It was as though Jeremy was seeing the world with new eyes. "Mike Peters, you've done me a great service just now. Would you like to come to my house, get cleaned up, and have dinner with me?" Jeremy wasn't thinking about consequences or about the young man in front of him; he wasn't thinking about anything real. He was only reacting to a gentle voice, the withdrawing of the dagger from his gut, the calmness of the man standing next to him.

"Pardon me, sir? I don't really think that is possible. Well, even if I cleaned up, I don't have any clean clothes and I don't want to be a bother."

"No bother at all, my friend. You seem a little . . . well, lost. I would like you to be my guest for dinner and I'll provide you with some clothes." Jeremy was already walking toward his car, opening the door for his guest.

"But, sir, I am really dirty. I can't get in that car. It's so . . . so, clean." Mike ran his hand over the hood as if caressing a dear pet.

"Nonsense, get in," Jeremy insisted.

"Yes sir." He brushed himself off, which did nothing to dislodge the stains on his clothes. He took one foot and attempted to wipe off the street grunge on the other foot, but he sighed and dropped his leg as he got into the car.

Jeremy pulled out of the deserted parking lot and headed up Old Coach Canyon Road. He handed Mike a bottled water from his side door, and the homeless man finished it in one swig.

"When did you last eat?" Jeremy handed him a second bottle.

"Uh, not sure, sir."

"I see." Jeremy drove in quiet tension.

Mike cleared his voice. "You said something about someone you lost. I'm sorry for your loss. Was it peaceful?"

Jeremy strained for a moment before he let out a half-smile. "No, no one died. You see, Mike, there's this girl. I mean this woman—" Jeremy confided in his new friend. "I think I may love her, and wow, I can't believe I just said that." He spoke faster, "I don't think I've ever really loved anyone except my mother . . . and that didn't turn out so well. . . . Never mind. It's just that I met this woman on the other side of the world . . . and I can't stop thinking about her and now she's in a hospital, I think, I'm not sure. You see there was a big X over the message and, well . . . Sheila wouldn't answer and I don't know what I am supposed to do exactly. Do you know what I mean?"

"Yes sir, I do. Is her name Sheila?"

"No, no . . . of course not. Sheila's my assistant, and she wrote the X, and she won't answer her phone."

"What does the X have to do with it?" Mike sat up straight, poised to piece the information together.

Jeremy slowed the roadster to an idle in front of the wrought iron gates of his estate. He waited while the gates cleared his bumper and revved the engine before accelerating up a steep incline.

"Excuse me, sir, where are we going? This is private property. I don't think we should be—" Mike shot up straight and looked over his shoulder, then back at Jeremy. The man's knuckles appeared white—under the grunge, as they gripped the dashboard.

Jeremy watched the homeless man's eyes dart back and forth rapidly then rest on Jeremy's. He placed his hand on Mike's left shoulder. "It's okay, man. It's my place."

"I don't like this. What do you want from me?" Mike's tone elevated to a shrill.

"Whoa, hold on man, it's all good here. Calm down, my friend."

Mike looked at the two men approaching the car in the lighted entry. "Who are they?"

Jeremy held his arm out to his staff as they approached the car. "They work for me. I'm an actor . . . this is my home . . . they are like family."

"And . . . what do . . . you want . . . from me?"

"Just someone to talk to who won't judge every word I say. Someone who won't play me."

Mike looked at Jeremy, then glanced back at the men who halted ten feet from the car. He lowered his blackened hands off the dashboard. "Okay, sir. I can stay for just a meal."

"Perfect, and by the way Mike, can you drop the *sir*?"

"I'll try, sir."

Jeremy got out slowly, gave the *okay* sign to his staff and opened the door of the car for his new friend. Jeremy nodded toward the entry while Mike moved his feet on tip toes across the whitewashed travertine driveway.

George walked ahead of them, opened the front door, and held Mike's glance as he walked through the threshold. Mike nodded, standing tall as he held eye contact with George.

It took Mike close to an hour to shower, clean up, and try on a variety of clothes that were laid out for him. Every move he made was countered by—*is this a set-up . . . a trap . . . had they found him?*

George knocked on the guest room door and escorted Mike to the dining area. "Jeremy's a good man. You are in safe hands. I understand you served?"

"Yes, sir, many tours, many places."

George swallowed. "My son served in Iraq. You can trust Jeremy. He has a good heart. I'm here if you need anything."

"Thank you, sir." Mike nodded.

Mike tucked in the Tommy Bahama silk shirt then pulled it back out as he approached Jeremy. The Docksider shoes didn't fit right, so they made a scuffing sound as he walked on the newly waxed dining room floor. He stood at attention behind a chair at the long, hardwood table.

"Sit, my friend, sit. You clean up well." Jeremy was already dishing up his food.

"Yes, sir. . . . I mean . . . thank you, Jeremy." Mike inched his way into the mahogany chair, unable to take his gaze off the food on the table. Once seated, he bowed his head and whispered something for a few moments, then made the sign of the cross before picking up his fork.

The herb pork tenderloin was cooked to perfection. Roasted apples and potatoes infused with spicy mustard accompanied the fine cut.

Fragrances of sage and thyme entered his being like a much-needed breath of fresh air. Jeremy watched as Mike slowly took bite after bite.

"How did you get where you are?" Jeremy asked the unlikely dinner guest.

Mike glanced up from the meal. "I'm pretty sure I should be the one asking you that question." He pointed around the room filled with precious antiques and the panoramic view of the ocean.

"It was easy, I just pretended to be someone I'm not." Jeremy sliced the pork into thick pieces and handed Mike the large serving spatula. "But I asked about you. What's your story?"

Mike laid down his fork without making a sound, while he took a moment to gather his words, to venture back into his own painful past. Not sure whether he had the strength to talk about it, Mike spoke haltingly. "When I was first transferred back stateside, my hopes of resuming where I left off were snuffed out. I did five tours, two in Iraq, three in Afghanistan. I fly helicop—" Mike choked. He took a sip of water from the crystal wine glass. "Rescue ops mainly, you know, get in fast, get out faster."

Jeremy stopped chewing and laid down his fork, listening intently.

"I look at every pothole in the road as if it were left by an IED explosion, and then . . . I see his body, my buddy . . . I pick him up and get him to the 'copter . . . it never stops. A loose cable in the road reminds me of the detonator for the roadside bombs . . . I can see them from the air, lying there ready to explode, but I can't do anything about them . . . I break into a cold sweat." Mike lifted his fork to resume eating, but put it back down, finishing, "Every firework I hear, every loud noise with a crack, brings me back to dodging incoming mortars. I wanna hit the pavement, cover my head. It all takes away any thought of freedom that I was actually there to fight for. The real shell shock is coming home to the people you love, who have moved on, or don't know what the hell you are talking about. You can't explain that stuff to anyone. It ends up feeling like jail and you're always pleading to get out, but there's no way out. I know I won't ever be free. I've damn well lost everything."

"And your family?"

"Had a girlfriend, but after too many screaming nightmares . . . well, she said she just couldn't do *crazy* anymore. I'm guessin' it looks pretty scary. They don't tell yah that part in boot camp. No one talks about any of this stuff."

Jeremy hadn't resumed eating. He had played a veteran in one of his movies, yet he'd never experienced the emotion of loss he now felt listening to Mike Peters. "I'm sorry man, I've never really understood why anyone would join the military and give up their lives to go to war, but I now have an idea of what it means when people say 'thank you for your service'."

Jeremy dipped another potato in the béarnaise sauce. "So the booze got you?"

"No, none of that stuff is for me, no drugs, no sauce, just tryin' to keep to myself, yah know . . . just keep to myself."

Silence landed and both men stopped eating.

"Enough about me, sir. Who is this woman you are so in love with?"

Jeremy lit up. "She's incredible, quite unusual really, but so incredible. I can't stop thinking about her."

Mike kept chewing and nodding his head, adding a smile periodically while Jeremy rambled.

"She has opened my eyes to so many things." Jeremy looked around the room. "I've never met anyone like her, and now I can't get to her."

"Well, it doesn't look like you have a shortage of money." Mike looked around the room.

Jeremy smirked. "What are you saying?"

"Well, it doesn't sound too complex either. You met someone special. She's far away and sick, and well . . . you're still sitting here."

Staring at the man like he just unraveled some great mystery, Jeremy leaned back in his chair. The thought crystalized. Jeremy put his fork down and looked out the window that faced west, framing the hills and the ocean off in the distance. "What if she won't see me?"

Mike looked at Jeremy. "What am I missing? What'd you do?"

"It's what I didn't do."

"Then go make it right. Like I said . . . you're still sitting here and life's short." Mike looked at the platter of desserts set in front of him.

Jeremy threw his napkin down and stood. "Stay here as long as you like. You'll be well taken care of in my absence." He walked over to Mike and grabbed him in a bear hug. "George is my right hand man. Let him know what you need. He's great . . . does everything, knows everyone. And by the way, he lost his son two years ago. The kid came back from Iraq with a nasty bacterial infection, lost his leg, and then the kid died. That's all I know. He doesn't like to talk about it."

Mike looked up at Jeremy with eyes glazed over. He placed his closed fist over his chest. "Thank you, sir."

"The gratitude is all mine. Now try that crème brûlée and don't leave any behind." Jeremy left the room to pack.

29

REAGAN had a mixture of emotions standing under the towering outstretched arc of a sign—*Sydney General Hospital*. She held the glass door open for Maura as they entered the massive institution.

"So many islanders in one place," Maura whispered, then shrugged. "Funny speak." She hid her hands behind the flowery design of her sarong.

Forcing a smile, Reagan let the door swing closed behind them. "Big island, many people . . . I know what you mean. It's hard to understand their slang." She looped her arm around Maura's. "You know I don't want to be here."

Maura stopped walking and faced Reagan. "I know, but island sick not good. You can't save Joni. We need you strong."

Reagan knew she was about to face the objective testing and critical eyes of professionals who would label her with the very diagnosis she was trying to fight. She would be faced with the harsh reality of the contagious nature of the disease, which she had fought hard to disprove. She would have to face her fears with honesty, not knowing her fate. She reached for Maura's hand, pulling it out of her pocket in full view for others to judge—not just Maura, but herself. "I need this hand in mine as I go forward," Reagan told Maura.

Reluctantly, Maura extended her hand to Reagan.

While working in the States, Reagan had grown accustomed to the sterility of hospitals. She never succumbed to the white lab coat and instead dressed as casually as the administration would allow, hoping to appear genuine and compassionate, avoiding the professional pedestal. She'd tried to explain this approach to her colleagues, well aware of their egos. "If I stay on the patient's level, we can partner in their health management. I share what I know and they share what they know, and we come up with a solution or strategy in healing."

The inevitable response ricocheted back at her. "Dr. Caldwell, if we all had that approach to medicine, we wouldn't have any patients. Come on, get real, we write a script and move on. It's a numbers game."

Their comments were circular, repackaged to help them digest it better, but the same theme—give the patient a prescription of the latest name brand, then a second to combat the side effects of the first—around and around the mismanaged care went. If patients actually got better because of an intelligent, sound, compassionate approach, how would they make money? She knew that certain meds intervened at the right time was needed, but not to the numbing degree doctors handed them out.

Looking at the sea of white coats moving all around the enormous entry, she reveled in her decision to leave the U.S. and Western medicine, as she knew it. Returning as a patient was never in her forecast.

"Miss Caldwell," the voice behind the counter announced. Reagan and Maura got up together. The receptionist noticed Maura's deformities right away and asked in an overly pretentious voice, "Are you contagious, ma'am?" The people in the waiting room looked alarmed. Some parents covered their children's eyes, snugging them closer. Others walked out of the room in fear of contracting some strange disease.

"No, she's not contagious." Reagan raised her voice.

"That's not necessary, Reag—"

Reagan saw the sweat gathering over Maura's brows. She cast her eyes down at the receptionist. "Where is your professionalism?"

Maura attempted to stand. "I go sit over there."

"No, stay here, Maura." Reagan's voice had a small crack in it. She turned back to the receptionist. "Are you sure your negative attitude isn't contagious? Is this how you treat patients who need help? Besides—" Reagan's voice got louder. "I'm the patient, not my friend."

"Can I help?" a man in a white lab coat asked.

Reagan turned to face a doctor who appeared to be in his twenties. His nametag said: *Dr. Walsh, MD, Director of Internal Medicine.* His blond hair and stark blue eyes made him look more like a movie star than a doctor.

"I would like to help," he repeated.

Reagan was speechless.

"Are you even old enough to be a doctor?" Maura put into words what Reagan was already questioning.

"Yes, but I do get called Dr. Doogie often." His smile had a sincere warmth.

Reagan softened. "I'm sorry, we're a bit tired and traveled all day to get here."

"Completely understandable." His dimples deepened.

The receptionist chimed in with a flirtatious nod toward the young doctor. "Shall I show them to your office, Dr. Walsh?" She beamed at him.

"No, give us a moment." The doctor reached in his hip pocket for his pad and pen. "This is Dr. Yiung's personal cell. He would prefer you use it rather than his office number." He smiled as he handed Reagan the slip of paper.

"I don't understand." Reagan got agitated again. "Are you trying to pass us off? Or are you trying to save yourself the administrative hassle of dealing with the CDC?"

"No, not at all, we're more than willing to assist. I don't mind working with the Centers for Disease Control in the least. My buddy is on the board. But why would I need to contact them? Aren't you that doc over in Fiji, the one working with Hansen's patients? Thought it was pretty benign."

Reagan was taken aback by his words. How would he know who she was? She froze in place.

"I'm sorry. I didn't mean to upset you. Dr. Yiung is a . . . well let's just say he is pretty holistic . . . and a specialist of sorts. Trust me."

"But . . . how do you know—"

"We've followed your work for years. It's an honor to meet you, and Dr. Yiung is really looking forward to your call." He turned to Maura. "So nice to meet you. I wish you both the best of luck." He winked at Maura. "Call me if it doesn't work out." He turned and walked away.

Reagan stared at the name and number on the small piece of paper, "Dr. Yiung."

30

*S*TEPPING onto the tarmac in a bomber jacket and long pants, Jeremy was hit by a blast of hot air. He forgot it was Australia's summer. Sweat trickled off his neck as he slung the half-filled leather backpack over his shoulder. His eyes were puffy and red. He was exhausted from the sleepless fifteen-hour trek. He slid on his Ray Bans and walked toward the sliding doors.

While scanning his passport, the customs officer asked, "What's your purpose of travel to-daay?"

Jeremy looked at the official, confused. "Today?"

"Yes sir, to-daay."

Jeremy's head was throbbing. He'd had a few drinks during the flight, champagne was the worst offender and little to eat, no sleep, no shower, no clean clothes, and no quick answer. "I'm here . . . to see . . . my girlfriend. She's in the hospital."

"Sorry, mate. Bad circumstances, hey? Off yah go then and better luck to yah." The man handed Jeremy his passport and nodded.

Stunned at the man's quick response, Jeremy put the passport back in his pocket. Someone had listened to him and understood, even if it was a slightly overweight Aussie official with a strange accent.

Walking away from customs, Jeremy looked around as if expecting someone—George to help direct him, Jones to complain about someone or something, his bodyguards or anyone who knew him—but there was no one familiar. He glanced at his phone several times, unknowingly, waiting for some sort of direction. He let out a deep exhale and headed toward the only name he knew, *Sydney General Hospital.*

Jeremy passed the baggage claim area still looking at his phone, hoping it would tell him where to go. As he looked up, he froze. *Reagan?*

Jeremy ran around the baggage turnstyle and touched her shoulder.

The woman turned toward him. The resemblance was uncanny. She was a bit taller and less muscular, but her stance was confident and natural like Reagan's. Her hair was darker, not as sun bleached. Her facial features were similar but more made up—the dark eyeliner accentuated the woman's seductive eyes. Reagan had very blonde eyelashes and a habit of looking away if he stared at her.

The woman spoke with her alluring gaze. "Hey, aren't you that actor . . . uh, sorry, not good with names."

He extended his hand. "Jeremy, uh . . . Jeremy Black." He stared at her, keeping her hand in his for too long for a first acquaintance.

"Nice to meet you. Are you filming here?" She released his hand and reached for her leopard-skin luggage.

"No, just here to . . . uh . . . see a friend."

The woman responded to his heavy stare with a flirtatious smirk. "I'm available for a drink if you like."

Normally the invitation would have landed well—he would have returned the flirtation making it easy for both of them, but her forwardness made him uncomfortable and convinced him to turn and walk away. This was new territory for Jeremy. He couldn't blow it. "Maybe another time," was all he could muster. He headed for the exit sign and hailed a cab.

REAGAN glanced at the name and phone number Dr. Walsh had given her. She made the call and got a message saying the doctor wasn't available. She almost hung up, but at the last minute left a message. "My name is Reagan Caldwell. I got your number from Dr. Walsh at Sydney General . . . said you might be able to help me." Reagan paused, but then out of habit, left her number without any preconceived ideas of the doctor even calling back. She felt helpless having traveled all the way from Fiji to Australia and then being referred out to some doctor, who was somewhere else. Not knowing if it was because of Maura or because they didn't want her disease in their hospital, Reagan felt the old anger well up, the incrimination she had feared but expected.

After sliding her phone into the side pocket of her backpack, it vibrated with songbirds—her tropical ring-tone.

31

"HELLO," Reagan answered nervously.

"This is Dr. Yiung."

Reagan's shoulders rounded forward and she looked down at the ground. Her voice softened. "Yes . . . yes, this is Reagan Caldwell. I was given your number by—"

"I know who you are, so glad you called. Sorry I couldn't break away from my last patient." The voice was energetic and positive, perking up Reagan.

"Thank you so much for taking the time to talk to me. But you need to know I likely have stage-two Hansen's. I just thought you should know. I started a dose of dapsone on the island, but the supplies were very low. I need to reserve them for the islanders. I follow a regime of fruits, herbs, and breadfruit. Maybe it's not the best balance, I mean—" Her words sped up and she rattled on citing 'clinical evidence' here and 'side effects' there.

Maura mouthed, "Slow down, you're not making sense."

Reagan kept going. "So, I completely understand if you can't see me, or can't help me. I realize—"

"Sounds like you better head straight over. Come to Sydney Annex. I want your labs, STAT." The doctor responded.

Reagan looked at Maura as she hung up the phone. "He wants to see me right away."

Maura held Reagan's hand and whispered, "You went a little island crazy there . . . slow down."

"It's just that we've come so far and . . . well, I thought he wouldn't . . . never mind."

"Do I slow you down too much?" Maura's eyes opened wide.

"In a good way, yes. You slow me down just enough. Come on, let's get a cab." Reagan matched Maura's pace and walked to the curb.

Pulling up to the small medical clinic, Reagan couldn't believe the line of people at the front door. The handmade sign at the top of the door said, *Free Clinic*. Reagan figured this was where all the destitute cases were sent. She conjured up thoughts of why she'd been referred here. *What is this?* She let out a disapproving exhale. *I get it, no insurance, head to the free clinic.*

"Uh-uh, just give it a chance." Maura rested her hand on Reagan's shoulder. "Jus' like you tell the girls when trying new poi. You no know . . . unless you go."

The line wrapped around the corner of the building and all kinds of disfigured people were waiting. There were amputees and people with cleft palates, aged blind people, and Parkinson's patients who could not stay upright in their wheelchairs. Reagan wondered why she was there, as well as why these people had to be shunned from a standard facility to a free clinic, waiting outside in long lines.

"Excuse me, ma'am." A small elderly man, stooped over his walker, nudged her. "Can you see how long the line is? I can't lift my head to see that far . . . might have to come back tomorrow."

"What are you here for?" Reagan asked.

"Oh, I need to get a prescription for my neck pain." He shifted his head to one side, straining to see her. "Is the line around the corner?"

She reached into her backpack, handing him her bottle of pain meds. "Here you are. Make sure you take only one per four hours and not on an empty stomach."

A stout chuckle chimed in behind her. "I hope this isn't your way of stealing business from us." Reagan turned around to see a small Asian man wearing a loose shirt with a design she couldn't decipher, in well-worn jeans and sandals. He reminded her of some of her surfer friends back in California. The diminutive man extended his hand: "I'm Jay Yiung. So nice to meet you."

The look on their faces showed similar disbelief. Dr. Yiung gave Maura a hug and then did the same with Reagan. "I'm a big admirer of your mother's work, Dr. Rosalind Caldwell . . . quite impressive, even in our part of the world, revolutionizing gene therapy. She must be very proud of your work."

Reagan looked at Dr. Yiung with a blank stare. Her first thoughts were: *Are you kidding me. Not this again. I haven't come all this way to hear a glowing report of my mother's genius.*

She escaped the limelight of her mother's work years ago, and, in good conscience, found her own identity away from her mother's admirers and connections. Reagan made sure that her mother had no idea what Reagan was doing on the island, or why she was there. Reagan had assured her mother when she left it was a cool surf trip. And Roz Caldwell was deeply disappointed.

As far as Reagan was concerned, she would keep it that way. She smiled politely at Dr. Yiung. "Yes, her work is impressive."

Dr. Yiung looked at Reagan and became more serious. He chose his words carefully, "I am ready to help you."

Reagan was taken aback—the way he comforted her with just his glance.

"Come, follow me to the lab." He waved them in his direction.

"But, what about all of these other patients in line? It's not fair that I get special treatment."

"Trust me, as soon as I get your blood drawn we'll have a decent wait period for your labs, so I'll be putting you to work."

She hoped his competence was in line with his confidence. "What if I'm contagious?"

"I believe in your theory, and what better clinical trial to run?"

Reagan and Maura followed him toward the clinic entrance.

Maura turned to Reagan and looked confused, "Your mother a doctor? You never say this."

Reagan looked at the sidewalk, embarrassed that she had never told Maura this small yet powerful detail in her life. "It never came up and it doesn't always help."

Maura pulled back, her hands cringed, her brows shrunk inward. "I don't understand." She would never admonish Reagan, but this statement showed disrespect to elders. It was not acceptable in her culture.

"I'm sorry, I know it is difficult to understand, but my mother and I have chosen different paths. We are at once alike but very different." Reagan rephrased her response in a way that might be acceptable to Maura.

JEREMY arrived at the entrance of Sydney General Hospital. Keeping his sunglasses in place, he approached the check-in desk. He paced for a moment, thinking . . . then smiled coyly at the receptionist. "I'm here to see my sister, Reagan Caldwell, and want to surprise her. Can you tell me what room she's in?"

"Fill out this nametag and let me check for her room." The hospital volunteer turned to the computer.

Jeremy was relieved she hadn't recognized him. He picked up the pen and wrote the first two letters of his name on the sticky paper, then stopped, looked at the volunteer at the desk, then continued to write *Jenson Caldwell*.

He felt uneasy at this performance, knowing his showing up under false pretenses could further drive Reagan away from him. He had attempted several times to communicate with her from afar, to explain how the film had been distorted in editing, but she never answered any of his messages. Even if she did, how could he explain that the movie needed to sell tickets, so it turned the truth upside down to draw attention to the disfigured, portraying them as contagious monsters? Jeremy felt the loss of their potential relationship deeply and wanted to explain how she'd inspired him to adopt a new way of viewing life. He owed her so much and yearned for her forgiveness.

Now Jeremy would find the answer—if she would just give him the time to explain. "Sorry, luv, no patient by that name here," the woman said.

"What do you mean? Of course she's here. I saw the message." He stopped abruptly. It hadn't dawned on him that she might not be there. Had he misread the message, or worse yet, had something dire happened to her? "Please check again. I know she is here. I beg you." Jeremy lurched forward leaning over the counter. The years of pretense had culminated in this moment. He was praying for a different answer, a different explanation. He was pleading for Reagan's safety. "Please be alive!"

A young doctor walked up from behind. "I think I can help. My name is Dr. Walsh."

32

$\approx\!\!\approx$

*A*S Reagan and Maura waited for Reagan's blood tests to come back, they toured the clinic.

Dr. Yiung asked, "Maura, will you help this young boy read while I show Reagan some of our clinical disciplines? He has autism but loves to follow the words, so point to them as you go." He handed Maura several books and indicated for Reagan to follow him.

"You know she can't straighten her fingers, right?" Reagan admonished.

He smiled and let out a chuckle. "Of course I know that. Why do you think I asked her to point to the words?"

They walked down a long hallway with windows open to the outside greenery. Reagan loved the natural beauty. There were no white plaster walls with sterile hospital smells, no closed treatment rooms or secluded passages with No Admittance signs. The space was open and inviting, like an artist's gallery. They passed a room filled with music and musical equipment. Some patients were playing instruments, while others were listening.

"Music changes brain function, relieving pain, anxiety, and overall suffering," Dr. Yiung explained. "It acts as a conductor for our soul and well-being while boosting oxytocin levels."

Reagan smiled, fully understanding this mind-body connection and the way the mind could tap into the body's natural painkillers. She thought of the humming she had grown accustomed to on the island. The tone and inflection of the words were her oasis in times of grief.

The doctor continued, "We don't charge anyone, but rather ask that those who can pay, do."

"So you don't bill insurance?" Reagan raised an eyebrow.

"What good would that do?" The doctor grinned.

They passed several patients in one room talking and supporting each other. "It is an interesting sort of secondary discipline, patients comforting patients. We triage all day long without a patient feeling that their issues are any less important than someone else's. We ask that those who can help while they are here to pitch in where they feel they can be of service. These patients are sorting and categorizing supplies in exchange for their blood pressure meds."

The volunteers were focused on their work, careful not to make mistakes. The quality control was impeccable.

"We are never understaffed. In fact, I am always looking for things for our patients—I mean our volunteers—to do."

Reagan looked around at the spotless and efficient facility.

"Dr. Yiung, do you want me to present your paper in the *Archives of Ophthalmology* as well?" an older woman with a patch over one eye asked.

"Whatever you think, Miss Hennessy. I trust you will get it published where it will be read."

Reagan was stunned. "They're doing your research?"

The doctor had a great laugh. It was filled with a child's giggle and a teacher's ingenuity. "No, they're not doing my research. That would be inhumane." He giggled again. "Too tedious and excessively time-consuming. They're just checking it for errors and publishing it. It's a great way for them to learn about their own diagnosis and self-treat based on their new understanding of etiology and epidemiology."

Reagan listened wide-eyed, yearning for this new view of medicine.

They walked through the clinic witnessing the hustle of activities throughout a calm and well-organized environment. The doctor peered inside a kitchen-like room, asking a young woman washing Pyrex cylinders used for chemotherapy treatments, "Hey, Jules, how's the headache?"

"Almost gone, doc," she responded with an air of accomplishment.

Dr. Yiung turned to Reagan. "Jules has chronic migraines. So she comes here at the onset and we have her start cleaning the Pyrex, which requires 140-degree water temp. She wears thick rubber gloves to prevent burns, which serve as an insulator for the heat. The heat in her hands draws the pressure from her head, dilating blood vessels and eliminating her headache." He smiled, raising one eyebrow to emphasize his lesson.

"Why not just give her Imitrex?" Reagan thought it was her turn to enlighten the doctor. Maybe he was living in the dark ages and wasn't aware of modern meds.

Jules and the doctor exchanged an empathetic glance as he answered wryly, "Then who will clean the Pyrex?" They shared a smile that was filled with deep understanding, a blend of complexity and simplicity.

Reagan was intrigued as she took in this revelation. Her awareness of traditional medicine was now being challenged. Down the hallway, Reagan pointed at two older men cleaning a huge window. The job appeared endless, and they were diligent in their efforts to reach up high to clean the glass. "Let me guess," Reagan said. "Cross midline activity to stimulate the brain after a hemiplegic stroke?"

The doctor smiled. "No, but very creative. You are getting the idea. Frozen shoulder."

Reagan smiled thinking of how clean all the glass and mirrors would be in any given medical institution if patients with frozen shoulders were to release their own adhesions while accomplishing a needed task.

"How did you start this concept?" Reagan looked in every direction trying to figure out each patient's diagnosis or the condition related to his or her task. It was ingenious.

"Simple," the doctor responded. "I got tired of watching the poor and marginalized treated so badly, so I refused to accept medicine as I knew it. I simply had to make an adjustment, to hopefully open someone's eyes, anyone's eyes."

She smiled. Never had her inner emotions regarding medicine been so validated. The global health inequities had almost forced her to leave her profession, which is why she left the States. Now she had a revived enthusiasm about practicing a new style of medicine, incorporating her patients as her partners rather than the typical partners called board members. Reagan's paradigm shifted. Dr. Yiung talked about remedies toward access to medical care for everyone, not just those born with global good luck. He spoke of vaccines and drugs being a critical arsenal for weapons of mass salvation. She relished his words and purpose: He believed in himself, and more important, in his partners—his patients.

Next was a small lab with people looking into microscopes and writing on a big whiteboard. The room was circular, with abundant windows. The natural light illuminated each list of compounds on the board, as if emphasizing their importance.

"What goes on in here?" Reagan noticed everyone was casual in appearance yet focused on the task at hand.

"These are our chemists. We try our best not to use pharmaceutical companies for our medications. I don't believe in trading lives for dollars." A few of the chemists looked up with mild grins resembling those of a teenager who gets an inside joke. "We use natural compounds to develop exactly what is needed for the patient."

Reagan was intrigued. Her biggest complaint in medicine was the over-prescription of toxic medications, which often led to monstrous complications.

"Potency may be lower," he explained, "but so are unnecessary side effects."

Reagan reflected on the numerous patients she'd treated back in the States with negative outcomes, only to be shifted to other meds with similar consequences. "Can you make dapsone?"

"We can make whatever we want, whenever we want." He smiled, knowing she understood perfectly how this would affect her patients in Fiji.

They continued toward his office, which had a small deck with doors opening onto a garden laced with flowers of all kinds. Reagan recognized many herbs, but some of the more exotic plants were a mystery. The doors were wide open, exposing a welcome view of mango trees cast against the harbor's seascape. With a sense of fresh realization, Reagan felt the breeze gently roll in. Her senses were clear and renewed, ready to embark on a new journey. It was as if the breeze itself began the healing process.

Dr. Yiung faced Reagan. "I am here to give my patients a purpose. I include them in their treatment by having them do the very things that I discovered will help them control their symptoms." He offered Reagan some tea, which she gladly accepted, knowing this was an invitation to learn. She opened her eyes and ears sensing the best lesson was yet to come.

"These people are in pain because they have lost their role in life. They have been ill-treated, not by doctors, but rather by their own community. The judgments imposed on them are unjust, thoughtless, and simply cruel. Pain then ensues due to loneliness or lack of acceptance. When people aren't connected to others, they lack drive or motivation, thus they wallow and retreat." He looked out the doors and finished, "I help them find their purpose so they can reconnect and start living again."

Reagan brought the cup to her lips, but this time felt the aroma fill her senses. She was fascinated with the simplicity of what she had just heard. She thought of the injustice her friends on the island had to endure, creating their lonely solitude, until their ultimate banishment. She had never correlated their unjust treatment to their pain level. No wonder they were so desperate to connect with her on their deathbeds. It was their final attempt to be accepted and cared for by a loving human being.

The doctor was refilling Reagan's tea when she asked, "How will you let others know about this approach?"

He adjusted his glasses. "What do you mean?" He held his eyes on hers.

"Well, are you going to let the medical community know about this? It seems empirically evident."

He chuckled in a teacher-like fashion. "Reagan, my dear. It's kind of like your island project. If it's important, it gets around. We've been admiring your work for years and learning from you."

Reagan was baffled. How would anyone know about her work? She hadn't shared it with anyone. "But I haven't published any of my work." She was slightly apologetic thinking about it now. "If anything, I've kept my work private due to its controversial stigma."

The doctor shook with laughter. Since Reagan didn't understand, she found it almost insulting. He caught his breath enough to explain. "That reminds me of the joke of how do you keep something hidden from your mainstream doctor?"

She shrugged.

"You hide it in the literature." Again he burst out laughing, like it was the first time he had heard the punch line.

Reagan was starting to understand Dr. Yiung. He had the courage to step out of the status quo thinking and acceptance of how things are. He was willing to fight for his passion and apply fresh concepts to his practice. He truly cared for his patients, as Reagan cared for hers. She smiled back. "But why are you against the literature? It's how we share our findings." She knew the answer but wanted to hear his view.

"You mean the tainted pharmacological findings intended to sell more short-term meds, further enforcing their planned obsolescence?"

Now Reagan burst out laughing. It was a belly laugh that she hadn't felt in years. It felt so good. The chemical change in her brain softened the tension in her muscles. They both felt a connection, one closer than most colleagues ever experience. It was a moment when the eyes finally open completely, understanding the lesson—a sort of "Aha" moment.

A woman in a wheelchair rolled into Dr. Yiung's office waving some papers. "Labs are in. Let's get to work!" The woman propelled herself in front of a computer and swiftly scrolled through stats and comparisons across the world. "Hey, are you gonna help or just wait to be helped?" she barked in a coarse yet hopeful tone. "I'm Ali, and yes I'm a paraplegic amputee, and I don't want your pity because you are much worse off than me." Reagan hadn't noticed her amputated arm until the woman mentioned it. She chuckled and felt at ease with her newly assigned medical team.

"Ali, meet Reagan, from Fiji," Dr. Yiung announced.

The woman looked up with a large smile. "Ah yes, R.I.P. So nice to finally meet you."

Reagan looked to Dr. Yiung in confusion, wondering if her lab results were that catastrophic.

Dr. Yiung smirked. "It's short for Reagan's Island Project."

Reagan softened her concern. She missed this kind of wit, this reliance on humor in the face of a serious situation.

"Your levels of interleukin-6 are very high, but your GABA levels will offset it." The doctor spoke as if talking about a tree that had mold on it and the plan would be to rid it of the mold with a sulfur-based treatment and pick the fruit the same year. "If we add more lycopene to your diet, we can block the action of free radicals and protect you at a cellular level. Next we keep you to a strict multi drug therapy program, combining rifampicin, dapsone, and clofazimine." He smiled at her, slowing his explanation. "No worries Reagan, I'll guide you." Dr. Yiung looked back at the report. "There must be some toxin you've been exposed to that is inhibiting your vitamin A production. So you'll need to take daily IV vitamin infusions." Reagan thought of all the deficiencies her body must have gone through living in the tropics, given the limited variety of foods available.

"Can you stay here for six months of treatment, or is there another doctor on the island who can help you with all this?" Reagan thought of her people on the island who would go unattended for six months. She thought of the hardship they would face without her there. Maura's daughter needed attending, there were Phaeole's next visits, and other near-death people needed her guidance.

"No, there's no one there to help or take care of—"

A voice interrupted; it was firm and intentional. "I'll take care of her." The intonation was strong and forceful.

Reagan turned toward the voice, choking out words in breathless array, "Je . . . Jeremy . . . what—how . . . how did you find me?"

33

*T*HE gentle breeze was soft and inviting as it blew through the open glass doors of the office. Dr. Yiung glanced at Jeremy. "Welcome. Do I know you?"

Reagan interrupted, "He's a friend . . . uh, from Fiji."

Dr. Yiung surveyed Jeremy, absorbing his attributes. He crossed his arms as if summing him up and whisked his upper lip with his index finger. "Uncanny resemblance. You remind me of someone, maybe from a movie?"

Jeremy flashed his smile and raised an eyebrow.

An awkward moment passed and Dr. Yiung giggled. "Ah yes, I remember the film. There was a doctor who smuggled some sort of illegal drugs. Funny the guy looked just like you, but surely—"

Jeremy smiled. "Could be anyone."

The doctor reached out his hand, inviting Jeremy in. "You have shown up and we are happy about that. There is much work to be done, so please let's move forward and learn about Reagan and what we are facing here."

Reagan was the first to break through the next long pause. Staring at Jeremy with her heart racing against a flush of sweat, she asked, "How did you know? How did—" Her hands trembled as she pushed the chair around, not sure whether she should fall back into it or hold onto it for support. Her thoughts spiraled back to the moment on the island when she realized Jeremy had left. Reagan didn't have the opportunity to say goodbye or even thank him for appearing during two emergencies. It was odd then and it seemed odd now. Sweat soaked through her blouse. Reagan didn't like losing control and her internal turmoil fueled the moment.

Dr. Yiung and Jeremy hadn't moved. Reagan's strange reaction held their attention. "I just . . . as you know, I meant—" None of the words made sense. She was stuck in a quagmire of thoughts that were usually so clear, full of mathematical calculations, then balanced by science. But now they were scrambled.

Jeremy walked past Dr. Yiung to Reagan and pulled her entire body into his. "I wish I'd known earlier," he whispered. "I wish I'd never left you without saying goodbye." Releasing the embrace, he placed his hands on her cheeks and gently kissed her on the lips. "I've thought of you every single moment since then. I can't even get through a full day without thinking about what you are doing. I know what you are thinking, but I'm here to stay, for as long as you want me." He kissed her again, this time deeply.

"Friends . . . Hmmm . . . excuse me . . . I'm here too, you know," Dr. Yiung interrupted. "Let's save all that for later. We have some actual work to do."

The doctor had the unique quality of dispersing tension with laughter. Reagan was particularly relieved by his levity. As their lips parted, Reagan took Jeremy's hand. The heat between them was palpable and her heart raced. Time seemed erratic and inconsistent as the doctor's words helped bring her back around.

"The virus can be overlooked by. . . ." The doctor's words trailed at first, but Jeremy was already focused on him, so Reagan did the same.

Reagan gripped Jeremy's hand firmly while the doctor explained the confirmed diagnosis, procedures for IV dosing and injections, including tapering doses and taking blood samples. He spoke to Jeremy as a colleague, trusting his competence and ability.

"Reagan will be able to talk you through all this. It's just a little bit tricky doing your own blood draw." Dr. Yiung winked at Reagan.

"Call that impossible." Reagan launched back.

Jeremy pressed his shoulders back and took a deep breath. "I can do that, doc. I've had to do a lot of stuff I don't really know, but I can do it when I see it."

Dr. Yiung looked at Jeremy. "That's a remarkable skill to have. If you can follow Reagan's directions, it would be immensely helpful."

"I can do this. She's worth everything."

Reagan's emotions washed back and forth like a disturbed sea. She was at once happy and slightly numb by the sudden shock of his appearance. She faded back to just moments ago—his lips on hers—the soft yet intoxicating act. Jeremy was saying something to Dr. Yiung, but Reagan was reliving the sensation. *Was this real? It felt so real.*

"Reagan, what do you think?" Dr. Yiung interrupted her daze.

"About what. . . ."

The office door swung open. Maura appeared with a large grin followed by an ecstatic squeal, "Oh, my dear Lord, you answered my prayers." Maura hugged Jeremy. "It's true, it's true. I see that you watch over her. I dream it, I see it clearly now."

Jeremy nodded. "Don't you worry, my friend, I'm not going anywhere. I understand what's needed."

A peculiar silence followed.

Dr. Yiung, Reagan, Jeremy, and Maura shared glances without speaking. It seemed a sacred moment.

"I think you've got this handled. But I'm at your disposal for anything, Reagan." Dr. Yiung bid them farewell and watched them leave the clinic.

Reagan looked up at the window, framing Dr. Yiung, and waved her bags of supplements, retrovirals, and antibiotics to him as a victory gesture. She linked her arm on Jeremy's elbow on one side and Maura on the other and walked toward the cab drop-off and pick-up area.

The approaching cab came to a slow halt at the entrance of the clinic. The door opened, allowing its passenger to exit.

"Dr. Walsh, what are you doing here?" Reagan extended her hand to the boyish doctor.

"This is my side hustle." He winked.

Reagan laughed at his comment knowing there was no reimbursement for his services at this clinic.

"This is my real classroom. So glad you made it. Did it work out for you?" The dimples in Dr. Walsh's cheeks deepened.

Jeremy stepped off to the side to take a U.S. phone call. Reagan wanted to introduce him to Dr. Walsh but couldn't get his attention.

"Yes, it worked out quite well." She looked at Jeremy.

Dr. Walsh smiled in Jeremy's direction. "Lucky guy."

"Yeah, I hear he's quite a star," Reagan said in a low voice.

"Uh, that's hardly what I meant. The guy almost had a coronary when we told him you weren't at Syd Gen." Dr. Walsh raised his eyebrows to Reagan.

DR. YIUNG watched Jeremy and Reagan and a few others gathered outside the clinic entrance. He considered the three he had just met—a young female doctor with a questionable blood panel, whose work was known beyond her borders, a courageous Fijian woman suffering from advanced stages of Hansen's disease, and a mysterious man—maybe famous, who had shown up at the right time, appearing to be in love. The doctor tapped the side of his cheek as he smiled.

Ali rolled back into his office. Her facial expression was filled with gloom. "I have the results of the additional tests you ordered." Her eyes were still focused on the paper in front of her as she handed it over. "It appears that the Hansen's diagnosis is the least of her problems," Ali blurted.

The slight breeze came to a halt. Dr. Yiung shifted his glance from the paper, then back out the window toward Reagan and Jeremy. He drew in a deep breath hoping to view the situation differently. The words in front of him were perplexing and unavoidable. He whispered in the breathless room: "How could she be alive?" He reread the words on the page, somewhat in disbelief.

"When will you tell her?" Ali wheeled her chair in front of him to clearly see his eyes.

"Not sure," Dr. Yiung whispered, crumbling the paper and looking away.

"Not sure when, or if, you'll tell her?" She moved her wheelchair closer to him, blocking him from moving.

"We will see." He shifted his glance back out the window, beyond the complex structure of the enormous entwined banyon tree. "I've always trusted I'd have the answer. I never imagined . . . this."

The bright sparkle in the doctor's mercurial eyes collapsed. There was only a darkness gathering like a southerly storm. A terrible foreboding stirred in the humid air, the breeze stagnated. "I think—"

Ali persisted, "Yes, doctor, what would you like me to do?"

"I . . . I'll let you know." He froze, staring at the picture of him and a Buddhist monk in Pali, arms wrapped around each other, smiles emblazoned.

Part 2

34

*R*EAGAN was disturbed by the texture of the crumpled paper in front of her. How did the wrinkles in the page get there, and why? Someone had read this then discarded it or withheld it from her. The results were one thing, but the insinuation that this threatening level of plutonium was withheld from her was the issue she couldn't comprehend.

"What does this mean?" Reagan straightened out the paper. She waited for Dr. Yiung's response.

"Do you mean, why didn't I tell you earlier?"

Their eyes met. She held the paper up in the air, pointing at the diagnosis—*Radiation poisoning*.

Jeremy turned from the window to capture Reagan's fearful expression.

"I was just here yesterday and you laid out the plan. It was supposed to be easy, just scrub away the mold." She threw the paper on the desk.

Jeremy moved closer. He swallowed and clenched his fist.

"Yes . . . I am baffled. Why didn't you tell me?" Reagan's eyes were wide open.

"It means that I thought very carefully about this moment and I knew you would ask me this very question. I knew you would question my practice and my methodology." Dr. Yiung let out a sigh of relief and sat down in his chair as if the worst of the inquisition was over.

Reagan could see for herself. The nuclear medicine scans showed her levels of plutonium escalated beyond a normal person's capacity. The high cortisol levels and low DHEA—a death sentence to her adrenal glands. She knew the radionuclides in the scan had no opinion or agenda in her knowing, so full disclosure stared at her on this crumpled piece of paper that may have never been revealed.

Jeremy was at her side. She would have to explain to him later—the implications of it all, what could happen, what would happen.

"I'm not questioning anything of you, Dr. Yiung. I simply don't—" She choked on her next words and cleared her throat. "I simply don't understand . . . how this could be . . . I mean . . . I. . . ." She avoided Jeremy's glare. "You and I know where this goes."

"Where what goes? What the hell are you talking about? You said Hansen's is treatable." Jeremy moved away from Reagan and toward Dr. Yiung.

A heaviness saturated the room. Pointing to the lab report, Dr. Yiung revealed the minimum facts. "Reagan has a rare form of radiation poisoning. Usually, for this to occur there would be a major nuclear catastrophe, but somehow she is showing high levels in her bloodstream that may have woken up with the Hansen's. We need to run further tests to determine treatment, but I don't have the needed equipment. You live in L.A. right? I'd get her there as soon as you can. L.A. Medical Center is your best choice. They have a state-of-the-art facility and faculty who specialize in nuclear medicine. I can forward all test results and recommendations." Dr. Yiung faced Reagan. "I'm just amazed you are living with this in your system. Usually there would be symptoms. How was this so hidden?" He rubbed his eyes in confusion. "I've seen extreme radiation cases over the years, but there's usually an origin. But this . . . this seems insidious." He looked to the ground. "No one lives with these levels of plutonium," he hesitated, "for long."

Jeremy's confusion shattered the desperate silence. "What?"

The doctor kept his gaze on Reagan, waiting for her reaction to the last two words. Dr. Yiung tried to reassure her. His voice softened. "Reagan, for some reason beyond medical explanation, you are managing to host this while your white blood cell count is normal. I didn't tell you right away because I couldn't understand it myself."

There was silence in the room.

He finished in an apologetic tone. "I didn't tell you for fear of opening Pandora's box of medical arsenal that you will likely now experience. The stress of it all. . . ." He waved his hands in the air, shaking his head. "Well, you know the effects of cortisol, but we have no choice."

Reagan felt unbearable tension compressing her gut. "Yes, I'm well aware of the effects of cortisol."

There was a strange amalgam of feelings: beauty everywhere, the fragrance of the flowers, the swaying trees, the dedicated loving people; everything she used to combat the effects of stress. Reagan always addressed it as part of her treatment and philosophy on the island. Surfing, playing in the ocean, her artwork . . . it was all therapy to combat the negative effects of excessive cortisol being emitted from stress. She used the beauty of the island and her work with those afflicted with leprosy as her personal nourishment.

Reagan caught a glimpse of the mangoes hanging off the tree outside Dr. Yiung's office, and she sniffed the gentle breeze wafting in the scent of a south wind. She noticed the hair on Jeremy's skin as it pressed against hers in support. Relieved she had dropped off Maura that morning at the airport, she managed a smile. "So, are we off to L.A.?"

Jeremy dropped his shoulders and embraced her. "You bet. My place isn't as cool as yours, but I'll take good care of you."

Dr. Yiung faced her directly. "You are strong, my dear. After all, you're still here. Go . . . go to L.A."

As they left Dr. Yiung's office, Jeremy called the States. "Hey, George, Jeremy here. We're coming home. We need to get to L.A. Med Center. Can you make some calls? Find out who's the best . . . you know, make it happen. By the way, how's my new friend doing? Are you taking good care of Mike?"

Jeremy's trusted house assistant and personal driver, George, relayed, "Done! I'll get it all arranged. Your new houseguest—Mr. Peters . . . I mean Mike . . . well, Mike's pretty interesting. The first day here, he insisted on handling most of the staff's jobs and everyone was getting nervous. So I made a call, like you said, and got him back in the pilot's seat over at Topanga Air. Do you have any idea where he's been and what he's done? The guy's got more hours than most commercial pilots. He flew air rescues in Iraq, advisory pilot to Special Ops, taught at Central Intelligence . . . and all. But he had disappeared, seemed to go missing last year. I did some research and we located his records . . . amazing guy."

35

*L*AX assaulted Reagan's senses from all directions. Loudspeaker announcements, beeps, horns, whistles, and people rushing around with phones attached to their ears, pummeled her. Then the putrid smell of something.

"What is that smell . . . my eyes are burning . . . cigarettes . . . oh yeah . . . smog." She had forgotten about the toxic atmosphere the moment she left L.A. ten years ago.

"Taxi, ma'am?" a shriveled man yelled at her with a cigarette dangling from his lips.

"No, it's mine—I was here first!" yelled another driver, followed by the obnoxious sound of a horn incessantly blaring for someone's attention.

Reagan looked around for Jeremy, like a lost, frightened child searching for her parents. When a man with an oversized bag bumped into her while talking on his phone, barely acknowledging her existence, she started to hyperventilate. This stress wasn't what Dr. Yiung was referring to, but it was already showing the toxic effect on her body. Was he right about sharing with the patients only what they need to know? She questioned why she had come—*why is Los*

Angeles the only place with radioactive poisoning experts? If only she could have stayed south of the equator.

"Reagan! Over here." Jeremy's voice helped temper her frayed nerves.

She hurried to him and latched onto his arm as he hailed his driver. The black Maserati GTS pulled up within seconds. Reagan ducked into the sports car, still gripping Jeremy as he closed the door.

Cars wailed by while Reagan got a first glimpse of Jeremy's wealthy lifestyle. She had never considered it with the exception of hearing he was a big deal back in the States. People pointed at him, others jostled to ask for his autograph. Everyone knew Jeremy Black.

"Sorry, sir, traffic is a mess," the driver explained. The man behind the wheel appeared to be in his fifties. He was impeccably dressed. His chauffeur's hat rested squarely over his slicked back hair, revealing only a hint of gray in his sideburns. He checked the mirrors several times before pulling away. "Straight home, boss?"

"Yes, George! Home please," Jeremy answered.

The fans jumped up and down, waving their hands and getting dangerously close to the window as the car pulled away.

Reagan caught a glimpse of George in the mirror. She waved her fingers, mouthing *hi*. He quickly looked away. She figured it wasn't his place to acknowledge new faces in Jeremy's car. It was a strange comparison to the Fijians, who were so friendly to anyone. She sighed, but noticed the driver glance at her again. She smiled at his blushed cheeks in the mirror.

"George, meet Reagan."

"Pleasure to meet you, ma'am." He held her gaze for a moment.

Reagan liked his gentle charm and felt the tension of her arrival relax.

The drive along Pacific Coast Highway also helped with the recovery from the airport chaos. Reagan hung her face out the window and inhaled deeply. The ocean brought memories she hadn't thought of in years. Passing Malibu, checking out the light offshore winds creating feather-like forms off the first point break, brought her back to her childhood. Although she hadn't been in California for years, she'd grown up here. She and her closest childhood friend, Andy, surfed all day—first point at dawn for hours. Then they'd eat steamed clams and fries on the pier, returning at sunset to surf the third point by themselves. He was her trusted surf buddy—connected through their love for the ocean. She wondered why she thought of him now. Maybe the surf spot provoked it, or maybe it was the waft of salty fries seeping into her senses. She remembered his gregarious personality . . . remembered she never got to say goodbye.

"What are you thinking about?" Jeremy swept his finger over the distended vein on the back of her hand.

"A dear childhood friend." Reagan kept her gaze on the long board surfer gracefully walking to the nose of the surfboard and back before kicking out of the wave. "We used to surf here as kids."

Reagan's index finger caressed her upper lip, creating a calming effect. She was relaxing into her memories when Jeremy brought her hand to his lips, kissing the back of it. Reagan relished the tender gesture. She had missed Jeremy—thought she'd never see him again, but now they were together. She smiled at the thought of them being a couple. It had been so long . . . so terribly long. The last relationship—a compilation of lies and deceit—imploded right here in this town. She washed the memory from her thoughts; this moment seemed so right.

36

*T*HE long drive up to Jeremy's estate was impressive. Reagan thought she knew Malibu well, but she'd never had a reason or opportunity to enter the private gates of the Hills Estates. Trumpet vines of every color climbed invasively up the edge of a cobblestone wall. Two travertine gargoyles were perched at the entrance of the final gate exposing the main entrance to his home. Several staff members were present as the Maserati came to its final halt. The door opened and George extended his hand to Reagan, helping her grasp the magnitude of what she was about to enter.

"This is home." Jeremy took her hand from George.

Reagan hesitated at the grand entrance, not sure she was ready for the next step, but the ocean view in the background helped her ease into Jeremy's world. Even when she had lived in L.A., she rented a modest apartment on Santa Monica Boulevard to be close to the hospital yet not too far from the ocean. She never considered spending more than what was necessary on her living conditions, even though she might have been able to afford it. Jeremy showed her around the house, proudly pointing out the fruits of all his accomplishments. She missed her modest quarters; she missed the simplicity of her room in Fiji; she missed her family on the island and the dolphins playing around her skiff.

"This is an original Monet." He gestured to the array of color and light bouncing off the French lilies. "It cost a small fortune, but what else am I going to spend my money on?"

Reagan bit her lip to squelch her response.

"This Andy Warhol was given to me after I won an Emmy for portraying him in an artistic documentary. I seem to do well portraying artists. I'm not sure why. Do you know how much this is worth!" Jeremy beamed.

He went on to point out life-size marble sculptures and abstract replicas of everyday objects, and, of course, the numerous golden statuettes lined up on the mantle. After a while she wasn't hearing the name of the artists or the value of the piece; it was becoming too much for her to take in.

Reagan remained stone-faced hiding her revulsion of the profuse abundance in the face of so much poverty around the world. *What am I doing here?*

They proceeded through the open kitchen where several people were busy preparing food.

"Is there an event going on here tonight?" Reagan asked innocently.

"No, this is just every day around here."

Reagan struggled with the complexity and pompousness of everything, including her feelings of disdain for his wealth and lavish lifestyle. She was drawn back to his life as an actor and the poor portrayal of the islanders in the film. She considered all the things he could do with his power and money. He could build a hospital or house hundreds of homeless. She tried to look away from all the materialistic trophies, but everywhere she looked there was another piece to gloat about. This was his life, an overwhelming collection of golden assets. Reagan felt nauseous—her stomach tightened and a horrific pain crept up her spine.

"I'm not feeling well." She bent forward holding her belly, unfamiliar with the intensity of everything she was exposed to—the house, his staff, sports cars worth more than six figures, and now this stabbing pain. "I think I'm about to get sick." The rumbling wave ripped through her body. "I need to . . . lie down for a—" The room went black as she collapsed to the floor.

THE tips of Jeremy's fingers grabbed her head before she hit the hardwood floor. "Hold on . . . I got yah."

The concerned staff gathered around offering to help.

"It's okay, she's just exhausted. She's been through a lot," Jeremy said calmly. He scooped her up in his arms, carefully protecting every part of her. He carried her into his room and laid her on the bed.

Reagan's eyes opened. "I don't know what came over me, I just lost—"

"Shh," he whispered, placing his fingers on her lips. "Rest. You've been through so much. I've got you."

Jeremy took off her shoes and pants, and placed a pillow under her head. He opened the cedar chest at the end of the bed, pulling out a silk duvet that his mother had sewed for him. It was a special treasure, a tarnished memory he wanted to keep pristine. He had never used it before; he'd only wanted to keep it safe. Jeremy inhaled the momentous scent and wrapped it around Reagan, tucking the edges gently under her spine. The smell of the coverlet reminded him of his childhood—a confusing mix of love and fear.

Stroking her forehead, Jeremy watched her eyes close. This was new territory for him. Most of his past relationships were a shallow arrangement made to satisfy very simple needs. He had never met anyone like Reagan, never felt this way about anyone—a pull so strong he felt he might die without her. He struggled with his thoughts. *What if she can't get through it? I've found the love of my life and she may not. . . .*

Jeremy watched her body surrender to the fatigue, in his house, in his bed, while straddling the emotional abyss.

37

*T*HE sign at L.A. Medical Center was enormous.

"You can't miss that." Reagan smirked. "I think they paid more for that sign than Dr. Yiung's entire clinic."

As they exited Jeremy's car, a woman next to them screeched, "Oh my God, it's Jeremy Black. Oh my, I loved your last movie . . . you were such a hero. I just adore—" Another woman in the parking lot latched onto the sighting. "Can you please take a picture with me? My daughter is your biggest fan."

Reagan balked at the attention Jeremy drew from everyone they walked by. They quickened their steps to get into the building before the mob intensified.

"Let me get that door for you, Mr. Black." A female volunteer glowed.

"Well, hello there, Mr. Black," said another.

A sheepish grin grew on Jeremy's face as he downplayed the attention.

"Can I show you to your department, Mr. Black?" It was endless. Reagan grew more irritated with every intrusion.

"Maybe I should do this by myself."

Jeremy gripped her arm and pulled her in close. "Come on, Reagan, you know it's just part of the game. I could care less."

When they finally arrived at the Department of Nuclear Medicine, the first evidence of the level of security and health warnings were clearly posted. "If you are pregnant or ill, do not enter." Reagan halted, stone-faced, realizing the weight of the words. The severity of what was behind those doors added to the immensity of her physical distress.

"Come on. We're neither of those, right?" His eyebrows raised while he motioned toward the steel doors.

She smiled thinking of the small miracle that would have had to happen for her to be pregnant. She hadn't been intimate with a man for a long time.

"Hello, miss, how can I help you?" The attendant barely lifted her eyes off the computer screen.

"I'm here to see Dr. Roscoe," Reagan answered.

The woman glanced up for a moment. She handed Reagan a clipboard with numerous intake pages. "Fill this out and have a seat. We'll call you when we're ready for you."

Reagan read the repetitive questions: Where have you traveled in the last ten years? Where did you go to college? What is your profession? Primary and secondary insurance . . . all previous medical conditions and medications. The list went on and on.

"Why do I need to answer all these?" she asked.

"Insurance company wants them, ma'am. Please just fill them out."

Reagan huffed at the thought of relying on insurance to keep her healthy. She appreciated her life in Fiji where she could protect her own health and the islanders' without lining the pockets of unnecessary middlemen.

"This is preposterous," Reagan complained to Jeremy. "They want to know my level of education, where I live, where I've been . . . none of this is any of their damn business. I don't even have insurance. Let's get out of here!"

"Please, Reagan—please stay. Look, this is regular stuff, just paperwork. I can help . . . give it to me. Really . . . please."

The receptionist fumbled quickly out of her chair. "Oh, Mr. Black, I didn't notice you there. She doesn't need to fill those out now. We can take care of them later. Come, let me take you to the doctor's personal office. Would you like some coffee, tea?"

Reagan rolled her eyes, let out a sigh and took advantage of the medical inequity right in front of her. "Is it possible to get some water?"

The receptionist turned and walked away mumbling, "Sure, honey, anything you say."

Walking into a private room with no windows, Reagan sat on a treatment table. Dreary outdated artwork hung on the walls. The incandescent light was stark and she wondered if her sunglasses were with her. Over the sink were posters with different drug company names—endorsing their latest miracle cure in big letters. She let out an audible, "Huh."

Jeremy shrugged. "What?"

Reagan shook her head; it was too hard to explain.

The door opened and a nurse in a white lab coat walked in, extending her hand to Reagan. "Sorry for the wait. My name's Lydia. I'll be finishing your intake that appears . . . well . . . unfinished." She held up the paperwork with only Reagan's name on the top.

The nurse asked numerous questions, this time more relevant, and different from the clipboard in the waiting area.

"Yes, I have been in Fiji for ten years."

The nurse kept her gaze down at the paper.

Reagan watched her curiously. The woman was attentive, scrawling notes faster than Reagan could speak them.

"Yes, I'm a physician, also as stated in the notes from Dr. Yiung. Yes, I have extreme levels of plutonium and other metals in my blood work, but I presume you will retest all those for your records." Reagan was losing patience.

The nurse stopped writing.

"Look, I'm just here for some scans. When can I see the doctor?" Reagan got off the table and moved toward the door.

"Hey now, you listen to me!" The nurse looked straight into Reagan's eyes. The assertive and stout African-American woman inhaled a deep breath, preparing for a short lecture. "This information is meant to give us all the lil' details that we need to help yo' ass. I don't care if you're a rocket scientist. I still need to know this stuff. So sit your butt down and talk to me so I can help you."

At first Reagan was surprised by the strong, gruff demand, but returning the nurse's stare, she sensed something powerful and felt a strange sense of safety with her.

Jeremy chuckled and the nurse turned to him. "And you pipe down, mister actor-man. I'm not happy with your last film . . . of all the sappy plots, I swear. You're on timeout as far as I'm concerned."

Jeremy and Reagan smiled at each other for the first time all day. The nametag on the nurse's lab coat read Lydia Williams. Reagan felt an immediate affinity for her and tried to cooperate with her questions. She liked how straightforward and quick-witted she was, all while pouring out more wisdom than one could sit still for.

"Where did you grow up?" Lydia resumed her pen to paper.

"Here in Los Angeles. The Valley . . . rather . . . but here, you know—L.A. area."

Lydia had brilliant white teeth, so when she smiled it took over her whole expression. "Yeah, sure, I know da area."

The conversation grew more relaxed. Reagan enjoyed the woman's Southern slang and wild hand gesturing. There was no pretense and she seemed genuine in her intentions.

"And you're treating the Hansen's? You on dapsone?" Lydia didn't flinch.

"You don't seem as fearful as others." Reagan anticipated her response.

"More likely to catch a cold than that ol' disease. Ya know those people got a bad rap. It's the ignorance that gets ya. My mama's friend used to help out at Carville. Oh, the things she told me. People so scared and all the while those folks suffered. They just kicked 'em to the curb. Do you know they even took away their vote? Not a lick a luck for them. Don't get me started."

"Thank you, you do understand." Reagan dropped her shoulders.

"Tell me more about your pain. How intense is it? Are you medicating?" Lydia flipped over to the third page of the medical intake sheets.

"It's pretty bad when I have it, but it's not always there. Seems worse since I arrived here in—" Reagan caught herself mid-sentence. "Interesting, this is what Dr. Yiung was referring to."

"Who?" Lydia asked. "There's no Dr. Yiung here."

"Never mind." Reagan didn't want to elaborate on his prediction of the effects of stress, and here it was, in full view.

"Don't you never mind me, girl. I'm here to mind my job. I need answers, every morsel you can throw at me. We got a mystery to solve here and it ain't no good playin' around it."

Jeremy let out an abrupt laugh.

Lydia snapped. "If I be talkin' to you, sir, then I be talkin' to you. But I'm not and—" A potential second lecture was on the runway, but Dr. Roscoe's entrance saved Jeremy.

The doctor first extended his hand to Jeremy. "Such a pleasure to meet you, Mr. Black. I am a huge admirer. That film about the real estate meltdown and big banks, that was awesome. You are so—"

Lydia cleared her voice in an abrupt manner. "Doctor, this is Reagan. She is here to see you, sir." She rolled her eyes, exhaling a small huff.

The doctor turned to Reagan. "Oh, yes. I understand you are here for extended testing, but—"

"I am? I thought I was here for some scans . . . a basic confirmation of. . . ."

The doctor glanced down at the chart, flipping through the pages, before looking back up at her. "I can't really help you without new MRIs, CTs, and DEXA scans. Then we need thermonuclear imaging and X-rays. I also need blood panels and genetic DNA mapping."

Lydia turned away, as if avoiding the collision in front of her.

"Why do you need to map my DNA?" Reagan whispered in confusion.

Jeremy straightened himself and faced Lydia.

The sound of Lydia's nails tapping on the table was the only audible sound.

Dr. Roscoe shook his head before looking at Reagan, "I also need to quarantine you here, due to the Hansen's disease."

Reagan looked to Lydia for support, but she had no comeback. Reagan stood up. There was an intense ringing in her ears. She felt like she was about to faint, but instead she gathered all her willpower and made for the door. "Over my dead body." She felt panicked and confused, not sure how they had originally gotten to this office and all the twists and turns to get out.

Jeremy yelled down the hallway, "Reagan, wait, for chrissake, wait."

He caught up with her at the elevator. Reagan was trembling while pressing the button excessively to close the door and get away.

"I don't understand. We need their help, Reagan. You can't go on like this. They can help . . ." On and on he pleaded, all the way to the car.

"I didn't come here to be a caged, experimental animal. Frankly, I'm not sure how I even got talked into returning to all this."

"Because we need to know . . . what to do, right? Isn't that what Dr. Yiung said? He didn't have the equipment to test you, right?" Jeremy held the car door open for her.

Reagan was silent. She stared out the car window, looking away from the group of people gawking at Jeremy.

He pulled out of the hospital driveway. Cars sped by and horns honked as he merged into traffic.

Reagan's concerns escalated. She alternated between defending herself and the unrelenting tears. "I shouldn't have come. It's all wrong," Reagan sobbed, drowning out the words. "I left long ago for good reasons." She gasped for air in between words.

Jeremy gripped the steering wheel with both hands. The veins on the side of his temples distended. There was no script to follow; he'd never known how to help . . . how to reach out, beyond his own vulnerability. "Please calm down, Reagan. I love you."

There it was, the inescapable emotion, laid out before her. Reagan's breaths slowed, her heartbeat steadied as she wiped the final tears from her eyes.

He pulled the car over and turned to her. "I thought I'd lost you once. I won't lose you again. We will do this together. I love you."

"But—"

He placed his hands on the side of her face and drew her close to him.

The gentle wisps of colors in his eyes—she was so drawn to when they first met, were vibrant. She held his gaze. Her heartbeat picked up again.

Their lips met and she softened. A surge of uncontrollable energy pulsed through her body. Her skin against his, their lips passionately kissing—she felt as if she were on the inside of a steep, treacherous wave, about to close out. It had immense power that attempted to overwhelm her. If only she could hold on, feel the centrifugal force of the wave and let it pull her to safety.

After they returned to his home, it was only minutes before they were in his bed, entangled in the rapture of the moment.

Their lovemaking was sheer intensity. The months of not being together, coupled with the stress of Reagan's future, unleashed into a powerful natural force.

38

"**M**R. Black, Mr. Black, there's someone very official here to see you."

The panicked voice came from behind closed doors. He glanced over at Reagan, fast asleep and unaffected by the intrusive knock.

"Mr. Black, come at once—they have a warrant."

Jeremy pulled the satin coverlet over Reagan's shoulder and ear, hoping to disguise the disturbance. He put on a pair of pants and tiptoed toward the door.

"Where you going?" Reagan turned toward Jeremy, her eyes glassy.

He walked back to her and placed his index finger on his lips. "Shhh . . . just rest . . . it's nothing." He kissed her lightly. "You are so beautiful."

Reagan tried to sit up, but fell back into the down pillow. "Yes, I'll stay put. This feels too good."

Combing his hair with his fingers, Jeremy followed George to the front entry. "Who is it, George? What time is—"

"Well past midnight, sir. They just appeared at the gate, showing badges. I'm sorry, sir, I wasn't clear about what they wanted or what to do." George slowly opened the heavy door, laden with security devices.

Jeremy drew in a deep breath, preparing for the next scene.

A man in a white uniform stood at the entry, offering his ID and a badge with clear lettering: CDC Protection Agency. Another man stood beyond him, leaning against an idling GMC van in the driveway. Jeremy squinted to make out the logo on the side of the vehicle.

He tamped down his agitation. "What's this all about?" Jeremy stepped forward, squaring his shoulders in front of the man.

"Sorry to bother you, sir, uh . . . Mr. Black. We've received some information and needed to follow up."

"In the middle of the night?" Jeremy raised his voice.

"Like I said, Mr. Black. We have our orders. We understand you're housing our suspect, Miss Reagan Caldwell, who has a seriously contagious disease. Leprosy, they say . . . and there's a recent outbreak in L.A., so we've been ordered to act quickly, even if it is the middle of the night, sir."

Jeremy caught the strong glare that George had thrown his direction. He launched back at the man in the white uniform, "Suspect? You guys are way off base, and likely trespassing. Where's that warrant? You can't just come to my door and throw out accusations you know nothing about."

George laid his hand on the back of Jeremy's shoulder. "Sir, if I may." He turned to the man. "We drove her to the airport at ten p.m. tonight. She's flying back to Australia."

Jeremy lowered his shoulders and stuck to the script laid out in front of him. "Yeah, but that's none of their business either."

The man looked perplexed. "Oh, we were told she was here, that they have surveillance footage of her leaving the hospital in your car, that black Maserati parked outside."

"Yah, well, that was hours ago. She's long gone. Would you like to come in and look for yourself?" Jeremy took a few steps toward the front door.

"No . . . no, sir, that won't be necessary. Sorry to bother you. We'll just double-check at the airport. I gotta tell you, my wife is a huge fan of yours, and if she heard I hassled you I'd never hear the end of it."

Jeremy looked down momentarily, swishing his bare feet over the granite stone. A strange squeak was emitted. "Would you like an autograph for your wife?"

The man put away his I.D. and snatched a pen from his pocket. "That would be great . . . ten brownie points for me."

George had left the men and returned with a signed, glossy and outdated photo of Jeremy. He slipped it into Jeremy's hand as if it was a "get out of jail free" pass.

"Here yah go, and sorry I jumped down your throat. It's just late and I got a big shoot tomorrow. It's a total pain to be woken up like this."

"My apologies, sir, and good night."

As Jeremy closed the door behind him, beads of sweat rolled down his brow. *Brownie points! What the hell was that about? Reagan . . . a fugitive . . . that's crazy.* He captured George's unspoken stare. "Sorry I didn't tell you, George." Jeremy lowered his head. "It's not that contagious."

"I know, sir. No need to explain. How can I help?"

The staff had gathered. They were in their sleeping attire and looked bewildered. "How can we help, boss?" one of them asked. "I can hide her in my car and take her to my house."

"Or we can hide her in the wine cellar," another added. "There's a permanent lock down there. No one's busting into that place."

"No, I'll cover for her and say—" George insisted.

"That's ridiculous, she would never—" another person responded.

Everyone had their opinion on how to hide Reagan, how to protect her, how to keep her safe and out of reach from the men in the white uniforms.

"I say we should . . ." George interrupted for the third time.

Reagan walked into the room. "None of that will be necessary. I will turn myself in." It was preposterous. She hadn't done anything wrong, yet she was now a medical fugitive. The bounty hunters had come for her.

"No you won't. That's ridiculous." Jeremy's purpose and confidence, lost for months since his return from Fiji, were now back in full force. "No one is taking you away from me. I'll make sure of it. You're here, in my home, a part of my life, and no one is going to change that."

The staff froze. This was a new Jeremy, never seen before. Jeremy had never spoken in that tone, with such determination. Then another bold knock at the door sent everyone back into a frenzy.

"Take her down to the cellar."

"No, put her in the town car."

"I'll take her to my place."

Everyone talked over each other as Reagan walked to the door and opened it.

"Oh my God!"

39

"LYDIA!" What are you doing here?" Reagan asked, confused. "How did you get through the security gate?" Jeremy added, looking toward George.

"Easy. I'm from the South and we know all about timin' things. Just had to wait out those nasty collections boys from the CDC, and I slipped right in." Lydia smiled as she batted her eyelashes at George.

George was frantically checking the security system. "Boss, I swear, all the cameras were working, no change in the signal or alarm system. I don't get it. How did you—"

"Honey, like I said, I have my ways and I have my means."

LYDIA WILLIAMS was raised in Macon, Georgia, known in the history books for slavery, cotton fields, and segregation. Lydia had fought her way out. She was smart and brave—the attributes necessary for survival. If something got in her way she'd always figure a way around it, like walking past a fully secured gate and alarm system, with a big white van and official lookin' folks hangin' around.

Reagan had heard her abbreviated story at the hospital.

Top honors at Emory University, full scholarship to the nursing program and any internship she desired, but Lydia had worked at four different institutions in her first three years as a nurse, while trying to fit in.

Lydia never danced around what she wanted to say. When a rep walked in, she was fully loaded with verbal ammo: "I see what you got there, boy. I know by the packaging. It's what's killin' our babies, them sweet-tastin' meds and soon enough them babies are lovin' those pain killers and soon enough they are dead. So smooth . . . they go down . . . just like sugar, huh?" Her heavy stare and strong slang continued: "Why should my patient give a hoot about your bonus? How about you take them small little boxes out of my office and let the doctor decide for himself what's best for his patients."

One by one the drug reps stopped dropping by to promote their wares in her office, and the hospital heard about it from the pharmaceutical companies. It wasn't long before the conciliatory lady from Human Resources reminded her about hospital hierarchy—she was not a doctor—and although her paperwork was impeccable, so in depth, accurate to a fault, she thanked her for her employment and released her the same day.

Maintaining the belief that things happen for a reason, Lydia felt she'd been touched by God when she was accepted into the research department at L.A. Medical Center, where patient contact would be minimized and paperwork maximized.

The day Reagan and Jeremy had come into Dr. Roscoe's office, Lydia had filled in while his regular nurse was out sick. Lydia knew she was not supposed to engage patients, but she liked Reagan once she got her to relax and finish her intake.

Now as she faced Reagan at the entrance of Jeremy's private estate, Lydia spoke slowly. "Hey, girl, you need my help. So where can we talk?"

Reagan hugged her, understanding their strange connection. Reagan wasn't sure why she felt relieved, but she did. Lydia was there to help. She sensed a power in Lydia akin to Maura's. Lydia, like Maura, was home and safety.

Jeremy whisked them both into his home office. "What is this all about?" He closed the door behind them.

"I'm still not happy with you, movie-star man. I be talkin' to this woman, seein' that she is special." She turned toward Reagan. "I'm here to tell you, I'm real good at what I do. A lot of folks don't understand where I've been and what I've seen, but that don't matter to no one, it seems."

Lydia's chest heaved with every breath. She was a big woman with strong shoulders and erect posture. There were no signs of wrinkles or sagging; she seemed to have the wisdom of someone much older. "I know stuff that most folks don't know, but I'm not talkin'," she continued. "I know the code. I obey when I'm told to obey, if it makes sense."

Jeremy raised one eyebrow. "Like coming here, breaking onto my property, and—"

Lydia raised her hand, signaling for Jeremy to stop his unwarranted accusations. "You shush! I'm not finished and I don't appreciate being interrupted." She glared at Jeremy. The intensity in her eyes and her outstretched arm set him back down and silenced him. "I've spent too much time in that dungeon. You know, ol' dusty archives. There's some strange stuff goin' on—hidden files, things out of place, the hushed-up voices when I walk by. And so many . . . I mean so many of da same symptoms. Jus' plain crazy."

Reagan was confused by her words. "Lydia, what are you talking about? What dungeon? What hushed-up voices?"

The white in Lydia's eyes expanded. "I be tellin' you. They send me to the basement, yah know . . . where medical records collect dust. That's my job since they don't want me crossin' paths with too many patients. Seems like I don't walk n' talk the way them do. That's how I lost my last job. So they jus' keep me doing paperwork, yah know, archive stuff. But then I trip on lots of stuff that makes no sense, not how it's supposed to look. They never dreamed a girl like me comin' where I'm from could figure this stuff out. Then you come along, I felt somethin' yah know, in here." Lydia held a fist over her stomach. "Like you were there for some reason, God only knows why I was there to meet you. But I knew it had to do with them files and them patients."

Reagan realized her body had become extremely tense—her jaw was locked down. She felt overheated and leaned against Jeremy, gripping his elbow.

Lydia lowered her voice. "We called those boys glow sticks. It was no joke, either. You could see 'em coming way down the hall." Lydia was now standing as she elaborated on her secret. "We wasn't suppose to say nothin' to them, and nothin' to nobody. But we all knew." She shook her head back and forth with a remorseful nod. "And the test results. . . . Oh, sweet Jesus . . . they were off the chart. We'd just keep checking and double-checking in case we made a mistake."

Reagan placed her hand on Lydia's forearm. "I still don't—"

"Your levels of plutonium and argon. They're not normal, not natural. God wouldn't put that in anyone's hands. This is a manmade problem. But I'm not talkin' and I'm not tellin' you this right now. I've already been fired, hired, and re-fired, so I can't say nothin' to no lawyer boys or under oath. I will deny it, even if you force it out of me." Her brows were arched up toward the heavens in a retractable promise. "I just want to help you. You need to know the truth. After all . . . you're a doctor. You should know the truth." Lydia wiped her brow with the back of her sleeve and let out a slow wheeze of oxygen. "Sweet Jesus, praise the Lord, I've seen too much."

Reagan was still perplexed trying to put together the pieces of a puzzle Lydia had created.

Jeremy finally spoke up. "What the hell are we talking about? What are glow sticks?"

40

~~~~~~

*L*YDIA put both hands on her hips. "So I once got a doc's license revoked for overprescribing antibiotics to an ol' lady for a common cold."

"And what's that got to do with glow sticks?" Jeremy insisted.

"Nothin', but the doc kept writin' scrips for any ol' symptom, jus' to quiet his patients. He knew it wasn't right. That nice ol' lady got MRSA . . . end of story."

Reagan threw her hands in the air. "No surprises there."

Lydia rolled her eyes. "So when that doc's attorney came roun' asking questions, you know I'm not cuttin' nobody any slack. I told the lawyer-boy the whole truth about this doc's lazy-ass practice . . . pills, pills, and more pills. Doc got fired and no more license to boot, then the guy went crazy . . . depressed and all."

"Okay, so you've been down this road before, but not all doctors are bad. What's your point? You said I should know the truth." Reagan straightened up a bit and tilted her head.

"It means I be thinkin' twice about talkin', but people ought a know. Especially you, being a doc an' all."

Reagan looked at Lydia trying to decode her message. It was all so scattered.

Lydia let out a large sigh. "You know, a glow stick, like a lighthouse warning, or a torch, like a radioactive walking zombie." She smirked slightly before shaking her head. "The boys from the power plant, they all come up glowin'. Not all at once, more like in batches. Not sure why, but they been comin' here for treatment over the years. But soon enough they never come back."

The room went silent with those last sentences spoken. Reagan's spine shot up straight like a steel rod, fully understanding Lydia's reference. Her pain level was fierce; a burning blaze ripped through her neck and into her temples.

"No." Reagan knew how and when she got radiation poisoning.

Jeremy could barely grasp the thread of conversation. "But Reagan's been in Fiji. There's nothing radioactive there. I mean there was that fallout in Japan, but that's too far away, right?"

Reagan paced the room with her hands pressing into her temples. "Oh no, oh my God. No, this can't be." Memories swirled in her head, colliding into each other, causing a chaos of emotion. Her pain ratcheted up many notches. She looked to Jeremy for support, for him to hold her up—to rescue her from the very real nightmare she was now living. Her legs trembled. Reagan's vision blurred as the memories assaulted her.

"What is it, girl? What aren't you saying? Just say it. What do you know about that power plant?" Lydia pleaded. "Tell me what you know . . . I'm just tryin' to help here."

Reagan thought about the beautiful right-hander she and Andy had surfed, wave after wave. They never tired of it and had the stamina to surf all day, until the sunset colors chased them back up the cliff. It was one of their favorite surf spots—one of the best waves in California. Everyone surfed there.

"I surfed the Cliffs for years, Andy and me, hundreds of times." Her eyes welled up. "It was just so perfect . . . I never would have—"

"So, there was a power plant where you surfed? What does that have to do with anything?" Jeremy swallowed.

Lydia leaned in.

Reagan spoke as if in a trance. "There was a shortcut path, much shorter than the common trail all the surfers took. We had to trespass under a wire fence, but it was so much quicker." Reagan's heart ached. "Oh, Andy." He was her first true love, without the physical intimacy. They were too young, too shy, to alter what they had. Maybe they knew better than to change their friendship. Reagan drew in a deep breath, churning over her worst fears.

Jeremy clutched her hand in both of his. "What is it? I don't understand any of this."

"At the top of the trail, there was a warm shower . . . just outside the power plant, where we would rinse off, drink from, and bask in for as long as we wanted. We just wanted to warm up on those cold north-swell mornings. It was heaven . . . I thought."

Lydia bowed her head. "Damn," she whispered. "Don't fret, girl. We'll figure it out." She moved next to Reagan, rubbing her arm. "Let's get Andy in for some testing and see—"

Reagan turned to Lydia, eyes flooded with tears, begging for a different explanation and having trouble speaking his name. It came out in broken syllables.

"An . . . Andy's goh . . . gone. He's dead."

41

~~~~

AURA had finished washing the last towel at the outdoor community sink when she caught sight of Roger running toward her. He had never stepped foot on their island. At least not as far as Maura could recall. "Roger? Everything all right?"

Huffing for a breath, Roger took off his hat. "Reagan's not coming home . . . she's headed to L.A. to get . . . help." He looked away from Maura. "She needs further testing . . . of some sort . . . something about. . . . Well, since Dr. Yiung didn't have what she needed."

Maura clung to the sink's edge trying to follow his masked words, which were all broken up, seemingly covering for something. "Why? She knows what to do . . . she has 'nough medicine and supplements. She carry 'em out of Dr. Yiung's office. I see it myself. They tell me they come home right after me."

"Well, there's more." Roger's glance wavered. "Turns out . . . she . . . uh, Reagan has . . . some sort of radiation poisoning." His eyes met hers.

A small crowd of islanders had gathered around Maura. Their attention was on Roger.

"We need to help Reagan." Maura's voice was assertive as she turned to the islanders. She spoke like the chief would have. "She needs our prayers, our strength. Everything she has ever given us, we now give her."

"How can we help?" someone asked.

"What does she need?" another chimed in.

The islanders grew restless. What would happen to their Reagan?

Maura didn't have the answers. In desperation, she thought of Phaeole. She had no choice; she needed his help. Clearing her throat, she announced to Roger and the others, "I go now . . . up the mountain. Phaeole will help us."

"Mama, please no—" Her eldest, Lelei, began to question her, but she knew not to overstep her mother's orders.

"Start kava ceremony, pray for her. I be back soon. I find the answer for our Reagan."

Maura set off by herself, against her late husband's and Reagan's wishes. Maura had been checking in on Phaeole periodically, but never by herself. He was a trusted sage, she reminded herself, washing the rumors of cannibalism from her mind. Maura had yet to tell Phaeole of Reagan's diagnosis of Hansen's disease, and now the news of this poisoning made it imperative that he know. There was no time to wait for someone to accompany her, no time to discuss whether Maura was safe trekking up the hill alone. This time she simply needed to act, for Reagan's sake. Phaeole could help, he would know what to do, but Maura had to get to him before it was too late.

After days of monsoon conditions, the rains had finally ceased. Maura proceeded up the arduous path, clearing the passage as she made her ascent. The overgrowth of vines acted like a secondary restraint. She was cautious as she foraged ahead to prevent harm to the precious plants, but she needed to get through the dense vegetation as quickly as she could. Then there was the newly softened mud, which grabbed at her feet like quicksand, making her efforts more difficult. She pulled one foot up high, releasing it from the suction, only to place the next foot down and repeat the task.

Each step was heavier than the previous one, with the added weight from the mud.

Why is this taking so long? Maura was fatiguing fast. *I just need to get to him. Phaeole . . . why are you so far away?* She stopped for a moment and sat on a rock. Her legs were covered with a tar-like sludge compressing her legs like a tight bandage, preventing her muscles from supporting her. *This isn't working. My legs can't take this . . . I have to turn back.* As her eyes stared at the dark green chasm of moss with broken branches around it, she noticed a movement. A greenish-brown toad with large textured bumps on its back sat looking at her. It had a stubby tail pointed upward. The toad made a croaking sound. Maura stared back and remembered Phaeole's whimsical tale: *Ah, of course, the poptail etsy toad. I see you clearly, even though you blend in forest perfectly.* She smiled. "Oh, look at you, my friend, you look like me. Show me the way."

The toad jumped away with a staggered gait, fumbling along the thatched branches. Maura stood tall, straining to see his direction, laughing at the wee-toad messenger.

I understand. I'm coming. She left her fatigue and fear on the rock and proceeded up the ravine. It grew steeper and windier, but she had her guide.

When Maura finally arrived at Phaeole's door, she straightened her dress and whisked the debris off her shoulders. She swiped the mud clumps staining her legs, but it was painted on like an ancient etching.

"Phaeole, it's Maura. Can I come in?" she yelled as loud as she dared. No response. She peered in the windows and walked along the lanai searching for his whereabouts. "Phaeole, are you in there?"

She peered through the palm-frond door.

"Phaeole, Can you hear me?" She intensified the volume. Maura looked around for someone, something, anything that would answer her question. *No, not today. She needs you, Phaeole. She needs you. Please, please!* She glanced to the sky.

Maura thought of the chief, of his unending determination and fortitude. Her own courage was now being challenged amidst her adversity. She thought of what her late husband would have done. The rain started slowly but then picked up its intensity. Her tears trickled then poured with the rainfall.

"Phaeole!" she screamed.

Maura buried her head in her hands. *Not Phaeole, not now. What happened? Are you finished? Was it jus' too much?* She wondered what she would do when she finally had enough, when the pain and disability became too much to endure. Her tears streamed. *Oh dear Lord, it's too late. I should have come yesterday.* Maura looked up to the sky, searching, her hands together: *Now what do I do? Now there is no Phaeole to help, no one to turn to, no Phaeole to help Reagan.*

"Who goes there?" came a voice from the back stairs.

Maura jumped at the sound of his voice. "Oh my Lord." She moved toward him, hugging him with vigor and relief. "Phaeole, it's you . . . you're alive . . . I thought—"

"Oh dear child." Phaeole jumped when Maura grabbed his shoulder. "Why Maura, calm . . . calm . . . what's this all about?"

"Where did you go?" Maura was still crying as the words swept out of her mouth.

"To the waterfall. I needed to hear the splash of the water and feel its breath."

Maura looked perplexed. "How did you get there?" She squeezed Phaeole's hand. "How did you find your way?"

Phaeole smiled. "I always know my way. The smell pulls me onto the path of the great ascent. Then the raging sound builds its intensity until I feel the rain." He raised his nose upward, "Then I smell my way home."

Maura stood in disbelief.

"I also needed to go pick these." He pulled a bunch of white flowers out of his pocket.

Baffled, Maura recognized the sacred plant immediately. How could Phaeole have known why she came? What she needed? What Reagan needed? She stared deep into the blind eyes of the crippled man and tried to untangle his myth and great powers.

"I had a premonition . . . Reagan was wilting away as a petal realizes its last breaths. She needs these to heal. She needs these to bleed out her poison." He felt his way to the kitchen and pounded down the petals, pulling out the stems and disposing of them. His crippled hands performed surgeon-like maneuvers as he sliced and diced the venomous beauty in front of him.

"But, how did—"

"Would you like some tea?" he asked, with one eyebrow raised.

Maura sat with Phaeole sipping kava tea and explained what had happened to Reagan. She told him all about Australia and the wonderment of Dr. Yiung's clinic. "He even had me read to a small child and point at the words. It felt good." She had tears in her eyes recalling the feeling. "I didn't know my fingers could straighten."

"Yes, the power of purpose." He brought the wooden bowl to his mouth.

Maura set her bowl on the dilapidated table. "She needs to come home, Phaeole. You can cure her. You know what she needs."

Phaeole smiled, an uncharacteristic warmth was emitted through his gentle answer, "We are her home, her family. Her medicine and religion are here on this island. She will come . . . be patient. She will find her way." He sipped his tea and inhaled deeply.

42

$$\sim\!\!\sim\!\!\sim$$

PEEKING into several stage doors at the Motion Picture Studio, Jeremy finally found him. He kept on his dark aviators and low-brim hat, while sliding through the massive steel door. The cast and crew were busy ending the day's shoot. The cameras were shut down, lights were dimmed, extension cords wound, and small huddles of people dissipated. The hustle of the studio dwindled. There he sat; Jean Michael was slumped back in the directors' chair, rubbing his eyes.

"Hello, Jean! How have you been?" Jeremy flashed his perfect white smile.

It took a moment for Jean Michael to look up. When he did, a wide grin replaced his dour look. "Ah, Jeremy Black. He returns." He stood and gave Jeremy a bear hug.

"You good?" Jeremy slapped his back.

"Well, depends who's askin'. If you're my wife, then I'm just fine. If you're my drinkin' buddy, bottoms up."

"What if I'm Jeremy Black askin', cuz you kinda look like shit."

Jean Michael lowered his head before looking around at the remaining crew in the room. The lines at the edge of his lips turned downward, acting like an anchor holding back his smile. His deep crows feet branched out wide, making his eyes appear small. He lowered his voice. "Honestly, Jeremy, I'm dying here, just plain fatigued. Nothing good on paper—just the same ol' formulaic, mindless crap."

"Sorry to hear—"

Jean Michael put his hand out. "Which reminds me, I'm really sorry about that last gig in Fiji. Really? *Hidden Beings.* Of all the cockamamie titles." He sat back in his chair, pointing at the chair next to him for Jeremy. ". . . and the implausible, tortuous plot." He shook his head.

"I'm equally to blame. I just had no idea where we were going with it all." Jeremy shook his head and regrouped. "Look, Jean, I wanna put that behind us. I got something big! We could redeem ourselves . . . I want another shot at this." He held onto Jean Michael's shoulders and begged for the role, like a rookie actor.

"Jeremy, it's great to see you, but I'm stuck knee-deep in the thickest crap you can imagine. Worse than . . . before. I don't know, I'm not up for any more wild goose chases, but okay, go ahead . . . lay it on me."

Jeremy looked around for any bystanders, and lowered his voice. "Well, here it is, trust me, it all sounds a little crazy, but it's real."

Jean Michael crossed his arms and glanced at Jeremy. "And you'll trust me, being the epitome of a Hollywood producer?"

Jeremy burst out laughing. "I would hardly say you are the epitome of anybody around here."

"Compliment accepted, enough ass-kissing. So what do you have for me?"

"I have information on a real story for you . . . potentially . . . dangerous."

Jean Michael tilted his head, listening with full attention.

"This story needs to be told." Jeremy got right to the point. "Reagan has been poisoned, and a local power plant is part of a cover-up of some sort."

"What do you mean, Reagan has been poisoned?" It was as if he had been shocked back to life. "Is she okay? I really liked that gal."

Jeremy continued, "Reagan somehow contracted radiation poisoning from surfing in the ocean in front of the power plant, and well, maybe directly from some of the runoff."

"Are you sure? Sounds a little far-fetched. I haven't seen anything in the news."

"Not that far-fetched at all since hundreds of employees and anyone near that plant seem to have been affected. We met a nurse who has seen them come and go from the hospital for years. Glow sticks, she calls them . . . Well, never mind, but they all seem to have radiation poisoning."

Jeremy's body language gave the story backbone; his spine shot straight up, his arms made large circular movements, his fingers pointed back and forth. He summarized everything Lydia had told them. No script was needed—Jeremy was not acting.

"And another thing," he went on, "an employee mysteriously disappeared some time ago. He appears to be the whistle-blower of some classified information." Jeremy had hooked him.

"Jeremy, you are absolutely sure about all this . . . this is serious stuff. You can't go walking around implicating the government or big business based on your girlfriend's strange illness. I mean, I'm really sorry, but it just sounds like a stretch. I would have heard about it by now . . . this is L.A., for God's sake."

Jeremy pulled in a deep breath. "There's not much time. This nurse . . . she came up with a guy's name: Charlie Grant, and he's presumed dead. That's the official story, but I have a lead. The thing is, I'm gonna need a little help tracking him down."

"If this is what you say it is, Jeremy, you need to be careful."

"I know. Any suggestions?"

43

*T*HE road seemed to be caving in under the impress of the harsh summer heat, the black asphalt erupting in sharp edges and unending potholes. Jeremy kept checking his map for a missed turn or wrong direction. There was no River Ridge Road on his map, no winding stream as described by his informant. He pulled over to look at the map again, hoping for a misspelled word or abbreviation in the directions he'd scribbled.

He must have been sitting on the side of the road for some time. The sun was lowering its glow and would soon extinguish his sense of direction. As he surveyed his map, an old green Chevy truck pulled up next to him. The window rolled down and Jeremy was relieved to see a young man at the wheel with a half-cocked grin, suggesting it was not unusual to find wayward travelers on this unmarked road.

He lowered his sunglasses. "You lost, man?"

"Do you know where Charlie lives?" Jeremy decided to leave off the last name "Grant," posing more as a friend than someone official.

"Sure, Chuck's my neighbor. Follow me up the road." The young man pointed.

That was easy, the kid didn't even recognize me. Jeremy turned the key in the ignition and followed the truck. *He must not be an accomplice to Charlie's secret life.* The road winding up the hill was lined with an assortment of olive trees, which disguised the view of the twisting path. It inexplicably narrowed as they drove on, leaving the pavement behind. All was dust and impending darkness. *Pretty easy to evade the world up here.*

The twists and turns could have left Jeremy with no visibility ahead, if it wasn't for his determined pressure on the gas pedal to keep up with the Chevy. Another rut and pothole, *clunk, thud.*

Jeremy was glad he had borrowed Jean Michael's older Toyota, the one used while filming in Mexico. It was a tough beast, though it hadn't been driven for ages. It had a minor oil leak. *What if this whole escapade ends with me broken down in the middle of nowhere? What about the kid up ahead? Who is he? Why did he suddenly appear?* His thoughts made him a bit edgy. *Who is Charlie Grant and why does he live so far off the grid?*

The vegetation grew more dense, with a chaos of broken branches and uprooted trees. The road twisted through somber hills, now falling into a gray hue. Finally, a rusty old gate stopped their progress, with no hint of habitation in sight.

The dust settled as the door to the old Chevy opened and the driver yelled over, "That's Chuck's place through there." The young man smiled and waved enthusiastically. "He ain't much of a talker, so good luck." He got back in his truck and drove off, leaving a dust storm behind him and Jeremy choking on the trailing exhaust.

Jeremy sat for a few minutes. He needed to clear his lungs and his thoughts and focus on the wrought-iron gate. He was amazed the gate was unlatched, allowing for an easy entry. He proceeded down a steep embankment and across a rock gully. Finally, a simple dwelling with a modest front porch appeared.

The overgrown ivy acted like a security system, protecting someone from either entering unnoticed or escaping unharmed. Jeremy approached the front door with trepidation, unsure as to what or who was behind it.

Could Charlie Grant possibly answer some hard questions related to Reagan's poisoning? What, if anything, could he do about it? He knocked lightly a few times then took a few steps back to collect his thoughts. No response. He thought of what Lydia had told him about the power plant and the cover-up by the companies, hiding their mistakes behind a smoke screen of lies. He knocked again, this time increasing the amplitude of the bang, desperate for an answer. The door remained shut; he grew anxious and impatient.

He went to knock a third time but was interrupted by the fuming rage of a man behind a shotgun, standing on the edge of the porch. Startled, Jeremy jumped back, having not heard the man's approach. The adrenaline poured into his system as he stared down the threatening metal barrel. He stood paralyzed by fear, unable to move in any direction.

The hoarse voice behind the rage demanded, "What do you want?"

Jeremy was in shock, not by the man's surprise appearance or size but by the anger in his red face. He swallowed. "Are you Charlie Grant?"

"Who's asking?" The man's stature was intimidating, leaving Jeremy momentarily distracted from his purpose. Yet there was something about the man's eyes that convinced him he wasn't a killer. He was simply desperate and very much alone with his secrets. Jeremy shook off his fear and resumed acting, hoping to break through the resistance in front of him. The man was unkempt, shaking as he held the rifle, spit sliding out the side of his mouth. His aggressiveness didn't appear to come from physical strength.

"My name is Jean Ravaa." Jeremy took Jean Michael's advice to disguise his identity, in addition to the oversized blazer and gold-rimmed glasses. "I'm a reporter for the Orange County Register. I'm not here for any trouble." He raised both hands up in the air. "My boss gave me a couple hundred bucks to come see if Charlie Grant is still alive or not. Something about he might have gotten sick and died like the others." Jeremy, now playing the role of a hack journalist, did what Jean said—keep it simple and straightforward. "So I just need to know if that guy is you, and if not, then I'll go." He lowered his hands, mirroring the man slowly lowering the shotgun. Jeremy continued, "I understand you may have been around the nuclear power plant a few years ago."

The man tilted his head, squinting his eyes against the last rays of sunlight. "How did you find me?"

Jeremy moved one step closer. "Would you mind if I asked you a few questions?"

The shotgun quivered in his braced arm, prodding more answers. "Did Bill tell you? Or Kenny? Who told you where I was? I'm not fallin' for any more tricks."

"No one. I found you on my own."

"That's not likely." The man's aim steadied. "What do you want from me?"

Jeremy spoke fast, "Really, I'm just a reporter trying to help the others, or their families. . . ."

"What people? What families? Who you talkin' about?"

"People who got sick." Jeremy decided to risk everything, just for a few clues, anything that made sense of the unraveling story.

The shotgun lowered a bit more. The man opened the door and gestured that he could enter. Their eyes fixed on each other for a few moments.

Jeremy took short steps toward the entry, unsure if it was a gracious offer or a well-laid trap. The one thing he did know about Charlie Grant—he was a very smart man, smart enough that people wanted him silent. Jeremy crossed the threshold with caution, looking for anything that might suggest this guy was not a maniac or a cold-blooded killer.

The small cottage-style room was filled with mechanical tools: a few pipes cut in half, discarded wrenches with too much rust to allow their usage, several vats of liquid with crusts of sediment around the rim.

"Looks like the scientist is still at work," Jeremy pretended the sight didn't disturb him.

"People call me Chuck," he said with an upward tilt of his head. He still held onto the gun with both hands.

"Amazing place you got here." Jeremy tried to break the tension. "It's nice to be away from the city for a change."

"Save the small talk . . . just sit down," Chuck launched back. "I'm gonna talk to you real quick and then you get on your way."

Shifting side to side in a stiff-backed wooden chair, Jeremy tried to remain quiet. It creaked with every move. He had prepared a mental list of questions, of course, but wasn't sure how to approach the first one.

Chuck sat back in a cushioned armchair. Jeremy wondered if this meant he was relaxing; the shotgun didn't suggest he was.

His voice remained husky and gravelly, like the words were working pretty hard to get out. "Yah know, they let me go just a few weeks before my pension would have kicked in. Damn greedy sons of bitches, holding out like it was ransom money or somethin'."

Jeremy was confused by the comment but didn't dare interrupt him.

"I worked there for twenty-nine years and ten months, then boom." Chuck slapped his gun against the chair leg.

Jeremy jumped back.

"I worked primarily as a wrench man. I was qualified to do much more, if they paid me. But you see, that's not quite how it works, not by a long shot. We had to wait 'til someone rolled over to assume any admin positions, so we just did the low-level job of changing out pipes and cleaning the lead lines. It seemed like somebody didn't want us knowin' what was going on, so we stayed down there with the pipes, nice and quiet. Who else is gonna do it?" Chuck tapped his heel in a repetitive pattern, which in turn shook the cheap windowpanes. The tip of his gun banged along, out of rhythm.

Jeremy listened intently, then interrupted the chair rocking, toe tapping, gun banging and jittery windowpanes. "Do you have any family?"

Chuck shook his head. "Not for me. Too dangerous, too much trouble." Then he was up and pacing, annoyed by the change in topic. "You don't understand, do you? I never intended to make trouble. I just wanted them to know. I just thought maybe they missed something." His hand went up in the air, swatting at nothing.

Jeremy sat up straight, anticipating his next words. Chuck cleared his throat with a series of harsh coughs. The deep hack finally halted, leaving the man hunched over in pain. It seemed like something was stuck in his throat that wouldn't come loose, like the truth trying to escape.

"Are you okay, do you need some water? I can wait, I'm not in a hurry."

Chuck went on as if in a trance. "Their egos are just too big to accept that someone down in the basement would know somethin' about anything." Chuck sat down and went back to tapping his heel.

"What was going on? What did you see?" Jeremy asked, softly. His heel stopped clicking. The windows stopped shaking.

Chuck took a deep breath, then exhaled with a slight cough, straining against the pressure on his lungs. "You ain't stupid. You just don't know. There's not much time left for me. I'm gonna tell yah cuz of that. Not because I know you, or like you, or know your goddamn paper. I don't care. I just want one person to know the truth."

Jeremy swallowed in anticipation, being careful not to interrupt the man's train of thought, careful not to put any more words in Chuck's path.

"For starters, the couplers . . . they were put on backwards. So idiotic . . . I just couldn't believe my eyes." Chuck's hand covered his mouth while his head shook back and forth in disgust. "How could anyone make such a stupid mistake?" He stared into midair.

Jeremy remained confused—he knew nothing about how mechanical things worked. "Why did that matter?" he asked, careful not to add on the five other questions that popped into his frantic mind.

Chuck was now up and pacing again. "Do you realize what travels in those tubes connected by the coupler?"

Jeremy shrugged.

"Yes, you guessed it—radioactive water. The fuel starts as uranium, but then after it's irradiated, it turns into plutonium and strontium. Do you know how deadly those are?" The pacing stopped for a moment, but then picked up again. "I told them the minute I saw it. They didn't seem to care. Safety wasn't exactly their strong suit, and inspections were haphazard in the plant. The most active fault line in the country is just across the highway, and even a modest earthquake could easily disable the backup systems. Such idiots. You have no idea."

He sat back down and lowered his head. The muscles in his spine couldn't hold up his head and all his years of silence any longer. The toll was too severe.

"There's more . . . a lot more. Everything wore out faster than Indy car tires . . . leakin' radiation all the while. And you think an oil spill is bad news. Man, you ain't seen nothin'."

The wheezing penetrated the room, or was it sobbing? Jeremy didn't know the facts; he was pretending to be a reporter, and this guy was claiming a serious conspiracy of some sort.

Chuck lowered his voice, "They labeled these as 'incidents,' not accidents, which told you what they were avoiding. They knew there was an issue and reporting it would be too costly."

Jeremy processed all the implications, not just for Reagan, but the entire community of workers, residents, surfers, beachgoers, and sea life within miles of the reactor. How would he tell the story—the magnitude of the fiasco?

"Hasn't the plant already been decommissioned?" Jeremy had been prepped by Jean Michael about this one detail.

Chuck raised his head slowly. The man looked spent. He let out a deep, exhausted breath, then dropped his head again. "Of course it's been shut down, but that's just part of the story."

Jeremy sensed he was witness to a man who was at the end of his rope and the end of his time. He listened for more reveal on the witches' brew so radioactive that everything it touched was affected.

"I'm sick of runnin' scared, so I'll just stay put here. They told me if I just keep my mouth shut, they'd leave me be . . . and maybe, just maybe, they will dole out my pension on a regular basis."

"Is that what you live on?"

"Well, that ain't happened yet. They know it's only a matter of time and it won't matter." Chuck leaned back in his chair, exhausted. "Can you believe it?" He stared at Jeremy with his eyes wide open, begging him to understand before sinking into the folds of the old pillows propping him up. The gun slowly slipped to the floor next to him. "Can you believe it?" Charlie Grant repeated. He reached for his handkerchief, while coughing up a large red clot of blood. He folded it as inconspicuously as he could and hid it in his back pocket.

Jeremy pretended not to notice the morbid sign. Could he believe it? Would anyone believe it?

44

THE pounding in Reagan's head persisted all the way to the top of the steep flight of stairs. There was little light, so her distorted vision added to the blinding pain in her temples. She didn't understand why Lydia had insisted on her meeting with a pharmacist at this hour. He worked out of his home, compounding a variety of medicines to treat cancer patients.

"But why now? Why so late at night?" Reagan asked, suspicious of the neighborhood and the concealment of it all. "Probably no FDA stamp of approval on these meds, which makes them all the more valuable."

"He used to treat the patients who came from the power plant," Lydia explained.

"So why not go to his office? In daylight?" She pressed for a better answer.

Reagan suspected there was more to the story. Lydia's sudden tight lips made her suspicions grow.

As she knocked on the door, Lydia gave out a morsel of information. "He quit his practice a few years ago, sayin' he be needin' an early retirement. We all thought that was odd. He was the head of the pharmaceutical cancer research unit. I hear he be makin' this drug;

everybody be clamorin' for it. Oh, they be knockin' down his door to know more . . . lot of secrets 'round him. Then, suddenly, out of nowhere, poof, he's gone. Stranges' thing I ever did see. It's like he's a magician or somethin'."

The latches on the door slowly unhinged, one at a time, suggesting tight security. A slight middle-aged man opened the door and gestured to them to enter. He looked wary of his surroundings. He spoke in a whisper and looked over their shoulders. His left eye twitched excessively.

"Paul, this is Reagan, the lady from them islands."

The man barely looked at her. He adjusted the thick-rimmed glasses on his nose and held out a bag of white and yellow pills in a plastic baggie labeled with a black marker. Nothing official referencing the physician who ordered the meds. No one's name or instructions on how to administer them. Just a bag of pills and the word *sulfur* written in black Sharpie.

"What's the purpose of these?" Reagan asked, careful not to disclose her medical identity.

"It counteracts the radionucleotide, combats further consumption of the plutonium, and rinses the toxins," he recited in a low, quivering voice.

Reagan sensed his response was too calculated, too rehearsed. "What about conflict with my iron levels?" she countered.

"Are you a doctor?" His eyes met hers, staring through the magnified lens of his glasses.

"I . . . um . . . studied chemistry." Reagan was flustered, remembering what Lydia had told her—she was not to disclose she was a doctor. It would jeopardize everything.

Confusion erupted and Paul pushed them toward the door. "You know the deal, Lydia. You need to leave."

"Paul, you know I'd never bring nobody by that be a problem. She's my friend and she needs your help. That's all."

The women were halfway out the door when Reagan turned to Lydia. "He knows about what happened. What aren't you telling me?"

The door shut abruptly behind them, followed by the successive click of three latches securing the hidden truth.

By the time Lydia and Reagan returned to Jeremy's home, Reagan's pain level had escalated. "Lydia, I need some meds . . . quick. My joints are screaming at me. Hurry, please. Damn this cortisol. My neck and shoulders are on fire. Grab my arm. I can't quite—" Reagan nearly rolled out of the car before Lydia could get hold of her body, now in tremors.

Jeremy raced out of the front door and was at Reagan's side. "What happened?"

Reagan grabbed him and buried her face in his chest. She wouldn't let him see the fear in her face—the catastrophic series of events leading to this moment. The Hansen's was becoming the least of her concerns. The pain was ratcheting up, yet when she looked into his eyes and saw his fear, she calmed down. "I just need my pain meds. Can you get them for me?" She needed to distract him, not let him inquire about their meeting with the "pharmacist." Reagan had no idea what had happened at the power plant but suspected that Paul had vital information. Someone had gotten to him.

Jeremy brought the meds and a glass of water to Reagan as she entered the front door. "The chef has made a beautiful meal." He pointed toward the dining room table. "What's on the menu, Marcus?"

A voice from the kitchen answered, "Filet mignon with béarnaise sauce and tarragon." The chef came out of the kitchen, facing them as he continued, "Overstuffed portobello mushrooms with dijon and honey glaze, homemade herbal bread with seasoned butters, and of course, dulce de leche ice cream for dessert." Wafts of a variety of sweet and savory scents filled the room.

Reagan looked at it all and reached for Jeremy's arm. "I need to lie down."

"I can make you some butternut squash soup, or how about some ginger tea?" The chef held up two tea bags.

Reagan's face had blanched deathly white; she shook her head apologetically. "I just can't . . . my stomach and my head. . . . Thank you, I appreciate every—" She felt more nauseous by the moment.

"It's them new meds," Lydia conceded. "They tough on yah."

Reagan climbed into bed and collapsed onto the pillow. She needed to rest . . . close her eyes . . . make the pain go away. Jeremy got into bed; she rolled into his chest and tried to stay settled. At first his soft arms and protective embrace provided a gentle comfort, but the throbbing throughout her body made it impossible to sleep.

When Jeremy finally started to twitch, Reagan let out a heavy sigh. She was tormented by the questions that ran through her mind. *How can I be dying? Is this what Andy went through? It's been five years. How'd I make it? He's gone.* Her anxiety level rose with each passing minute, deep into the abyssal night. There was a void in the pit of her stomach. She needed to get back home, back to her island, back to her family.

How can I tell him? How can I convince him? Reagan missed Maura and the kids, Roger, her ocean, and her dolphins. Everything she had worked hard to nurture and protect was now missing from her life. She might die in L.A. so far from home. The thoughts were endless until she finally drifted to sleep.

The turbulence of the ocean thrashed her back and forth. Reagan clung to her surfboard looking for the dolphins. She was stuck in the eye of a major hurricane, not able to get to land. Tossed above the surface and then forced back down toward the ocean floor, there was no one around, no one to help, not even her ocean friends. The blue water turned gray and then black, taking away her sight. She clung to the surfboard even harder, but her fingers were not there to secure her grip. Her hands were gnarled stubs, and they slowly slipped off the board as she struggled to hold on for dear life. Her screaming was soundless at first. Then with a desperate plea for deliverance, her voice shattered the silence.

"Reagan, you're okay. I'm here. You're okay, my love." Jeremy gently shook her awake. He took off his shirt, using it to dry her soaking wet body.

She grabbed for what she hoped was real—being alive. There was no hurricane, her hands were not gnarled; she was holding onto Jeremy with all her might.

"I need to go back." Reagan panted. "The dream . . . the dream. Please." She gripped Jeremy's upper arm. "I need to get home to Fiji."

Reagan could see it all with clarity—how the end would be if she stayed. The endless tests, the storm of high-tech machines coming at her from all directions, then heavy meds, pills to counteract the heavy meds, an array of assailants to kill her slowly. It was a vicious cycle that would weaken her immune system until it couldn't fight anymore. Surrender was inevitable; the surfboard slipped out of her grasp. There was no more time to explain it all to Jeremy. She had to leave.

"Let's try a few more doctors' visits. They'll help you. They are the best money can buy, Reagan, please try . . . maybe stay here a few more weeks to—" Jeremy's words splintered apart, useless.

Reagan was out of bed, looking frantically for her clothes and bag. "No, I won't wait weeks or even days. I must leave now." She was unsteady on her feet and sweating profusely. "Where is my bag? Where is my passport?" She paced the room in search of whatever could help her get home. "Where is my—" The last thing she felt was her head hitting the floor.

45

*R*EAGAN slowly opened her eyes and looked around Jeremy's room. "Did I faint?"

Jeremy nodded while propping her body more upright to help her breathe. Reagan's elbows collapsed as she tried to sit. Only moments ago, she was frantic to find her passport and belongings to get home to Fiji. Now she was on the floor, unable to hold herself up, with pain streaking down her arms to the very ends of her fingertips.

"I don't know what's happened to my energy. It's completely gone, and the pain . . . I just don't understand it. Why is this so debilitating?" She looked to Jeremy for an answer. "Maybe I underestimated the pain from Hansen's. Or do you think this is the radiation poisoning?" She rambled on with her questions.

Jeremy lifted her off the hardwood floor. "Maybe it's the stress Dr. Yiung was talking about. Is that even possible?"

Reagan's fingers strained to hold onto his neck; the little strength she had was fast diminishing.

Jeremy lowered her onto the bed. "How can I help? What do you want me to do?"

"I just need to go home. I will not die here."

Jeremy looked away momentarily before bringing his gaze back to her. "Of course you won't die here . . . or anywhere. I should have never left you back in Fiji. This is all my fault." He placed his hand over her wrist.

"Ouch . . . careful, that hurts so much. I'm sorry, I know you mean well, but everything just hurts . . . everything." Reagan's hand recoiled from his touch, and it fell to her chest. "I miss my family—Maura and the kids, the ocean, my sea friends, the waves. . . ." Tears flowed as she buried her head into the pillow.

"Okay." Jeremy stroked her forehead. "I will book the flight." He said the words knowing it could be a fatal mistake leaving modern medicine and all his contacts that allowed them access to the very best science the U.S. had to offer. He dreaded the thought of her being helpless at the resort in Fiji, with only her bag of medicines.

"Now rest. We'll fly out tomorrow." He slid next to her in bed, placing his arm around the back of her neck. The tension in Reagan's spine muscles released, followed by a steady inhale, exhale, and a series of twitches in her body. He kissed her cheek and held her head against his chest. She continued to fall deeper asleep, her body finally surrendering into his arms.

LAX was filled with its usual mayhem. Reagan glanced out the window periodically watching for their airline's sign, then dropped her head back onto Jeremy's shoulder. She couldn't help but hear Lydia's comments firing every few minutes.

"There you go, just cut us off. Jackass!" she yelled out the window. "Of all the idiotic. . . ." Lydia had joined them in transit to the airport, but that's as far as she would go.

Reagan agreed she would be more helpful staying in L.A. to coordinate her metal counts and treatment regimes. "Lydia, calm down. It'll all be okay."

"You sure you don't want to join us?" Jeremy grinned. "There's a world of chaos here. You could leave it all behind."

Lydia had never left the United States, and although she had a new kinship with Reagan, she wasn't ready for the journey abroad, even though Jeremy had offered her a small fortune to come along and help out medically. Reagan looked forward to Lydia meeting Maura someday, knowing they would connect on a certain level. They were two human beings, thousands of miles apart, who somehow shared the same innate nurturing and care for those suffering, as they had suffered. But it would have to wait for another time.

Jeremy helped Reagan out of the car, offering a wheelchair that she declined. "Then wait here while I check us in," he ordered.

Jeremy turned to Lydia without Reagan noticing and handed her a piece of paper. "Any chance you can get a copy of Charlie Grant's medical records? I think he is somehow connected to all this."

Lydia tucked the paper into her jacket pocket while keeping a protective eye on Reagan. "Sure, but only if you take good care of her." She hugged Jeremy and he darted into the terminal. She turned back to the trunk of the car and hauled out Reagan's backpack.

A white van pulled up next to their car, one of the men inside asking, "Are you Reagan Caldwell?" Lydia quickly caught the question, glancing up to notice the letters on the side of the van: *CDC Protective Services.*

She leapt in front of the van, sparing Reagan the interrogation by the investigators. "Who wants to know?" Lydia's chest heaved in defiance, blocking Reagan from their advances.

"In the car, now!" Lydia ordered Reagan.

With only a quick glance at Jeremy's driver, Reagan mustered the strength to get into the car and George pulled away, leaving Jeremy in the terminal and Lydia on the curb with the CDC bounty hunters. The men hustled into their van and attempted to follow the car carrying Reagan.

Lydia let out a bloodcurdling scream. "Help, they stole my purse! Help, police!" Pandemonium erupted; cars zigzagged in and out of lanes to cut off the presumed criminals. Lydia continued her screams, with a slight tear of laughter—mingled with loss. The CDC van was caged in as the car carrying Reagan slipped out of sight.

46

JEREMY heard sirens and ran out of the terminal toward Lydia. "What the hell . . . what happened?"

"Oh, sweet Jesus, they be after her . . . took off in that same white van. She's in the car with George, but they onto her. You gotta get her outta here. She's sick, Jeremy; she need to be on 'dat plane."

Jeremy looked at Lydia. "I've got an idea. Can you call a cab? Here's some money. I appreciate everything you've done for us."

Lydia motioned to him, "Shoo now. I be jus' fine. Go to her."

Jeremy was frantic but he had no choice. While he had only known Mike Peters a few weeks, he felt an immediate sense of trust and acceptance of the homeless veteran he had rescued. Jeremy understood his story—the trauma, which is why Mike was his only hope. He was a pilot used to dangerous situations and had returned to flying while Jeremy was gone.

The phone rang six times before Mike answered.

"Yes, they are hunting her down," Jeremy explained. "The driver will meet you there. . . . No, don't bring any guns." The trust was alive, but Mike's judgment was to be questioned. He hadn't recuperated from the trenches and still had a great deal of post-traumatic stress that blurred his decisions. Yet he was Jeremy's only option.

"Thanks, bud," Jeremy finished. "I owe yah."

The homeless guys' military past had created deep wounds. Mike seemed near dead when Jeremy had met him—dirty and shoeless. He, himself, was desperate for a friend. *How strange, I'm an actor; he's a soldier and here we are . . . desperados.*

Jeremy proceeded to the private terminal. He flashed his smile and recognizable face to all security personnel. "Thanks, guys, gotta run . . . my plane's about to leave. Film crew and directors are all waiting for me. Damn traffic. I appreciate you letting me take the shortcut through the pilots lounge." He looked over his shoulder for the men Lydia had warned him about. The distance between Reagan and him seemed to be widening, but he would find his way to her soon enough. *Mike, I need you, bud. Stay cool . . . stick to the plan.*

AS Reagan exited one car, she attempted to smile at Mike. Her right leg trembled as he supported her elbow. "Thanks, Mike. Glad to finally meet you. Jeremy's talked about you." She hesitated, "I didn't think we'd be meeting under these circumstances."

Mike smiled. "Yep, I sure didn't expect this assignment. Jeremy was a mess without you, yah know. That's how we met. He was like . . . staring out at the ocean. Then he asked me to dinner, which was . . . well, a surprise. Next thing I know, I'm hangin in the hills of Malibu, in a mansion and he's chasing after you. Pretty amazing really."

He did not appear to be the scruffy homeless man that Jeremy had initially described. Reagan had wondered why the two men had met under such strange circumstances. Now, she understood. Mike stood strong and upright, even though he was obviously embattled from within, and had been attacked by the "enemy." His shoulders were broad and he looked protective. There was something about his eyes, much different from the softness of Jeremy's that looked directly into her. It felt awkward at first, but she trusted him and felt safe.

She hugged him, feeling his muscular arms squeeze her in return, giving her a brief renewal of strength. "Where are we going?"

"I hear you want to go home, right?" Mike opened the passenger door.

"Yes." Her voice trembled with emotion, "but—" She collapsed into the front seat.

"Gotta roll." He fastened her seat belt.

Mike sped along side streets, appearing to know his way. He turned down an empty road toward a fence marked: *Restricted Area. No Entry*. He drove by the sign without hesitation. The road beyond the fence looked endless with all its harrowing turns. No sight of anyone following them so he eased off the accelerator, somewhat more relaxed after passing the sign. He re-engaged in the conversation. "How did you two meet?"

Reagan smiled, sensing his awkwardness at their just having met and being thrown together in this reckless plight to get away. "In Fiji, while he was filming." She looked out the window. She didn't have the strength to describe it all. Her feelings ran strong yet her state was fragile, immobilizing her words. The memory of how she met Jeremy was blurred, but her emotions were clear—she loved him.

"Are you an actress?"

Reagan laughed a hearty chuckle, even though her weakness shouldn't have allowed for the expenditure of energy. "No, recovering physician."

"Jeremy didn't mention you were a doc. What do you mean, recovering?"

Reagan smiled thinking of what she was actually recovering from— losing her belief in mainstream medicine, but that would have been a crazy thing to say.

Mike glanced at her. "You don't look like an addict."

"No, not that kind of recovery. I've been finding my way back to medicine by actually helping people." She explained the inexplicable.

"But you are helping people, right? What could be wrong with that?"

Reagan looked at Mike. She could hardly find the words to summarize the struggle. It was too hard to retrace her steps back to her basic hard-won beliefs—her Hippocratic Oath. "I was just trying to help . . . do the right thing for the patient." She cleared her voice. "I saw this huge labyrinth. Do you know what I mean?"

Mike shrugged and nodded. "Maybe so, maybe not."

"It seemed like it was about . . . the drugs and the money, not about the patients. It's like medicine was all of a sudden a commodity." Her eyes fluttered. "I'm so tired . . . I just wanted to help." She leaned into the headrest. Moments of silence passed before she asked, "Weren't you trying to help people, too, in Iraq or Afghanistan?"

Keeping his eyes on the road, Mike shrugged, repeating, "Maybe so, maybe not."

The restricted entry led down a private road to an open dirt runway. Mike pulled over and helped Reagan out of the car and into the small Cessna 152.

"Sorry, didn't have much notice to prep this flight." He dusted off the seat, shifting a mess of paperwork so she could sit. "It's a short hop. Try to get comfortable . . . just rest."

She was about to question where they were going and where Jeremy was, but exhaustion took over.

"Close your eyes and relax. Jeremy will meet us soon." He turned to the cockpit, adjusting the instruments on the panel. He flicked switches back and forth and made checkmarks on a clipboard with an intense focus.

Reagan took a deep breath and felt the burden of the chase affecting her ability to stay awake. As she fought to keep her eyes open, she half-glanced at Mike's forearm, noticing a faded tattoo. The image was an Air Force eagle with a dagger in its mouth, and the words: *Death Before Dishonor*. Below it . . . a smaller, more faded image. It was the number 43.

Her stare must have been obvious, as Mike held her glance. "That is the number of brothers who fell in my arms. Forty-three men took their last breaths on my watch." He bowed his head and remained silent.

Reagan placed her hand over his arm, slightly touching the number with her index finger, then tracing the numbers gently. She suddenly felt a deep connection with Mike, sharing their experience of loss. It had cut deeply into both of them.

"You know, you were meant to be there, holding them. It was so important. The last thing they saw was the love and comfort in your eyes." Reagan's hand slipped off his arm. Her head rolled to the side.

He revved the engines and slowly pressed the throttle forward.

She welcomed the darkness.

47

*T*HE small Cessna shook more than a commercial flight, yet the turbulence acted like a rocking chair; the engine's constant buzz was monotonous and reassuring. But as the plane changed direction and started its descent, Reagan's breathing became labored and she woke with a dry throat while aspirating a forceful choking cough.

"Where are we?" Reagan was barely awake. Her pain and weakness continued to affect her memory. She tried to ignore the pain, but the inability to reorient herself was terrifying. The full effects of the stress-induced hormone were now showing. "He was right."

"Who?" Mike asked.

"Dr. Yiung was right . . . stress of it all . . . just so weak, I can barely lift a. . . . Damn cortisol."

Reagan glanced out the small oblong window, searching. Nothing . . . familiar. "Where is the ocean?" The chronic fatigue was wearing on her. She had a strange sensation of being out of her body, feeling like a bird gliding back to its destination.

Mike laid his hand on her arm. "You are safe, my friend, no one can hurt you now." That wasn't the first time he had said those words while flying on a rescue mission. He kept his hand on hers. Mike had flown on many military rescues, usually in combat areas, with air strikes blowing up his visual proximity. This was different. At least his current path was without air pursuit. His attention was still as sharp as in previous rescues, but this time his precious cargo needed his subtle touch. Unbeknownst to him, he was able to provide it. His own hand softened as Reagan's breathing became more settled.

The landing was soft and cautious. Reagan slowly lifted her head and caught the familiar glance and warm smile of Jeremy on the ground. His chartered plane had arrived at the private airstrip ten minutes earlier than the Cessna. Jeremy was at the foot of the gangway as the door opened.

"NO time to waste, my love. Our next flight is ready for us." He pointed to the military cargo plane with engines running. Mike had arranged for a special ops flight to carry them to Fiji. Jeremy had no idea how he had finagled such a prestigious and secretive flight; he could only assume the man had called in a big favor. That story would have to wait as Jeremy noticed the exhaustion on Reagan's face when she smiled. Mike carried her down the steps carefully, wearing a concerned look.

"She needs a gentle touch, yah know." Mike adjusted Reagan's small backpack in her lap as he handed her to Jeremy.

"Thanks bud, I got 'er." Jeremy was a bit clumsy carrying her at first, but Reagan snuggled into his neck and wrapped her arms around his neck.

"She's all yours. You're right about how special she is," Mike finished with a peculiar glint in his eyes.

The bulbous fixed-wing aircraft was filled with crates of military supplies. The plane was bound for Guam with one unscheduled stop. The cargo area allowed for passenger jump seats along the side. Jeremy and Reagan were the only passengers.

The pilot tipped his hat, welcoming the couple aboard. "Not much cabin service, but there's plenty of snacks and water in the forward hatch." He pointed to an overhead cabinet. "Wear these Bombers and earplugs, too." The pilot handed them two oversized thick jackets and a small plastic case. The engines roared on takeoff, and within minutes the wheels were retracted into the belly of the plane.

Reagan fell fast asleep, her body surrendered to the fight and flight of the day. Jeremy placed his jacket over the one she was already wearing. Her breathing sounded less congested, the creases along her brow softened, and her lips eased into a childlike sweetness—an innocence of sorts. She looked beautiful, even as she lay stricken with an unimaginable toxin at war with the ancient disease.

Jeremy was enamored by her bravery. His own fear of her uncertain future was washed away as she slept in his arms. Only recently had he discovered his ability to comfort and a reason to be selfless. Reagan had been the strong one, the teacher, the adventurer. The juxtaposition of her weakened state compared to when he met her was astounding. Jeremy, all of a sudden felt strong, just as Reagan's strength diminished.

All these thoughts collided as Reagan's body pressed against his chest. She took a deep breath and adjusted her position. He pulled her closer, hoping to keep her still for a few more moments. He relished this feeling in his heart—the feeling of real love, a genuine caring for this person who now depended on him.

48

*T*HE gentle popping in Reagan's inner ears slowly brought her to consciousness. She was disoriented for several seconds yet became aware of Jeremy's warm skin and scent. She smiled and sank into his chest. She hadn't felt her usual agitation of encroaching pain upon awakening. This time was different. She kept her eyes closed hoping to savor the moment a bit longer. She felt a lightness, an inexplicable withdrawal from the illnesses that clawed at her system. The light nudge of Jeremy's shoulder helped her open her eyes. Sitting upright, Reagan saw what she had been longing for. Like some beautiful dream, there it was—the final steep turn brought the landing strip in view. A strange energy pulsed through her—home, finally home.

MAURA and Roger had been waiting at the Nadi airport for hours. The last message they had received was from Jeremy saying they had been sidetracked but were finally on their way. He mentioned something about not being on a commercial flight, so the arrival time was vague. What started out as small talk between Roger and Maura eventually led in several directions—children, family, staff, and all the associated details of their narrow island life.

"How have you managed all these years? I mean no disrespect, but it is painful, isn't it? I simply couldn't imagine." Roger leaned forward in the airport chair with his elbows propped on top of his thighs. His glance was on his own hands and fingers. "You seem so accepting . . . so happy."

Maura shrugged, further stashing her gnarled hands into the deep pockets of her handmade smock. "It's not that hard, livin' for your children, your loved ones, it's what you gotta do."

A traveler passed by and stared longer than necessary. Maura looked away, tucking her face farther into her scarf. She had relived the hatred, fear, and uneducated view of Hansen's disease while she was with Reagan in Australia and didn't want to draw unnecessary attention.

"You were married once?" Maura asked.

He avoided looking directly at her. "Yeah, once, long ago."

"Any kids?"

Again, no eye contact. But this time his body language changed. Roger bowed his head and stared at the tiles under his sandals. He cleared his throat. "It was a long time ago." The tone of his voice softened, "She would have been thirty or so by now."

Maura was silent.

"Her name was Laura. Precious little Laura." His eyes filled with tears. "She was only alive a few hours. Her mother blames my smoking as her cause of death. The doctors called it SIDS." Tears slid down Roger's cheeks. His hands trembled. "I haven't told many people about her."

Pulling one hand out of her pocket, Maura placed it on the back of Roger's hand. "I'm so sorry, Roger . . . so sorry." She kept her hand there for several minutes as they sat in silence.

"Reagan!" Maura jumped out of the chair, letting go of Roger's hand.

Reagan and Jeremy walked toward them, but it was not the same

Reagan who Maura and Roger had last seen. Reagan looked aged and withered, an altered version of the person they knew and loved. She was gaunt, staggering as she walked, mostly supported by Jeremy. She had been gone only a few weeks but was already frail, white as a ghost, with dark circles under her eyes. Yet there was her smile, still full of life and reassurance.

Maura shuffled toward Reagan while Roger wiped the remnants of his tears. He drew in a last mournful breath and exhaled.

The group hug lasted a few minutes and was only interrupted by travelers moving around them. Maura held both of Reagan's hands and surveyed her body up and down. Making light of her appearance, Maura broke the silence, "What, no good food over there?"

Their tearful eyes matched in emotion. "Nothing like your cooking."

Roger looked away.

"I'll be okay." Reagan placed her hand on Roger's arm. "Really Rog, it will all be okay."

Reagan knew her friends well. She could read their worried body language and see past their quivering smiles. She closed the circle by linking arms with Roger and Maura. "Can someone please get me to the ocean quickly?"

The bumpy taxi ride came to an end at the water's edge. They transferred to a small inflatable Zodiac and powered out to the mooring where their boat was anchored. The twenty-one-foot whaler was as good as home to Reagan. She missed this little vessel that she had logged so many hours on, making many crossings to the island where the islanders lived and spending so many hours playing with her favorite sea mammals. Reagan's energy awakened. The blue-green ocean and its salty breeze were her body and soul. She sat up straight, somehow stimulating her postural muscles to work—a reason to hold her up. The rock of the boat gently nudged her to sway at just the right time. The splash of saltwater refreshed her senses. She licked her lips, recognizing the familiar taste.

The final turn into the bay at the resort was exhilarating. She felt her return to nature—the ocean, dolphins, waves, and her family. It suddenly occurred to her that there had been no pain since she had arrived in Fiji. She probed her elbow and wrist joints searching for the wince, but no pain there either. She turned her neck from side to side, surely to find the deep ache—no pain. A slight smile crept over her face, acknowledging the decrease in the constant stress she had felt while away.

The words came back—*Home*, then, more audible—*Home*.

Her eyes followed the shift in the wake as the boat throttled back, cautious to protect the shallow reef ahead. A sudden flap and cackle announced the landing of the cormorants as if welcoming Reagan back home. *Plonk, slap*—she heard the impact on the water from the bat rays jumping high out of the ocean only to land with a graceful *swish*. There was a strain in Reagan's cheeks from smiling. She hadn't felt the stretch of her face this way in some time—the effect of pure pleasure. Then, just as she thought she couldn't handle any more gifts, Romeo and Juliet breached out of the water in elation. Reagan smiled, thinking there was still time to recapture her missed moments.

49

*J*EAN MICHAEL continued to scan a script while overhearing some demanding voices outside his office door. He was accustomed to all kinds of intrusions, mostly from amateur screenwriters attempting to get their manuscript into the famous director's hands by sneaking in the back door. But these were loud, overly aggressive male voices— not trying to pitch a script.

"We're here to see Jean Michael Raava," one of the men brusquely announced.

"Whom shall I tell him is here?" There were no appointments on the schedule.

"Agents John Wheeler and Max Smith." There was silence for several seconds. "County Investigative Services." He flashed his badge.

Jean Michael separated the blinds giving him a view of the two men. He motioned to his assistant, declining their entrance. But before his assistant could respond, he changed his mind and walked out of his office. "I'm Jean Michael. How can I help you?" He needed to test the waters and see if this was related to Jeremy's recent trip to the back hills of Orange County.

The agents waiting for Jean Michael were facing the prestigious plaques and awards in the waiting room. "County Investigative

Services" was their cover and few people ever questioned their badges. Their informant had called with a report of a man going to see Charlie Grant, and the license plate was associated with the owner of the vehicle, Jean Michael Raava. Now as the agents looked at their suspect's name on the wall, there would be questions of why a filmmaker was poking around.

Jean Michael extended his hand in a greeting. The heftier of the two men accepted the handshake. The other kept both hands on his notepad, poised to start scribbling.

The hefty man spoke first. "We need to meet with you in private."

Jean Michael leaned in and read the nametag. "What's County Investigative Services?" He opened the door for the men and motioned for them to enter his office. Hairs raised on the back of Jean Michael's neck. The mystery of the men with badges intrigued and excited him.

"Please have a seat." Jean Michael gestured.

One man sat while the other remained standing, scribbling away before anything was said.

"We are investigating an incident involving a vehicle. We have traced the vehicle and license plate back to you."

Jean Michael was unfazed. "So what exactly did my vehicle do that you are so worried about? Seems like I'd know if I was in an accident."

The stares across his desk were penetrating.

"At least give me a clue what you're talking about, without all the cloak and dagger stuff. Otherwise, gentlemen, I need to get back to work."

"Sir, we can't discuss specifics . . . we simply need to know who you talked to."

"Well, you'll need to discuss specifics or I can't help you. I talk to people all day long. Most of which . . . well, a bunch of nonsense."

"Let's cut the crap." The agent standing closest to Jean Michael puffed up his chest. "We know it's your piece-of-crap 4Runner and we know you've talked to Charles Grant. We've been tailin' you. Now tell us why."

"Why would you be tailing me? I don't have a clue what you're talking about. I sold that old truck about a year ago after I trashed it in Mexico on a film shoot. It got all beat to hell. You are chasing the wrong guy. You're wasting your time. I really do have to wrap up here. I wish I could help you, but I can't." Jean Michael realized he had meandered into the realm of bravado, which he really didn't possess. Words came fast and furious; his heart rate had increased exponentially. Moisture collected above his brow. His acting skills couldn't hold up much longer under close scrutiny.

The agent who was seated looked up with a cocky grin. "You know, we can make life miserable for you."

"Come on guys, let's give it a rest. If you are linking me to a car I sold last year, how 'bout you go find that guy and chit-chat about your Charlie character to him. I can call security and help you find your way out."

50

*L*ONG shadows of light cast from the hallway extending into Jean Michael's office. Hours had passed since the characters with badges had left. He had sent his secretary home at seven p.m. Only the security guard was left on the property.

There was a small lead with Charlie Grant, but there had to be more. Jean Michael rubbed his strained eyes with the palm of his hand. The abrupt vibration of his cell phone startled him. "Yes, Jean Michael here."

"Umm," the caller went silent.

"Who's this?"

"My name . . . my name is Lydia . . . and I'm the . . . umm . . . nurse that. . . ."

"Oh yes, Lydia?" Jean Michael softened. "Jeremy mentioned you might call. Do you have any news?"

"Well, yah, maybe. Jeremy was vague as a night crawler. Who exactly am I talkin' to?"

Jean Michael cleared his voice. "Of course, I work with Jeremy, and I know about Reagan. Would you rather meet in person?" There was a delay and a crackle to his phone, ". . . if that's okay with you."

"Such a . . . absolute . . . yah get my drift?" Lydia's words came and went.

"Sorry, I didn't get all that. Bad reception here. Did you get something on Charlie Grant?" He jumped out of his chair and moved to the hallway for better connection. "You there?"

"Like I jus' said, somethin' be way wrong here. Paperwork and clues scattered all over this joint. Nothin' suppose to make sense. But I see it now; I see the trick. They be stashin' bits an' pieces in different locked cabinets."

"What kinda clues?" Jean Michael clenched the phone.

"Well, for one, there's info here and info there in different files. It should all be in a patient's chart. But there be holes all over—yah know, a lot missin'. Had to stumble onto these here mixed-up files. Bits of it won't be doin' anyone any good, but when yah put it together, well, holy Jesus. All of it in special archives. Luckily—"

Static on his phone cut her off. "Wait, say that again. Luckily what? Lydia?"

"I said, lucky no clearance was needed. Open doors for me here in the concrete basement. They think I know nothin' so it's a slice a pie."

Jean Michael felt a twinge of fear and excitement. She sounded sharp with a quick wit, which kept him intrigued.

"I 'specially like the files labeled, *Investigative Services; Confidential* . . . in red."

"But how'd you get access? Aren't those locked up?"

"Oh honey, let's jus' say they be unlocked now, okay."

Jean Michael let out a hearty laugh, "I'm looking forward to meeting you, Lydia. You're my kinda gal."

"This Charlie guy, he be real sick, right?" Lydia asked in a solemn tone. "Cuz there's a few different pictures bein' painted here. The handwritin' is definitely a doc's, so hard to be certain, but what I can make out says excessive days off, left for personal reasons, intolerant behavior and this here says. . . ." she mumbled something.

"I didn't get that." Jean Michael paced in his office.

"Says . . . medical hazard and inability to comply."

"Who Charlie? He's the whistleblower, so I get it." Jean Michael rubbed his eyebrows. "And Lydia, the guy really is sick. Jeremy met him."

"Yeah, him and many more jus' like 'im. They all have da same problems—GI issues, headaches, nausea, bloody sputum. But that could be with anyone admitted here. So then there's the altered bone marrow and white blood count . . . that be different. And to top it off—like it needed more, they all got real high metal counts. Like off the chart."

There was a moment of silence. Jean Michael asked, "You still there? Lydia?"

"Oh yeah, I be here, but I jus' saw somethin' else, again an' again. Oh, sweet Jesus . . . what is this?" she gasped.

"What, Lydia, what is it?"

"For the love of. . . ."

Jean Michael perched at the edge of the railing in the dark hallway. "Please, Lydia, what is it?" He heard her heavy breathing on the other end of the line.

"Those bastards . . . it's the same damn doc on all these cases."

There was silence from both of them, a sudden realization of the harsh reality of the cover-up. Thoughts of Charlie Grant entered Jean Michael's mind. He walked back into his office with the phone still at his ear.

There it was—the unassailable facts all lined up. Adrenalin pumped into his system, a feeling he hadn't had in some time. A powerful story—an exposé that could bring government and utilities companies to their knees. The pieces were slowly falling into place—innocent people had been subjected to poisons over the course of years, a total cover-up, files buried in the basement of a well-known medical institution, with only a few people alive to tell the truth. Lydia had uncovered exactly what he needed.

Jean Michael sat down in his leather chair and let the view unfold. "Lydia, you've really taken a risk. I can't tell you how grateful. . . ."

"It would be a bigger risk," she interrupted. ". . . sayin' nothin'. We'll talk more soon."

51

*O*NCE home, Reagan's mind and body relaxed and she slept long hours. Waking periodically to see Jeremy next to her was comforting. Her eyes fluttered open briefly and she felt his body next to hers, or in the distance, she saw the outline of his body swinging in the hammock on her lanai. She would smile then sigh, before falling back into her dream state. But the days and nights blended. She was unaware of what day it was, or any memories of who had visited, or what words had been spoken. Food was offered to her, but her appetite was gone. There were moments Reagan realized she was fading—she was losing the battle within, yet didn't have the energy to talk about it.

One morning, she limped to the lanai to watch the fruit bats diving and foraging for food. Reagan loved their dance, their union with nature. She attempted to pick a guava, but exhaustion and weakness took hold and she collapsed on the wicker chaise. The hammock looked so inviting but it was several feet away. How would she get in and out of it? Like the perfect contours of a seashell worn down by the crushing shore-break, her senses were lackluster and dull. Reagan closed her eyes, pulling in the sweet memory of plumeria; she worked hard at seeing it, smelling it, trying to touch it, so close to it. . . .

"Good morning, my love," Jeremy interrupted the moment.

She accepted the taste of his lips. Touching the stubble on his face, she felt the stirring of energy. What had seemingly disappeared over the last few weeks was awoken as she kissed him again. The warmth of his lips and small chemistry change was all she needed. Reagan flashed back to the memory of their first few meetings and how inept he was—fast forward to this strong man who now cared for her.

"I've brought you some tasty treats." Jeremy returned the gentle kiss.

"How about some bananas?" Roger walked toward them, holding up a stalk of four ripe yellow bananas and a handful of guava from the trees that surrounded the modest shelter.

"Here, let's get this pillow behind you where it will do some good." Jeremy gently slid a pillow behind the small of Reagan's back.

Handing her a freshly picked bunch of miniature bananas, Roger chimed in, "I see he's spoiling you again. Please eat these, my dear. You need your strength, 'eh. You want to get to your boat, don't you?"

Reagan managed a shallow smile and pulled at a single banana connected to the stalk, but her hand slipped away. She looked at Jeremy defeated, "Would you mind . . . I'm a bit tired."

Jeremy pulled the banana from the stalk—pretending it was difficult, and half-peeled it before handing it to Reagan.

She took a bite to ease their concern. The texture of the fruit sent a curl of tension to the back of her throat, barely allowing the small bite to be swallowed. She breathed through her nose and closed her eyes, insisting it stay down. She could win this small battle, if only for them. "I will finish this later." She closed the peel. The nausea had not subsided and her appetite was completely gone. Jeremy was at her side as she pressed farther into the curve of the chaise like a small, vulnerable child. She was used to the fetal posture, hiding her weakness and inability to hold herself upright. Reagan pulled her knees high into her chest. Her frail shoulder could barely hold her sleeve in place. What used to be strong sinewy muscles were now bones holding up weakened flesh.

"I need to go to the island today." Reagan lifted her head a few inches off the pillow. "I must see the children and Phaeole." Her head fell back, her drowsiness again relieving Jeremy and Roger of denying the daily request. She was asleep in moments.

Weeks had passed, and although Reagan was out of pain she was too weak to leave the bure and too despondent to do anything. Maura visited several days a week, coaxing nutrients, trying different herbs, fruits and aromas; strategies different from Jeremy and Roger, but nothing seemed to work.

Reagan tried to comply but it took all her energy to say, "I'm just too tired right now. As soon as I wake up, though, I promise."

An hour later, Maura would attempt to feed her and again face rejection.

Reagan's body withered daily—she was under one hundred pounds and losing the desire to live. She survived mainly on intermittent sips of coconut water and pieces of grapes.

Then one morning, when Jeremy had started his ritual of food offers, she opened her eyes with renewed energy. "Okay, I will eat, as long as you make me one promise." She gathered herself in an upright position, preparing to negotiate the deal.

"Anything, anything at all." Jeremy held Reagan's hands in anticipation of her willingness to eat. He kissed them gently before releasing them and foraged around the bure for her favorites: nuts, mangoes, coconut, dried fruits, all that had been stockpiled for weeks anticipating the return of her hunger. Jeremy piled it all in front of her hoping she would pick up some morsel on her own.

"Don't you want to know what the promise is?" She picked the roasted coconut pieces from Jeremy's hand.

"It doesn't matter, I will give you the world, anything you want. There is nothing I won't do for you." He seemed to have broken through some unspoken barrier. If only she would start eating. "Look at these passion fruit, the color and smell. Hmmm. . . ." He dropped them in her lap. "And how about these Ghirardelli chocolates Lydia sent over? She said she only snuck one and the rest are for you. Roger's kept them in hiding, in the fridge."

"Oh dear, I haven't called to thank her . . . for everything, really. She's been so amazing." Reagan sucked in a deep, labored breath. "What would I even say at this point?"

"I'll let her know. Don't worry about it. What do you mean at this point?" Jeremy stood still.

Reagan considered relinquishing her request. She was so grateful at that moment—aware of how much Jeremy loved her. It was like watching a movie and the climactic scene was unfolding. How could she interrupt it? She glanced around the room; it reflected every detail of the life she loved and the life she had lived.

If only she could surf one more time or swim with her dolphins and feel their sleek skin. She could feel them now, dancing in the water. They'd guide her to the surf break. They'd be there for her after her long ride through the close-out.

They will be there. . . .

She closed her eyes. "I want to die. I am ready to die, and I need your help."

52

*J*EREMY froze, stunned by her request. Then he paced, unsure of how to react. "I love you. Do you understand? This isn't a movie or some twisted love story. I can't consider this . . . I won't. It's crazy. You can get better. You only need to eat something . . . that will make you better. You know that and you are refusing for some reason I don't understand."

"I don't expect you to understand. I love you with all my being, but I can't put you through this. I can't put myself through this. It's useless."

Jeremy collapsed in the corner chair and buried his head in his hands. His right hand trembled, and then clamped his fingers shut.

Reagan softened her tone. "I'm a good doctor and I will instruct you." She sat up straight. "The vein is easy to palpate and prepare. When it distends, you simply pierce the needle and—"

"No, you are not listening to me. I love you and I will not do this. You just need to eat all this healthy food and you'll be fine. You told me so, yourself—if we came back here, you'd be okay." His eyes were flooded as he whispered, "What happened to my warrior? My muse, my purpose for living."

"You were my person. . . ." He didn't bother correcting his statement to: You are my person.

"I can't," he choked on his own words. "I won't."

Reagan bit her lower lip, trying to tolerate the escalating pain level. She let him continue.

"You showed me how to be strong and stand up for others. I won't let you take your life. I won't do it." His hands were clenched with tension that surged throughout his whole body. The room was stifling, not even a whisper of a breeze came through.

"But I'm suffering." She kept her voice low and controlled. "I'm going to die and I don't want you to watch me suffer anymore. Which is worse?"

Jeremy's pacing resumed. His repetitive steps and turns were manic. He shook his head back and forth. "I can't. I won't. You can't ask this of me."

Reagan felt dizzy and nauseous. She couldn't come to grips with his rejection of her request. She would never do this to someone pleading for help. But she also realized he wasn't a doctor, and he couldn't comprehend the desperation of suffering—especially hers at that moment.

"Please just consider it and we can talk more about it later," she knew it was useless. "I can ask Maura to—"

His stark glare halted her sentence. "So . . . if not me, you'll get someone else to do it. This doesn't make sense. None of it. . . ." Jeremy stopped his restless pacing and looked at her. His energy drained out of him all at once. His cheeks were drawn and receded. There was nothing for him to grab onto. Months ago, this beautiful woman had entered his life, changed his life irrevocably, and now she lay on her deathbed begging to end it all. It was inconceivable. Dropping his head, he attempted to speak. "I thought you were the one . . . the one person I would be with for the rest of my life. I thought you would be my wife, my partner. I thought you loved me."

The silence was deafening. Reagan could not find the words to defend her emotions. She had no strength to further explain her suffering, progression of disease, and loss of purpose. She thought he loved her to death. Her glance shifted to the floor and remained there until the bamboo door closed behind him, leaving her alone. She closed her eyes over it all . . . so tired, so very tired.

53

*J*EREMY'S plane landed hard on the runway at LAX. He lurched forward in his seat as the tires grabbed the tarmac, jolting him into reality. At first he wasn't sure where he was, or more importantly, where Reagan was. He rubbed his blurry eyes, trying to shake off the lethargy that ran through his achy body.

What happened?

The pilot's voice of welcome seemed more like a message of doom. How could he have left Reagan for the second time?

His thoughts doubled back on him, surrounding him. *Why? My beautiful Reagan, swimming with her dolphins, the taste of salt on her skin. What if . . .?*

He had sworn his commitment to her, his lost love, found and lost again.

What if I never see her again?

Jeremy wandered out of the terminal numb to everything that surrounded him. He was oblivious to the usual stares from fans who questioned if he was really Jeremy Black, or some scraggly look-alike.

George pulled up next to him and quickly got out of the car. "Sir?"

Jeremy looked up at his right-hand man with bloodshot eyes— the man who always arrived, always protected him. Here he was again, just in time. Jeremy's bag was slung over his shoulder, unduly weighing him down. He was hunched over, no smile, no entourage, no Reagan, only a vacant stare in his eyes.

"Are you okay, sir, can I take your bag?"

"Yeah, I'm okay. Let's go. Let's get out of here."

Like the highway choked with traffic, there was nothing but tension on the ride home. Then there was the windy road up the canyon with nothing but desolation.

As they waited for the gate to open, George asked again, "Sir, are you okay?"

Jeremy finally heard the words, as if flowing toward him from a long, dark tunnel. "Yes, George, by all means, the gate. Yes, proceed. I can't quite . . . I mean . . . I left Reagan in Fiji and I'm a little, you know . . . it's just that . . . well, I'm exhausted. Long flight."

"Yes, sir, I understand." George held the car door open waiting for Jeremy to emerge. When he didn't, George asked insistently, "Sir, do you need an assist?" Looking over at Mike Peters, George nodded for him to help.

Jeremy looked up blankly, "No, I'm just wondering—"

"You remember Mike, he's here. There's lunch inside. Come along, sir."

George and Mike had long conversations after Jeremy had abruptly picked up the homeless man, left him at the house, and then flew off to Australia. It all seemed crazy to George and the house staff at first. They were not about to trust Mike, his wandering around the house looking at everything, touching things that were never touched. Then a pipe burst. Mike was the first one to react, and much to everyone's amazement, he figured out how to turn off the water main, find tools, and fix it in incredibly short order. The bathroom reeked of raw sewage made worse by gushing water, but Mike didn't hesitate to finish the job and clean up the mess. Jeremy was halfway around the world, but cheers went up for Mike that night. They nicknamed him, "the Fixer."

Mike grabbed Jeremy in a bear hug. "Man, great to see yah. You look wiped. Let's take a load off."

Jeremy curled over into Mike's embrace and broke down sobbing, attempting to talk but not able to put the words together. "Reagan . . . so awful . . . can't she see . . . kill her. . . ." The sobbing broke up any sense of it all.

Mike pulled Jeremy off his chest and stared into Jeremy's eyes. "Say it again, slowly."

"I couldn't do it, Mike . . . just couldn't . . . she wanted me to, but I wouldn't." Jeremy collapsed on the granite entry steps.

Mike crouched with him. He held Jeremy's broken and fragile stature as the shuddering continued.

"She wanted me to end her life . . . begged me to . . . I had no choice. I love her too much. I simply had no choice."

"What do you mean she asked you . . . to kill her?" Mike straightened Jeremy to standing, locking his gaze. "Did you kill her?" he whispered. There was no response.

"Jeremy, did . . . you . . . kill . . . Reagan?" Mike's embrace tightened around Jeremy's shoulders. He shook, at first gently, but his grip strengthened with each passing second.

Jeremy slowly shook his head. "I couldn't do it. I wouldn't do it."

Mike cradled Jeremy's head as he wept. He knew despair so well, he'd met it so many times in the war zone—a child, a young soldier, limbs blown to bits, endless sadness, despair. Mike had thought he had nothing left; he embraced the man he thought had everything.

54

*T*HE winds were easterly and not in favor of a smooth landing. Dr. Yiung latched his seat belt snugly as the plane lined up with the landing strip for a second time.

"You'll get it this time," he prodded the young pilot, aware of his nervousness. The man appeared to be in his late twenties and had flown inter-island many times, yet he still lacked the confidence of an experienced pilot in extreme weather conditions. The other three passengers were busy collecting their belongings, finishing their final sips of beverage and closing up their laptops, assuming all would be fine. Dr. Yiung stayed focused on the pilot and placed his hands firmly on the man's shoulders.

"You got this. The winds will lift, then draw, and let go. Follow the rhythm and lower your wing softly. Keep your eyes on the horizon."

The pilot re-engaged his pressure on the wheel and re-calculated the visual field in front of him. He lowered the tail, compensating for the upward draft from the wind. The wheels touched down for an instant then lifted off the ground again. He leaned farther into the steering wheel, adjusting its direction with more confidence. Finally, all wheels were down and secure on the ground. Dr. Yiung released a quiet sigh.

"Good work, my friend, that was a tough one, excellent job."

"Thanks, Doc, you have good energy. The winds are a bit finicky today, we're getting pretty close to cyclone season. You just never know."

As always, Dr. Yiung was focused on the moment and how to solve any given problem that presented itself. He knew he needed to get to Reagan without delay, but the inexperienced pilot had been put in his path for a reason—a reason he wasn't sure of at the moment, but he knew it would be clear soon.

Dr. Yiung had traveled nearly two thousand miles. The realization of Reagan's illness had come to him late one night as he turned off the lights in his office. The room went dark, but the moon was brilliant. It lit up his office as if it were daytime. He marveled at the power, the energy streaming into the room, casting shadows in every direction so that his desk was suddenly reconfigured as an odd shape on the wall. He thought of Reagan immediately.

That's it . . . it's been there all this time—the answer, right in front of me.

From that moment on, Dr. Yiung knew he had to get to Reagan as soon as he could, to tell her, to help her realize what it was she was battling.

Angus picked up Dr. Yiung for the transit to the island. The splash of the waves on the bow of the boat seemed playful enough, but when the dolphins joined in for the ride, Dr. Yiung let out a gleeful laugh.

"Of course, this is where Reagan finds her peace and purity, her reverence and acceptance." He laughed again as one of the dolphins breached the water with his entire body, welcoming him to their world.

"Please sit, Doc, get bumpy now, crossing is comin', not long, we be there," Angus said, as they cut through the oncoming seas.

Dr. Yiung admired the lush landscape of the island surrounded by the crystal-clear, teal-tinted water. *Beauty amidst beauty. I hope I'm not too late.*

Years ago, before he had started his alternative approach to medicine, Dr. Yiung had worked with a young woman with a rare form of breast cancer. She had a tumor referred to as "massive" per medical standards. Dr. Yiung had utilized the standard oncological advances in Western medicine, with no change in her status. Weeks progressed and the patient got sicker and less responsive to the drugs. The mass had doubled and the cells multiplied like a fast-growing milkweed. He referred her to a specialist thinking he had exhausted his potential to help the dying woman.

Then one morning Dr. Yiung had a premonition of sorts that showed the patient's tumors shrinking by flooding her with ingredients similar to those of the chemo meds, but in their natural plant form. He thought the potency of the attack drug could be increased to inundate the cancer cells like a smart bomb. The approach was conceptual at best, but he was so drawn to the vivid apparition that he had to pursue it. Dr. Yiung hiked deep into the Northeastern Australian rainforest seeking help from a local Aboriginal healer who showed him how to pluck the natural form of phytochemicals, including resveratrol and myricetin, from plants. He learned about the delicate balance of the food's nutrients and the phytochemicals in the plant to coerce a correction in the imbalance of cancer cells. The complex yet simple synergy helped the body return to its healthy homeostasis.

He later learned how to apply the plant-based nutrition to all of his pharmaceutical regimes to attain a purer approach to his patients' problems. Dr. Yiung returned to his cancer patient asking her to trust him and let go of her current Western treatment protocol and try the homeopathic approach. The natural compound showed positive progress within seven days, and at the end of a full month of treatment her tumor had shrunk more than fifty percent. Dr. Yiung was hopeful and optimistic for a full recovery until her kidneys failed from the high levels of radiation to which she had been exposed. He had tears in his eyes as he read the autopsy results showing the severe mass in her breast had fully diminished in size and was not related to her immediate cause of death.

A splash of water from the deep ocean ground swell flooded the bow of the boat, and Angus slowed to an idle.

"You okay, Doc?" The question was a welcome distraction from the morbid memory.

"Oh, yes, onward we go," the doctor pulled back to reality. He thought of the delicate balance between beauty and loss as he washed away the memories of his previous patient to focus on his current one.

55

*T*HE glare of the sun, once a perfect introduction to Reagan's day, was now a burden. The rays felt like daggers piercing her eyes. She dreaded the exertion of rolling her body away from the illumination. Her bones had begun to ache again—not the same sharp pain as in the States, but rather a deep crushing pain from the inside out. She had grown accustomed to the muscle pain and weakness, but the return of the deep and dire bone pain robbed her of the little energy she had left. She was desperate to get back to the island to see her extended family before she died, and she had to make Roger understand.

"I need to go to the island today." The labored release of words was strong, but her voice was weak and dispirited.

Roger looked up from his book and drew a deep breath. "That boat ride across the channel, even in the morning calm, makes my stomach turn."

Reagan's frail body exposed every twitch and twinge. Her atrophied muscles were no longer supported by her skeleton. There was no possibility that she could make the journey without severe pain or a splintering of her weak bones.

"Maybe after some food," Roger cajoled her, as if she were a child. "Then we can—"

It was the usual ploy, played over and over again.

Reagan sat up with renewed vigor. "No more managing me," she insisted, with a strength she had not been able to muster for weeks. She was seated on the edge of her bed, dressing herself. "If today is my last day to breathe, I cannot leave without seeing my family." Her eyes opened wide, retaliating against the harsh sunlight.

Roger closed his book and stood up. Wherever this renewed energy was coming from, it was the essence of Reagan. "I guess it's no use—"

"I have lived and breathed for them. I feel their love and know their loss and the endless pain they've endured." Reagan started to stand on her own: "I am one of them. I belong with them. They are my real family, my final stage. They are who I want to be with before I die." She sat back down, her thin legs were so weak—her physical strength battled her will power. "I want to see my family."

"Okay." Roger could no longer deny her wishes; she was on her final journey home.

Sachi was her guardian for the transit. He lifted Reagan into the boat and lowered her onto the padded seat as if she were an exquisite but fragile seashell.

Roger tried to keep his emotions in check; he wanted to appear rational but struggled with every word. "I understand what you want . . . what you think you want, but you will be more comfortable here. I can't stop you from going, but I want you to know . . . I want you to—" The words knotted up in his throat, blocking any more sounds.

He nodded to Sachi and tapped the side of the boat—an indecipherable gesture of remorse. He loved Reagan as a friend, and perhaps, as the daughter, so long ago lost.

Her body language answered Roger's final words as she settled into the aft seat, hanging onto the rail. She untied the stern line from the cleat in a slow and methodical manner and let it slip into the water. Reagan's determination in casting off the boat was her final resolution. She said calmly, "Roger, thank you, I love you, too."

She half-smiled—a pretense of victory. She gave a small wave of her hand blowing a kiss in the wind, but her arm fell to her side.

Roger followed the wake of the boat, unable to look directly into Reagan's eyes. He knew it was Reagan's sole intention to convince Maura to start the process of her transition. It was unbearable—an impossible thought.

What if Jeremy were here—what would he do? He'd get on a boat and chase after her. He would want me to stop her . . . but Roger knew he couldn't change the course of events; they were inevitable.

The sea was calm once inside the protected reef. Romeo and Juliet were close in tow, underwater, their fins not breaking through the surface. The cormorants flew single file leading the procession in perfect unison. Reagan closed her eyes smelling the ocean air and welcoming the mist of boat spray on her face. The taste was heavenly, filled with salt, sea foam and a thin layer of fine sand. She was home and headed to her family. She thought of Jeremy and struggled with all her will to block the tears.

"Sachi, do you remember when Jeremy tricked you into taking him to the island?"

"Oh, yes, ma'am. I'm sorry for that. I didn't know what he was up to."

"What did you think of him then?"

Sachi cleared his throat. "That's not for me to say, Miss Reagan."

The breeze created by the forward motion of the boat and the wet spray chilled Reagan. The tropical heat was in full press, yet she shivered and wanted to curl up but the narrow seat would not allow it. The edges of the boat felt hard and unforgiving. She wanted the crossing to be over; she wanted Juliet and Romeo to leave her in peace and stop inviting her into the sea to play with them. Most of all, she wanted to avoid any more thoughts of Jeremy.

He's a coward. How dare he leave? Yes, that's it, he's a coward . . . he couldn't stay and hold my hand and . . . watch . . . me . . . die. Her throat narrowed. It was difficult to swallow, tears dripped along the inlaid curves of her hollowed cheekbones. *I'm sorry,* she whispered to the wind. She wept silently for their lost love, crushed by her illness, soon to be severed by her death.

Sachi slowed the engine and they drifted into the landing. He was careful not to bump the wooden dock. Reagan was pulled from her deep sadness by the sight of Maura's three children waving madly at her, jumping up and down and shouting as loud as they could, "Auntie Reagan, Auntie Reagan, come quick, we have a surprise for you!"

Reagan pretended she could manage on her own, but Sachi propped his shoulder under her armpit and torso assisting her, without calling attention to her dire weakness.

Maura moved ahead of the children so they wouldn't tug on Reagan or try to be lifted up for an embrace, which Reagan always did when she arrived on the island. Maura got to her first and turned to the children. "Auntie is a bit tired, so, easy hugs, girls . . . easy hugs, like with Papa."

Lelei, the oldest daughter, shot a glance at her mother, and back at Reagan. "What do you mean like Papa? Do you mean sick Papa?"

"Now come along, girls, Auntie is just tired from her long trip. Go get her Mama's Li'l Helper. I saw him at the straw bin."

The children ran along, two of them skipping and giggling. They loved Mama's Li'l Helper, and enjoyed "saddling him up," which was only throwing a rope over his head and twisting it into a halter, with a bit left over to lead him. Twisting the rope correctly was a fun puzzle. It always took several tries to get it right. It was a big job for the girls to get the small donkey ready for the difficult trip up the mountain. He resisted; they giggled.

Once the girls were out of sight, Maura embraced Reagan. "You are tired, my friend. Let's go up the mountain. Phaeole is waiting for you."

Reagan glanced up the hill, and took a deep breath. "Why are we going up there? Maura, you know why I'm here. It's my time."

"Let's talk later. Mama's Li'l Helper will take you."

"But why . . . I—"

"Phaeole. He needs you. We go to him."

Joni dragged Mama's Li'l Helper between Maura and Reagan. The small donkey wiggled the rope off his ear, which was now bent in place. He didn't seem in the least interested in a trip up the mountain, but nevertheless the girls and Maura boosted Reagan onto his back. Giggling continued, for no good reason other than the sight of Reagan atop the small animal. With her legs dangling above the ground, a small crease of a smile swept over her—a wave of pure joy that could not be suppressed.

Reagan had forgotten about Mama's Li'l Helper. He was used primarily to help haul small loads, especially supplies coming off boats, or anything Mama needed help moving. Sometimes the children rode him, but no one much heavier. His small stature and narrow spine made it difficult for an adult. Reagan's lighter weight allowed this much-needed respite from the hike. She massaged the animal's soft neck and released the trapped ear from the makeshift bridle, "Thank you, my friend."

The donkey gently shook his neck.

"I can get off when it gets too steep," she whispered into the furry ear.

"No, you stay on him," Maura snapped. "Li'l Helper is plenty strong. Look at all he does 'round here."

As they started their climb, Reagan thought of her dear friend and how she could never have imagined this outcome. They had shared so much together—laughter and sadness—life, sickness and death. They were at once: mother, sister, friend, confidant, healer, helper, joined together by an unlikely journey.

Reagan swayed back and forth with the donkey's surefootedness adjusting to the altered terrain. He was slow and offered precious moments to look around, to see the path unfold, to hear the sounds of crickets and frogs in the low-lying brush, to hear the breeze sneak through the oddly shaped screw pines and towering banyans. A mix of richly colored flowers were strewn across the hillside like a Monet canvas. Her senses were intensely alive.

Pink and purple trumpet vines were draped along the ridge of the cliff, and Reagan noticed how their petals opened like two hands offering solace. All of these impressions seemed new to her, as if she had never seen them before. She inhaled more deeply than she had in months; the smells of plumeria and jasmine bloom were intoxicating. The deep-seated pain in her body diminished with every step the donkey took upward.

56

*A*S the copper-red deepened into evening twilight, Jeremy felt the constricting heaviness in his chest. He stared into the empty void of approaching darkness wanting to touch Reagan one more time, knowing he couldn't get to her. He couldn't return with his heart full of longing just to watch her die. His body was taut with despair. He slammed his clenched fist into the wooden desk, ripping open the tender flesh over each knuckle. Blood spewed over the antique mahogany, which was never meant to be touched, only dusted. The rush of sensations was overwhelming. The impulse to pace and try to catch his breath at the same time alarmed him.

"Why can't I breathe? Is this a heart attack? Mike . . . George. . . ." His call for help was frail, almost soundless; no one could possibly hear him. The strident sound of his cell ringing snapped him out of a spiraling anxiety.

Jeremy was frozen in place. The ring tones persisted. Finally, he grabbed his cell like a lifeline, ready to yell "help."

"Hello," he answered, pressing his hand into his chest to help stem the flow of blood.

"Jeremy?"

Silence.

"Jeremy, are you there? This is important. It's Jean Michael."

Silence.

"I don't have much time. Jeremy, for chrissake, answer me."

"I'm here, Jean, I'm sorry, a bit of a connection problem." Jeremy slowed his heart rate and settled himself. "What's going on?"

"You have no idea what I've just—"

"Jean, I'm here, go ahead."

The connection went dead. Jeremy pressed Call. Jean Michael's number rang and rang—no answer.

Jeremy kept checking his cell and redialing. The blood from his wound oozed onto the screen of the phone.

He went into his private washroom and grabbed a monogrammed hand towel to wrap his hand and another to mop up the blood on the desk. He stared at the desk for some time, unconcerned about the stained surface. Normally, even a slight swath of dust would bother him, but now it didn't matter that a large bloodstain spilled over the cherished grain. His world was collapsing inward. Jeremy was not a fighter. He knew nothing about heroics, unless he was acting out a script. He looked at his phone one more time. He had to get to Jean Michael.

Being alone with his thoughts was unbearable, so Jeremy got into his roadster, his hand still wrapped in the bloody towel, and headed toward Wilshire Boulevard.

JEAN MICHAEL shut off the lights in his office and headed out the back door. Lydia's call had made him anxious. It was important to connect with Jeremy. "What the hell . . . answer the damn phone. . . ." As he walked across the dimly lit parking lot, he saw a shadow from over his left shoulder, and at the same moment heard Jeremy's voice on the other end of the line. He reached for his car keys, hoping to set off the alarm, but the heavy metal object hit him squarely in the back of the head.

It was over in seconds. Jean Michael lay in a pool of blood on the pavement.

JEREMY tried to recall the backstreets he could wind through to get out of freeway traffic, but at night it was a maze of flashing lights, roadwork, and an endless stream of headlights going in every direction. He dialed Jean Michael again to no avail. His anxiety took over, no call back. Jeremy finally found the right street to turn into the studio back-lot. Horns were blaring along with flashing detour signs, all adding to the stress of not knowing why Jean Michael wouldn't answer his phone.

Beyond the security gate, a chaos of emergency lights appeared— two fire trucks, one ambulance, three police cars.

"Oh, God, no, this can't be happening." The bile churned in his stomach, knowing it must be Jean Michael. Jeremy slammed on his brakes and got out of the car with an equal mix of panic and nausea.

A police officer intercepted him. "Sorry sir, you can't go any farther, this is a crime scene."

"Crime, what crime?"

"We don't have specifics, sir." The officer held his hand out to stop him as a gurney loaded up a body into the ambulance.

Jeremy pressed against the officer's hand on his chest, trying to catch a glimpse of the victim. "I think that's my friend, that's Jean Michael Raava. He's a director. I'm Jeremy Black; we work together. He just called me, but I was busy, I couldn't pick up . . . I did pick up, I just didn't understand what he was saying and then the phone went dead."

"Sir, will you step over this way, please? We will need to have a word with you."

"Can you tell me how he is? Is he alive?"

"Sir, I'm sorry, we have very little information. He's being loaded into the ambulance. It appears you've suffered some kind of incident yourself." The officer nodded toward Jeremy's shirt and hand. "Can you explain that?"

"Of course I can, I hit my hand on a desk."

"I see. Any particular reason? You were walking by a desk and decided to hit it?"

"Oh, come on, officer, this is ridiculous, I need to find out how Jean Michael is. This is serious."

"Yes, sir, it is serious and I need you to calm down and answer a few simple questions."

"Did you hear me? I'm Jeremy Black."

"Yes, sir, I did hear you the first time. You seem a little agitated. Have you been in a scuffle of some sort?"

Jeremy realized the trap that was being set for him. He had the presence of mind to slow down, to fall back into his acting role where he could pretend to be calm. "Officer, I'm just worried about my friend. We were talking on the phone and, wham, nothing. I got worried that he got jumped by somebody . . . it does happen in L.A., you know, so I came right over. I'd like to follow them to the hospital."

"I'll need to see your driver's license and car registration, and I'll be back in a minute to talk about your friend. Please get back in your car and stay put."

The ambulance sirens went off and everyone turned their attention to clearing the way for their exit. Jeremy sat in his car playing with his keys, tossing them back and forth in his hand. He stared at his bloody knuckles, blood-soaked shirt and hand towel on the front seat of the car.

57

*P*HAEOLE'S modest wooden hut finally came into view. It seemed like it had been years since Reagan was last there with Maura, but it had only been months. So much had happened, life had completely changed. Reagan slid off Li'l Helper, letting the rope fall to the ground. For a moment, she couldn't move. She stood like a statue frozen in time.

Maura motioned to take her arm. "I've got you. Not much farther."

"I'm okay, really, I'm okay. I just need a moment." Reagan followed each rustling sound as she prepared to move her foot forward. Frogs croaked out of tune; lizards slithered under protective layers of dense foliage; there was a faint communal buzz in the star jasmine engulfing Phaeole's lanai. A gaggle of parrots, lories, and fruit doves created a cacophony of sounds that wound their way through the ancient banyans. Reagan stepped carefully as if on sacred ground; the beauty was profound. She wondered why this feeling was so powerful, so overwhelming. It carried her forward, supporting her. *Why is nature embracing me now . . . is this my end stage flowering?*

Her delicate thoughts were broken by the sound of Phaeole's shuffle and his sudden appearance in the uneven doorway. Reagan stared at him. She'd forgotten his imposing stature—even hunched over, crippled by leprosy, and blind, Phaeole's presence was impressive. His smile beamed like a lighthouse beacon—a welcome sight after being lost at sea.

Reagan's thoughts were blurred by weakness. Grabbing the rickety porch railing, she pulled herself step by step to him. Maura shuffled behind her, struggling to keep up with Reagan's burst of strength.

Phaeole stood with his arms outstretched toward Reagan. They were curved and buckled like the roots of the banyan, but they reached for her.

Reagan fell into his arms. The musky smell was a welcome scent, mixed with her salty tears. "I'm so sorry, Phaeole . . . I don't know why I ever left. I should have stayed. I could have helped you and the children. I was wrong to leave. It took all my strength."

"Now, now . . . you've had a long journey. This is your place to heal. Come, let's have some tea."

Maura followed them through the threshold and gently embraced Phaeole. "We made it. God willing, we are not too late."

The vines of the trumpet flowers were flowing from the outside into Phaeole's kitchen. He brought bowls of tea to Maura and Reagan, his gnarled hands keeping the tray balanced. Reagan noticed his ability amid his disability. She followed his fluid movement until he sat next to her, facing her directly. She sensed his need to talk.

"You've come home." Phaeole rested his hand on her shoulder.

She emptied the small bowl in two gulps.

"Slow down, dear Reagan, it is potent, and meant to be sipped slowly to be effective."

Reagan responded, not really listening to his words: "I am sorry, Phaeole, I was supposed to be here for you, to help you on your journey, but now it is my time. I've grown so weak. I see no way of going on."

Maura sat more erect, gripping the bowl in her fists. It was the first time Reagan had admitted her desire out loud. The silence was crushing.

"Have you considered that you may have taken the wrong path?" Phaeole asked calmly.

"What do you mean?"

"You left what heals you."

Reagan looked past Phaeole, knowing his words were true.

"Maybe it's not your time." He used the exact words Reagan had once used to derail his desire to end his life.

Reagan's posture slumped in exhaustion. She grabbed at her neck and shoulder, rubbing them anxiously, trying to relieve the ache. Her frail arms offered little relief. She wondered if Phaeole and Maura really understood. *Do they have any idea what the pain is like? Every day is a subtle, endless torture. It has to end. It has to be stopped.*

Her illness had robbed her of the ability to fight, leaving her helpless and decimated. There was no more joy, or love, only the vacuous space of a painful existence.

She cried like a child. "But I can't do anything. Don't you see, I'm so useless. I could barely hang on to the donkey going up a hill. I used to trot up that mountain myself. I can't surf, dive, or help anyone . . . Hell, I can't even help myself."

Reagan looked into the blank stare of Phaeole and the thought rose up in front of her like a brilliant orange flame—*dear God, what have I said, he is blind, crippled, frail . . . and I cry for myself?*

Phaeole drew in a deep breath. "I understand. It's hard . . . every day. But God gives us just enough strength to accomplish our purpose."

A slow, calming smile rolled from the left side of his mouth to the right in a gentle wave of affirmation.

Maura sat still perched at the edge of her seat.

A pulse of energy enveloped Reagan. The heaviness in her spine eased up a bit as she considered his words. She pressed her arms deep into the saggy pads on the wooden bench. "Well, I believe my strength is at its end. The suffering . . . it's just too much to bear any longer. Besides what has God given you?" Her cynicism toward him was uncharacteristic and tinged with anger.

Phaeole's graciousness and wisdom reached out to her again. "To start with, he gave me just enough laziness, which I like to call patience." He pointed toward the unfinished art pieces and clutter in every direction. "He also gave me the right amount of memory loss, so if I choose to forgive then I can easily forget."

They all smiled.

Phaeole's eyes looked straight into Reagan's. "Lastly, God gave me the gift of seeing. Not as you would have it, but I can certainly see things you cannot. I admit, I have been very angry at times. I could not understand His ways, taking the color out of my world, making my hands into tree branches, but I have come to understand slowly, patiently, stubbornly—The Truth."

This phrase jolted Reagan. The room flooded with the smell of jasmine and a parrot let out a strange screech. She gathered all her energy to speak through the tangled thoughts, "What do you think God has given me?"

His expression softened with a broad smile. "You know the answer, my friend." Phaeole chose his words carefully, as a father does leading his child to the answer. He gazed into the darkness that held Reagan. "He has given you just enough adversity to enhance your empathy, your understanding and compassion."

There was silence for a few moments as Reagan contemplated his words. She opened her eyes wider. "Do I lack those qualities?"

"That is not something I can judge. Those are your gifts and your gifts are being expanded."

Reagan listened intently.

"You see, life comes and life goes, in all forms. Those flowers," he pointed to the dried-out bunch of wildflowers on the table, "see how the crumbled remnants scatter like ash. The animals. . . ." He pointed to the birds perched outside his window. A small lory cocked its head and chirped before taking flight. "It's the ebb and flow of the groundswell in the ocean, drawing deeply from the bottom, taking in and gathering energy and then slowly pushing nature's force upward, redelivering force with its push in the curling waves." He glanced at Maura and then at Reagan, as if he could see them clearly. "Our lives, everything we know, comes and goes." Phaeole slowed his words as he faced Reagan directly. "Reagan, my dear, there are many people who will help with 'life comes'." He adjusted his posture, sitting more upright, to help articulate the magnitude of his next words: "But only a few very special people can help with 'life goes'."

Their space was silenced. Even the slight breeze that had so gratefully wafted through the conversation abated. It was eerie, as if a ghost was passing through the room. Reagan thought of the chief and how she had ushered him into the next world. He had begged her over and over again to let him go, yet his spirit was not at peace. He wanted the painful journey to end; he railed against it, until his final release. Reagan contemplated medicine's greatest paradox: Doctors train to manage illness yet they must also release their patients from illness.

"Don't lose your purpose," Phaeole concluded. "People should not suffer as they do here." He glanced out the open window. "You give us back our dignity in life and in death. You are our Kōkua."

Reagan had overheard the Hawaiian word for 'helper' on one of her trips to Nadi to pick up an emergency supply of medicine. She didn't have the required paperwork, so they called her Kōkua and that seemed to resolve the situation. It had been a common term used in the South Pacific in earlier times, referring to anyone who offered their skills and their love in support of the islanders. The fishermen had also called her Kōkua, because she tended to the reef, talked to the fish, and played with the dolphins.

Honored by Phaeole's thoughtful reflection, Reagan adjusted herself more upright. She tilted her head toward him and wondered if his words could be the catalyst for the mixture of medicine needed to help her survive. No one had ever helped the islanders with leprosy before; their suffering was unbearable to their last breath. No one had held a dying hand or told them it was okay to want to end their life, before she had arrived. No one had ever devoted their life to their misfortune and disease, until Reagan. Perhaps part of her illness was her painful love for the islanders. There was, perhaps, no clear answer to medicine's greatest paradox.

58

A FAINT rustling outside of Phaeole's entry stirred Reagan. She looked toward the clanging bamboo strands.

"Hello." The jovial voice carried in on a light breeze. "May I come in?"

Reagan bolted upright, sparked by the familiar voice. "No, it couldn't be."

Maura grinned and released a deep breath, collapsing the walls of her chest. She whispered, "They're here."

The giggle was unmistakable. "Well—what's all this?"

Reagan turned to the doorway. "Dr. Yiung?"

He bounded inside like some magical wizard, not in the least winded from the last leg of his tiresome journey.

Dr. Yiung's smile illuminated the room, sweeping the dark energy straight out the back entrance: "Looks like an intervention if I ever saw one." He continued his levity with the energy Reagan had grown to love while in Australia.

"How did you—" Reagan was standing.

"What . . . find you?" He raised his eyebrows then waved Roger to step inside.

"Roger? What is going on here?"

"Someone had to get the good doctor to the island. Besides I've never met your legendary friend." Roger stepped toward Phaeole, reaching for his hands. "It's good to finally meet you. I'm sorry I haven't made my way up the mountain until now."

Phaeole bowed toward Roger's gesture. "I've heard about you and your place where the people come and go. You've helped Reagan help us and we've never had a chance to say thank you, until now."

Dr. Yiung moved closer to Phaeole. "I promise, I wasn't really eavesdropping, but your words rolled straight at us. We had to duck." The doctor laughed. "Your words are strong and beautiful at the same time—life comes and life goes." He reached for Phaeole's hands, gently opening the gnarled fists, entwining his fingers into the deep crevices of scar tissue. "My friend, I think we are of the same fabric and share the same understanding."

Phaeole's mouth twisted into a smile. Maura had told him about the giggling doctor and his creative treatment techniques used in Australia. Though Phaeole was on guard, he immediately liked the doctor's demeanor and attitude. He had not met many men from the outside world, and those he had met were cruel, harsh, and not to be trusted. They saw no beauty in the human spirit, especially one that was cloaked in disintegrating flesh. The laughing doctor seemed quite different.

Reagan interrupted the conversation. "I don't understand. Can someone please explain to me what is going on?"

"Oh dear, you will have to forgive me. I'm forgetting about my patient, my young friend here." Dr. Yiung went to Reagan and sat next to her on the wooden bench. It was rough-hewn and slightly awkward, but his gesture signaled everyone to sit down.

Reagan grew quiet wondering what elixir Dr. Yiung had brought with him, what advice he would share—he had come all this way for her. His broad grin escaped with the breeze, and the forthcoming sentence was molded by a serious expression, uncharacteristic of the doctor.

Dr. Yiung took both of Reagan's hands, just as he had Phaeole's, and spoke slowly. "Reagan, what if . . . what if your sickness isn't your sickness?"

She squinted, trying to comprehend the message.

"What if it is a mere accumulation of toxins that are preparing to leave you?"

Maura tilted her head to the side. "I don't understand—"

"What if you've had to go through all this struggle for the final phase?"

"I am preparing for the final phase. That's why I came back to the island . . . to be with my family and to say goodbye. I can't go on with this horrible, torturous illness."

Dr. Yiung adjusted his glasses. "How do you feel now?"

"Well, I am . . . I guess, I'm a little more comfortable now that I'm home and my friends are here."

"What about the ache in your joints? How does that feel?"

"I feel a bit achy, but not as bad as when I was in the States. That was excruciating."

"Why was that?"

"Well, it was all wrong. All the machines and the radiation and the meds, the assault on my system—none of it was going to help me, it made me terribly sick."

"What helped you?"

"Jer—" Reagan tripped over his name and quickly moved on, "Leaving helped, coming home, helped."

"Okay, now we are home and now I can help you. I'm sorry I sent you into the thicket of Western medicine. I have been conditioned . . . you see, and I've had to work so hard to overcome my training, but I default to it when I don't have the correct answer. Now I have the correct answer and now I know you are well on your way to health, if you will trust me. It took me some time to understand. I had to see the shadow on the wall to understand. Never mind . . . again, I'm so sorry I encouraged you to go to the States."

"It's not your—"

Dr. Yiung put out his finger, halting the words on her lips. "I've been thinking about you and this strange poisoning. The specialists I sent you to indeed forgot to be generalists first." Dr. Yiung shook his head back and forth slowly in regret. "It's like treating the common cold with antibiotics. It's not necessary and often harmful."

He bowed his head momentarily before lifting it again to continue, "Treatment should always be relevant, about the cure, not the illness," he looked around the room at the colors of the natural light bouncing off the walls. "Like this rainbow, it is a reflection of the outside beauty projecting itself inward. Our physical bodies can do the same thing."

Reagan scanned the room and felt a sense of calm. She cast her eyes toward the open windowsill, where a green-orange finch perched, his brilliant colored crown was cocked in their direction as if listening in on the lecture.

The room was silent for a moment, then Dr. Yiung went on. "If we allow ourselves the nutrients we need, then nature can heal us. The outside light reflects inward." Dr. Yiung faced Reagan squarely. "Sometimes we need to get out of the way of ourselves, you know, quit blocking the light and let nature do its job."

Roger chimed in confused. "Wait a minute, what are we talking about here, what light? You mean the light that appears when you die? This isn't what I thought we were going to talk about."

Maura placed her hand on Roger's to quiet him.

"Quite the opposite. I'm referring to the light and the shadow I was mentioning," Dr. Yiung answered. "Just quit thinking about any of this as a death sentence. There is a tenable solution here, and my friend Phaeole understands it as well as I do."

Phaeole nodded. He seemed to understand the answer, but convincing Reagan remained the challenge.

Reagan was trying to grasp what Dr. Yiung was saying—what he was implying—she knew the facts and statistics. No one lived long with radiation poisoning, especially if compromised by Hansen's. She figured she had six months to live. Her organs would shut down their function, not able to stave off the poisonous contagion. Her olfactory senses were already in jeopardy, not allowing her to eat with any pleasure, and her muscles were atrophying with a vengeance.

"I'm sorry, I'm too tired to understand. Can you—"

Dr. Yiung accelerated his delivery. "Excessive plutonium is radioactive and can accumulate in the bones. It was used as a deadly war agent years ago and as nuclear reactor fuel, and is one of the heaviest elements. We know it played a role in World War II and the atomic bomb. I'm not sure how you got exposed to these levels, but I've been baffled by the fact that you've survived until now. You've somehow managed to combat it all these years, but once the Hansen's appeared it must have triggered a release of some sort . . . your immune system started to shut down and the toxins got the upper hand."

Reagan had moved in closer to Maura; she appeared exhausted by the depth of the explanation.

Roger added with concern, "With all due respect, doc, you're not helping us understand how Reagan is going to survive this."

Phaeole was the only one in the room fully aware of Dr. Yiung's explanation. He had relaxed into the back of the chair and nodded. He had been called upon to heal before, though he had never relayed the story to Reagan. Only Maura knew about the strange occurrence.

Years ago, Phaeole had provided safe harbor for a young family who had suffered from a grave illness and were dumped, like so much garbage, on their island. They were left there to die—a mother, two young children, and their father. No one was certain what they suffered from and they couldn't explain it. They spoke a different language, unknown to the islanders. They used gestures to communicate. When the parents were overcome by weakness and death seemed imminent, the children were taken on donkeys to Phaeole.

Recognizing their dire condition, he immediately treated them with the native plants he cultivated near his bure. Both children responded within days; their small systems were cleansed of the toxins and their energy rebounded in force. Their survival only added to Phaeole's myth—that he held power over life and death.

The parents, however, did not make the journey to see Phaeole. Whether they were decimated by their illness or their circumstance, no one knew, but they surrendered quickly to their fate, leaving behind the children who were embraced by the islanders. Phaeole knew the power of his medicines, though they never cured the affliction that riddled the island. Even on the small island, the mythical stories got twisted and reshaped—Phaeole was considered dangerous instead of a healer. He had learned to accept their judgment and went about life as best he could, cultivating his garden and sending the right mix of medicines to those who acknowledged his skill. He sketched the healing plants until his eyesight failed, and now he was very close to his final gesture.

He turned toward Reagan. "I think you understand what the doctor is saying. It's just difficult to see it, until you feel it. We are asking your illness to retreat, to leave you, but you must be in agreement."

The colors in the room were changing, a lone ray of light continued to stream through the open-air window casting a myriad of colors along the walls. Everything appeared to be moving, swaying like palm trees, but there was nothing to account for the motion.

Dr. Yiung pointed to the refracting rays of light. "You see, that is what I mean. There is your answer. The light and the shadow. One is real and one is an illusion. You are the light, your illness is an illusion, a shadow."

"Please . . . this is too hard." Reagan's eyes welled up.

Dr. Yiung continued, "Reagan, it is time to consider new thoughts, be open to not ending your life, but rather restarting your life." Glancing around the room, he directed his words to each person.

"Treatment may not be as difficult as you think. We are all here for you."

Dr. Yiung broke the somber mood and leapt up from his seat as if wielding a magic wand. "Imagine this: the periodic table is an actual table balanced on a ball instead of legs." His arms were wide stretched, as he went on: "If your levels of plutonium are excessive, then the table tilts."

His hands dropped, exaggerating the point.

"To right the table, imagine going to the element opposite the one which is excessive to help balance the table, or in this case balance the toxic effect of too much plutonium. If you look across from plutonium, you see that iron is at the top. I imagine there is limited iron on this island, knowing the plantation-style produce. Simply add more iron to level the table."

Reagan and Maura glanced at each other, only partially understanding his explanation. Reagan seemed almost annoyed, "Dr. Yiung, you can't honestly believe it can be that simple."

"Honestly, I do. Interestingly enough, your levels of potassium are high, thanks to all those tropical bananas. So if you look across from potassium, you get to krypton."

Reagan perked up, envisioning the Periodic Table of Elements. She knew them like she knew her own name; it was just hard seeing them through the haze of her illness and in an organized fashion in midair.

"But isn't krypton a gas?"

"Yes, of course, but right above it is arsenic, which is very reactive and used as an effective pharmaceutical agent to inhibit effects on the central nervous system." He smiled across at Phaeole as he sipped his tea. "And this, my dear friend, is loaded with friendly arsenic."

Roger spit his tea back in his wooden cup. "Arsenic? Can't that kill you?"

Dr. Yiung smiled again. "Paracelsus, the famous physician and astrologer, once said, 'All things are poison and nothing is without poison, only the dose permits something not to be poisonous.' It's the balance." He concluded.

Reagan was beginning to understand the treatment plan. She felt the first glimmer of hope, the first realization that she could beat this toxic assault. "I think I see where you are going . . . balancing out the toxin's effect. It's sort of simple."

Dr. Yiung's smile widened. "Yes, you've got it. Arsenic is one of our strongest medicinal elements. It is similar to selenium, which plays a role in our immune system, boosting resistance to overoxidation, kind of like antioxidants. Arsenic and selenium are reciprocal and may play a role in cleaning up toxic metals. For years it was used to treat malaria. It has its homeopathic application and if consumed in the right doses—voilà." He gestured like a magician. "The table is in balance again."

Roger stared at him, a bit dumbfounded. "So I'm not gonna die from this tea?"

"No sir, you are not, and better yet, it will rid Reagan of her toxic buildup and she will not only live, but she will live a full and wonderful life."

The room was silent again. Reagan looked off in the distance as if calculating numbers in her head. "It makes sense, I can't deny your theory."

Maura lifted her bowl of bitter tea. "What do you think, Reagan? We drink."

A new sense of hope washed away the despair. There were no guarantees.

"It will take some effort," Dr. Yiung explained. "But you will have plenty of support. If you agree, we can return to Australia together. You won't have to stay too long, but I do need to keep an eye on your metal count. We have some balancing to do."

"I hadn't thought of . . . of leaving again. I don't know if I can. If only—"

Maura interrupted, "If only what?"

Reagan turned abruptly to Roger. "Does he know . . . does Jeremy know about all this?"

Roger shook his head. "No, I'm sorry. I didn't even know." He paused and rubbed his eyes before falling back into the wooden chair.

Reagan searched the room. "I'm really not—"

They looked at her in anticipation, even Phaeole kept his eyes leveled at the direction of her voice. He presented an eerie sight, apparently able to penetrate her thoughts with his will. Dr. Yiung waited. There were no giggles, no sounds.

Reagan broke the desolate silence with a rush of confused words. "I need to get to a phone. I need to reach Jeremy. I have things I need to say to him. I asked him the impossible and he left because he loved me. He didn't leave me. I sent him away. He has a right to know the truth. I feel empty, completely empty. I was wrong . . . I need to tell him . . . I know that sounds crazy, he'd never come back. Why should he, but . . . he just has to know."

Roger broke through her conflict. "Not crazy at all, my dear, let's get to the phone."

59

*J*EREMY tapped his heel anxiously while watching the police officer pace with half a cigarette hanging from the corner of his mouth. He appeared beat-up, shabby, and well past his prime. The officer looked at Jeremy periodically while talking into his radio. Jeremy pressed harder on his wound, hoping to stop the blood from dripping onto the pristine leather floor mat.

"Mr. Black. Thanks for your patience. Everything checks out." He handed Jeremy his driver's license. "But I still have a few questions. Again, I'm not clear on how you know Mr. Ray-va?" The officer mispronounced his name for the third time.

Jeremy was getting antsy. "Look, I need to get going. As I said, Jean Michael is not only a film director, but a good friend, and we are working together on a film. Is that clear enough for you?"

Jeremy's hand and head were throbbing and he still didn't know what was going on with Jean Michael. He glanced away, cautious not to give out any more information than absolutely necessary.

"Yes, I do understand. I'm completely clear that you are some famous actor and this Ray-va fellow is a director. But the problem we have here is that he was clubbed over the head, and he is in critical condition. You appear out of nowhere, and for some reason you have blood all over you. From where I stand, I've got some questions. You seem a little fidgety. Is there anything you'd like to tell me that might help me figure this out? I've got all night."

"No problem at all." Jeremy jumped back into acting mode. "What I know is this—I had a bad day . . . just broke up with my girlfriend and smacked my hand on my table . . . AT HOME. I was frustrated. Then I got a phone call from Jean Michael. While I was talking to him, I used my shirt to stop the bleeding. After the call, I grabbed a towel. My friend was in trouble. . . ."

"Okay, what did he say?"

"Well, he didn't say much. We had phone problems."

"How did you know he was in trouble?"

"He sounded worried."

"Worried about what?"

Jeremy realized he was being led down a path he couldn't turn back from. He searched his mental scripts for a character who would fit the moment. "We're always worried about new scripts, always working on dialogue and then there are endless production issues. It's complicated. I don't expect you to understand the intricacies of the film world. I know you are out here protecting all of us and I appreciate that, really I do."

"Thanks, Mr. Black. That's a real sweet, heartfelt speech. But we have another problem here."

Jeremy shifted in his seat, sensing the end was near; he hadn't played the right role.

The officer leaned toward Jeremy, bending into the open window of the roadster. He smelled musty and his words were laden with corrosive coffee breath. The mix of the guy's foul body odor and his own dried blood made Jeremy queasy.

The officer continued, "Central says you were recently pursued for harboring a medical fugitive from the CDC. Quite a story. Car chases, private planes and all sorts of intrigue. A real good story. A female, too. Reagan Caldwell. Sound familiar? Is that the 'girlfriend' you've been desk-slamming with your fist? Do you see my problem here? I've got a lot of questions, and you don't stop fidgeting with your keys."

Jeremy looked away. "I have no idea what you're talking about."

"Okay, Mr. Black, suit yourself, but we are going to need more information from you, probably best if you come to the station."

"How is he?" Jeremy burst out, no longer able to contain his anxiety.

"I haven't been given an update on the victim, but I assure you, when I know—" The officer's radio squelched and he retreated to his car to listen to the communiqué.

Jeremy strained to hear, but a wave of panic curled up through his gut toward his throat. He slid the keys into his ignition with only one thought—he had to get out of there.

The officer returned to the roadster. "Okay, you're free to go for now, but we'll need a statement within forty-eight hours. Here's the address. We'll look forward to seeing you and your best friend." He winked. "Your lawyer."

Squinting to make out the officer's badge, Jeremy replied, "Officer Burns. Have a nice day."

Burns curled his lip upward, creating an awkward wrinkle on one side of his face, and nodded his head. "You do the same, sir."

Jeremy drove along Pacific Coast Highway, mumbling to himself, unable to put the sequence of events together. He tried to get a handle on his emotions, but every turn fed into his confusion. He reviewed every move he had made since hitting his hand on the table. There were so many scenes in his head, like a complex movie script. A horn honked behind him. He looked up at the green light and moved through the intersection.

Jean Michael called. Phone went dead . . . CDC . . . Reagan . . . Jesus . . . what's going on?

Another honk.

Jeremy checked his speed and locked onto the center divider.

I can do this . . . focus. Jean called. Phone went dead . . . CDC . . . Reagan. . . . . Jeremy repeated the sequence hoping to understand it. He felt a cloudiness, an inability to hold onto any thought long enough to make sense of it. Another honk from the car behind him.

Asshole, just pass me. He kept driving, unable to focus on anything. An emptiness that arrives just before a dreadful, numbing depression, enveloped him. He was driving through a dark, echoing tunnel. Now as the light led him through the last stretch of tunnel, he heard a fourth honk, this time louder and more insistent than the previous. His nerves were frayed, he felt listless. He exited the tunnel and pulled over to allow the car to pass him. He certainly didn't expect the car behind him to do the same.

Thank God, it's not the cops.

A car door slammed and Jeremy squinted in his rearview mirror to see who was approaching his car. He couldn't identify the heavyset man moving through the disjointed reflection of headlights. He reached for his cell to dial 911. As he went to push the final digit, he recognized the familiar New York twang.

"Ah, Mr. Black, we meet again."

"Officer Burns?" His mind raced again, holding the phone in desperation. All he had to do was push the final number 1. "Am I in some sort of trouble?"

"No, but your director friend may be. Nothing is adding up. After I left you, my shift was over, but I did some more checking. There are some strange things going on and I think you might be in danger."

"In danger of what?"

"Look, son, I went to all the trouble to follow you . . . to tell you. I live thirty-five miles that way." Burns pointed to the southeast. "It's a helluva drive, but this case stinks from miles away."

"Officer, I'm really at a loss here. I'd just like to head home and get cleaned up . . . been a long day."

Burns shifted his weight back and forth, straddling a question he couldn't ask without retribution. "It appears your friend tripped on some information he shouldn't have, and there are some people looking to shut him up." The look on his face was sincere, yet Jeremy wasn't about to trust him.

"So he's alive?" Jeremy gripped the steering wheel with both hands. The officer nodded.

"What kind of information?" Jeremy asked cautiously.

"Don't play stupid with me. Consider what your friend just went through, maybe ask yourself why. And when you come up with the answer, you let me know what kind of information."

Jeremy remained in actor mode, not giving a hint that he was the one who visited Charlie Grant. He shrugged and looked away.

"You think you got some blood on your shirt now, wait till they rearrange your whole face."

Jeremy looked at the guy, only half-shaken by his words, but nonetheless ready to take the game seriously. "Why would anyone want to rearrange my face, as you say?"

"Why don't you tell me?"

There were a few moments of silence.

"Who is this woman you are protecting? This Reagan Caldwell."

"She has nothing to do with this." He shifted in his seat, avoiding the detective's glance. "Maybe it has to do with our new project." Jeremy changed the subject but quickly regretted his words.

"What's the new project about?"

Jeremy was growing more uneasy by the moment. He was tired and confused, his nervousness showing in the restlessness of his hands. *What does this guy know? Why did he follow me when he just told me I was free to go less than an hour ago?*

"Gone silent on me?" The officer glanced around at the cars slowing down before passing them. "The guys on Mr. Raava's case are currently being investigated by Internal Affairs. You know, a little pay-off here, turn your back there." Burns cleared his throat. "Mr. Raava's on their short list. It's gone way upstairs . . . know what I mean?"

Jeremy watched him intently. His distrust was peaking and he wasn't ready to surrender Reagan. No one knew she was in Fiji. He was so confused about who they were after. Was this the CDC for Reagan or related to the power plant and Charlie Grant?

Jeremy's skin prickled, with beads of sweat soaking his shirt. His phone vibrated and he grabbed it, relieved by the interruption. He answered it without glancing at the caller's name. "Hello."

"Jeremy?" The voice was soft and melodic, distant, almost female.

"Reagan, is that you?" He turned away from Burns. "I can't hear you. Speak up, please."

The caller's voice was barely audible. "It's Jean Michael. You must go. Get out of here, now! Leave the country. They know."

Straining to hear the words, Jeremy was doubtful it was even Jean Michael's voice—the tone was so meek. He yelled into the phone, "Who . . . who?"

The phone went dead. Jeremy stared into the red icon.

"So, how is the missus?" Burns asked.

Jeremy fell for the bait. "It wasn't her, it sounded like Jea— I couldn't hear—"

Burns' mouth stretched toward a cocky grin. "You know what you need?"

Jeremy looked at him, exasperated. "I'm sure I have no idea."

"You need a new phone."

"What?"

"You have alotta bad connections. You said that back at the lot . . . always this phone problem."

"Thanks, officer, I'll make a note." Jeremy started to roll up his window. "And now if you will excuse me, I'd like to hit the road."

"Son, all I'm trying to tell you is to watch your back. I advise you to come to the station as soon as you can, for your own safety. You answer some simple questions and we will fill you in on the bigger picture."

"The bigger picture? Are we talkin' motion pictures here?"

"Yeah, the movie where you and your buddy get polished off with a semi-automatic. It's a doozy."

60

*T*HE final steps down the mountain were easy for the sturdy donkey—the feed bin was close, so he would not miss a step. Reagan handed the reins to Maura's eldest daughter, Lelei, and gave her a hug. "Li'l Helper deserves a few extra handfuls of grain today."

Lelei wrapped her arms around Reagan. The young girl had recently hugged her dying father the same way. The islanders gathered to say goodbye. Heads were bowed in respect and the chants of sorrow followed Reagan toward the boat.

"Senga, Senga," Joni yelled as she pulled on Reagan's arm. Maura shot her daughter a stern glance. The English word "No," spoken by a child to an adult, was forbidden, so Joni cleverly used the Fijian word to disguise the ache she felt seeing Reagan leave. She feared Reagan was dying like her father.

Dr. Yiung and Roger moved quickly toward the skiff. Roger motioned to Sachi to start the engine and prepare for departure.

Joni continued to pull at Reagan's hand with tears in her eyes. Reagan turned to the young girl she had spent so much time caring for, nursing her through terrible fevers and watching her fight back each time. She stroked Joni's salt-ridden hair with an unsteady hand.

"I want to go with her." Joni tugged at her mother's dress. "Please, Mama, please. Can I go with Auntie Reagan?"

"My dear, Reagan goes on her own. She loves you as big as the sun. She needs to get well for all of us."

Joni sobbed. "But I don't want her to die, Mama. She will die if she leaves us . . . just like Papa."

Reagan glanced at Maura, and then back to Dr. Yiung and Roger. "I won't leave you, any of you. I promise, I won't leave you." She grabbed Joni and lifted her, gathering the strength needed to convince not only Joni and the group, but herself, as well. "I promise," she whispered in the little girl's ear.

The boat, with Roger, Reagan and Dr. Yiung, pulled away from the dock, leaving a trail of white water blending into the ocean's blue-green hue. The thought of never seeing them again crossed Reagan's mind. She could hear the faint chant from the islanders; it followed the boat's narrow wake then dissipated over the crystalline sea.

The dock slid slowly out of view. Reagan resisted the urge to turn toward the islanders, knowing it would be too much for her. "I'll be back," she whispered in the headwind created by the boat's forward movement. "Sachi, can we take a small detour to my reef?"

Sachi kept the boat on course and looked to Roger.

"Reagan, don't you think we should get back to the resort? We have a lot to consider—packing, getting you safely on the plane—your phone call." Roger abruptly stopped his to-do list.

Dr. Yiung filled in the gap of silence. "I think it's a good idea."

Sachi turned gently to starboard, changing course without comment.

The trade winds were offshore, a harbinger of the seasonal weather changes. Sachi slowed the boat as they approached the reef. Everyone was immersed in the view of dolphins jumping and playing in the boat's wake. Their tail flukes flicked in the air before disappearing into the water for a few seconds, then their sleek heads resurfaced. The beautiful dance repeated itself over and over again.

Reagan luxuriated in watching them surf the small crests of waves shaped by the broad stern of the boat.

Dr. Yiung let out a childish giggle. "Reagan, I see why you love it here so much. Look at these creatures. I wonder what they think of us in our half-sunken boat." His comments set off a ripple effect of chuckling that broke open into laughter.

Roger joined in. "We must look absolutely silly, stuck in our old piece of wood with a smelly piece of metal that pushes us along."

Reagan's expression and body language were in conflict. She wanted to laugh, but her body didn't allow it. "They are so precious, look at them. I wish I could spend my days with them right here," Reagan said as the dolphins broke through the surface of the stern wake.

The doctor broke the levity. "Well, that's the very point. You'll be back in no time, swimming with your friends and surfing your waves."

Reagan looked into Dr. Yiung's brown eyes wanting to believe him, but unsure of the possibility.

Sachi let the boat drift in neutral near the coral shelf. Reagan breathed in the salty air, as if it were her last breath. The boat rocked gently and she realized there was no pain, no fear, only comfort and beauty. "This is what I need . . . my ocean life."

Reagan's broad grin illuminated the boat. Watching the dolphins play along the wake, she wondered if this was the healing of light pushing through the shadow that Dr. Yiung had referred to. It had sounded like so much mumbo jumbo at the time, but she was beginning to understand it. Since the moment she searched for the row of freckles on her back, her trip to Australia, then the news of radiation poisoning on top of the early stage of Hansen's, it had felt like too great a burden to carry. She still felt guilty that she had asked Jeremy to take her life. It was her burden, not his. Reagan couldn't bear to think about their loss of love. She thought the island lifestyle would keep her sense of self alive even if she didn't survive. The malevolent gusts of wind swirled inside her, taunting at the thought of Jeremy and her being a couple.

The manta rays glided over the reef edges, flapping their wings, signaling goodbye to Reagan. She leaned over the edge of the boat, swooshing her fingers in the water.

Sachi explained the gesture, "Miss Reagan talks to the rays and all her friends here. She tells them now she is going."

Roger and Dr. Yiung sat quietly while she talked to her ocean friends.

Reagan looked at Sachi, "Time to go pack. I'm ready."

They made way to the resort dock. The minute the boat's bow closed in on the ramp, Reagan was up and moving toward Roger's satellite phone. She lifted the receiver and held it for a moment.

What will I say? What if he doesn't take my call? Ring, ring, ring. She inhaled deeply, lifting her spirits slightly. Ring, ring, ring. *I just want to hear your voice. . . .*

"You've reached Mr. Black's private line," the female voice started, "Please leave your name and number. . . ."

Reagan sank into the chair. She hung up the phone but kept the receiver at her ear until she realized he would not be there for her. She walked to her bure and packed her belongings, shut the window and door, and went straight back to the dock to leave for Australia.

Gathering on the dock for goodbyes, Roger showed his concern. "I'm afraid the weather's turning. If you don't leave now you may not get out for several days, maybe weeks."

"Yes, Reagan, I'm sorry, we do have to get back to the clinic. Theoretically, I'm on vacation here, probably pushing it a little if we have any delays."

Sachi took Reagan's backpack and put it in the boat. "We must go; waves are getting bigger."

Roger stepped forward to hug Reagan for one last time.

"I'll miss you, my dear, take good care of yourself. We'll be here waiting for you. I'm sorry we didn't get through to Jeremy. I'll keep trying. We're in for some bad weather."

"Yes, indeed, she'll be back." Dr. Yiung turned to embrace Roger. "You're a good man," he giggled, "and a good tour guide."

Moisture gathered in the deep corners of Roger's eyes.

Sachi, once again, helped Reagan into the boat and adjusted her seat. It was going to be a rough ride.

"Mr. doctor, please, we must go."

Dr. Yiung hopped into the boat and wrapped two towels around Reagan to protect her in the stern seat. He positioned himself between her and the hard corner of the gunnel.

Sachi dropped the lines and pushed off.

Reagan lifted her head to see Roger's shallow, lifeless wave goodbye, before his hand dropped to his side. There was nothing more she could do except watch the outline of Roger's body diminish as the small boat bucked the mounting waves heading toward the main island.

61

REAGAN didn't expect the crush of frantic travelers at Nadi International Airport—families, travelers, businessmen—all leaving ahead of the bad weather.

Sachi harped about the weather during the boat ride over to the mainland, but Reagan never fathomed each flight departure sign would read: Delayed . . . Delayed . . . Canceled. Incoming flights had already been rerouted or grounded.

"Excuse me, what's going on?" Reagan asked the airport attendant.

"Nasty storm comin', ma'am. Maybe a cyclone. Many cancel, they go nowhere today, ma'am."

Dr. Yiung insisted that Reagan take a seat as he negotiated travel for their special circumstance—someone with a medical condition traveling with her doctor. He'd all but given up hope when a young mother holding a crying baby in the crook of her arm, and a two-year-old pulling at her hand in another direction, turned away from the counter saying, "No worries, luv, I'll go back to the hotel and wait it out. This is hopeless." She turned to the doctor exasperated. "All yours, mate, I can't handle another bloody minute of this cryin'."

Dr. Yiung moved quickly to the counter. "Where was she going?"

"She had two tickets on the last flight out." The overworked Fijian woman seemed anxious to end her long day.

"Great, we'll take them." Dr. Yiung looked up at the flight number and destination. "Crazy luck." He handed his credit card to the person at the counter, "Closer to home and better than staying landlocked at the airport." He returned to Reagan flapping the tickets in the air. "We're off, last plane out. Do you need anything before we board?"

Reagan's eyes were sunken, with a rim of gray craters below each eye. "I'm ready."

Getting back to Sydney as quickly as possible was imperative. The past few months, the transition had created a strenuous journey back to civilization for her. It drew on every ounce of Reagan's being. Once away from the island, what was left of her strength would diminish quickly and, possibly, the pain would return with a vengeance.

Dr. Yiung did his best to get Reagan through the boarding procedure. He should have insisted she use a wheelchair. Leaning heavily on the doctor's slight frame, Reagan made them both stagger, appearing like a drunken, off-kilter couple.

The boarding sign blinked as the final announcements streamed through the handset static, "Final call. Final call for all those boarding AKL 1015. Final call."

Reagan stumbled and shivered. She had raised bumps on her arms and a feeling of feverishness. She remembered the symptoms from Jeremy's house—the terrible fatigue and the sense that she couldn't hold on.

"Are you okay, do you need a moment?" Dr. Yiung grabbed her waist this time, trying to keep her upright.

"No, keep going, we must make this flight." Reagan's body had been pushed to its limits. If only they could get to their seats.

After takeoff, the flight attendant asked if they would like a beverage. They responded in unison: "Water, please."

Dr. Yiung pulled out his pencil and paper to begin the calculations. He would use the entire flight to plan the counter-attack against Reagan's toxic build up. He moved the pencil rapidly along the horizontal edge of the lined paper then flipped it ninety degrees to vertical and repeated the rapid translation of characters.

Reagan tried to follow his movements and their meaning.

"You should rest, my dear. By the time you wake up, I'll have all this measured out and we'll be on our way home."

Reagan turned to the doctor. "I haven't had the opportunity to thank you. Not only for taking your 'vacation' in Fiji, but for trying to save my life. Even if my outcome isn't the best, we will all learn about the immense power of your natural compounds. I don't want to let you down."

Dr. Yiung kept drawing lines, formulating equations—arrows pointed at incomprehensible symbols. "It's not a question of letting me down. Don't let yourself miss the opportunity for a full life. You are tired, please rest."

Reagan massaged her arms to ease the constriction of blood vessels. She wasn't sure what was causing all the tension. Her body's response fluctuated wildly between chills and sweats. Pulling the blanket over her head, Reagan closed her eyes and surrendered to a deep, comforting sleep.

DR. YIUNG jumped at the sudden jerking motion that started in Reagan's right shoulder. It progressed down to her hand, jolting her awake. He rubbed her arm to quiet it. "Are you okay? More pain?"

Reagan spoke through a cloudy mist of confusion. "Something hap— It's probably a small cramp. I'm missing my bananas." She attempted a weak smile, casting off her memories of childhood night terrors.

"Of course, I'll go forward and see if I can find one."

Reagan lowered her head back into the pillow and closed her eyes, oblivious to the increasing turbulence jostling the plane.

Her dreams continued. She was with Jeremy in the ocean, avoiding a lionfish. They swam against the current, reaching for each other, struggling to stay away from the venomous beauty. Reagan reached for his fingers, but they kept slipping. She was pulled farther and farther from him and into colder depths while Jeremy floated to the surface. Only the deadly lionfish swam in the current; Jeremy was gone.

"WOULD you happen to have a banana, still in the skin?" Dr. Yiung's request seemed unusually urgent to the flight attendant.

"Is there a problem, Sir?"

"It's my patient, she's cramping from lack of potassium and we need a banana."

The Australian attendant reacted immediately, as if blood was spilling down the aisle.

"Yes, of course, no worries, we have fresh bananas."

She returned quickly with two bananas. The "fasten your seat belt" sign went on, just as the plane lurched from side to side.

"Sorry, doctor, you should return to your seat immediately."

"Yes, of course. Can you tell me how much longer until Auckland?"

The attendant looked anxious, "Best you take your seat; the captain will be making an announcement shortly. There's a bit of bad weather."

Dr. Yiung understood the alarm in her voice. He swayed with the plane, holding each headrest as he made his way along the aisle, back to his seat.

Reagan glanced out of the blanket at the banana being handed to her. She took a bite and slithered back into the darkness.

The intercom crackled and the captain's message began: "This is Captain Stevens, I'd like to reassure you that while we are having a bumpy ride, we will be out of this front in less than an hour. If you can bear with us for a moment, I will update arrival details as they become available."

Dr. Yiung put on his noise-canceling headphones and adjusted the volume of his favorite "Symphony 1997" with Tan Dun and Yo-Yo Ma. It completely absorbed his thoughts. He felt the stomach-churning drop of the jet, possibly a few hundred feet, and the subsequent rev of the engines to regain altitude. The vibrant symphonic sounds calmed him.

He stared at Reagan, waiting for her to be jolted awake, but she remained in another world, safe from the immediate discomfort of the plane. It was becoming increasingly difficult to jot down calculations. At one point, his pencil nearly ripped through the paper in his notebook. They had been in the air for five hours, yet the flight time from Nadi to Auckland was only about three hours.

He pressed the red button for the flight attendant at the same moment Reagan rose up, looking possessed. Her eyes were wide open and staring straight ahead. "It's wrong. We are off course. I can feel it. The pain . . . it's back again. Where are we?" Reagan's breathing was labored and she grabbed the doctor's arm.

Dr. Yiung was unnerved by Reagan's sudden burst of awareness, as were the passengers who overheard her loud announcement. He offered her another banana.

Reagan's voice got louder as the flight attendant made her way down the aisle toward her. "I can feel it. We are way off course. Can you feel it?" She shook the doctor's forearm. Forcing big exhales through her nose, Reagan tried to breathe through the pain, but it continued to escalate from the very depths of her marrow. Her insides were squeezed as if she was diving underwater to seventy-five feet. She tried to grab another inhale, but her lungs couldn't expand.

Panic ensued as Reagan reeled from the pain. Her back went into spasms with no relief in any direction. Sharp, stabbing daggers went up her spine, through her shoulders and down her arms. She quivered in despair and her voice deteriorated to a whimper.

Dr. Yiung pulled the blankets tight around her shoulders and arms creating a cocoon. She started to calm but still winced from discomfort. He pulled the blanket tighter and tucked it around her legs and behind her back. Another deep breath; it was working. She gave in to the comforting effect of swaddling.

The flight attendant stood close by shielding them from onlookers who were already edgy from the extreme jostling. She held three more blankets, offering them to the doctor.

Reagan's head fell backward into the pillow propped up to catch her. The power of the blanket offered temporary reprieve.

"What on earth is going on? We are quite overdue for our destination." He spoke quietly to the attendant, cautious not to wake Reagan.

"We have been rerouted. Didn't you hear the captain's announcement?" The attendant whispered. He took the headphones off his ears. "There will be another update within the hour. We are dodging a strong cell."

He glanced out the window seeing only thick cumulus clouds piled high against each other, with no land in sight. The doctor put the headphones back on and escaped into the safety of his symphony.

"Please fasten your seat belts as we make our final descent," suddenly boomed over the intercom, jolting Dr. Yiung into the upright position.

Reagan slithered snake-like out of the dark cave of blankets, unsure of where she was or the time of day. The pain was still intense, but a surge of excitement jump-started her system. She strained to see New Zealand's oblong shape with its smattering of offshore islands scattered over the beautiful sea below. She assumed they must be on a northern approach, perhaps slightly offset by the storm, the orientation looked familiar but different.

"Where are we?"

Dr. Yiung had gone back to his fastidious writing and calculations, almost embarrassed that he had dozed off for so long wearing his headset.

Reagan glanced out the window again, recognizing the land and seascape, the layout of the islands, the sharp volcanic peaks piercing through low clouds. "Oh no, it can't be. How could it be?"

62

*R*EAGAN pressed her nose against the thick window just as she had as a child, imagining the towering peaks collecting swirls of whip-cream clouds. They looked delicious then, now she felt betrayed. Grabbing Dr. Yiung's arm, she shook him. "How is this possible? I don't understand."

Just as Dr. Yiung tried reassuring her, the long-awaited announcement interrupted, "Hello folks, this is your captain speaking; again, we apologize for the rerouting. It was absolutely imperative that we continued northeast. A cyclonic front had developed in the Coral Sea and was joining forces with a southerly 'buster.' Highly unusual. Our Hawaii-bound passengers will arrive home early and our New Zealand-bound passengers will be reticketed for return. We advise that you stay in the lounge boarding area and await further instructions. Accommodations will be handled if the layover is extended. Thank you all for your patience. We will be on the ground shortly. Welcome to Honolulu."

Dr. Yiung looked at Reagan quizzically. "Did he say Honolulu?"

The noise of the plane's landing gear overruled their discussion. The passengers around them dutifully adjusted their seats and seemed much less surprised at the outcome.

Reagan continued out of sorts, "Surely we didn't fly all this way without an announcement . . . without them telling us."

Dr. Yiung bowed his head and sketched his pencil back and forth. "Well, I think there were a few announcements, but I was deep in . . . ah . . . concentration." He held up his pad of paper to prove it. "I've nearly worked it out. I've almost got the right proportions for you."

Reagan arched her back, feeling the strong surge of pain returning. She took a deep breath believing she could pull in some energy, but all she felt was the compression of her chest and lungs. She tried rubbing her lower back, but her arms were sore. All her symptoms were spiking and she was under full assault.

"I don't think I have much time." She hesitated to say the words out loud. "My pain is getting worse and deeper, just like the last time I was in—"

"I have a working theory." Dr. Yiung glanced at his watch. "I monitored you every hour of the flight, interpreting the progression of your movements." He pointed to the graph and symbols scratched in all directions.

"About?"

"It started about a hundred miles north of the equator." He pointed to a sharp line projecting upward.

"What do you mean?"

The plane went into its final fibrillation as the wheels hit the tarmac, broadcasting an immediate jerk that unsettled passengers for the last time. The flight attendant was quick to announce, "Please remain in your seat as we taxi to our gate."

"Well?" Reagan pointed to the odd-shaped map with zigzagging marks, a spider web of numbers one way and symbols another—everything in shorthand. "Is this some sort of code? If so I've got nothing left to decipher it—nothing left in the tank, so just tell me in plain English."

Dr. Yiung turned the graph so Reagan could orient herself. He spoke slowly, while anxious passengers organized their baggage. "You started grabbing your neck right here, just north of the equator." He pointed to the map. "You also started twitching, right here, possibly a neurologic effect, maybe a bad dream."

She tilted her head trying to interpret the explanation, but it was difficult to get her bearings.

"Then as we got farther and farther north of the equator, you moaned and reached for your back. I presume you were in more pain at that time, but I didn't want to wake you. You see, right here."

As carefully as Dr. Yiung explained the location on his map of equations and extrapolations, it was too difficult for Reagan to grasp. The doors to the arrival area had been opened; the moist tropical heat flooded the cabin as passengers pushed and shoved to exit.

Reagan remained in her seat, not anxious to move in any direction.

Dr. Yiung continued, "Then, when we were descending, you really jumped at something uncomfortable. I'm not sure if it was the intensity of your pain or something else."

The doctor explained that in the graph the straight lines projecting upward correlated with the latitudes on the map. There were other annotations showing happy or sad faces, which only confused Reagan.

"So you think I have more pain north of the equator?" Reagan tilted her head awkwardly. "Like it has something to do with gravitational pull?"

"Yes, you're getting it." Dr. Yiung smiled. "Opposite equatorial energy and magnetic influences." He giggled, the hallmark of his wisdom.

Reagan shook her head, still not understanding.

The doctor made one more attempt, knowing they had to prepare to leave the plane. "Your body is incredibly attuned to variations in time and spatial being. It's unusual, to say the least. You displayed protective torsions at different longitudes, and then the rapid transition from latitudes, south to north, created the most difficulty."

Reagan felt the confusion mounting. "If this is really true, then why do I still have pain sometimes south of the equator? It never leaves completely."

"Cortisol knows no boundaries, and you wear your woes. Your body carries the residual stress factor with you, like carrying your backpack. Or maybe you are just globally intolerant, a new diagnosis I just invented."

Reagan half-smiled as she reached for her backpack tucked under the seat in front of her.

The flight attendant approached them. "Will you be needing a wheelchair? The cleaning staff needs to start working."

Dr. Yiung looked around at the empty seats. "What's happening now?"

The attendant leered at the doctor but surrendered to his endearing grin. "My good doctor, all New Zealand-bound passengers are headed to the lounge to be reticketed. You are welcome to refresh yourselves, enjoy the lounge restaurant and await word about the next flight or accommodations." She added with a smile, "If you miss an announcement, you are welcome to ask an airline attendant. They will assist you."

"Thank you, you've been very kind. We'll make our way."

Reagan stood up slowly, awkwardly, adjusting her bag. It was heavier than she remembered, with all her belongings bulging out of the zippers that she had struggled to close.

63

$\mathcal{A}$ SWEATY, overweight businessman turned toward Jeremy. "Hey, bud, you should look where you're going."

Jeremy peered out from under the wide-brimmed Panama hat, disguising his facial features—especially his eyes. He glanced at the man with stringy gray hair and a scruffy beard. "Sorry, in a hurry." Jeremy kept on moving, out of place in his white silk shirt and light gray Armani satin trousers. He slouched as he walked along, which only accentuated the odd disguise. The throng of people moving in every direction, pushing and shoving, annoyed him.

"Hey, man." A small hand tugged at his sleeve. Jeremy whirled around expecting to see a young child. "Do you have any change?"

Though startled, he could only think of Mike Peters and their first encounter, but this was different. He didn't want to be seen and this petite teenager, with tattoos scrolled all over her arms and legs, appeared harmless.

"Look, can I just give you this? I'm in a terrible hurry."

The girl looked up at him. Dark shadows circled her eyes. She held out her hand.

Jeremy rifled through his wallet, agitated, hoping to rid himself of the second intrusion. "Here you go, take care."

She held the bill in her grimy hands, flipping it over and over again. "Holy shit, look at this, will yah." She stuffed the fifty-dollar bill into her baggy shorts held up by a piece of rope and yelled down the bustling hallway. "Thanks man, a fifty spot, that's some cool shit."

Jeremy was horrified at the encounter and started to run, not really an athletic run, but a combination of fast walking with a skipping motion as he dodged everyone around him. He noticed a security guard at the end of the long hallway and took an immediate left into a café bar. He stood panting, unable to catch his breath, wondering if he was being followed. Jean Michael had warned him—the situation had become dangerous, but would they follow him here? He should have called Mike first, but there wasn't time. He'd missed several calls; one was probably Lydia warning him. Jeremy was tired and confused. He was used to being surrounded by a protective entourage when en route to film locations. The wide-brimmed hat was ridiculous. He hated hats—they only obscured his good looks, but now it was essential.

Jeremy surveyed the service counter, but it felt too exposed for him to sit down. He'd take his chances in the crowded corridor. He suspected every male he passed was Burns, still tailing him. The angry ex-New York cop must have been so pissed off when Jeremy left him in the dust. But he hadn't done anything wrong. Or had he? Jeremy's head spun with unanswered questions; he felt hot and queasy. For the third time in one day, he banged into someone, but this person was on the floor of the lounge and he almost tripped over the crouched body.

"I'm so sorry, I didn't see you, I'm terribly sorry." Jeremy was embarrassed at his awkwardness. There was something bumpy underneath his hard-soled shoes and he jolted his foot upward.

REAGAN and Dr. Yiung were the last passengers to deplane. A sense of chaos hit Reagan. Lines of distressed travelers cued up to all airline counters. Finding another flight back to Australia was her immediate concern, but the storm would likely hold them over for a while. Reagan's shirt stuck to her skin. She wiped her brow with her sleeve.

"I'll check the monitor for possibilities." Dr. Yiung motioned toward the departure screen. "Why don't you settle in here for a bit?"

"I'm off to the loo." Reagan used her Aussi slang. "It's been a long flight and a little freshening up will do me good."

"I don't think you should wander off on your own. Please wait a minute."

Reagan ignored the doctor as if in a trance of exhaustion. She could see the ladies room sign ahead; it was close enough. "The exercise will do me good." Her backpack cut deeply into the boney curves of her shoulder blades; they ached. "I'm sure I can make it."

But the floor fell away and she collapsed, toppling over her backpack. A crunching sound, followed by the splaying of various bits of her life across the dirty floor; the seashell she always carried was the first thing to be crushed into powder. Her passport and slender wallet slid away, as did her notebook for sketching and the small pencil attached to it. Reagan became teary-eyed and mumbled, "I don't see how . . . I don't see how this happened. Why—"

She searched for Dr. Yiung knowing he must be close by. She sobbed openly, attracting the uncomfortable stares of travelers. Reagan felt a sudden bump and an awkward lurch of a body trying to avoid her.

"Oh god, I'm so sorry." The shadow of a tall man leaned toward her. "Reagan?" The gentle voice echoed toward her as if coming from a long dark tunnel. "Reagan?" Again, she heard the familiar tone, but she struggled to respond.

She stared at the man.

"Reagan, is that you? What—" He kneeled next to her, pulling off his hat. "You're here."

Reagan looked at Jeremy, stunned, unable to gather her thoughts, unable to stop the flood of tears. "Our plane . . ." She stumbled. "You're here . . . how did you know? I've missed you so much."

He leaned over her. Using his thumbs to slow the rush of tears he kissed her deeply, with every part of his being. "I love you. I've missed you so much. I never thought I'd see you again. Will you ever forgive me?"

Dr. Yiung approached the couple, with onlookers gathering to watch the emotional moment. The doctor's giggle preceded him. "Why am I not surprised?"

Jeremy looked up. "Dr. Yiung, what are you doing here?"

"Well, I might ask that of you. Ours is a simpler explanation— we got rerouted from New Zealand because of terrible weather. Our plane was headed for Hawaii, in any case. And you? Where are you headed?" The doctor crossed his arms and stared at Jeremy with a grin that demanded an answer or threatened to sour the moment.

"I was . . . um . . . you see, there's been a bit of a problem, and then I decided to leave. And then it became clear . . . I had to get to Fiji. My flight goes through Honolulu." Jeremy kept on, "What are the chances? It's the craziest coincidence."

Dr. Yiung raised his arms. "Well, that's just it, my friend. There are no coincidences."

After an overnight stay along the Ala Wai Canal, they were back on track with flights rescheduled. The ordeal had drained the last of her energy. Yet she felt a strange peacefulness, as Jeremy traced her fingers with his. Reagan succumbed to sleep upon takeoff.

"Can you tell me now, what the plan is . . . I mean how's she doing?" Jeremy whispered.

Dr. Yiung filled in the many details of their travels and his understanding of her illness and treatment. He looked more serious and more depleted than at any time Jeremy had seen him. "I've discovered some helpful anomalies in Reagan's physiological presentation of her illness. The malaise and fatigue, the mottled appearance in her skin, the slight flutter in her lung sounds. . . ." He looked over to make sure she was still sleeping. "It's taken me a bit to understand the inter-relationship of the toxins and Hansen's—how they played off each other. Maybe one condition is her savior. It took a little more time to discover the answer. It appears our bad weather and rerouting to Hawaii provided some answers. We needed to look below the surface. I'm rambling on a bit. Are you following?"

"I'm not exactly sure. Your mention of coincidences is bothering me. I'm trying to piece together a few things that happened in L.A. First there was Mike."

Dr. Yiung raised his eyebrows. "Mike?"

Jeremy continued, "Long story. Then there was Lydia and Charlie Grant. Jean Michael got jumped and I was implicated somehow, but I don't really know why or how, and then there's this cop. He's a real piece of work . . . and Reagan is here and alive, after wanting me to—I don't get it."

Jeremy looked at Dr. Yiung hoping he'd continue with his explanation, but instead he said, "No, you've got it. You understand completely. You are here. Reagan is here. We will be in Sydney in—" Dr. Yiung looked at his watch and laughed. "Oh dear, I've done it again. I didn't set my watch after hearing the announcement. Never mind, the clinic is aware of our arrival. I emailed what I could about my calculations."

"Calculations for what? What are we dealing with? Doc, I want Reagan back. I love her and I won't let her die, but I'm not clear how—"

Dr. Yiung returned to his gentle, lighthearted demeanor. "You will have to trust me for a bit. We've come to the answer and it will work. You must understand it will take more time to balance the equation and quite a bit more of your time to get her healthy. You see, in part of my calculations, I saw Reagan's energy decline in mathematical proportion to distance, and then I observed how your love, clinically speaking, brought her back to life."

In an almost priestly fashion, the doctor leaned over and touched the top of Jeremy's hand, which held Reagan's. "We can get her healthy again."

After eleven hours in the air, the plane made a gentle landing in Sydney, Australia.

64

*J*EAN MICHAEL rubbed his forehead trying to ease the persistent headache. He had twenty-one staples in his head and a concussion.

A surly detective had made several trips to his office and was on the verge of harassing him with questions.

"So, tell me, again, why is some guy gonna wait in the dark and jump you? What do you got that he wants? What's the connection here, because I'm just not seein' it? And then there's your pretty boy actor, claimin' to be your friend, who disappears instead of helping his ol' buddy out. You see where I'm goin' with this? It's got a bad stink." The detective tapped his notebook against Jean Michael's desk.

"I'm sorry, detective, I've given my statement and, actually, I've made several statements. I've tried to be as helpful as I can be. I have no idea why someone would attempt to . . . you know . . . hurt me."

The detective dropped by way too often. His visits only increased Jean Michael's wariness, agitation, and pounding headaches. He always checked to make sure the detective had completely cleared the building before making any calls. Slightly paranoid, he lifted lamps and looked under his desk, thinking his office had been bugged to get additional information, but he consoled himself with the thought *that only happens in movies.* And that annoying detective didn't strike him as being a bright guy; only his intense interest in the case was worrisome.

Jean Michael looked out the window toward the parking lot; the official vehicle was gone. He pressed the numbers on his cell carefully, preparing what to say. The phone rang three times and then he heard the deep, cautious voice of Lydia. He whispered, "Lydia, is that you? Things are getting really strange around here. The detective keeps coming back. I've been through all the files, but I'm having trouble making sense of them. I can't find any reference to Charlie Grant."

Lydia was not one for whispering, so she launched straight into it, "I'm tellin' yah, it's all there, right smack dab under your little white nose. Now I can't be goin' to your place and explainin' to y'all. So you are gonna have to look and see for yourself. Take your finger and run down them lines. You see the patient's name, you see the diagnosis and you see the notes—like 'treatment terminated' or 'unresponsive to treatment'. Well that's referring to all them glow sticks. You get my drift? Look at how many names . . . pages. I seen your Charlie Grant . . . he's on one of them damn pages. Keep lookin'. You will see the words next to him—'handled.' Now what does that mean?"

Jean Michael felt his head ready to split wide open and start bleeding again. "I'm not sure. It could mean they handled his pension and let him retire, but that's not what Jeremy said."

Lydia drew in a deep breath before releasing an avalanche of words. "Of course, he didn't get no damn pension. He was alive when Jeremy saw him and he had no damn pension. I'm suspecting he is dead by now. That means 'handled' to some folks. And you better watch your shiny white ass. I swear there is somethin' so ugly goin' on I can't even speak it and I don't even want to know what I know."

"What are you saying?" Jean Michael choked on his words.

"All I'm sayin' is look right at them words in front of you. It's all there. Take it all in. Let the glow sticks tell you. Then do somethin' about it. And watch your back." Lydia clicked off as if suddenly interrupted.

Jean Michael looked at the stack of papers, the edges of the pages curled from repetitive shuffling. Back and forth, name after faceless name, he thought of their lives, their families, and then he saw it—the pattern of 'terminated' and 'handled.' He rubbed his eyes trying not to see the truth of it, but it was yelling at him. They'd all died from radiation poisoning. An "accidental" leakage caused terminal cancer in these pages and pages of people—workers at the nuclear power plant, people who lived near the plant, swimmers and surfers who enjoyed the nearby beaches. They all became "glow sticks."

The outer door to Jean Michael's office was locked. He surveyed his desk. Did the detective notice anything? I always move the papers. I'm sure I did. Charlie Grant . . . whistleblower. What happened to him— 'handled?'

He picked up the phone. It was a long shot, but he needed to warn Jeremy about what was really going on. Things were so upside-down, so unbelievable, yet Lydia was very believable. She had risked so much. Now it was his turn.

It took three calls to get the country code, area code, and cell number correct. The ring sounded distant with a static buzz. Finally, he heard Jeremy's voice.

"Jeremy, where are you, how are you?"

"Jean, my god, great to hear your voice. I'm doing amazingly well. I'm in Sydney, Australia, with Reagan. We are seeing Dr. Yiung. Jean, she might get better. She may live!"

A few seconds of silence passed.

"How are you doing, Jean? Are you okay? I'm sorry I left so abruptly. I wanted to come see you in the hospital, but things got out of hand."

"I know, I know, that's why I'm calling. It's potentially a very dangerous situation. You know, our nurse friend . . ." Jean Michael lapsed into pretend code words hoping Jeremy would pick up on them. "She gave me all the information and it is what we thought. I think we should proceed with the film, but we might have to fictionalize it more than I thought. Documentary is out. We'd be so liable."

Jean Michael strained to hear Jeremy's reply. "I'm sorry, we have a bad connection . . . I'm losing you. Are we a 'go' on the film?"

Jean Michael felt frantic to get the message across. "Yes, but it's quite involved. I'll need your help, but I'm not sure it's safe for you to come back to L.A. right now."

"I'll help . . . for sure. Up-front financing, no problem, but I need to be here . . . with Reagan . . . for now. Treatment just started and it could take some time. I can't leave her again. I won't. We'll figure something out."

The connection was full of static. Jean Michael yelled into the phone; his words rolled out sounding more like a desperate plea. "Sure, I understand. I'll keep working on the script, do more research, I'll get everyone together. We'll get it right this time. This is big stuff and it will have to be done quickly . . . discreetly."

"Quickly? We don't do anything 'quickly' in film." Jeremy laughed, not understanding his meaning.

"People are dying here; we've got to get ahead of this."

"I'm losin' you, buddy. I'll try again when I'm closer to a hub. Email me. Good to hear your voice." Beep. Silence.

"WHO was that?" Reagan tried to lean closer to Jeremy, but she was hooked up to an IV infusing Vitamin C into her veins. This was the first part of her treatment, to boost her immune system and help flush the toxins. Next to follow, a botanical concoction consisting of floral meds and a fusion of oceanic healing kelp.

"Jean Michael. He sounded good, but sorta . . . stressed. The connection was bad."

The mention of Jean Michael set off an alarm for Reagan. It meant talking about what happened in L.A. She didn't want to think about it now. They'd been so happy and she was finally getting stronger. She wanted all thoughts of L.A. to disappear, vaporize. She asked reluctantly, "How is he? Has he heard from Lydia?"

"He sounded okay, still pursuing the idea for our film. You know, we are all a part of it now. One way or another, it's touched us all."

"Let's not talk about it now. I need to focus on getting my health back and I couldn't bear it if you left again."

"No, no. That's not my intention at all. I'm not going back. I can't. I'm here for you. I love you and I won't leave you."

He wound his arm around Reagan's shoulder, pulling her as closely as he could without disturbing the tubes hooked up to the centrifugal machine. He whispered in her ear, words that made her laugh, then cry, and made her love him even more, "For nothing can be ill, if she be well."

Reagan shoved Jeremy away. "Oh you clown. You've never performed Shakespeare."

"How do you know? Maybe I tried out for the Romeo part once. Or maybe I Googled Romeo and Juliet, cuz of your dolphin friends. There is so much more I'd love to learn about you. I'll memorize the whole play if you like."

65

*T*HE lush green backdrop meeting the satin blue skyline should have been a calming distraction for anyone, but Reagan bit the corner of her lower lip nervously as she scanned Dr. Yiung's text. He relayed only a small part of her latest test results, the most significant—her metal counts. Focused on the numbers, she put her fist in the air: *0. 01, 0. 04, trace . . . they're within normal limits. Thank God. Six months of cleansing and I'm almost home free.*

Dr. Yiung had compounded the exact prescription from natural ingredients with the fewest side effects, and the greatest amount of filtering and destruction of the poison. Reagan had completed her final round of sulfone drugs to effectively control Hansen's. With the exception of some malaise and fatigue, their time in Australia had given her the revitalization and strength needed to win back her life.

What if Jeremy had given in to my wishes? Reagan dismissed those needling thoughts. It had been one of the most painful moments when Jeremy turned to her in disbelief and said, "I can't . . . I won't help end your life." She remembered the distress in his eyes, both of them wanting to love each other, then the impermeable sound of his footsteps as he left. To find him again as she knelt on the departure lounge floor at an unplanned stop, trying to pick up the bits and pieces of her life, was nothing less than a miracle.

Reagan pressed the phone to her chest, whispering, "Thank you." Dr. Yiung had indeed been a partner in her cure, as much as Jeremy.

Standing at the edge of the winding stream, Reagan looked in every direction for Jeremy, eager to relay the news. It was their last week in Australia. Jeremy had insisted on one more fetch up the river. They had spent their spare time in the Blue Mountains, hiking, scrambling up and over boulders, admiring the lush vegetation and incredible views. They explored, fished, ate dried figs and brie, and made love, indulging in everything that came naturally to them.

Reagan tired easily in the afternoon, so she stayed at the water's edge. She spotted Jeremy showing off his newly acquired fly-fishing skills. She tried not to laugh at his awkward approach, holding onto rocks for safety as he slipped into the crystal clear waters. Reagan imagined it took all of his focus to impress her with his accomplishment. He cast his line with ease into the meandering river near their cabin. It teemed with a variety of trout and perch, gorgeous to observe, difficult to catch.

She beamed, with both pride and surprise, at his transformation. She had never imagined it possible.

His arms had become well-defined and tanned. His soft, smooth good looks now bristled with untrimmed stubble and sunburnt hair. His hands had become coarser, but more sensitive to the touch. He no longer dabbed on smelly cologne; instead he had a strong natural scent, the aromas of ginger and eucalyptus that pulled Reagan irresistibly to him. They immersed themselves in lovemaking and living in the moment, leaving behind the darkness that had threatened.

Encouraged by Dr. Yiung's text, Reagan waved her arms to get Jeremy's attention. He raised his index finger up toward her and she nodded. He spooled the line and wound up his arm, waiting for the change in texture of the water to forward cast his line beyond the ripple, landing it lightly on the surface and fluttering in exactly the right place. Reagan could see his breathing settle from where she stood. It appeared slow and content. She sensed all his energy focused on the river. Then his arm jerked abruptly.

"Aha, gotcha, little guy." He pulled up the golden-brown beauty. Its long, sinuous body flapped in the air as Jeremy held it up for Reagan to admire. "Check out my catch!"

"What a prize!" Reagan laughed. She lapsed into Australian phrases, "Sorry, luv, kiss 'im goodbye. Time to pack up and get to Sydney. I don't want to be late for our appointment. Could be slow-moving traffic back into town."

Jeremy eased the hook out of the fish's mouth with the expertise of a plastic surgeon. "Careful, little one, don't want to leave a scar. Off you go."

Reagan had heard his words to the fish and placed her hand on her chest as he released it back into the pristine stream. The small pang in her heart was real. A rush of adrenaline swept over her as he trudged toward her in his soaking wet shorts.

"What's that on your hand?"

Reagan opened both hands, shrugging.

"Ah yes." He took her right hand and turned it over, gently kissing the back of it. The gesture weakened her resolve. "Can't we have another few minutes?"

They fell into each other in a tender embrace, tasting each other, not able to pull apart. Reagan desperately held onto the sensation, not knowing what lay ahead. Their energies combined seemed combustible, even though both of them had known the lowest point of rejection and despair. They shared their love completely. There remained questions; reality stood in front of them like a heavy wooden door they'd have to push open.

Reagan held off on saying anything about her text from Dr. Yiung and the metal counts. What if she hadn't interpreted them correctly?

She was quiet on the drive back to Sydney, reluctant to let go of the beauty and peacefulness they had found in the stark mountain rock sculptures, overwhelming green lushness and the constant rush of water. The road expanded into two lanes; the traffic increased as the skyscrapers of Sydney emerged. Reagan felt anxious, touching Jeremy's knee as he drove uncomfortably on the left side of the road.

"What are you thinking?"

Reagan didn't hesitate. "I thought it would be wonderful to always come back here, to remind ourselves what these trees actually smell like."

"Well, I'm sure that is entirely possible, but today we head to the city and try to get a 'seal of approval'. Then we can go off and play."

Reagan laid her head against the seat and let her eyes capture the light playing on the mirrored buildings. "If only it could be so simple, always."

FAMILIAR faces gathered around them as they entered Dr. Yiung's clinic. Comments were hurled down the hallway at them allowing Jeremy and Reagan to shake off the city noise and relax a bit.

"Miss Reagan, I reckon you're in love with that silly bloke. You're all red-cheeked and such."

Reagan felt the rush of heat. "Half my luck, eh." She didn't really know the full meaning of the Aussie phrase, but assumed it meant, "I'm lucky."

Jeremy and Reagan had become clinical residents, on each of her visits for infusions and meds. Using their unique skills to assist with varying patient ailments, they found a sense of joy making a small difference in the lives of others, which further deepened their love for each other. Jeremy worked with dementia patients, having them memorize lines from a play. "More practice," he would say, igniting their limbic system within the temporal lobe of the brain to keep it active. "Visualize your line, like you are living it. Store it and repeat it again."

"But I can't remember the word," a patient commented.

"Then think of how it tastes or smells, like this apple." Jeremy pointed to a bowl of fruit on the table. "You know it is crispy and tart. Store that taste. Your mind works with all senses, so use them all." He took a big bite out of the Fuji apple. "Oh yeah, and it makes a big sound, too. Now what is the name of this?"

"Apple."

"Fuji apple."

"Tasty apple."

The patients chimed in, securing the word in their brain.

"Did he say he wants an apple?" one person asked.

"No, he says he wants to plant an apple tree."

And another overlapped with, "No, he says apples are good for you."

The comments were circular and nonsensical, but Jeremy laughed along with the group. "Let's take it from the top again."

Reagan's job was different. She worked with patients in their last days of life. She sat and listened carefully. She did not judge them, but offered her own love and strength, and the ability to let go. The connection with each patient was unique. Her near-death experience had given her a new view of life and a deeper understanding of death. Her strength had been diminished and regained; her love and compassion for others had deepened immeasurably. She picked up an old woman's hand and held it.

The dying woman confessed her greatest regret, "Yah know, I never did tell Gina I was sorry for not goin' to her daughter's wedding. I never forgave her for that stupid kiss she gave my husband . . . thought she fancied 'im."

Reagan sat quietly, waiting, listening.

The woman continued in a shaky voice, "I reckon it was just a muddle, probably made a bigger deal of the whole thing than I needed to. Lost my best mate over it, even long after my husband was gone."

Reagan stroked her arm, careful of the distended veins and delicate skin. "We all make silly mistakes in life."

"Yeah, but mine was just plain stupid."

"Maybe we can call her tomorrow just to say hi." Reagan knew tomorrow was a long shot. The woman's skin was already mottled and her breathing sounded muffled. The woman's spirit seemed relieved and Reagan hoped she had helped release the burden.

"Yes, I think I would like that. . . ." The woman's voice drifted off.

Reagan matched her breaths to the woman's, noticing the slow descent of vital signs. The calmness was beautiful and quiet, so quiet.

Another patient confided expressively to Reagan, "You know, I never told anyone, it just didn't seem that important."

"But it seems important now, right?" Reagan waited.

"Well, yes, it does seem so, now that you mention it."

Reagan listened like they were the last people on the planet. Her eyes never left theirs, her attention fully invested. It was her best work—fully in the moment and not fixing a thing. The patient would again confess and confide, releasing their burden.

Many of those patients died in their sleep after their talks, having said what was needed. There was no medical assistance needed.

REAGAN had one foot wrapped playfully around Jeremy's ankle as they sat in Dr. Yiung's exam room. His office had the appearance of a living room, with a comfortable couch and all the instruments disguised as pieces of art—Dr. Yiung's theory of art.

Their hands were entwined and a little fidgety as they played a silly game of thumb war.

"It's okay, we know the metal counts are good, right?" Jeremy pushed Reagan's thumb backward so she would listen. "Stop with the worried look."

Reagan had an uneasy sense that something wasn't right. She'd only seen the very narrow tabulation. There could be something else Dr. Yiung had withheld while they were in the Blue Mountains. He was adamant about them not checking in until the new metal count results were in.

The door swung open. Stopping their flirtatious games, Reagan dropped his hand and clenched hers.

Dr. Yiung bounded through the doorway with his usual energy inflating the room, severing Reagan's anxious thoughts. "Guess you've been eating some rich Aussie lamb while you've been here."

Reagan immediately felt guilty. "You know I'm a vegetarian. What do you mean?"

"Sorry, misuse of cuisine. Good news, your weight is up. It means your immune system is kicking in and responding positively. So maybe some fish?"

"Yes, I confess, I do love fish. Then there's the Tim Tams too. Can't just eat one," Reagan chuckled. "And the pain is . . . I hardly feel a twinge."

Jeremy chimed in, "Doesn't that have to do with the south-of-the-equator stuff?"

"Hang on," Dr. Yiung interrupted, "before we get into that. Reagan, you are eating well, correct? You are feeling okay from day to day? Anything else?"

Reagan hesitated, not wanting to ruin the picture of good health and all the possibilities that lay ahead. "I'm tired, you know, it's just the cleansing and detox regimen and my system has had to work really hard. Don't you think?"

"You've been active. I mean in the sense of hiking . . . that sort of thing."

Jeremy interrupted, again. "Yes, we've been on long hikes and she's been getting stronger every day. Look at her. She's healthy."

"It's amazing what those happy hormones will do for you." The doctor flipped over the pages in her medical chart. "I just wonder why—" Dr. Yiung stared at one page for a moment too long for Reagan not to notice.

Bile flooded her stomach, rising toward her esophagus; the fear of bad news was overwhelming. "What is it?" she blurted out. "Tell me!"

"Not sure, numbers are just a little off." His voice softened. "Could just be a typo, or a mistake. You know we run the labs with volunteers. Maybe—"

"What mistake?" Jeremy was on his feet, leering over the doctor's shoulder as if he knew what he was reading.

Reagan pulled at her ribs, adjusting her posture. Jeremy was at her side quickly, with his hand on her shoulder.

"Well. . . ." Dr. Yiung continued. "I think we need to take a closer look at something. Do you mind if I take a quick peek?" He adjusted his crooked glasses on the narrow ridge of his nose.

"Oh, God, no," Reagan panicked. "A tumor—you must think I have something like a tumor. Please don't tell me I have a growth. I can't take any more—"

"Reagan, please trust me. Let's not jump to any conclusions. This will only take a minute."

Jeremy held Reagan close. The tension in his own grip caused Reagan to wiggle loose from his grasp. She felt a crushing sense of asphyxia.

Dr. Yiung asked Reagan to lie on the cushioned chair, which expanded to a fully horizontal position. He gently applied cool gel, spreading it around with the metal wand.

The silence in the room made it seem hollow and cold. Reagan shivered.

"Reagan, your chemical panel is good, very good, unusually so. Hansen's is in full remission and all the radiation poisoning seems to be out of your system, which leaves only a few reasons why you might feel exhausted and nauseous."

Just then, as if from outside the room, the tiniest blip of a heartbeat could be heard. All eyes locked onto the fuzzy ultrasound monitor.

Tears streamed down Reagan's cheeks and Jeremy pulled her in a deep embrace. "How could it be?" she whispered.

Dr. Yuing's smile broadened, as he shrugged his shoulders.

"Life comes."

To be continued. . . .

Acknowledgements

*T*HANK YOU TO THE TRIBE who supported my journey with Kōkua

All ocean lovers—The ocean is our rescue, strength, respite, passion and inspiration. May we all acknowledge and give thanks to the power of the ocean and all of its' inhabitants.

Neva Sullaway—Master of shaping words, dialogues and all things author-ish. Not just an elite editor, but a teacher, friend, patient and guide. I am so fortunate for Neva's expertise and unending dedication to my writing journey.

Stacy Vosberg—My sister, whose artistic renderings helped shaped scenes, giving them depth, color and emotion.

Brett Hoffman—My son, with his artistic view behind the lens creating such a beautiful cover.

Susan Lieberman—My friend and patient, whose encouragement to *keep writing* will stay with me always.

Pete Zamoyski—My friend and patient, who shared his emotion for Phaeole, and my vision of the healer on the hill.

Melissa Vosberg—My sis-in-law, who under the immense psychedelic path of a scorpion sting in Mexico, wanted the rest of the manuscript, PRONTO!

My sincerest gratitude goes to the Fijian locals who demonstrate compassion and love amongst true disparity. I will sit in a Kava circle with you always. And the man who worked at Kalaupapa general store in Moloka'i; your smile and abilities shaped the essence of my characters. Shaking your hand was my privilege. Really!

About the Author

STEPHANIE HOFFMAN MS, PT

*A*SIDE FROM THE MANY roles Stephanie Hoffman plays: Mother, Wife, Physical Therapist, Surfer and Humanitarian, her recent role as a Hospice volunteer has inspired many of the ideas in her first fiction novel—Kōkua.

Stephanie has extensive experience in the field of Sports Medicine and Orthopedics. Currently, she has a private practice in La Jolla Shores, California. Over thirty-five years in medicine has inspired her to educate others with new ways of looking at disease and injury, primarily with tolerance, compassion and understanding.

Stephanie's numerous surf trips abroad have presented her with extraordinary glimpses of those in need and the opportunity to share her skills in support of others. "It's not just a surf trip. . ." Steph's known for saying. "Let's see where we might be able to help."

From donating essentials in Mexico, Dominican Republic, Fiji, and Indonesia, to starting a school in Croix des Bouquets, Haiti, helping to rebuild the lives of children who lost family members in the 2010 Haiti earthquake, her experiences have culminated in respect and tolerance for those outside of local boundaries, pressing our awareness of those in need both nationally and globally.

"To the world you may be one person; but to one person you may be the world."

*Dr. Seuss

(One of Steph's favorite sayings from her neighbor; Ted Geisel).

Proceeds from this book will help fund Institut Edeline in Beudet, Haiti.

For more Information go to:

www.projectedeline.com

Stephaniehoffmanbooks.com

Made in the USA
San Bernardino, CA
05 July 2020